O'GALLAGHER NIGHTS

THE COMPLETE SERIES

Lisa—
gotta love
those sassy
nights (·‿·)

MIGNON MYKEL

Also By Mignon Mykel

LOVE IN ALL PLACES *series*
full series reading order

O'GALLAGHER NIGHTS

THE COMPLETE SERIES

MIGNON MYKEL

ISBN: 9781980323679

This is a work of fiction. Names, characters, places, and incidents are the product of the author's imagination. Any resemblances to actual persons, living or dead, are entirely coincidental.

Cover Design and Formatting: oh so Novel
Editor: Jenn Wood
All images and vectors have been purchased

ONE NIGHT STAND

book 1

Prologue
Mid-March

O'Gallaghers was the place to go if you were looking for a good time. The local sport teams hung out there after games, for one, but also because the O'Gallagher siblings were a sight to behold.

At least, in my opinion.

I grew up with the siblings, once upon a time. From the time I could walk and all throughout high school, my parents and I lived next door to the O'Gallagher family. Brenna, the youngest of the trio, and I had been best friends up until the fifth grade. Conor, the oldest, and Rory, three years younger than him, were wild, flaunted sex appeal like nobody's business, and were *fiercely* protective of their baby sister.

They also didn't seem to think she was every bit as wild and crazy as they were, which was actually part of the breaking point in my and Brenna's friendship. By the age of ten, I was no longer good enough for Brenna.

While I remained the quiet, timid Mia, the only part that was *wild and crazy* about me was the brown, curly locks on my head. Two years after our friendship ended, and I still held on to my baby fat while Brenna was the first in our grade to get breasts, then her period. She was the first to grow tall in our class, too. Sure, we eventually all caught up and she became the shortest in our class, but it didn't stop the boys from noticing her. She was a five-four, C-cup beauty with raven black hair and piercing green eyes, and we were only twelve years old.

By fourteen, rumor had it she lost her virginity in the back of a high school senior's van. A classmate of Rory's, no less.

By sixteen, the rumors started circling she was pregnant. She wasn't, I don't think, but it was a popular story, told again and again.

The thing with the rumors was that the people spreading them, the people responsible for them, were extremely careful to keep their words clear of Conor and Rory.

Brenna left for school in her conservative clothes and always returned home in them. She left clean-faced and was sure to wipe the make-up off before heading home.

I'm sure her brothers weren't stupid, but with everything else going on in their lives—senior year, college, and the like—if Brenna showed up clean and fresh and like the angel they thought she was, they could go on and pretend the same.

Even though our friendship had fallen apart over petty things, I never spread the rumors.

It wasn't that I was afraid of her brothers; quite the opposite, actually. At all of eight years old, I had fancied myself in love with fifteen-year old, Conor. He shared the same jet-black hair Brenna had, but his eyes were the type of blue you could see from a mile away.

So incredibly brilliant. Piercing.

As much as I had missed Brenna's friendship in our pre-teen and teenaged years, it was the easy smiles her brother always had for us that I missed the most.

Currently, I sat at a high-top table in O'Gallaghers, my eyes on the man running the bar, hoping to catch that blue brilliance, willing it to aim my way.

Conor O'Gallagher.

I hadn't seen him in fifteen years so I doubted he would recognize me—but I certainly recognized him.

Gone was the lanky, tall, clean-faced kid from our youth. In his place was a taller, broader man with a short, yet thick, black beard. The only time he flashed his smile was when he was flirting and he always paired it with a sexy wink. Tonight though, was ladies' night, which meant he brought the charm up one-hundred-fold.

The O'Gallagher siblings were second generation Irish-Americans; their grandparents were from Northern Ireland. Anyone with any knowledge of Irish history would know that the Irish didn't wear kilts, but rather tunic things called lein-croichs.

Ok, maybe I looked it up.

But I had been pretty sure kilts were a Scottish thing.

Anyhow.

Thursday was ladies' night, and Conor and Rory brought it up a notch by wearing solid black kilts—last week's was saffron colored— paired with the forest green shirt that was part of the bar's uniform. No other bartender did the same, just the O'Gallagher boys.

They also both wore tan work boots, which should have made the ensemble ridiculous but rather...

It was fucking sexy as all get out.

I had been coming in a few times a week for the last three weeks, trying to get the nerve to go up to Conor. Re-introduce myself. See if he wanted to sit and talk, ease him into what I really wanted from him. Yet, every time I came in, I sat at this table, away from the bar and away from Conor.

I licked the corner of my lips as I lifted the glass of Irish ale to my lips, my eyes still on the man of the hour.

Each time I was there, I was helped by one of the female barmaids. If I wanted to be helped by Conor, if I wanted him to truly notice me, I would have to sit at the bar but I still had to form a plan because I wanted more than to just sit and talk and catch up.

You see, for all of Conor's flirting, he always backed it up. Sure, he flirted with damn near every female in the place, but if he gave you extra special attention, you just knew where your night was going.

Allegedly at bar close, he took one of the remaining ladies up to his apartment for a wild rendezvous. Never a virgin; he wasn't quiet about his lack of desire to take a virgin to bed. He liked the wild women who knew their own way around the bedroom.

Thursdays, rumor had it, he brought two up with him.

I didn't want to be one of two tonight, no.

But I did want one night with him.

A night to learn the ropes of sex.

Because if anyone knew what he was doing, it was Conor O'Gallagher.

And I was going to be his first virgin.

Chapter One

Conor

I set the mixed fruity drink in front of the sexy blonde sitting at my bar and gave her a wink. Her drink choice needed work, but she would probably still be fun in bed.

Maybe she'd stick around for bar close.

I wiped my hands on the bar towel hanging from my belt and glanced up as one of my regulars-turned-good-friends came up to the bar, pounding on it twice with his fists, a huge grin on his face. "Yo, Conor."

I chuckled and nodded upward, working on a drink order one of my barmaids brought up. "What's up, Cael?"

Caleb Prescott was one of my regulars, yes. He played hockey for the city's NHL team and often came in with his brother or the team as a whole. He and I would sit and shoot the shit sometimes and I grew to like the guy. He was younger than me, my sister Brenna's age actually, but he was a good guy.

"I talked Syd into a date for the wedding." Caleb moved to sit in what had to be the only open stool at my bar and leaned forward on his arms. Caleb met Sydney during a dating show.

I take that back. Sydney was the casting person, and Caleb fell for her, hook, line, and sinker.

"She finally decided she was going through with it, hey?" I grinned and slid the glasses I'd filled over to the end to be picked up. "Your mug is good enough for her?"

Caleb grinned wide. "Fuck you, Conor. But yes, we decided on a date. And I want you to be there."

I stopped wiping my hands on my towel. Caleb and I were friends, yeah, but I didn't realize we were invite-you-to-the-wedding kind of friends.

"It's cool if you don't want to, or can't come. We're having it back in Wisconsin. But you're one of my few friends here that isn't on the team and Sydney likes you, so."

"Nah, yeah, absolutely," I said, reaching up to flip my baseball cap backward. "I'd be honored to go. Thanks for the invitation."

"I only asked because of Sydney," Caleb said with a smirk.

"Yeah, whatever, fucker. You love me."

Caleb shot me the bird before standing to pull an envelope from his back pocket. "Don't tell her I gave it to you bent to shit, though. She spent a lot of time on them."

I laughed and shook my head. The guy was whipped. I couldn't imagine one pussy for the rest of my life, but hey, if he was happy...

I reached for the envelope and put it back by the register and legal pad, which I would have to take back to my office before the night was over.

"You want a beer?" I asked as I turned.

Caleb shook his head as he pushed back from the wood. "Nah. Chief made dinner and we have a game tomorrow, so I need to pass. See you tomorrow though? You get those tickets?"

I nodded, holding my finger up to a pretty girl waving in my direction. "I did. Rory was fucking ecstatic. They're great seats, thanks." Rory's birthday was coming up and Caleb hooked me up with tickets to the Enforcers-Wild game the next night.

"Absolutely. Happy to help. Talk later," Caleb said, holding his hand up in the air in salutation as he turned to leave. I shook my head, grinning, and went back to work, heading down the bar to the girl who flagged me down.

"What do you have on under that kilt, Conor?" she asked. She was certainly hot, with her dark hair and grey eyes, and her most definitely surgically-enhanced chest. Maybe she'd be willing to play tonight. Her blonde friend beside her was pretty easy on the eyes, too. Maybe she'd be up for some play time as well.

I chuckled and lifted a brow. "Wouldn't you like to know."

Everyone with a true Irish bone in their body knew that kilts were a Scottish thing, and the kilts worn by the Irish were typically an American thing. When my brother Rory and I were trying to find ways to keep the bar from falling under the red line, we decided to go with the kilt idea. It didn't matter that kilts weren't a true part of our heritage, regardless of the Gaelic ancestry we had; we were Irish, and Irish-Americans liked to wear them.

That, and the ladies seemed to fawn over them.

So we wore them on Thursdays, which quickly became our best night of the week.

For the business and the bedroom.

I wasn't exactly private about my affairs. Many a drunk woman would stick around until bar close, hoping I'd pick them in my nightly game of eenie, meenie, miney, 'ho.

Some of those ladies were disappointed to learn that I wore boxers underneath, but only dimwits went bare under a kilt.

That and the phrase was "True Scot" and, like I said, I was Irish.

I walked down the bar to pour a lager that was ordered up from the floor when I could feel someone staring at me.

Keeping at task and filling a lager glass, my eyes scanned the bar as my ears kept focus on any requests from the patrons sitting at the bar. Finally, my eyes settled on the woman who had been coming into my bar a few nights a week for the last number of weeks. She sat at a high-top a few tables back from the bar, in the same spot she'd been a few other times.

I'm not sure what snagged my attention, to be honest, the first time I'd noticed her. She wasn't striking like the half dressed women who sat at my bar. No, she wore little makeup on her face and had a crazy mass of curls that looked like she fought to put back in the bun behind her head.

She never came in with anyone, never met up with anyone. It was only just ever her, sitting at one of my high tops, nursing some lager or another. I idly wondered what her story was, and what kept bringing her in. The bar had regulars, don't get me wrong, but she just didn't strike me as such.

When her eyes shifted and met mine over the bar and a couple tables, she quickly looked down.

Ah, so *she* had been spying on me.

She didn't look the adventurous type, but I had been surprised by women before. Maybe she wanted in on my fun tonight and was just too timid to make a move.

Sometimes it was the quiet ones that turned out to be the freaky-in-bed ones.

Recalling her drink, I poured her another and set it with the lager that had been ordered. When Emily, the quiet but beautiful—and therefore, great for business—barmaid we hired last week came back for the lager, I pushed the extra glass toward her. "High-top four."

"Sure, Con," she said with a small smile. I watched as she delivered it, my hands slowly wiping and bunching at the towel at my hip.

When Emily sat the glass down, Curly Locks looked up, wide eyed. I couldn't hear whatever Emily told her, but before Emily left the table, Curly's eyes met mine again. I offered her a wink then went back to manning my bar.

One of my bartenders, Greyson Stone, walked behind the bar from the swinging kitchen doors. Yeah, his parents were fuckers for naming him that. "Hey, bossman."

"What's up, Stone?" We clasped hands and pulled into one another, bumping chests with our hands between us. Typical greeting.

Stone came to work for Rory and me three years prior, when O'Gallaghers re-opened for business. I needed a trustworthy bartender and while I hadn't known Stone from Adam at the time, he'd proven to be one of my best employees and a pretty damn good friend. That and he didn't hit on my sister.

I filled orders as I talked to the man who wasn't supposed to be working tonight.

"What brings you in tonight?"

"Ah, Rory asked me to cover his last hour." Stone began going through coolers and chests, making sure all the fridges and condiments were how he liked them. The man was slightly OCD about it.

"What the fuck is Rory doing?" I glanced over at Stone, my peripheral on the lager I was pouring.

"Something about a girl," Stone said around a chuckle. He grabbed a towel and hooked it into the back pocket of his cargo shorts.

I shook my head. Everyone knew I'd take a woman home at the end of the night, just like everyone knew Rory wasn't above taking one home in the middle of his shift. "Always a girl."

"You take a break lately?" Stone asked before his attention was snagged by a customer at the far end.

We split the bar, each taking a side, as the night hit a busy spurt. Thirty minutes later, the rush ended for the moment, and I remembered Curly Locks. I looked toward her table, sure she would have left by now.

But nope, she was still there, nursing the glass I had Emily send over.

"Stone, I'm going to take that break," I said over my shoulder. I grabbed two bottles of water and, carrying them in one hand, made my way out from behind the bar. I tossed my towel on the back counter by the register just before clearing the bar.

"Hey, Conor."

"Conor, my man, how's the night?"

Everyone knew who my brother and I were. Not only had we grown up in this town, but O'Gallaghers had been a prime establishment since our parents opened the doors twenty years ago. Five years ago, the doors closed when our parents decided to do the empty nester thing, traveling around the country in a fucking RV of all things. When I mentioned wanting to take over, I refused to accept the bar as a gift. They went on and on about how it was us kids' namesake and I should be willing to just take it, but I wanted to give them a sensible down payment. Between Rory and me, we accomplished that in just about a year, and roughly eighteen months after the doors closed, we re-opened.

The patrons who came on Thursdays were generally the younger crowd. And the ladies, of course. I would say that on any given night, I knew at least half of our patrons from either back in school or around town.

I made general small talk with customers, some I knew, some I didn't, on my short journey toward my destination.

The entire time, my eyes were on Curly Locks. She knew I was coming for her.

There may have been loud conversation and music playing all around me, but the only thing I could hear was my breathing and the slight thump of my Timberland work boots.

The closer I got to her, the wider her eyes became.

Trapped, baby.

I've got you trapped.

Mia

When Conor first caught me staring at him, I battled the need to leave. But then he sent the pretty waitress over with another drink. It was rude for me to leave then, even if I knew I wouldn't drink it.

I had a limit, and I was pretty strict about it. I had to drive.

When the bar got crazy busy, I almost slipped out then. I wanted to be unnoticed. I wasn't ready to 'meet' Conor. I had to come up with a plan!

Unfortunately, I found myself glued to my chair and when Conor's eyes found mine yet again when the crowd dwindled…

I had been frozen to the spot, unsure of what to do.

He stalked his way toward me now, black kilt hardly moving around his legs. My eyes traveled down, taking in his hairy but muscular calves, ending in short socks and tan boots. I brought my eyes back up to lock on his and sat up a little straighter.

Did he recognize me? Did he know who I was?

He finally reached my table and put a bottle of water down in front of me. "Your lager is probably warm and undrinkable by now."

His voice had deepened more in the last fifteen years. I mean, I knew it was going to happen. It had started well before the last summer I spent with his sister. But it was low and gritty, and it alone had my heart pounding behind my breasts and my pussy getting wet.

I licked my bottom lip before bringing it in my mouth to bite gently. I watched as his eyes focused on the movement.

I hadn't been intending on the highly sexual movement to be anything more than a reflex of my nerves, but the way his nostrils flared and his pupils dilated… *Shoot.*

"You like what you see, Curly Locks?" His eyes slowly moved from my lips to my eyes.

So he didn't know me.

I wasn't sure if I should be relieved or embarrassed.

"I do." My voice held a huskiness I wasn't aware I was capable of.

"What are you doing tonight?"

Oh my God. This was happening.

I hadn't properly planned and wasn't expecting anything to happen tonight but oh my God.

It was happening.

I shifted in my seat and tilted my head to the side. I guess I was going to have to play it by ear. With a mental shake and a deep breath, I brought out my best bravado. "Nothing."

"I bet I could turn your nothing into a great night."

He leaned into the table, his forearms resting on the wooden top and he lazily slid his bottle of water from hand to hand, as if he didn't have a care in the world.

Well, he probably didn't.

He could have his share of women in this bar.

"I don't do threesomes." I lifted my brows in challenge.

"Ah, so you've heard about the *other* Thursday night special." He chuckled, one side of his lips lifting with the movement. "I can work with that. You see, Curly, I've seen you here in my bar, by yourself, a few times now. And I've felt your stare. I think you want to go upstairs with me."

There were so many things my mind wanted my mouth to spit out.

You know me.

How are your parents?

What has Brenna been up to?

I'm really damn proud of you and Rory.

YOU KNOW ME!

But I fought to keep those words back. Instead, I focused on his intense gaze and ignored my heart battling in my chest. "So what if I do?"

He winked and pushed away from the table before uncapping his water and taking a long, long drink from it. My eyes watched as his Adam's apple bobbed with each gulp. When he put the bottle back down, it was more than half gone.

"Stay put and I'll make your wildest dreams come true." He recapped the bottle and walked back to the bar much in the same fashion he had when coming toward me.

Proud. Confident.

Cocky.

Damn, I couldn't wait.

Chapter Two

Conor

I'd been damn near positive Curly would leave in the hours between our chat and close, but nope. She sat at her high top, one leg crossed over the other, nursing the bottle of water I left with her. Sometimes she'd lean against the table, others she'd sit up straight. But always, her eyes were on me and my movements.

I knew what women like her saw when they watched me.

A man whom she considered was just out of her league. A man who would never take a moment to appreciate the plain shirt and jean-clad legs, hair in a mess of a bun, while women with perfect hair and perfect faces and perfect tits falling out of their hardly-there shirts leaned over my bar.

But pussy was pussy. Tits were tits.

And every now and then, it was fun to throw something different in the mix.

I glanced over my shoulder at the clock before turning back to the last of the bar's customers. "Closing time, ladies." As was usual, I was the last to be in the bar. My cooks left at eleven; the last of the barmaids left an hour ago, and Stone left an hour before that.

"What are you up to tonight, Conor?" a fucking gorgeous brunette asked me. Her eyes met mine, but not before checking out my junk.

Not that she could see much of anything under the heavy fabric of this kilt.

I was up, all right, but it wasn't for this brunette. It was for the one who kept her heavy gaze in my direction, who kept licking her fucking pink, full lips. Kept drawing in that lower lip. Kept squeezing her fucking knees together as she sat with her legs crossed.

She was just as impatient as I was.

Most of the women generally were.

The brunette at the bar leaned over as she pushed her glass forward, a twenty under it. Assuming it was to cover her tab, I took the bill and turned to close her out. When I returned with her change, she winked. "You keep it. But tell me, Con. How much does a girl gotta pay for you to take her virginity?"

There was no fucking way this woman was a virgin. Not with how provocatively she dressed nor how strong she was coming on.

Her girlfriend beside her giggled into her hand. Either she was a happy kind of gal, or she had one drink too many. Considering I always watched out for my customers and their limits, I would say she was a happy girl.

"I don't fuck virgins, sweetheart."

I reached over with my towel to wipe down the bar beside these two. My rule against virgins wasn't anything bred from a terrible past or knowledge of horror stories of the whole *deflowering* process.

Nope.

Actually, I just didn't think it was fair to the woman.

I wasn't there to coddle, I wasn't there to make sweet love.

I wanted to throw the woman down on the bed, rip her out of her clothes, and enter her without the preamble of foreplay and being sure she was ready. They were always mostly ready, some tighter than others, but always thick and hot and welcoming.

The pain, the tears, the *blood*; yeah, no thank you.

"Well, that's too bad, sugar," the girl said, pushing the change I just left her toward my end of the bar. "I'll just have to come back. Have a good night, Conor O'Gallagher."

The women left, leaving only Curly Locks in the establishment. I flicked my towel over my shoulder and rounded the bar, grabbing my legal pad and Cael's invitation on the way. I continued to walk toward the door, but addressed her. "You're still game?"

I looked over my shoulder, sure she would nod her response, and was pleasantly surprised to find she now stood near me. She grinned up at me, not looking nearly as naïve as I had pegged her as, and nodded. "Still game."

Looking down at her, I couldn't help but feel that I knew who she was.

It was something in her eyes.

She looked strong yet slightly wary, a look I'm sure I'd seen a thousand times before. Maybe that was why.

"Alright then." I locked the front door and flipped a switch, turning off the neon advertisements and the "Open" sign.

I couldn't help but want to take her hand, but that wasn't me. What was that about? So instead, I walked ahead of her. "Follow me then, Curly."

Mia

I nibbled on my lower lip as I walked just behind him.

Fuck, I was nervous.

The entire time between now and when he had left me at the table with just a bottle of water, I thought about what would be happening tonight.

I wasn't a stranger to sex, per se. I had toys. I knew my body and was comfortable with it. Sure I was a little on the bigger side; my yearly biometric screening labeled me as "over-weight" even though I was about twenty-three percent body fat. I spent many years as a child battling my weight and finally as an adult, found a way to shed most of it. These days, I had muscle and was toned, but the pudge in my tummy and the extra under my chin when I tilted my head down... they bothered me.

But I fought hard for my body and I was fucking proud of it.

So yes, I was comfortable with my body and knew what got me off. At least, what got me off by my own hands.

I had vibrators, dildos, and this fancy little toy that sucked and pulsed around my clit. But the actual penetration from a real, live penis was what was new to me, and I couldn't help but be a little fearful for it.

Tonight though... Tonight was my ultimate dream come true.

I followed behind Conor as he walked toward the other end of the bar, flipping off the last of the lights. He pushed through the kitchen swinging door, hardly even holding it for me but for the tips of his fingers as he continued on through the kitchen.

I slipped through before the door swung closed on my face.

He obviously didn't bother with sweetness or gentlemanly acts. Was this all part of his show? To scare away the girl who wanted that sweet gentleman? He wasn't going to scare me away though. Nope.

I quickened my step so I was closer to him, but only in fear that I would truly end up hit in the face by a door. At the end of the kitchen, he turned a corner and reached into a room to flip off the light. Before he pulled the door closed, I recognized the room as an office.

Still, I followed him until we reached the end of this back room. After locking one more door, he opened up the last of them and reached into the hall the door led to. He flipped on a light in the hall, revealing a staircase, before turning off the light to the room we just cleared.

Up the stairs we went, to what I assumed would be his apartment.

Great observation skills on my part, you know.

He opened the unlocked door at the top of the stairs. This time he waited for me. He stood against the open door, his back propping it open and his muscled forearms crossed over his chest.

"You change your mind yet, Curly Locks?" His eyes were challenging me.

I cleared the last of the steps and, chin held high, gave him a challenging look of my own. "Nope. No, I have not."

I slipped into the dark apartment in front of him.

Chapter Three

Conor

Maybe I was wrong about this chick.

She had a bit of a bite, and I liked it.

I reached over to hit the switch, bathing the living area of my apartment in bright light. Stepping away from the door, I stood back and waited for the door to latch before moving toward Curly.

"Grand tour," I said, giving my general spiel with a heavy sigh. I tossed the pad and invite down on the coffee table before gesturing in the direction of the couch. "Living room." I pointed to the kitchen, which was clear due to the lack of wall between the two spaces. "Kitchen slash dining." I stepped past Curly, skirting my comfortable, well-worn leather couch, and headed toward the single hall in this place. Assuming she'd follow, I pointed to a door as we passed it. "Half bath." I kept walking to the end of the hall, heading toward the only other door, and walked into the bedroom.

This fucker was bigger than the living room and kitchen combined.

I had a California king in the middle of the far wall. A leather ottoman thing at the end of the bed. A dresser. A huge ass television. Door to the attached bathroom. Nothing horribly special in there yet, but I wanted to at least redo the shower. Nix the tub.

When Rory and I bought the bar from my parents, one of my projects was renovating the apartment above as well. Rory had his own place due to some investments he made in college, so I got to call the apartment my own. It had been a two bedroom with an office, and I wanted it to be a bitchin' bachelor pad.

Dream it, do it, you know?

"Bedroom. Where the magic happens," I finally said, turning to watch as Curly walked into the room behind me.

Usually the woman would say something at this point, or start stripping—something—but Curly just looked around. I followed her with my eyes as she stepped past me, moving along the wall and taking it in.

"It's a bit big for just you, don't you think?" she finally asked. She had stopped near the bed but turned toward me.

"The room or the bed? The bed is sometimes too small." I smirked at the memories.

Four women. One at the head, sitting with her legs spread. Another between her, eating her out. Me eating *that* one out while on my back and another woman bouncing on my cock, my hands buried in the fourth's wet, slick, bare pussy while she rubbed her tit and girl two's tit.

Good times had been had in this room.

Good times.

Curly looked like she was torn between shock and rolling her eyes. I liked the shock factor.

"Strip," I told her, reaching behind my head to pull off my shirt. No more talking shit. Down to business. I wanted her naked and spread on my bed.

I had an ache in my cock that having her fucking eyes on me caused. All damn night, she stared. Every fucking time she bit that damn lip of hers, I got a little harder.

It had been a long night downstairs, and I was long and thick to prove it.

When my shirt cleared my head, I saw that she had done the same, leaving her in just those fucking skinny jeans and a bra.

Her tits were fucking huge on her body. They weren't the perkiest I'd seen, nor the fullest, but tits were tits. Her belly and hips were soft, but she had a small gem hanging in her navel, showing me she wasn't one of those insecure girls who thought a little extra meat meant she was fat. The piercing proved it; she wasn't afraid to show off her belly.

I moved to sit on the bed, grinning to myself when she shifted at my nearness. I had a huge fucking bed and yes, I was going to sit next to her as I finished undressing.

I leaned forward to remove my boots and socks. I stood again so I could remove the kilt and my black boxers from underneath.

"You're moving slow, Curly."

I dropped everything and stepped out of the puddle of clothes, standing bare in front of this curly-haired woman.

I saw her rake her gaze over my body, lingering on my thick, hard cock that was pulsing and purple, straight the fuck up and down, needing a pussy to envelope it.

Her fingers faltered at the button of her jeans. That's right, Curly, I was fucking hung.

The women loved it. Often I was told it was my best asset.

And let's be honest. I wasn't looking for a relationship, so who the fuck cared if the best thing about me was my cock and what I could do with it?

"Get on with it, Curly Locks, or else your jeans won't make it home with you."

I liked nothing more than ripping clothes off a woman, and depending on the chick, I would do it without the warning I just gave her.

Curly lowered the zipper on her jeans antagonizingly slow, but when I caught her eyes, I saw just a hint of mischief there. Girl knew what she was doing.

She lowered them with a bit of a shimmy and when they were off, leaving her in her bra and, to my disappointment, plain cotton boy shorts, I grabbed her hips and pushed her back onto the bed. Her eyes flared wide for a moment but I dropped my mouth to the top of her tit, sucking and biting.

She let out a breathy moan when my mouth continued its way down until my I surrounded her covered nipple.

I sucked her into my mouth, my teeth gently biting down around the globe, and my tongue pressing against the pebbled peak there. I scraped my teeth back as I lifted my head, leaving a wet circle where my mouth had been.

Curly lay under me, her hips moving against the bed but she kept her hands to herself. I needed more participation from her.

"Hands on my cock."

I pulled down the fabric cupping her breasts and groaned at the sight of her erect, puffy nipples. Damn, I loved puffies. The way they felt in my mouth, an extra cushion around a pebbled, hard peak.

Her hands finally grabbed me and in reward, I dove for her other nipple, sucking her deep into my mouth while my hands went to her underwear. If she were in a fucking thong, I'd rip the damn thing off her.

Or pull it to the side and sink into her.

But she was in fucking granny panties, and I had to actually remove the damn things.

I suckled on her tit while her hands slowly moved up and down my shaft. My girth was my truest asset, and I could feel she had her hands locked together, completely covering me with her hands, as she moved up and down.

I pulled back from her tit, allowing my teeth to bite down a bit harder than what could be considered gentle, and reveled in her open mouthed moan. Fuck yes, Curly.

Sitting back on my knees, I covered her breasts with my hands, kneading and pushing the globes together then apart. I fucking loved real tits. Her hands faltered on my cock but that was ok. I pushed back, my hands still on her chest, until I was partially leaning over her. I moved my hands from her tits only so I could finally undress her fully.

I pulled the offending cotton from her, leaving her bra on and under her tits, pushing them up, and groaned at the site of her bare pussy.

With her curly hair and normal attire, I would have pegged her for all natural. Maybe bikini-kept, but not fucking bare as a baby's bottom.

Still kneeling, but now between her legs, I took her ankles and folded her legs up and out so her wet, pink pussy was on display. My mouth watered as I saw her squeeze, a drop of her wetness seeping out of her. She was fucking soaked.

There would be no dry, uncomfortable penetration. She was going to be a slick, slippery glove and my cock wept its own precum in anticipation.

Needing a taste of her, I leaned down and into her, sweeping my tongue over her beautiful folds. My hands were still on her ankles, but I could feel as her knees dropped inward toward my head. She moved her hips as if trying to get away from my mouth, but I wasn't having it.

One taste of her honey sweetness wasn't going to be enough.

I wasn't one for the foreplay, but her taste was fucking addicting.

I let go of one of her ankles so I could wrap my arm around her leg, laying my forearm over her hips to hold her down. As I put my mouth to her again, this time sucking and moving my face against her, I put my hand to the back of her other leg, pushing her thigh closer to her hip. The action trapped my hand against her but it also opened her up for me. Not wide with full access to her clit, but long, giving me access to her entire pussy and the puckered rose at her back.

Her hips bucked under my arm as I went to town on her. Sucking, thrusting, biting, nipping. My tongue flicked over her clit, then entered her pussy. I sucked and feasted on her wetness as she bucked and moaned and whispered my name. Her hands were in my hair, fisting the locks so fucking hard it hurt.

Give me more, Curly.

Pain with pleasure was the best line to cross.

I released my hold of her leg and her heel dropped to the bed beside me. I wasn't giving her an inch, though, as I sunk two fingers into her wet, waiting pussy.

Her breath came out as a sob and her hips jolted with the intrusion.

She was swollen against my fingers and so fucking tight, I wanted to weep at the thought of her surrounding my fucking cock. It was going to be a tight fit, if the feel of my fingers in her was any indication.

Because two fingers was nowhere close to my girth.

I pumped and pulsed my fingers into her quickly, so fucking fast my forearm was tight and I knew it would be slightly sore later in that night. But her squirming, her moans, her fucking squeezing so hard I thought my fingers would squeeze out of her, only egged me on to go harder and faster.

I sucked her clit into my mouth one last time before she shattered around me.

Mia

God damn, this was so much better than my toys.

The high I felt as I exploded around his hand was unlike any orgasm I ever gave myself.

I loved his control. His mouth was fucking magical and his fingers…

Damn.

Earlier, when he had me grab his cock, I was slightly fearful of his size. He was a bit bigger than my largest dildo.

I had always been sexually minded, having started to masturbate at around twelve. Being a twenty-something year old virgin wasn't something I had planned; I just never found time to date and never wanted to participate in meaningless sex.

Not that this with Conor wasn't meaningless.

He didn't even know who the hell I was. I think that gave the definition to meaningless.

The thought of sex always left me wet. Reading sex always left me uncomfortable with need. So finally last year, I decided to do something about it, and bought my first toy.

Which only spurred my desire for more.

When I started experimenting with penetrating toys, I started small, gradually getting to what was marketed as a normal sized penis.

Conor was not the same size. He was well-endowed in comparison.

I'd always questioned the thicker penises when watching porn, but now I knew they could be real and true.

He was thick from base to just before his head, where he narrowed slightly before the rim of the head of his penis flared out. He was red with a slightly purple hue, with thick veins running up and down his length.

I knew that him entering me was going to be tight and probably a little uncomfortable, but I wasn't about to tell him I was a virgin.

I was on such a wonderful high, there was no fucking way I was allowing him to stop.

I lay there, my chest heaving as I came off of said high. His fingers were still buried deep inside of me but his mouth was no longer on me. Nor was his arm holding my hips down.

He was sitting back on his knees when he slowly, God, so fucking slowly, removed his fingers from my slick channel.

His curled fingers hit another nerve ending, causing me to squeeze down around him as I moaned. He chuckled and took his fingers from me. I watched in fascination as he put his fingers deep into his mouth, his bearded cheeks seeming to hollow as he sucked and pulled his fingers back out of his mouth.

Before I could tell him my thoughts on the action, his hand was fisting his cock and he grunted. "On your stomach."

I had a moment of panic. Maybe now was actually a really good time to—

Before I could further contemplate it, his hands were at my hips and he flipped me over, pulling me up on my knees so my ass was in the air. I rearranged my arms so my hands were at my shoulders, leaving my cheek pressed to the cream pillow that matched the dark tan spread under my body. Behind me, I heard the tear of foil just before I felt Conor's hands on my ass, pulling my cheeks apart.

I looked over my shoulder just as I felt the tip of his covered cock at my pussy.

Could he tell? Surely he wouldn't be able to tell I hadn't truly had sex, right? It would just be a little snug.

I risked looking up at his eyes, but his eyes were focused where his cock head rested. He removed one hand to position himself and I had to bite down on my lip at the excitement that this was happening.

I was nervous, sure, but I was more excited. Feeling the head of his cock right there…

And when he slammed into me, I had to turn my head into the pillow to muffle my yell.

God fucking damn, that hurt!

It was an unbearable stretch and I could feel tears prickling behind my eyes. I groaned open-mouthed into his pillow as his hands kneaded my love handles, his hips pushed all the way to my ass.

"God*damn*, you're so fucking tight, Curly." His voice was gritty and sexy, but I was too busy concentrating on relaxing my muscles. Deep breath in, letting it out slowly against the pillow.

I squeezed my eyes shut as he pulled out unhurriedly and thrust in again.

I could feel him sliding against my slickness, and the tightness was slowly becoming bearable. It was still slightly uncomfortable but he was moving in and out of me slowly, allowing me to become accustomed to his girth.

For the moment anyway.

His hands squeezed my hips as he continued his slow thrusting. "So wet, so tight."

Finally feeling composed, I turned my head so my cheek was to the pillow again. I tried to push up on my arms, but he moved a hand to between my shoulders and pressed me down.

"Right there. Stay right there for me, Curly."

He pushed himself to the brink again and I could feel as he shifted on his knees. Doing what, I wasn't sure. Moving closer?

With his cock still lodged deep in me, he moved my knees together as he straddled them. The new position with my legs together made the feel of him in me impossibly tighter, but I could feel every ridge and line of him as he began his slow pumping once again.

I needed more now, though.

The feel of him in me, thick and veiny and *full*, was bringing out something in me I had never felt before. I pushed my hips back to his, meeting his thrust with one of my own.

He chuckled above me. "Oh, you want more, do you? I'll give you more of this cock." His hands moved from my hips to just above my ass, pulling the extra there up and squeezing the handfuls. I ought to be embarrassed or self-conscious, but he didn't seem to mind as he squeezed and began pounding into me at a quicker pace.

"So fucking tight. Damn, Curly. Take me. Take all of me. That's right, woman. Take my cock."

His grunts intermixed with dirty words as his hips went from his quicker pace, to faster, shorter strokes, the head of his cock hitting me in all the right places. I thought for sure I was going to explode around him.

"I'm close," I managed to whisper.

"Tell me how much you want this cock. Tell me with your filthy mouth, woman. Don't you fucking come until you do."

My heart was pounding and I could feel nerve endings sizzle. How did one *stop* an impending orgasm? I didn't know, but I also didn't want him to stop doing what he was doing, so I did as he demanded.

"You're so big and full. I love when you hit—" I stopped on a moan as he did just as I was about to tell him.

"That? You like that. Tell me more. I'm gonna come so fucking hard, tell me."

I wasn't sure if he was informing me he was going to come, or if I was supposed to repeat him. Either way, it was likely true.

"I need to come, Conor. I have to come. I'm going to come so hard."

"Fucking hard."

"So fucking hard." I squeezed my eyes shut as my orgasm was right there, right at the brink. But I wasn't falling yet. I was right there and I needed to fall over the edge, I needed it so badly.

Conor wrapped an arm under my boobs and lifted me back to him, my back to his chest, as he continued to pound up into me. But it was his other hand that gave me the reprieve I was looking for.

His thick, calloused fingers were at my clit and he squeezed the nub between two fingers, just hard enough to send me flying.

I threw my head back against his shoulder as my mouth dropped open on a soundless cry. With all the porn I had watched, I just assumed a powerful orgasm would bring out the vocals, but I stayed whisper silent, like I did when getting myself off.

"Goddamn, Curly. Fuck!" His cock pushed up into me and I could feel him throbbing against my own pulsing and tightening. It was a heady feeling, the battling beats warring inside my pussy.

Before I was fully sated, Conor lowered us more gently than I would have guessed he was capable of until my stomach was back to the mattress. My legs straightened and before I could revel in the feel of his weight on my back, Conor pulled out of me and stood from his bed.

"Damn. I may just keep you around for a repeat after my cock is rested." He chuckled to himself and I rolled to my back in time to see him frown, moving his hands to roll the condom off his softening dick. "The condom broke. Probably because you were so fucking tight. You're on the pill, right?" He didn't sound anxious. "I'm clean. Get tested regularly. You clean, Curly?" He moved to the bathroom, leaving me alone in his room, in the middle of his huge bed.

Those were not words a girl wanted to hear when she *wasn't* on the pill. Especially when said so nonchalantly.

My doctor put me on a number of birth control pills in my teens to help with hormone regulation due to my period being incredibly irregular, but they all made me severely depressed. I stopped trying to find one that worked. By twenty-two, my hormones finally settled but my period stayed regularly irregular.

"Um." I could tell him no, I wasn't o birth control. I'm sure this wasn't his first rodeo with a broken condom, not with how easily he announced It. Or I could just tell him yes and be sure to go to the doctor right away in the morning.

If I had had time to plan this night with Conor, I would have made an appointment with my doctor prior to the planned night, but that hadn't been in the cards.

I sat up then, pulling the cups of my bra up over my breasts and looking around for the rest of my clothing, suddenly feeling very dirty. My *bra* hadn't even been off!

I heard a toilet flush and Conor walked back into the room. "You didn't answer me, Curly."

"Um, yeah. I am." I shook my head and forced a grin on my face, looking around until I spotted my underwear. Good God, I wore *those* today?

My face slightly red, I stood and reached for them. I pulled the plain cotton on as Conor grabbed a clean pair of boxers from one of his dressers. He turned toward me as he stepped into the fabric and I risked looking at his penis, curious what it looked like flaccid.

He wasn't nearly as long, but he was still pretty thick. It was impressive, really.

I grabbed my shirt and slipped it on over my head before finding my jeans. This whole getting dressed immediately after sex was awkward. It wasn't something I wanted to do ever again.

Conor came over to the bed as I was hopping into my jeans and I noticed another frown marring his face.

"What the fuck?" It came out as a surprised whisper, his brows drawn in as he stared at the bed.

I looked behind me and bit my lip.

So much for that theory.

Chapter Four

Conor

It had been a fun, even if slightly quick, session in the sack, and I was ready to hit that sack for other reasons. It was nearing three thirty and I'd been up since five the morning prior. Curly was getting dressed and when she'd been putting on her shirt, I admired her soft stomach and full tits once more before she bent to pull on her jeans.

Which gave me a better view of those tits.

It was over her shoulder, though, that I noticed the small dark marks on the spread.

I walked closer and took a better look, my eyes frowning.

"What the fuck?"

She'd been too wet to tear, even with how fast I pushed myself to the hilt.

Which only meant...

No.

She was tight, but I had only heard stories of girls being so tight, with breaking through the hymen, that it was nearly chokingly tight around the guy's dick.

My frown still in place, I looked down at Curly. She was now standing at her full height, her hands clasped in front of her and her eyes...

Shit, her eyes looked worried.

"Were you a fucking virgin?" I didn't recognize the incredulous tone in my voice.

She bit that lip of hers again and my damn cock warred with my head.

The panic was morphing into some sort of anger. Or heated unease. "I said—*were you a fucking virgin*?"

I didn't fuck virgins. I didn't.

Fuck. She was going to want to come back, she was going to cling. I didn't do relationships, and I certainly didn't do second-times, unless the second time was with a group.

Curly lifted her chin defiantly, still not answering me. "I'll see myself out. Thanks for a great time, Conor."

I reached for her arm to pull her to a stop. I was angry, yes, but when she flinched at the movement, I had a moment of realization that between my anger, my words, my actions, and then I'm sure with the way I looked…

"Get your hand off of me," she said between clenched teeth.

I let go of her arm and held both my hands up. I tried for a more placid tone, but even I could hear it didn't quite make it. "Were you. A virgin."

I could see her battling the answer. I could see her battling answering me.

Fuck.

Her chin still lifted, her brown eyes met mine and held. There was a long moment of silence before she opened her mouth again. "Yes."

Fuck.

I didn't want to be insensitive but…

I was. I was insensitive.

"Why didn't you say anything?"

"I didn't think you would notice." She moved to walk out of the room and I followed. Willingly, even.

That was a bullshit answer if I'd ever heard one. "How the fuck wouldn't I notice?"

She didn't bother to stop or turn her head to look at me. "You didn't until well after the fact."

Ok, so the lady had a point.

"Look." She finally stopped in the living room, turning toward me. "I was curious and I'd heard about you and I just wanted the damn thing taken care of. That's all. I'm not going to cling. I'm not going to beg you for tomorrow night. In fact, you probably won't ever see me again." She smiled slightly, but it looked menacing almost. "Thank you for tonight, Conor," she said again. "I'll see myself out."

She turned again and moved to the other side of the room in record time. I tried telling myself I didn't care, she was just another chick, another hole on another night.

But when she reached the door and looked over her shoulder at me briefly before pulling the door open and stepping out, I was hit in the gut again with her familiarity.

But I didn't know her.

Shit, she was just another woman I took to bed, who I didn't get her name. Names didn't matter.

But for whatever reason, I had a feeling her name mattered. A feeling that her being my first, and fuck she'd better be my only, virgin, mattered.

I shook my head.

I was too tired for this shit.

Tomorrow night I'd take two girls. That would take my mind off Curly for sure.

Chapter Five
Late August

Conor

"Get your fucking phone out of the ice chest, Rory."

Rory and I were getting the bar ready for the day. It was all of ten on a Sunday morning but with a noon baseball game, we were bound to start getting busy the moment we opened the doors at eleven.

"Dude, yesterday there was a Articuno in here."

I frowned at my kid brother. "A arti-what?"

"Articuno. You know, Pokémon Go?" Rory closed the ice chest and scanned his phone around the bar and into one of the fridges.

"You are fucking twenty-nine years old, Rory. Pokémon is for ten year olds."

Rory shook his head, his longer wavy hair shaking with the movement. "No. Definitely more adults playing. It's like a flashback from childhood." Still, Rory didn't look away from his phone.

I walked over to him and snatched the device from him. "Well right now we need to get the bar ready, so catch your Pikachu on your own fucking time."

Rory grabbed for his phone but I did the dick move and put it down the front of my pants.

"Fuck, Con! Shit, that's nasty." Rory's face was contorted and I couldn't help but laugh as I went back to my earlier task. "You owe me a new phone, fucker."

"I didn't put it down my boxers. Relax, man." I shook my head, grinning. I was stacking glasses when Brenna came barreling into the bar from the swinging kitchen door.

"Oh my God, you'll never guess who I ran into last night!"

I looked over my shoulder at my twenty-five year old baby sister. Her black hair matched my own, but had the same waves Rory's did, although hers was much longer.

"Oh, please do tell," I said dryly. Whether Rory or I wanted to hear, Brenna would tell. She probably ran into one of her ex's that was a douche, that Rory or I took care of. Something or someone like that.

"Mia Hampton."

I moved to grab another pallet of glasses and glanced at Brenna. "Mia Hampton?" Remembering the phone in my pants, I took it out and put it in my back pocket. Brenna caught the act and frowned a moment before continuing her story.

"You know. Curly Mia from elementary school? My best friend up until the fifth grade? She spent every freaking day at our house."

Rory chuckled. "Oh yeah. Fat Mia."

"Rory!" Brenna's brows were raised. "She wasn't *fat*. Don't be a dick."

"She was kind of pudgy," I said under my breath, remembering the round girl with the unkempt hair.

"You two are asses." Brenna crossed her arms. "Anyway, I saw her at the mall. Get this. Coming out of a *maternity* store." I fought from rolling my eyes. Didn't she have girlfriends she could talk to about this? "She's gotta be like…six months pregnant. I asked about her husband and she doesn't have one. Said the baby was an accident but she looked so happy. *God*! Remember how everyone thought I was the bad egg between the two of us? Shit. Who'd have thought she'd get knocked up on accident…before I did." Brenna stumbled on the last of her words and while that was concerning, I didn't question it.

"Great?" I didn't really care who was pregnant or that pudgy Mia from fifteen years ago was without a man and with a child. I wasn't about to call Brenna out on spreading stories though. She knew what harm could come from them and I didn't really want to see her bright eyes dim at the reminder.

"Anyway, I invited her out to dinner tonight."

I paused and looked at her. "Tonight's your birthday dinner."

She nodded, grinning.

I scratched above my eyebrow, slightly exasperated with her. "Why would you invite her to a dinner you were having with your brothers? Go do lunch with her instead. It's not like you work here."

"I do too work here, asshole." Brenna uncrossed her arms. "She just looked kind of lonely. Happy, yeah, but lonely, and I thought it would be nice for her to meet up with everyone again."

I shook my head. My sister was so softhearted sometimes.

Rory shrugged a shoulder as he faced the liquors on the back shelf. "So we do dinner with pudgy Mia—"

"Don't call her that!"

Rory continued, ignoring Brenna. "It's just one night, Con. Make nice, you asshole."

I couldn't help but feel like Brenna was setting one of us up with Mia. Rory, the Pokémon Go player, certainly wasn't up to dating a woman who was knocked up, and me? Fuck that shit.

"She's actually really pretty," Brenna added, her brows up and a sly grin on her face. And that fucking look was aimed at me.

Yep, totally trying to set me up.

I pointed at her. "Do not."

She feigned innocence and lifted her hands in the air. "I'm not doing anything, Con!"

"I like my life."

"I know!" She put her hands down. "I just thought maybe if you saw her again, you would maybe think twice about all the hoes in your life." She grinned at me. "Besides, I miss having her in my life. She was a good friend."

"You were fucking ten."

"Hey! That's a pretty impressionable time in a young girl's life!"

"She ditched you."

"Yep, she totally did," Rory added, as if he were actually a part of this tennis match and not an onlooker. Speaking of, the fucker wasn't working.

"Rory. Do something with the bar." Then to Brenna, "I don't do relationships, Bren. You know that. I'll make nice at dinner, but don't expect anything more."

The answering look on Brenna's face...

I didn't want to know what she had up her sleeve.

And quite frankly, at the moment I didn't care. I had a bar to run.

Mia

Living in the town I grew up in had its moments.

Moments where I wished I'd chosen a teaching job anywhere else.

Unfortunately, of the schools I was offered a job at, the neighboring town of Imperial Beach, where I spent much of my youth, had the better program. As such, I taught second grade at an elementary school I went to, and often ran into old classmates at the grocery store.

Or ex-best friends at the mall. Namely, an ex-best friend whose brother put this big old basketball in this tummy of mine.

You know. People like that.

When Brenna asked about my husband, I froze. When she rephrased to ask about the "baby daddy," I stumbled and looked at my feet. I wasn't about to tell her my baby's daddy was her older brother. I hadn't even had the nerve to walk into the bar to tell him; I sure wasn't going to tell his sister first.

But somehow I found myself doing just that, as I cried over an iced tea in the food court. I didn't know why Brenna was being so nice to me, but she was extremely easy to talk to and there I was, blubbering at her like a freaking fool.

"Conor? My Conor?" she had asked.

I nodded and told her how he didn't know who I was, and how it was just a one-night thing. How I never intended on seeing him again but after my irregular period was nearing three months late, I took the test and my stomach had dropped. What were the freaking odds I'd get pregnant my first time, and for Plan B failing too? It was as if the Gods were laughing at me, making an example out of the good girl who did one naughty thing.

Brenna simply hugged me and went on and on about how she and I could finally be close again. About how she was going to help me break the news to her brother. About how she and I could discuss it over dinner tomorrow night.

I was extremely thrown by this bombardment from Brenna but needing a friend, I took her up on her offer.

I had gone home and tried to find an outfit that didn't make me feel like a whale. Now wearing it, I found myself at a cute Italian restaurant just outside of town.

I sat by the front door, nervously chewing on my lip as I waited for Brenna to show. She told me to meet her just outside the door and text her the moment I arrived.

I held my clutch in front of me, nervous energy running through me. I was still a bit put off by the whole running into Brenna and her wanting to be my friend after fifteen years thing, but I would get past it.

The doors swung open and out walked Brenna in her raven-haired glory. It really was unfair that she'd been beautiful as a pre-teen and was even more gorgeous as an adult. What happened to that adage of the pretty ones turning out to be the ugliest after school was over?

"Come on in. I have a table already." Brenna smiled and held the door for me, allowing me to step into the restaurant before she moved in front to weave the way to the table.

I should have followed my gut when I felt the telltale signs of something being wrong the moment I left the mall—and Brenna—yesterday.

Because just a few tables away, a few feet in front of Brenna, was Conor.

I stopped dead in my tracks and, whether it was hormones or just me, felt tears build up behind my eyes. I was so fucking naïve.

Of course she didn't want to be my friend. She stopped wanting to be my friend in middle school when I was too fat to hang out with her. When she was getting all the attention from boys and I was in the middle of my extremely long awkward phase.

Was her inviting me tonight her being facetious? Was she being rude and wanting to point fingers at me? What the hell was her goal?

The buzzing in my head didn't allow for me to hear Brenna address the table but the moment Conor's eyes met mine across the short distance, my stomach truly dropped to the floor, my clutch following shortly after.

With a red face and burning eyes, I knelt down the best I could with my slightly protruding belly, and picked up my clutch. I stood as gracefully as I could in the black pants and flowy shirt that did *not* hide the evidence underneath and, with a swallow, made myself face Conor.

Made myself face the father of my child.

Chapter Six

Conor

The after game crowd had been a bit of a riot at O'Gallaghers, but Rory and I managed to slip out in time to make it to dinner with Brenna. Stone was manning the bar for me, and I had full trust in the man.

Never mind the fact it was Sunday, and we would only be open for another hour or so.

As soon as we made it to our table for our seven o'clock reservations, Brenna excused herself to go meet Mia.

I should have figured there was more to Brenna's excitement than her simply running into an old friend who was pregnant.

Because when Brenna came back, big-ass grin on her face, with Mia behind her...

My stomach fucking dropped.

Mia was Curly Locks.

Curly Locks was Mia.

The chick I fucked, the only virgin I fucked, nearly half a fucking year ago, was *pregnant*.

I would like to think that my sexual prowess persuaded Curly—*Mia*—to go get laid more often, that there was no fucking way in hell that that baby bump had anything to do with me, but I wasn't stupid.

Fuck.

Fuck.

I hardcore stared at her. She looked the same as all those nights ago, except for the obvious being pregnant. That and her curly mass of hair was down, a small top section pulled back with everything else falling just past her shoulders.

I was so fucking torn. Mia was goddamn hot and I can't say I ever found a pregnant woman sexy before. But putting my cock aside, she had known who the hell I was and still fucked me.

How the *hell* didn't she tell me who she was? So not only did I fuck a virgin, but I fucked a girl who used to follow me around like a sick puppy dog, up until she and my sister had a falling out.

The real kicker though, the one that got me in the balls, was just like she hadn't found it important to tell me her name, she hadn't found it important to tell me I knocked her up.

Mia's eyes met mine across the tables and I watched as her face went from bright red to fucking pale as a ghost, no doubt in response to the fire in my eyes. *That's right, bitch. I'm pissed.*

"Brenna," I growled low. I wasn't about to make a scene in this fancy-assed restaurant, but I needed a word with my sister. Brenna's grin faltered and the light went out from her eyes. I had a fleeting thought that maybe she wasn't being cruel in this meeting.

But then again, this was the girl who left my baby sister to fend for herself when the adolescent years started to get tough.

She shot a small smile over her shoulder at Mia before walking over to where I still sat at the table. Her brows pulled low, the growl in her whispered voice matched my earlier one as she leaned down, her face in mine. "You will fucking make nice, Conor O'Gallagher."

"I love you, and it's your birthday, but I am not dealing with *that*," I pointedly glared toward Mia, who was still clutching her wallet in front of her, "at your dinner. I trust you have her phone number, so send her away and I'll deal with her later."

I couldn't believe that Curly Locks was Mia. No shit her eyes had looked familiar. I'd seen them nearly every day from when she and Brenna were three until they were ten.

"I'm not sending her away!" Brenna whisper yelled at me.

"What the fuck game are you playing?" I glanced over when I noticed Rory stand and watched as he walked over to Mia, no doubt to make small talk for both her and his own sanity. Probably was bored being out of the loop.

It didn't explain the tightening in my chest or the red in my eye when Mia smiled at Rory and hugged him. What the fuck was that about?

"I'm not playing a game. You did this, Conor, you did." Brenna poked her finger into my chest. "*You* will make nice and *you* will make this right."

"She didn't even fucking tell me her name."

Brenna lifted a brow, standing straight and crossing her arms over her chest. "How many names do you usually take when you bring one of your 'hoes upstairs, Conor? She was just another and you knocked her up."

Again, that fucking tightening in my chest when Brenna essentially called Mia my whore.

What the actual fuck? I rubbed my chest, but did it where Brenna had jabbed her finger into my sternum.

"Why are you being nice to her, Bren?" I looked around quickly.

Surely we were making a scene with two of us arguing over hushed words, and two others awkwardly having a conversation. "She abandoned you. At fucking ten years old, Brenna! She should mean nothing to you."

Brenna's face morphed into one of almost sadness as she shrugged, her brows lifted. "Maybe I was the one to abandon her. And I don't want to do it again. We may not have been friends, but I always knew she wasn't one to spread the rumors."

I stared at my sister, heated anger still coursing through my body, before shaking my head. "It's your dinner. Whatever." I wasn't going to win this. My fault or not, Mia had known who I was. She also had known where to fucking find me and chose not to.

I shook my head yet again, turning my attention back to the empty table, and tossed my napkin in my lap roughly. Brenna sat beside me and once she and I were seated, Rory and Mia walked over. Rory, showing off his fucking cocky side, held out the chair for Mia and she sat slowly across the table from me, her eyes glued to the table cloth.

I kept my eyes on Mia. I had so many things to say, cruel words, fucked up words, but also questions. Curious questions. Rory sat down beside her and reached for the wine menu.

"This calls for something strong." Rory flipped open the small booklet and started to scan, as if the kid knew a damn thing about a good wine.

Still, my eyes were on Mia. She kept her hands in her lap, gripping her wallet still, I assumed, her eyes remaining on the table. I watched as she started to lift them, stopping where the table met my stomach, and her eyes cut over toward Brenna.

Mia shook her head and swallowed roughly. "I can't do this." Her voice was strangled.

Brenna reached across the table, holding her palm up. "Mia. You two need to talk. I know my brother, and this is going to be the least hostile place for you two."

"Yeah. Besides, it's totally Con's fault you're in this predicament anyway so let him deal with the stares," Rory offered.

I frowned at him. "Thanks."

Rory grinned and winked. "No prob, bro."

Mia glanced at Brenna's hand finally and she started to lift her own from her clutch. Quickly though, I watched as her face went from slightly red in embarrassment to blanched, to a really fucking concerning shade of green. Rather than reach for Brenna's hand, Mia brought the back of her hand up to her mouth and with wide eyes, shook her head. "I'm going to be sick."

She stood from the table quickly and I could hear as her clutch fell to the floor again. She looked around the area quickly, looking for the bathroom I would assume, and left the table in a hurry. I sat in my chair but turned to watch over my shoulder. I saw as she stumbled when someone pushed their chair out to stand, but she recovered and continued her trek.

Brenna took my shoulder and forced me to turn back to the table.

"She's twenty-four weeks pregnant and she's under the illusion that it's yours. And after the story she told me, I have to say I believe her," Brenna said, her voice in that low, dangerous tone again. She was pissed at me.

"She didn't tell me who she was," I repeated.

"That doesn't fucking matter, Con!" Her voice was low enough still to not carry, but it certainly felt like she yelled it. "She's pregnant and she's alone, and she's obviously scared of you! Did you see the way she looked at you? What the hell did you do? Tie her up against her will? Slap her around?"

Rory, the bastard, looked ready to laugh as he settled into his chair, arms crossed over his chest.

"I may have raised my voice when I learned she was a virgin."

"A...?" Brenna frowned. "She was a twenty-five year old virgin? No way. She's too pretty and too confident."

"She was a fucking virgin." I squeezed the bridge of my nose between my finger and thumb.

Rory still looked smug, but he turned his chin some and an inquisitive look crossed his face. "You ever get anyone pregnant before, Con? I mean, you do have quite the active sex life." As if he had room to fucking talk.

Brenna put her fingers to her ears. "Lalala, I don't wanna hear it!"

I frowned at Brenna but then turned back to Rory. "Not that I know of, no." I pulled Brenna's finger from her ear and said loudly enough in her direction, but not so loud the entire restaurant would hear. "The condom broke when I was in her tight pussy."

"You're such a pig," Brenna muttered before I turned back to Rory.

"I've only broken a condom maybe two other times and I've seen those chicks getting plastered afterward, so I'm going to go with no."

"Well, congrats, Daddy," Rory said with a shit-eating grin. Bastard.

Brenna looked over her shoulder to where Mia disappeared to. "I'm going to go check on her."

I stood before Brenna could. "I'll do it."

She and I needed to have words.

In private.

Chapter Seven

Mia

Thank God I made it to the bathroom in time. I didn't bother locking the door the single person bathroom, only caring to dive for the toilet before what was sure to be only stomach acid came up and out of my mouth.

I was too late in the game to be having morning sickness and actually, I had been extremely lucky my first trimester, never getting sick. I never had cravings, I didn't have the need to binge eat. The only change in my life was the fact I was growing another life inside of me.

Having not eaten since noon, the only thing that came up was indeed stomach acid. The burning in my throat, paired with the embarrassment of the entire situation I found myself in tonight, had tears falling from my eyes.

I was such a fucking fool for believing that Brenna would want to renew a friendship. Who sought out a friendship from someone you hadn't truly spoken to since middle school?

I should have figured she was going to throw Conor in my face. I never told her when we were little, but I think she always knew I had crushed on her oldest brother.

But what was a crush at ten? It was a whole lot of *nothing*.

I wiped the back of my mouth and reached for the toilet paper, needing to blot some of the wetness from my cheeks when there was a knock at the door.

"Just a minute!" I called out, a slight wavering in my voice that was no doubt due to the tears in my eyes.

I stood and straightened out my dress pants, trying to dust off the knees. When the baby moved, I put my hand over the front of my swelling tummy. "It's ok, baby."

I chose not to find out if I was having a boy or a girl. I still had panicked moments where I considered putting the baby up for adoption. Was I ready to be a mom? Was I ready to be a single parent?

I wanted this baby, but sometimes it was the fear of what I could offer the child, or rather what I *couldn't* offer him or her, that kept me up at night.

The knock on the door sounded yet again. Damn impatient woman. I glanced at the mirror after moving to the sink and grimaced at the splotches on my face. "Just a second, I'm sorry."

I turned on the water and just began splashing water on my face when the door swung open.

I jerked up and turned to face the intruder. "I said it would just be a min—"

Conor.

My heart stopped and yet again, I could feel the color fall from my face.

He stepped into the small space and closed the door behind him, doing what I failed to do and locking the door.

Locking the two of us in here together.

I swallowed hard and stared at him. He stared back.

I took in his dress pants and dress shirt, sleeves rolled up to show off the gray and black sleeve he had on his left arm. His beard appeared to be freshly kept and his eyes, framed with such dark, thick lashes, were locked on mine.

It wasn't fair he was such a beautiful man.

"Why didn't you tell me?" Conor broke the silence with a surprisingly calm voice.

Tell him what? My name? That I was pregnant?

"Because I was afraid of your response," I finally answered. It was the truth and fit both scenarios. I forced my eyes to meet his, and moved my gaze from his left to his right eye, back and forth as I tried to read his expression.

He hadn't been happy to see me out there.

But then again, I hadn't been exactly thrilled, either.

Just like I'd been attempting a plan to get into Conor's bed, I had been trying to figure out a way to tell him, oops, that broken condom left me a little pregnant.

"You keeping it?" His eyes jerked down to my tummy then back up to mine.

"It's a little too late to abort," I said a little harsher than the situation probably warranted for. Besides, medically that was a lie.

He shook his head and sighed. I could feel his annoyance with me. "I meant adoption. Are you giving it up?"

I put my hands on my belly as if trying to protect the little one tucked away inside. I gave Conor the truth. "I've considered the fact that I might not be what's best for this baby, but I think," I took a deep breath. Everything clicked into place. The baby rolled and I was reminded of every move, every hiccup, every uncomfortable dig this little peanut had done and I realized I wouldn't change it for the world. Regardless of Conor and what happened in the future, yes, I wanted this baby. "Yeah," I nodded. "I'm keeping it."

His blue gaze was once again locked on my stomach, this time not moving. "You want child support or something? After a DNA test, of course." His eyes met mine again and I fought the need to yell at him. Rather, I clenched my jaw.

"If I wanted something from you, Conor, I would have sought you out."

"Oh, like you did for your virginity. Because that's what that was about, right?" He crossed his arms over his chest. "You knew who the fuck I was, and still you sat at my fucking bar, eye fucking me every damn time you were there. You planned on me taking your virginity."

I lifted my chin and said through gritted teeth. "I didn't think you would notice." Quite quickly, my blood pressure was rising. This man! He had quite the nerve in making me out to be the bad guy in this situation. When I was pissed, my mouth ran. And it was about to run. "Because guess what? Your cock's not the only thing that's been in this pussy. Get over yourself, fucker."

There was a red haze around the room and I had to fight the mixed urge to vomit and to run. My heart was pounding in both anxiety and anger. I tugged on the lower hem of my shirt which ended up only allowing the bulge of my tummy to show off even more, and pushed away to try and get past Conor, needing to leave.

Damn Conor for being a gorgeous asshole.

Damn Brenna for being a conniving bitch.

Fuck me for being naïve and believing the best in people.

Conor was standing in front of the door but I attempted to squeeze around him anyway. "Let me out." I leaned against him in an effort to push him out of the way, but I knew I was going to fail this battle.

With ease, Conor put his big hands on my arms and moved me away from the door and against a nearby wall.

"I told you once before. Keep your Goddamn hands off of me." Again, I spoke through clenched teeth. It was that or I was afraid I was going to start crying. Damn fucking hormones.

"I seem to remember you liking my hands on you."

"Yeah, before your asshole colors truly came out." I refused to look him in the eye, instead choosing to look at his shoulder.

"You knew beforehand that I was an asshole. Everyone knows I'm an ass."

I worked on calming my heart before meeting his eyes with my own. "Please just let me go. I won't bother you with the baby. I promise." My voice cracked on the last word and I could feel the damn tears I tried so hard to keep at bay, fill my eyes.

This time it was Conor's eyes flitting back and forth between my own. His hands squeezed on my arms and once they loosened, I thought I would be able to run to freedom, never seeing him again.

But I was wrong.

Oh so wrong.

Conor

Now that I knew she was Mia from back in the day, now that I had that small amount of knowledge, the familiarity in her eyes made so much sense. I looked back and forth between her whiskey brown eyes and when I saw them watering, it hit me low in the gut.

I wasn't a guy who dealt with emotion. My sister's, sure, yeah. But never anyone outside of my siblings.

I flirted with women at the bar because they tipped extremely well when I did. I took countless nameless women up to my apartment at the end of the night and they always knew the score. Bring them up, get *it* up, in, out, go home. Every night it was the same story and rarely did any of the women linger in my mind.

I thought that Curly lingering in my mind was because she'd been a virgin. It made her, unfortunately, special. And not necessarily special in a good way.

Special in a way that had me seeing red for weeks afterward.

But eventually I worked her out of my system by doing what I always did. But the shock of seeing her again, being pregnant no less, had all the feelings I thought I pushed down and away, coming back up.

Feelings that maybe she was special in a different way.

I didn't want a special woman in my life. I liked my life the way it was, thank you. I liked different pussy and multiple pussy. I liked rough sex, and bondage sex, and anal sex. Looking at this curly haired woman in front of me, I didn't see any of that in her.

But damn if that didn't have me *not* turning away from her.

Rather, I did what I never did with women.

I loosened my grip from her arms, and just as I saw the relief flash through her eyes, I grabbed her hips and pulled her in tight. The swell of her stomach against my now hard, aching cock gave me pause, but not nearly as much as the need to kiss her did.

I didn't kiss women.

I didn't kiss men either, you fuckers.

I just didn't kiss. I put my mouth on pussies, dipped my tongue in them too, but my mouth never touched another's. Not really sure why, to be honest; kissing just never was high on my agenda. I always had other places I wanted my lips and tongue to be.

But at this moment, the only place I wanted them was on Mia's full, pink ones.

Her mouth opened on a gasp and I took the opportunity to sweep my tongue inside. My hands gripped at her hips, and I fought the desperate need to pull her closer than she already was. Any closer and I'd be inside her, fucking her against the wall.

Not that that was a bad idea.

I reached around her to grab a handful of her delectable ass, remembering the feel of the full globes filling my hands. She went up on tiptoe and finally, *finally* she was participating. Her hands were in my hair, her tongue battling mine. Mia tried pressing closer and she groaned in disappointment when she couldn't. I couldn't help but pull back just enough to chuckle.

"What do you need, Mia?" I whispered against her mouth right before I nipped at her upper lip.

"You," she whispered back as she moved her hands out of my hair, her fingers grazing through my beard. She traced her fingers down my neck, my chest, my sternum. Down, down, she kept going down.

I kept my body still, not wanting to rush her pursuit but my cock was fucking ecstatic at the trail her hands were taking. Her fingers lingered at the top of my pants, just above my belt, where my shirt was tucked.

Untuck it, I wordlessly pleaded with her. *Untuck it and stick your hands down my pants, Mia. Do it.*

She kept a hand at the top of my belt buckle and with her palm, trailed over and down to where my cock was standing up and at attention, as best as it could against my pants. Her palm covered me and I bit back a moan. Fucking God, I needed her hand to squeeze me.

But be careful what you wish for, because—

"*Fucking A!*"

She fucking squeezed all right. She fucking squeezed so fucking hard, my hands fell from her and she stepped back.

Her face was flushed but her eyes still held that sheen of tears from before, and *that*, ladies and gentlemen, is what gave me the truest pause. She'd been into the kiss. I knew that she had been; she was more fucking responsive now than she had been in March. So what was up with this look?

"I said keep your hands off of me, Conor," she said, her lip quivering just slightly but her eyes held fire. She pulled down on her shirt—more in a nervous habit, if I had to guess, than to straighten it—and pushed her chin up. "Not everything can be answered with sex. When you're ready to be an adult and talk to me, I'll be happy to do just that."

This time when she pushed past me, I let her go, watching as she left the small confines of the bathroom.

I should be pissed. Fuck, my dick ached for a whole different reason at this very moment.

But rather than be pissed, I was slightly amused.

Mia had claws.

I couldn't wait to tame them.

Chapter Eight

Mia

I stomped out of the restroom, berating myself the entire way to the table where Brenna and Rory still sat.

I *enjoyed* his mouth on me. It was an action I wasn't expecting, and the way he controlled the kiss... My God, the man was magical.

And I *responded*. I was supposed to be pissed at him! I *was* pissed at him!

Sure, this whole debacle was my fault but my goodness, I didn't expect a *kiss* from him upon finding out that I was pregnant and had kept it from him!

I furiously swiped under my eyes, trying to rid my lower lids of any lingering tears. Fuck this hormonal emotional bull, too. I hated that I cried on a drop of a dime and from the moment Conor turned his icy glare at me, to when he was trying to win me over by getting in my pants yet again...

I couldn't control the emotions.

Brenna noticed me coming first and immediately stood. "I am so sorry, Mia."

I held up a hand as I drew near the table. "Save it, Brenna. I should have realized you had something up your sleeve. I wasn't good enough for you growing up, and you obviously wanted to push all my buttons now." Brenna's mouth dropped open and she gaped at me. I was so livid, so *pissed*, with myself that I really could give two shits about Brenna's thoughts and reactions at this very moment.

I looked around the table for my clutch, finally spotting it where my chair was. I leaned forward but grumbled to myself when my belly got in the way. My goodness, I didn't know what I would do in even five more weeks. At twenty-four weeks, I looked like I was harboring a ball of some sort under my shirt, and I still had sixteen weeks to go.

I moved my lean into a crouch and finally was able to retrieve my clutch. I stood back up just as Conor reached the table.

"Happy birthday, Bren," he said, pulling her in to kiss her temple, "but I'm taking Mia home."

"Like hell you are!" I slammed my clutch to my side.

He glared at me, the blue of his eyes icy and fierce. "I'm taking you home. We are not finished." Each word was pronounced as if he were forcing each word out. As if his forced words would get me to comply.

Ha!

I wasn't some woman he could just...order around! I shook my head. "No. I drove myself. I'll get myself home." I turned on my heel before he could get in another word.

With my head lowered, I made my way out of the restaurant. We definitely made quite the scene and it was embarrassing to say the least. Before I could open the door, it opened from a masculine arm behind me and I fought the need to growl at Conor.

I walked through the door, my clutch held firmly against my leg, as I made my way toward my car.

"I said I was taking you home," Conor spoke from behind me. He was right on my heels, not that I turned to check.

"And I said I was doing it myself." I weaved through the cars in the parking lot, finding my gray Mazda-3. I popped open my clutch to find the little fob I tossed in there, hitting the button to unlock the doors.

As I went to open the door though, Conor's big paw slapped down, holding the door in place.

"I want. To talk. To you."

I whipped around, my back to my car, before I could decide that was a bad move. I was now trapped between a menacing Conor and his hard, delicious body, and my car, with no escape route.

"Then talk." I gave him my best stern-teacher voice, even though inside I was quivering with nerves. Or anticipation. I wasn't entirely sure which.

"Not out here."

I crossed my arms and drew in my brows. "You are *awfully* demanding."

"We need to talk, Mia, and I don't want to do it out in the open. My place, your place, *fuck,* the bar. Just not here."

He didn't move any closer, but he was already close enough. The toes of his boots met the toes of my shoes and with him leaning forward against the car, it brought his chest and neck close to my face. When I'd last been near him, he smelled good, yes, but he had the scent of the bar on him.

And other women.

Let's not forget the other women.

But tonight he was devoid the other smells. He was all Conor. All amber musk goodness.

I had to work to keep my mad on. It would be all too easy to fall into the charm of Conor O'Gallagher. When he flashed smiles or winks, when he was actually nice, he was incredibly attractive.

Come to think of it, I hadn't really experienced that side of Conor. I just watched it from the sidelines at the bar.

"Fine." I turned back toward my car. "But I'm driving myself. To my place. You can follow." I didn't want to be in his apartment. While it held a few moments of great memories for me, I didn't want to have a conversation with him in a place that he likely had forty other women in after I left.

I wasn't anything special. It wasn't like he went celibate after I went upstairs with him.

Conor dropped his arm from the car and stepped back. Oddly, I ached for him to brush his hand along my arm, my lower back, *anywhere*, but he didn't. He kept his hands to himself. "All right. I'll follow."

Conor

I followed behind Mia at her request. The entire drive to her place though had my mind swirling.

Where did she live? Was it safe for an infant? Did I really care if it was safe for a baby? Was I getting *invested* in this baby? If I was, what did that do for me and Mia?

Was there a 'me and Mia?' Fuck, did I *want* a 'me and Mia?'

Hell, I didn't even *know* Mia!

All these thoughts were confusing as shit. I liked my life. I liked the different women every night, and the thought of settling down—the fucking *idea*—was never one that played in my head.

But one look at Curly walking back into my life, with a baby belly at that, had everything shifting, even if just slightly.

Not too far from the restaurant, Mia pulled into a small, seemingly well-kept, apartment complex and I maneuvered my Subie into an open spot near her car port.

I was probably getting too old for the turbo charged, boosted Subaru, but it had been my dream car as a teenager, and I was holding on to her as long as her motor kept running.

So to all those fuckers who said I couldn't handle commitment, fuck you. I could handle commitment just fine.

I cut the ignition and peeled myself out of my car, not bothering to look across the lot before stalking toward Mia, who stood beside her own car waiting.

Thank fucking God, her eyes didn't have tears in them anymore. They still held that sass I witnessed in the restroom, but sass I could handle.

Before I could think up something to say, Mia turned and headed toward the building. I, having called this meeting, followed behind. I left enough room between us so I could check out the sway of her hips. One of the things I immediately noticed on Mia, beside her belly, was that her tits grew. I wasn't surprised then, to find her ass had a little extra bounce to it, too.

I wanted to put my hands on it, squeeze the round globes in my hands as I pounded into her from behind again...

Wait a fucking second.

I didn't do double dipping. I know I said we needed to talk, and I know I was having some mixed feelings on the drive over, but hell if my head didn't seem to want to keep Mia around. I was going to have to think about that little fact a bit longer.

Mia had me climb three fucking flights of steps. Three. Now, I know that's not a lot, but she was at the top of the apartment complex and if her belly was the size it was now? Surely she would be winded on this trip a few more weeks down the road.

"You should proba—"

She held her hand out to her side, angled back toward me without actually turning to address me. "Save it."

My brows lifted on their own accord, I swear it, at her abrupt dismissal of what I was going to say. "You don't even—"

Mia stopped in front of a door and turned toward me. "I said. Save it."

Well-fucking-then.

I stopped beside her and crossed my arms over my chest. Fine. I wouldn't say it. Yet.

She turned back to her door and unlocked it, stepping inside and holding the door for me. I took the door from her on my own way through and she moved away, toeing out of her shoes. Moving them with her toes, she placed them along the wall and hung her keys on a peg, putting her wallet in a small basket attached to the bar the peg was on.

"I'm going to change into something more comfortable. Just... Sit somewhere." She waved her hand dismissively as she walked away from me and like the involuntary brow raise a little bit ago, my lips were twitching to grin.

I let the door close behind me and bent down to untie my dress shoes, placing them near the shoes Mia set aside. They were next to a pair of running shoes, a nicer pair of sandals, and a pair of those plastic flip flops you could buy for less than five bucks.

Deciding to take a look around, I pocketed my hands and moved quietly through her place. There was a small bathroom and laundry room, and the next room I passed through was a living room area and one of the smallest kitchens I had ever seen. The place couldn't be much bigger than five hundred square feet. I wondered what she was paying for little digs like this.

Which had me wondering what it was, exactly, she did for a living.

Which, of course, had me curious about how that would all work out once she had the baby.

Fuck. This train of thought I had where Mia was concerned fucking baffled me.

It looked like the nicest piece of furniture in her apartment, and by that, I mean more expensive than twenty dollars apiece, was her couch. I went over to the sectional and sat down, surprised to realize it was extremely comfortable.

I mean...it was bright turquoise, but it was comfortable.

I sat forward, my forearms on my knees, as I waited for her to come back out. I wasn't a lady, but I couldn't think of a reason why her slacks and shirt were uncomfortable and why she had to change. It wasn't like she'd been in them all that long.

She arrived to the restaurant, barfed in the restroom, and left. Not that much time in her clothes.

Then again, she did barf, and was pressed against the restroom wall...

I couldn't help but grin at the memory.

So yeah, maybe that's why she wanted to change. Bathroom walls were dirty. Her panties probably were, too.

When a door opened at the other end of the room, I looked up to see Mia emerge, this time in cotton shorts and a dark t-shirt that hugged her stomach. Her crazy curls were pulled back from her face now, but I only glanced at them quickly before dropping my gaze back to her stomach.

Mia stretched at the bottom hem of her shirt. "They're getting too tight, sorry," she grumbled. Barefoot, she padded past me into the kitchen to grab a bottle of water, then moved back toward me only to stop at the counter seating area. She placed her bottle of water on the counter and pulled out a stool to sit facing me, but she didn't say anything.

I tried to work on getting my mad back, but I couldn't manage to find any anger as I looked at her sitting there in front of me, propped on a stool with her hands clasped between her bare knees.

"Were you going to tell me?" There. I would start with that.

She stared at me a moment too long, and I had my answer. No, she hadn't been planning on it.

"I was going to try," she said instead.

I nodded a few times, my eyes locked with hers. She looked uncomfortable but I gave the girl props, she kept eye contact.

"You should—" I started, but she spoke at the same time, "Look, I was—"

We both stopped and stared at one another before Mia sat up a little straighter in her chair.

"I was going to try telling you. I know that's not a good enough answer, but I was going to try. And I'm sorry I didn't tell you the first night who I was. I should have. It was childish of me not to tell you, just as it was childish of me to want to be with you for a night."

Well, I wouldn't say *childish*…

"By the time I found out I was pregnant, I was already three months along. Conor, it took me three weeks to try and talk to you, and even that I failed at. I just…" she shrugged her shoulders and looked down at her lap.

I didn't have the anger in me any longer. To be honest, I'm not sure it ever was true anger. When I found out I took her virginity, I was angry, sure, but more at myself. Omitting the truth is lying, yeah, but I probably could have handled her better afterward. And when she walked into the restaurant earlier, it wasn't so much anger as it was *shock* at learning the woman I had fought to get out of my head was a girl I had known when I was a kid, and that she was obviously pregnant with my child.

"What have you been up to, Mia?" I asked. The shock on her face was comical. It was not the direction she was thinking I would go, I was sure. Hell, it baffled me a bit too.

She contorted her face a few times as she worked on spitting out words, but finally she settled on, "I teach?"

"Is that a question, or is that what you do?"

Mia nodded. "I do. I teach. Second grade."

"So that's what, seven and eight year olds?"

She nodded again.

"How long?"

"I just finished my first school year."

"You get decent benefits?"

She nodded but shrugged as well. "If you're asking about the baby, Conor, I said I was going to be fine." Unlike the previous time she told me this, her voice held no bite.

I shifted in my seat and narrowed my eyes ever so slightly. "Do you *want* me in the baby's life?"

I don't know why her answer mattered, but I was surprised to find it did. I would have been fine going through my days, not knowing I'd fathered a kid. But knowing there was a kid out there that was mine? I'm not so sure I could do it and not have any sort of contact with it.

"I don't need you in the baby's life, no."

"That wasn't the question though."

"Conor, I don't know you anymore. I can't make that kind of decision. I don't know if there's a good guy under that front you put on at the bar, or if that front is really just you."

"Then ask me something." It caught me off guard, but I wanted her to know who I was. I wanted her to have that knowledge so she could make that decision. Granted, I was surprisingly afraid she would learn that what I put on for show at the bar was really just classic Conor O'Gallagher.

I found myself wanting to know if I could be the good guy who got the girl. Crazy as that fucking sounded.

Mia frowned at me but she didn't move from her spot. I could see the wheels turning behind her eyes. She leaned to her side so she could rest her arm on the counter, her head in her hand, as she scratched at the side of her head. Her eyes remained on me as she thought. "This is awkward."

"Anything, Mia." I leaned back to appear more casual, slouched against her couch with my arms thrown over the back, when casual and carefree were the last two things I felt inside.

Nervous.

Anxious.

Not worthy.

Those were pretty forefront in my mind.

Not to add the confusion of why those things were there.

"Well..." She sat up and rocked in her seat, as if to find a better position. Her eyes were fixed to my chest but moved up to my eyes. "I guess, what have you been up to the last few years? Just taking over the bar?"

"Yeah and no. I bought it from the parents and Rory and I worked on the remodel before opening the doors again."

"Did you go to school?"

I lifted my brow. I remember the day I left for college; it was probably the last time I'd seen a little Mia. "You know I did."

"Well, did you *finish* school, then?"

I nodded. "Business," I said, guessing her next question. I leaned forward again.

"Any serious relationships?"

I shook my head no.

Her brows rose. "None at all?"

I shook my head again. "Nope."

"So you really do just take a random woman up to your place at night. Every night?"

I didn't think lying to her would be a good answer. "Most nights."

"If we do this...co-parenting thing...that stops with the baby." She crossed her arms under her ample chest. "I don't care what you do in your free time, but you don't bring women up when you have the baby."

"I wouldn't." It was my turn to shift in my seat.

"How often are you willing to be away from the bar? You're there all the time now, aren't you?"

I nodded. "Usually, yeah, but I can take time off. What are you thinking? Do you need, want...someone to go to appointments with you?"

She shook her head. "Oh! No, not that. I was talking about when you'd have the baby."

Again, I nodded. Made sense. "I would, you know, go to appointments with you, if you wanted."

"No, that's ok." Mia's smile was forced. "Um. So yeah. What do you... How do you want to do this, I guess?"

"What do you mean?"

"Do we do this civilly between us, do we get lawyers?" She scoffed to herself. "Well, lawyers are probably a good idea, regardless."

"How about we just take it a day at a time?"

Mia swallowed and nodded. "Ok." Her eyes widened briefly and she smiled. "Do you maybe, do you want to feel the baby?"

"Like, touch your stomach?"

"The baby's really active right now. You might not be able to feel it as much as I can, but you might be able to. You know, if you wanted."

Did I want to? Kind of, actually, yeah. It was some weird fucking shit, though.

But this was the most open Mia had been all night and I was going to grab on to that olive branch. I pulled to a stand, rubbing my suddenly wet palms on my pants, and walked the short distance to where she sat. I pushed the sleeves of my shirt up a little more just as I reached her.

Mia reached out a hand and grabbed my wrist. I had to refrain from jumping at the contact. It was electrical, and fuck if I knew what that was about.

She guided my hand to the swell of her stomach and my palm touched just as something pushed from the other side.

Well, not something. Our kid.

Our kid.

I just felt our kid.

And suddenly I wanted nothing more than to be in this kid's life.

And in Mia's.

I would find a way to be in Mia's life, more than just as the father of her child.

For the first time, I found myself wanting forever.

Chapter Nine

Conor

I probably stood there for another five minutes, my hand in one spot on Mia's belly.

She'd ask, "Did you feel that one?" every time she felt a push or a kick, and I found I was disappointed that I only felt a few of the movements she felt.

Her hand was still on my wrist and she guided my hand to the top of the swell. "What about there?"

I tried to focus on my hand and what was beneath it, but I kept fighting my eyes from searching over her face.

This Mia was certainly a grown up Mia from my childhood.

The Mia then was, like Rory and I called her earlier, pudgy. She'd been a little rounder than most of the kids, but she was a laugher. She laughed and she smiled, and as much as I hated Bren and Mia hanging around, there may have been a few days I said no to a party or something just so I could hang out in the backyard with my kid sister and her tagalong friend.

When their friendship ended, I had already left for college, so not seeing her again after that point wasn't something I dwelled on. She was eight years younger than me, and my kid sister's once friend. She'd been a blip on my radar.

It was easy to see how I didn't recognize her back in March. She still had the crazy hair and the eyes that looked like they could see right through you, but she had grown up into quite the beautiful woman. No, she wasn't flashy like many of the women I spent my time with, but still, there was something about her.

Mia's gaze was down on our hands the entire time, and finally she glanced up to see me watching her. Her face flushed and she bit on her lower lip, much like she did again and again that night in March.

We had made good leeway tonight, came pretty far from the argument at the restaurant, and I shouldn't want to overstep the line.

But I wanted to.

And because I wasn't one to take too big of a step back, I did what I wanted.

As I slid my hand down the swell and over to her hip, I leaned down so I could press my lips to hers. Before meeting her lips though, I paused long enough to let her pull back.

But Mia didn't pull back.

No, no she didn't.

She leaned up. I could feel her hip tense as she pushed to stand on her stool just enough to make that contact, and then relax as I met her and followed her back down as she sat. Putting my other hand to her face, I kept my lips against hers light and the kiss slow. What I really wanted was to lift her up and find her bed, toss her down and fuck her senseless, but there was the kid between us now.

Shit, how did that work?

Mia pulled back and frowned up at me, so I mirrored her frown. "What?"

She shifted in her seat. "Don't start something you have no intention of finishing. Don't...*kiss* me because you feel like it will give you...I don't know, *leeway* with me. Just..." She maneuvered to stand and squeezed past me, her baby belly brushing against me. "We can't kiss, Conor. We just...we can't."

She was moving away, but fuck, I didn't want her to. I reached with both hands, grabbing onto her hips, and pulling her back as I moved forward. When I rocked my erection against her, she gasped lightly.

"Give me a chance," I whispered into her ear, rubbing my chin just under it.

Her laugh was cold. "Give you a chance? Geez, Conor, why would I want to do that?" She looked at me over her shoulder, but didn't move away from where I was pressed into her back. "This is probably just some…I don't know, fetish or something. You're curious about *fucking* a pregnant girl and—"

Everything kind of drowned out after she used the term 'fucking.' That's what I did, yes, but to hear it coming out of Mia's mouth? Can't say I liked it too much.

"—eventually you'll just get sick of me, of us, and you'll leave. Sorry if I don't want to play that game."

With my hands on her hips, I turned her to face me. Her face was still flushed, or rather, it was flushed again, and her eyes were wild. But her lower lip was trembling again.

"Look. This is new for me. I'm guessing it's new for you too. I don't see any chicklets running around." I lifted my brows, waiting for her to challenge me in the way she did. When she didn't, I continued. "I can't promise next week. Fuck, I can't promise tomorrow. But I want," I shrugged and swallowed. Shit these words were hard. "I'd like to try."

She stared at me like I grew two heads. Fuck, maybe I did.

"But…I mean…" Mia stumbling over her words was kind of cute. She was flustered and it was more than evident. "That's not *you* though, Conor. I'm sorry, but you're a flirt. And while, yeah, flirting isn't necessarily the end all, you don't just flirt to flirt. You flirt to get laid."

Point, Mia. "Just let me try." I don't know why this mattered so much to me, but it did.

Mia shook her head, raised her brows, and I'm pretty sure she rolled her eyes, all in one move that my sister did all too well. It meant she'd fold. It meant—

"Whatever. I guess you can try. But!" She held up a finger between us. "If you're serious, you are going to be monogamous."

I grinned crookedly. "So that means we'll be having sex."

Her hand shot out so fast, hitting my chest before I could stop her, but it didn't stop the laugh that burst out of me.

"I haven't decided yet. Just…one day at a time, Conor." She wiggled her hips from my hands, trying to pull away, but I just pulled her closer. Fucking belly of hers wouldn't allow her to be as close as I wanted her, but that was ok. I'd deal.

"Seal the deal?" I asked down to her, and her brows creased yet again. I let go of a hip so I could rub my thumb over the ridges there. "You're going to get stuck, you keep doing that."

"I just…I don't *know* you Conor, and this?" She waved a hand between us in the miniscule space between our chests, "This isn't the Conor I've been watching."

"You said you'd give me a chance."

"I don't want you to resent me."

"I couldn't resent you," I said, realizing it was true. "And you said you'd give me a chance. Day at a time." I slid my hand to the back of her head, grabbing her bun-contained curls in my hand and pulling her head back ever so slightly. "Give me my chance," I whispered, before lowering my lips to hers once again.

Now that I started kissing again, I couldn't seem to stop. At least, I couldn't seem to stop kissing Mia. Her lips were a drug. Her responses, a drug. She gave me a fucking high, and I couldn't help but want to stay on the upper she gave me. I squeezed her hip under my hand before moving back to grab a handful of her ass, causing Mia to moan under my mouth.

I let go of her hair so I could put my other hand under her ass, lifting her up. Automatically, her legs wrapped around me but she pulled her mouth away from mine, eyes wide.

"I'm too heavy for you!" She didn't make any moves to get down, though.

"Shut up, you're fine," I told her. Maybe 'shut up' wasn't the best word choice, but it was what I had. "We're going to your room. Objections?" I moved so I could press my lips against the column of her neck, biting and sucking here and there until I left a mark near her collar bone.

Mia's head dropped back with that move, but did not object to my statement, so I moved us toward the room she came out of a short while ago in new clothes.

The night had started to creep in, leaving her room dark. I blindly hit the wall with one hand, finding the light switch, dousing her bedroom in light.

I didn't have time to look around the place. I spotted what I wanted, where I wanted to go, and I moved us to her bed.

Thank fucking God she didn't say anything about the light. I wasn't having that argument right now. I resisted throwing her down on the bed, because of the baby and all, and moved up on her mattress on my knees, lowering her back gently once I reached the middle.

Her bed was likely a queen, but felt like a fucking twin compared to my own luxury bed. Far too small.

I pulled back and immediately started to tug down on her shorts. "Are you able to stay on your back?" I asked as I went to task. I didn't bother stopping as she answered.

"Right now, yes. In a few weeks, probably not." Her voice was husky and slightly breathless and I had to fight a grin of satisfaction. I did that to her.

I leaned back to completely take off her shorts, not at all surprised to find she was in those cotton underwear. Maybe I could talk her into lace or silk someday.

Hm. Yeah. Someday.

Depositing her shorts on the floor beside her bed, I moved my hands up to the hem of her shirt. The plain cotton was surprisingly thick and rough. I was a fan of soft, vintage style tees myself, but to each his, or her, own. My thumbs hooked under the hem and I pulled the fabric up, exposing her stomach inch by inch.

My eyes darted up to Mia's to catch her reaction and I was semi-surprised to find her eyes on mine already, her lip between her teeth, as if she were afraid of my response. I moved my eyes back down to her stomach, which was stretched and taut.

I will admit—it was a fucking powerful feeling knowing she held a baby in her stomach and that I put it there. Yeah, Mia and I had some way to go, but I wasn't kidding when I said I wanted to try.

Inch by inch, I exposed more of her stomach. Her belly button ring was no longer in, and her belly button itself was starting to pop out. Unable to resist, I bent down to press my lips to her stomach as I pushed her shirt up to her tits. I pressed my lips over and over again to the swell of her stomach and chuckled when the kid pressed against my lips. It was a soft, fluttery feeling, but I felt it and Goddamn, it made me feel like fucking Superman.

I sat back on my knees and pulled her up to sit so I could finish pulling her shirt off. I groaned out loud when her breasts were freed from the shirt, showing she wasn't wearing a bra. God fucking damn.

Her tits were indeed larger than I remembered, and her nipples...

Fuck, her nipples were huge and dark and begging to be in my mouth.

I peeled the shirt over her head, tossing it to the ground at the same time I sucked one of her nipples into my mouth. Mia's hands were in my hair, holding me close, as I sucked, running my tongue over the hardening peak. I licked, pulled back, licked again, sucked her into my mouth where I bit down gently and played with the peaked nipple with my tongue. I put my other hand over her cotton underwear, holding my palm over her. I could feel her wet heat through the cotton, her panties already wet.

I pushed Mia back gently to lay once again, and moved my mouth to give her other tit the attention it deserved, all while moving my lower hand up just enough to slide under the band of her cotton panties, finding the goods that lie underneath.

When my fingers brushed over her clit, I sucked hard on her nipple, eliciting a gasp from Mia. She was fucking soaked, her wetness making the glide over her clit slippery and easy. I rubbed quick circles there, moved my fingers back and forth over the nub, too, before sliding down and finding the source of all that wet gloriousness. With ease, I slipped two fingers into her, no preamble, no hesitation. My fingers moved in easily up to my top knuckle, and I slowly began to pull my fingers in and out.

Mia's hips moved restlessly below me as I continued my ministrations on her tit, going back and forth, showing equal attention to both.

"Oh my God, Conor." Her body tensed all around me and I could feel the telltale pulses saying she was about to come. I moved my mouth to hers, speaking against her lips.

"Let it go. Let go, Mia. Just let go." I moved my fingers in her faster, curling up into her walls, letting my palm hit her clit and add more pressure. Soon enough, Mia was crashing through her high, her arched back pressing that baby belly into my stomach.

I kept my mouth on hers, gently nibbling at her lips until she was finally through with her quiet moaning. *I need to get this girl to be more vocal*, I thought offhandedly.

Rather than give her reprieve to breathe, I crushed my mouth to hers, sweeping my tongue inside. This kiss was fevered and Mia was an active participant, her tongue and teeth clashing with my own. Her hands were in my hair, down my back, grabbing my still clothed ass. And my fingers were still lodged way up deep in her pussy.

She shuddered and bit down on my lip, not so gently, mind you, as I slowly pulled my fingers out. I left her with one more kiss before moving to stand beside her bed. In no time at all, I was out of my clothes and on my side beside her.

I turned her to her side to face me, one hand under my head so I could look down at her and my other hand moved to rest on her hip. For the first time since losing my virginity at fourteen years old, I didn't have a fucking clue where to start with a woman.

Forward, backward, fuck, upside down? What would be best for Mia?

Apparently I wasn't going to have to think long. Mia had her hands between us before I could even try to ask. Those fingers of hers were wrapped around my huge, aching cock and shortly after, my dirty bird lifted her leg to drape over my hip, angling her hips so she could brush the head of my cock over her folds.

Fuck, yes.

Mia

For a sex god, Conor was thinking too much. I could practically hear the wheels turning in his head.

I was probably a fool for wanting this with him, wanting to see if he could do the commitment thing, but every girl wanted to live out their childhood crush. I wasn't asking him to marry me, for goodness sake.

I moved so I could angle his cock where I needed it to be. Before I could attempt to sink down on him though, Conor rested his head down on the pillow, using that arm to pull my upper body in close, and slammed up into me. I let out a breathless moan and pushed my nose into his chest, squeezing my eyes shut at the tight intrusion.

"So fucking tight," Conor murmured into my ear. "God, I missed this tight fucking pussy. Didn't realize I could until this moment. So fucking right." His hips thrusted against mine and he held onto my leg that was over his side.

I loved that he talked dirty. It wasn't surprising, no, but it was just enough incentive to get me close to flying over the edge again. I moaned, greedy little moans, as he moved his hips in and against mine.

"Use your words, baby girl. Use your words. Tell me." His voice was in my ear, followed by kisses raining over my cheekbone. "Give me the words. Harder, faster. Anything. Tell me, Mia."

My only sexual partner had been Conor, and toys certainly didn't ask you to talk to them. I was so used to being quiet that even the thought of using the words was foreign to me.

When I didn't comply, Conor pushed his hips up into me and did some hip twist or another that nearly had me seeing stars. "You like that, Mia? Tell me. Tell me you like it, baby girl."

"Yes," I managed, shakily at best.

"Yes what?"

He was going to pull them out of me. He did the move yet again and I had to close my eyes against the onslaught of pleasure.

"God, yes, I like that."

"Conor works fine," he chuckled against my forehead. "Or Con. But I guess God works."

Before I could give him a sassy reply, my body was once again shattering around him. My God, what the hell did this man eat for breakfast? I had an idea of how often he practiced his moves, so I didn't really care to have that question answered, but really, the man was phenomenal in bed.

My jaw was dropped as I went through the waves of pleasure. My breath held. My eyes squeezed tight.

"Talk to me," he pressed. He flipped onto his back, pulling me on top of him. I had to press up on my forearms to be comfortable, baby belly and all, but my body was still spasming and the act took more energy than I had in me.

"Give me something, Mia." His cock was still sliding in and out of me, slowly as if he was having a hard time pushing his girth through the pulsing muscles.

Without thinking, I said the first word that came to mind. "Fuck." But the word wasn't as nice and quick and easy as one would think a one syllable word to be. Oh no. I drew that damn word out for a good five seconds, which earned me a chuckle from the man below.

My body was finally slowing off its ebb, just enough that I could glare down at him for laughing at me, but he took no mind to the look.

Nope, if anything, he sensed the energy was well and gone from me and he sat up straight, hugging me close, his knees bent, and began mercilessly pounding up into me, finding his own release. I wrapped my arms tight around his neck, holding him as close as I could, as he pushed his forehead down into my shoulder.

"Fuck!"

I have to say, his was a bit more exciting than mine was, all loud and full of passion. Who knew Conor had it in him? His body pulled tight, straining under and around me, and I could feel every muscle in his upper back as his cock jerked inside me, leaving behind warm wetness. It was something I hadn't felt the first time we were together, regardless of the broken condom. It was...

Interesting.

We stayed locked around one another for a number of minutes, as my breath finally calmed down and his body started to do the same.

Conor finally lifted his head and looked at me, his blue eyes set and determined, but with a warmth I wasn't prepared for. "You ok?"

I nodded.

"The baby ok?"

I couldn't help but grin. "You can't hurt the baby with sex, Conor."

"Well, I know, but..." Holy hell, Conor had a bashful side. I could see a slight blush rise behind his bearded cheeks. I grabbed said cheeks and brought his forehead to my smiling lips, pressing a kiss there, before pushing against his shoulders to try and stand.

I pushed myself up, biting on my lip when his cock dislodged from me, and stood in front of him. Belatedly I realized where his face would be when I did so, and before I could try to walk off the edge of the bed, Conor's hands were at my ass, pulling me close to his mouth.

"Conor, no!" I put my hands on his head. "It's...*messy*."

"Fuck messy," he murmured against my mound. Before I knew it, his tongue was between my pussy lips, lapping up the both of us. I had to brace my hands on the wall behind the bed to keep from falling.

I mentioned it before that I was a sexual being, even if I hadn't had sex, but these pregnancy hormones were no joke. Before long, I was coming against his face. "Jesus, Conor," I said around a quiet moan.

"You're getting better," he chuckled against me.

I frowned and stepped back, almost falling and having to brace myself with a hand on his head. "Excuse me?" I was getting *better*? Was that some offhanded remark about my inexperience? Where the fuck was he going with that comment? Was he fucking kidding me?

And then he had the gall to fucking laugh at me! *And* slap my ass?

Fucking jerk.

I stomped off the bed, as gingerly as I could without falling on my ass and making more of a show than I intended, and headed toward the bathroom. My small apartment didn't have the luxury of a bathroom attached to the bedroom. I had to stomp naked through my apartment to get to the bathroom at the front of the space.

"Mia!" Conor yelled after me, but I kept going.

And shit, cue the water works.

God fucking damn, the hormones!

"Mia. Mia, baby girl. Stop. Stop, Mia!" His voice was drawing near. Not hard to do. It wasn't as if there was a ton of square footage between the bed and the bathroom. He reached for my arm and I swung around on him so fast, he probably thought he was seeing the Exorcist.

"You're a jerk, Conor O'Gallagher! I don't know why I agreed to give you a chance." I brought my free hand up to my face. "I'm so fucking *stupid*!"

Conor was fucking laughing again as he brought me in for a hug. I was confused and pissed, and my nose was pressed against his chest and fuck him for still smelling good, even with the lingering scent of sex between us.

"You're misreading the situation, Mia." The smile was evident in his voice, the bastard. "I meant you were getting better at *vocalizing*." He drew the word out and it kind of made me feel, well, stupid.

"Oh." I dipped my chin down and Conor took the opportunity to press his lips to the back of my head.

"Why don't you clean up," he said against my head, "and then we'll continue to talk, kay?"

I nodded and finally moved my head so I could look at him again. "Ok."

He had the audacity to grin at me again, the crinkles beside his eyes deepening. I merely lifted my brows and pointed at him before turning and finishing the few steps to the bathroom, closing myself in the room, locking Conor out.

And then I grinned wide, my lower lip between my teeth, and refrained from doing a little dance with myself.

Chapter Ten

Conor

After pulling my briefs and slacks back on, I may have snooped around her room a bit. Mia had semi-mentioned she had toys and I was curious as all fucking get out as to what she had. Hands in my pockets, I walked around gingerly, slowly. On the other side of the bed was where I hit the jackpot. Plugged into the wall was a vibrating wand, and in a basket nearby was a freaking dildo and this other compact looking thing. I crouched down to pick up the pink device and turned it over in my hands. It had a hollow nub at the top. I put my finger over it and found the on-switch, chuckling when the nub started to pulse and squeeze my finger.

I knew she liked her tits and clit worked on, but I definitely wanted to see this one in action someday.

I turned the device off and put it back in the basket, and headed back into the living room where I could hear the shower running.

I lounged on Mia's comfy-ass couch, waiting for her to get out of the bathroom. For all I knew, I was going to be here for a while, Mia being female and all, but rather than be uncomfortable in her space...

I found I enjoyed the peacefulness it brought to me.

I could still hear the shower running behind the bathroom door and imagined the water dripping down her tits, falling off her tight peaks. Soap running down and over the swell of her belly, disappearing between her thighs.

I shifted in my seat and adjusted myself. Getting hard right now wouldn't do me any good.

I squeezed myself through the cotton and polyester blend of my slacks. Now that I started, I couldn't turn off the images of Mia playing in my head, imagining what she looked like in the shower. Those curls of hers relaxed and around her shoulders. Her eyelashes wet from the stream of the shower.

Her pink lips brighter from her constant nibbling on them.

The door to the bathroom opened, pulling me from my daydream. I was hard as a fucking rock under my hand and I groaned to myself, knowing that when I pulled my hand away, I was going to have major tentage.

Mia, bless her fucking sweet heart, stepped out of the bathroom wrapped in just a white towel, took one glance at my lap, and shook her head before walking past me toward her bedroom.

What I wanted to do was follow her and beat off to her changing, but at the same time, I really did want to prove that I could be in this for the long haul, with or without the sexual benefits.

Beneficial as they were.

I stood instead, pushing my hands in my pockets, and turned to study the photographs adorning her walls. I was surprised to find they were all landscape photos; not a single one had a person in them.

When I heard her walk back into the room, I asked without turning, "How are your parents?"

"They're good. They still live in the old neighborhood. Different house, though."

Mia moved to stand beside me and I looked down to see she was in the same cotton shorts as earlier, but a different tee, this one a little looser. Her hair was actually pretty long when it was wet, and with it straight from her shower, she almost looked like a different person.

I liked her crazy curls better though, I decided. It was more Mia.

"You don't have pictures of them."

She laughed lightly. "Ah, they're all on a hard drive. Or my phone. You know, the digital age."

I nodded because I actually did understand that. The only picture I had around of my parents was in the bar, from when they opened O'Gallaghers, and it was right next to a picture of Rory, Bren, and I at the re-opening.

Mia moved to sit on the couch where I had previously been, her hands clasped between her knees. The move pressed her tits together and I had to fight the onslaught of another fucking erection. Good God, the woman did things to me.

"So what now?" she asked softly.

Wasn't that the real question? What now?

"Well," I said on a sigh, my hands still in my pockets, I looked down at her and shrugged. "I'm not entirely sure. We already agreed to be exclusive while we're trying this out. Is there, like, a time limit or something?"

"Do you want a time limit?" Mia tilted her head toward her shoulder, her eyes inquisitive and on mine.

Did I want a time limit? Well, no. Not really. "I think I want to give this a good, real try," I told her instead. "Dates. I'll go to appointments with you. We figure out what's best for us and the baby."

Mia patted the couch beside her and I moved to sit next to her. "I'm kind of afraid that sex might cloud judgment," she told me. "Or really if I'm being honest, the lack of multiple partners for you."

I had an idea and as much as it baffled the hell out of me, it was going to throw Mia for a loop. "Then we don't have it."

She looked at me skeptically. "Seriously." Her voice was deadpanned and her brows were lifted up to her hairline.

I nodded a few times. "Yeah. Why not?"

"Because you're Conor O'Gallagher, that's why."

"I can go without sex." Even I could hear the slight disbelief in my voice. No, I really hadn't ever put myself on a celibacy streak, but I could do it. I knew I could.

Mia shifted in her spot and turned toward me, her leg folded to the side and between the two of us. Her clasped hands sat in the spot between her legs, in front of her pussy, her arms bracketing her belly. With her leg up, the cotton of her shorts stretched and I could almost, *almost*, see the land of glory.

She lifted a hand and snapped her fingers in front of my face. "Up here, Romeo."

I lifted my eyes to hers and offered her a coy grin. "I can," I repeated.

"Let's just say for, I don't know, a month."

"Of us trying?"

"Of no sex. Keep up, Conor."

Shit. I could do that. A month was nothing. "Alright. Deal."

"We don't have to go on dates, either. Maybe just dinner now and then."

"I'm taking you out on a date, Mia."

"Maybe just lunch after an appointment, then."

"Mia. I'm taking you out on a date."

"You're stubborn."

"Kettle, meet pot." I reached out to take her hand. "I'm taking you out to dinner. I'm going to your appointments. And in one month, we'll decide if sex is going on the table or not."

"You mean you want to *have* sex on the table." Mia, the sass, grinned.

"I think you're the one who's going to have an issue with the no sex clause," I said around a laugh.

Mia just shook her head, still smiling though. "Nah. I've only had one partner. And you're good, Con, you are, but..."

"You know you like it. Don't even try saying you don't. I'm better than your toys."

Her brows went up. "How do you know about my toys?"

"Well, you eluded to them once, but I may have found them."

Her brows stayed raised, but her eyes widened to join them. "You *snooped*?"

"I was changing and they were...just there." I grinned wide and reached up to scratch my chin.

Mia jerked her hand from mine, only so she could put both her hands over her face. "Oh my God, this is embarrassing."

I reached for her hands and pulled them down. "Nothing to be embarrassed about." I leaned in to kiss her lips once. I was starting to regret not kissing her the first time I had her in my bed. "It's sexy as hell. We're gonna play with them in a month."

Mia's devilish side must have wanted to play because, while she was still blushing, she bit down on that lip of hers and said, "We could always play with them tonight. And tomorrow night. We just can't have actual sex."

I really liked the way this woman thought, but, "No." I shook my head. "We are going to abstain one-hundred percent, Mia."

She pouted and it was fucking adorable. "I don't think you understand how pregnancy hormones work."

"You're all hot and bothered, yeah, I get that." I reached forward to brush one of her tightening curls behind her ear. "But I want to do this right."

"What's the male version of a cock tease?"

Shaking my head, I turned on the couch, pulling Mia with me, so I could lay back. Mia's ass stayed between my legs, snug up to my covered cock, and I pulled her down to lay on me. I wrapped my arms around her shoulders, holding her in place. "You'll survive."

Mia rotated her shoulders so she could rub herself against me. "But will you?"

"Barely," I groaned.

She turned, much to my displeasure, and pulled herself up to her knees, propping her hands on my bare stomach. "I don't want you to resent me, Conor." The words were said softly.

I reached up for her face, pulling her back down, and spoke against her lips, before kissing her. "I don't think I could, Mia."

Chapter Eleven
One Month Later

Mia

The past month flew by.

Conor had invited me to a wedding in Wisconsin and I'd been shocked when I learned it was for an NHL player. Apparently Conor and the groom had become fast friends through the bar.

True to his word, Conor didn't try any frisky business with me, and that weekend away was the first time he and I stayed in a bed together since the night of our talk. I was semi-expecting, shoot, I was hoping, he would try something, *touch* something, but other than holding me through the night, his hands didn't make any moves. If I had to guess, I would think he just liked keeping his hands on my belly to try to catch the baby moving, not the actual touching *me* part.

After that weekend though, Conor started staying the night.

Every night.

Said he liked to sleep next to me.

And that his California King was too damn big without me in it. That he'd take my little queen sized bed with me in it any day of the week.

Which baffled me because I personally would take the space of his large bed any day of the week. I was starting to get super warm at night and had to pee at least once a night, if not twice. Having Conor's big, burly form wrapped around me kind of became a pain some nights.

Conor cut back on his time at the bar, too. Said he wanted to spend more time with me, and that Rory and Brenna were more than capable of handling the day to day operations. We also may have had a slightly heated discussion about it a week or two ago.

He still tended bar Thursday through Sunday, and still wore a kilt for ladies' night, but swore he didn't take any ladies up to the apartment with him.

Which I believed full-heartedly.

I mean, he always crawled into my bed thirty minutes after bar-close so unless he was doing magic quickies...

More than that, though, I was growing to trust him.

He still had his cocky ways with his fast grins, but when he was with me, he was with me one-thousand percent. We learned a lot about one another over the last month too, catching up on the last fifteen years.

I also started back at school two weeks ago. While Conor slept until noon, I went off to work. He would sometimes stop by the school during my lunch break and eat a brown bag lunch with me in my classroom.

Seeing Conor in a little green chair did serious things to my heart.

But finally, we reached a month.

Today.

And I was newly two weeks into the third trimester and if I hit the 'don't touch me with that thing' phase after spending the last four weeks in sexual need-but-not-getting, I was going to...

I don't know, but Conor wouldn't be very happy.

I considered going to his apartment, but he was at the bar and he'd know something was up. As it was, he was only working the lunch crowd today, leaving the crazy Saturday night to Stone and Rory.

He'd be back to my place in an hour. I wasn't planning anything extravagant, and I didn't have any fancy teddies or anything. It was hard to find something and feel super sexy with this belly. Thankfully, my belly hadn't done too much growing the last few weeks; at least, I didn't think so. Ask Conor, and it grew leaps and bounds. I was the one sporting it, though, and I didn't really notice too much of a difference.

But my belly button officially popped out. And there was that line down my belly. And the stretch marks. They were all things these days.

Like I said. Hard to feel sexy.

I did order lacy boy shorts and a bra for the occasion, but wasn't planning on putting them on until right before Conor walked through my door.

We had found an easy rhythm for us as a couple. There wasn't any talk about what was going to happen after today, being the end of that first month, but I was comfortable with the thought this was happening, that this could be a long-term thing. That we could co-parent and everything would be right in Baby O'Gallagher's world.

We hadn't talked names, but we did discuss that the baby would take Conor's surname. It only made sense to me. However, the closer we got to D-day, the more we should probably start considering first names.

With a sigh, I walked back to my room to be sure everything was in place.

Conor

I never realized how exhausting not having sex could be. Every night I slept wrapped up in Mia. Every night, I went to bed with a case of blue balls worse than the night before.

But while I went to sleep uncomfortable, I found myself waking up more than comfortable. This thing between Mia and me had an easy rhythm and, as much as I didn't want to be the owner of the idea, I really think that the no-sex thing worked in our favor.

It was no secret that I liked sex, that before Mia coming back into my life, the longest I went without it was maybe two days. And I usually made up for those off days when I got back in the sack. Being with Mia, and not being able to sink into her wet heat, had its challenges, sure, but I think I decided I liked myself better as a person, and it reinforced that I could do the co-parenting and monogamy thing long-term.

Earlier this month, I brought her to Caleb and Sydney's wedding with me. I enjoyed showing her off, her standing at my side and my hand covering her belly.

These days, Rory teased her like he teased Brenna. Bren and Mia... I was pretty sure they were on good terms now, too. Neither talked to me about what they talked about to one another, but things were easy all around where Mia and my family were concerned.

Today, Stone showed up to the bar an hour early, but rather than head to Mia's, I went back to the office to try and do some bookkeeping that was due to be finished tomorrow.

Mia didn't know it, but right after I found out we were having a kid, I bought a copy of that book, *The Expectant Father*. I devoured the months we were already past, curious about what Mia had been through, and then I fucking studied the hell out of the months to come. When I got to her apartment one Wednesday morning after close, something she said triggered a piece of information I read. I let her go back to sleep, pissy as she'd been, and in the morning I made sure to wake up with her and her alarm and we talked about me cutting down on my hours.

I owned the fucking bar. I made enough money managing the place that bartending wasn't necessary. So we made a compromise that I'd work Thursday and Friday nights, Saturday afternoons, and leave Sunday for bookkeeping. That way when the kid was here, we'd have more flexibility once Mia went back to work.

As for tonight...

If I had my way, I was going to be up really late and wasn't planning on leaving Mia's arms until *maybe* tomorrow afternoon at the earliest.

We reached our month.

And I had plans for my baby mama.

There was also the fact that *The Expectant Father* mentioned Mia's libido could potentially drop, and I'd be damned if we went a month without sex, a month where right before the vow, Mia was downright *craving* sex, for her to put up the red light because she wasn't feeling it anymore.

I booted up my laptop and while my accounting program loaded, I opened up my email to check on the status of a ring I'd been looking at.

Yeah, yeah, it was definitely too fucking early to talk about marriage, but it was something that had been sitting in the back of my mind since watching Cael get hitched.

Damn internet was slow as fuck today.

I sighed and leaned back in my chair, closing my eyes while I waited.

Chapter Twelve

Conor

My cock was getting some crazy attention.

What a fucking crazy sex dream, I thought as I started to come to. My book mentioned I may have sex dreams which I thought was fucking bogus. Mia, on the other hand, oh yeah, she was having some crazy sex dreams, but this was a first for me.

Not only could I imagine Mia's hands rubbing up and down my cock, moving my zipper lower over the hardening length, but I could fucking *feel* that shit.

I groaned and shifted, trying to fully wake up, when a giggle that *wasn't* Mia sounded in the room.

My eyes snapped open, my booted feet pushed my chair back as far as I could, and I searched frantically for the intrusion.

Sitting where my feet had been by the desk, was one of our blonde regulars.

She smiled wide up at me. "Hey, Conor. You were so exhausted behind the bar today, I thought I'd give you a little...pick me up."

My heart was pounding, my hands on the arm rests of my chair. My body was fucking paralyzed, trying to figure out what the hell to do. I glanced down and saw my cock nearly completely out of my pants and just as I went to tuck myself in, just as I was going to stand up and order her out of the room…

My office door opened.

And Mia stood there.

Her face fucking fell, and it was a fucking punch to the gut. I thought I was paralyzed before? Everything fucking stood still right then.

I lost my breath, my heart was three times too big for my chest, and the erection I was sporting, the one I was sporting from thoughts of Mia, quickly deflated.

And then Mia turned on her heel, and my world spun into fast forward.

I tucked myself back into my pants quickly, not fucking paying attention to much of anything when I zipped, damn near zipping my fucking cock in the process. Fucking A, that shit hurt!

But it was nothing, fucking *nothing*, compared to the thought that everything I was working for this last month was about to just.

Go *poof*.

"You're not fucking welcome here," I issued to the blonde as I stormed out of the office. She just fucking stood there like a Goddamn doll, not caring about a damn thing.

Fuck.

I should have figured something like this was gonna to happen. I had a fucking reputation! Sooner or later, it was going to get around that I wasn't fucking sleeping around anymore. God-*fucking*-damn.

I peeled around the corner as Mia pushed through the swinging door separating the kitchen from the bar. I ran the length of the kitchen, narrowly dodging my weekend cook at the fryer, and ran through the swinging doors.

"Mia!"

She was close to the door.

If she got through that door, if she got to her car…

Shit, I couldn't think like that.

"Mia!" I lengthened my stride, reaching her just as she got to the front door. I slapped my hand over where the door and jamb met, and put my other hand on her hip.

"Don't *fucking touch me!*" she yelled, twirling around on me. Her yell was hysterical and before I looked into those whiskey eyes I was learning to enjoy so damn much, I knew, I fucking knew, they were going to be filled with tears. And these ones wouldn't be due to pregnancy hormones.

"You were *late*, so I thought I'd check on you. I should have figured you couldn't hold up on your end of the deal. How long, Conor? Huh? How long?" Her words were watery and she refused to look at me, instead looking clear to the side toward the back of the bar where our dart boards were set up.

I took her face in my hands and bent down to her level, forcing her to look at me. When she still refused to move her eyes, I leaned over, blocking her gaze. "Listen to me, Mia." My voice was low, quiet, almost a whisper, but the desperation was more than clear. "I didn't do anything."

Her eyes moved back and forth between mine and she let out a small sob, followed by a hiccup, and shook her head with my hands still on her. "I don't believe you. I don't believe you, Conor." Her voice lowered to a watery whisper, "I don't believe you."

"I didn't. I swear to fucking God, Mia, I didn't do anything." I wasn't above begging at this point. I straightened enough so I could press my lips to her forehead. "I fell asleep and woke up and she was there. Fuck, Mia, I thought she was you!"

Mia sniffled and tilted her head down, this time looking at our feet.

Well, she probably really only saw her belly.

God, her belly.

She couldn't walk away. She couldn't.

"She's blonde."

I tried really fucking hard not to laugh at that. Hand to God, I didn't mean to chuckle, but if that was the only thing Mia could come up with, then I knew this was going to be ok.

She swung her head up so fast, she nearly clipped me in the chin, causing me to almost laugh again but the glare in her eyes had me stopping. "She's a *blonde*, Conor. How did you think she was me?"

"I was sleeping, Mia baby." My voice was quiet again. This conversation was for Mia only, not the gawkers who kept glancing over at us. Stone, good man that he was, turned up the baseball game on one TV, and was talking loudly about the latest NHL trades with a couple of the patrons. "Come upstairs with me. Please."

She sniffed again and clenched her jaw. I could see that determined, *stubborn* side trying to win out in my girl but finally she just nodded. "But only because we're making a scene. Which we seem to do so well," she added in a smart-assed, off-handed mumbled way. I didn't bother stopping my chuckle this time.

She stepped out of my hold and skirted around me, heading back toward the doors we both just came barreling out of.

Just before getting there, of course the fucking blonde had to walk through.

I was ready to pull Mia to me, make an announcement to the entire bar that my cock was closed for business, but Mia beat me to the punch.

She pointed at the girl and said through her teeth. "He's mine." Damn, I loved that possessive tone in her voice.

Blonde, stupid assed bitch, just grinned. "He doesn't do seconds, sweetheart. Everyone knows that."

"I don't know if you noticed, but he's done seconds with me. And thirds." That was a great exaggeration on Mia's part, because I'd been sporting a hard dick and blue balls for a month, but the thought was the same.

Mia rubbed her belly and the blonde glanced down, eyes widening as if she only just now noticed the bump Mia was sporting.

It wasn't exactly small.

I reached around Mia and placed my hand on top of hers, rubbing the bump with her. "Just leave her, Mia." The baby kicked under our hands, giving its opinion of the matter as well.

My grin was huge as shit. The kicks and punches were getting stronger. According to my book, it wouldn't be long until Mia and I could watch, without touching, as the baby moved and I was fucking excited as shit for that.

That would be so fucking cool. Weird, but fucking cool.

"Well, when you change your mind," blondie said as she walked away, her eyes full of a promise I had no intention of unwrapping. Ignoring her, I took Mia's hand in mine and we made our way through the kitchen, up the stairs, into my apartment.

"I had a surprise for you," Mia found her voice after I closed the door, locking it behind us.

"What kind of surprise?" I asked, curious.

Her hand still in mine, Mia pulled me to the couch where she turned me and pushed on my stomach until I sat down with a grin. With her lip lower lip locked between her teeth, she moved her feet so she could straddle my legs, hoisting up the lower hem of the cotton dress she wore.

I took her all in, now that there were no outside distractions. Her face was still flushed from the emotion of downstairs, and her voice still had a bit of a quiver in it, but her eyes lost that wildness.

She wore a simple white, cotton dress, but it cut in at her shoulders in the racer-back fashion, leaving her shoulders bare. It also gave the illusion she wasn't wearing a bra, but I knew my woman's tits; she was wearing a bra.

The cotton stretched tight over her belly. Every day, at least that's what it felt like, her belly got a little bit bigger. I loved putting my hands on her and feeling our kid move around inside of her. Through the thicker, soft cotton, I could see where her belly button was.

When Mia woke up last week and saw it had popped out, she cried.

I laughed, yeah, because of her antics, but then I held her, rocked with her, and told her she was beautiful.

Because she was.

This woman with her crazy hair and not-flashy clothes, this woman who sometimes came home from work with marker up and down her arms and glitter in her hair, she was mine.

I focused back on the here and now, trying not to chuckle yet again as Mia attempted to put her knees on the couch beside my ass, to sit on my lap facing me. Unfortunately, our kid was in the way.

Mia growled and pushed against my chest so she could stand again. "It worked in my head."

"I'm telling you, Mia, your belly's growing."

"It's not."

I laughed at her scowl. "Yeah, Mia baby, it is." I spread my knees and pulled her to stand between them. I pressed my lips to her belly in question before lifting the lower hem of her dress. I was guessing her goal was to get naked, so I was only happy to oblige.

Imagine my surprise when the cotton panties I was expecting were actually a pair of lacy boyshorts in a nude color.

"Damn, Mia."

I could never again see another thong and be fine. In the last month, I had my hands on more pairs of thick cotton, thin cotton, bright colored cotton, and black cotton panties, than I ever had before in my life, and I liked it because it was *Mia*. But this lace she pulled out....

"I bought them for today."

I grinned up at her. "Ah, so you were hoping to get lucky on day one of month two."

Finally, she smiled down at me. "Well, yeah. It was your stupid rule."

"Mm," I nodded and, with the fabric of her dress in my fists above the swell of her stomach, I kissed her belly again, this time lips to skin. "But I think I proved myself to you, yeah?"

Mia put a hand on my shoulder and thread her other through my hair, brushing it back gently with a sweet, kind smile on her face. "Yes, Conor."

"And today?"

A look of panic, then insecurity, flashed over her features before she shrugged. "I'm not really sure what to do about that for the future. You have a reputation, you know."

"I'm putting a picture up." It wasn't what I originally thought I was going to say, but it was a great idea. "Next to the picture of my parents, and the one of Bren, Rory and me. You and me. Cael texted me a picture from the wedding."

Mia's brows raised. "You're putting a picture of us up?"

"Yeah, why not? Then the women will see."

She looked like she was thinking about it before she nodded. "Ok, I guess that could work. I don't know that they're going to be searching for pictures but..."

"And I have an appointment tomorrow with my tattoo guy." One that I scheduled on Thursday—after my last appointment with him.

Mia took one step back but only so she could lean away from me. "You have an appointment with your tattoo guy?" she repeated, her voice down an octave and her chin dropping to accommodate. She was fucking cute as hell.

I nodded once. This was what I originally was going to tell her. "Yep." I popped the 'p' and nodded once more.

"You don't have any more room." She was looking at my sleeve where yeah, every inch of skin from just past my shoulder down to my wrist was covered in black and gray ink.

I held up that same arm and with my thumb, tapped the base of the finger between my pinky and middle fingers.

Mia frowned. "But that's..."

"Yep. That's right."

Her eyes widened. "It is *way* too soon to be talking about *marriage*, Conor!"

Sure, I thought the same thing, but I felt that kick in my heart. I covered up the disappointment, though. "Shit, I know that, Mia. But you're the mother of my kid—"

"People have kids and don't get married all the time!" Her voice was taking on that edge of panic she sometimes had. Her panic, and her words for the matter, was doing serious damage to my ego. As such, I couldn't manage to hold the pissed off tone from my voice.

"Are we back to that argument? You want out of this, Mia? Just do co-parenting and see each other when we pass the kid off?"

Her face fell but she was completely open, every emotion all over her face. "Well, no."

"Then let me fucking mark my damn ring finger for you. It's not a wedding band. But you're the mother of my kid, and I want you there."

Mia stared down at me for what felt like for-fucking-ever and finally she nodded with a shrug of her shoulder. Crazy woman with mixed gestures.

"Ok. All right, sure. Yeah."

"Good." There was definite satisfaction in my voice. Have I mentioned I'm a sore loser? Yeah, I liked to get my way. "Now, back to our previous programming." I winked up at her and stood, my body brushing against her belly and making her step back in the process. When I was at my full height, I started to lift her dress all over again.

My eyes were fixed on her tits the entire time, fucking ecstatic to learn if she wore something lacy and fun on top too. You have to understand, my girl was a cotton panties and boring bra kind of gal. I tried to get her to buy a flowery print, in cotton even, at Target a few weeks ago, and she went with the regular white.

But she was wearing lace on her ass.

I needed to know if there was lace on her chest, too.

I nearly swallowed my fucking tongue, strangling Mia in the process because the dress was now up by her neck and head, when I saw what she had on.

My girl found herself a sexy side.

Shit, that sounded bad.

I found Mia sexy as all get out, strutting around with a baby belly that I gave her. She was smart, she was witty, she had class. But fucking A, her in lace was a sight to behold.

"Shit, Mia."

She wiggled and I shook my head, helping her out of her dress the rest of the way until she stood in front of me in just nude lace. The bra was unlined, unpadded, and I could see her dark areolas through the pattern.

Her smile was on the shy side, but her face was bright with happiness. "I did good?"

"Fuck, yes, Mia. But it's gotta come off."

She took my hand and turned. "Bedroom."

And I followed her. Like a lovesick fool. But my cock and balls would be happy, and let's be honest, with this view? Mia walking in front of me, arm stretched back so she could lead me to my room, dressed in lace with crisscrossing straps between her shoulder blades? Fuck, she could take me anywhere.

Chapter Thirteen

Mia

I had been excited about playing with my toys with Conor back at my place, but splayed out on his huge bed was a pretty decent compromise.

That was the other thing. My toys. Conor wouldn't play with them with me during our month of no-sex, saying that playing and touching was all considered sexual and he wanted complete abstinence. He wouldn't even let *me* play while he was around. Finding time to play with your toys while your, well, whatever Conor was –*boyfriend?*—wasn't around wasn't incredibly easy.

So tonight we'd be toyless which, let's be honest, would be completely fine. The man *looked* at me and I was wet. He put his hand on me and I was ready to shoot off into bliss.

I pulled Conor along to his bedroom, his hand squeezing mine. When we entered the room and I pulled us closer to the bed, Conor stopped and tugged me back into him, where he crossed an arm over the top of my chest and cradled my belly with his other arm.

"You're so fucking sexy," he whispered into my ear. I tilted my head to my shoulder, wordlessly asking him to press his lips to that magical spot. Smart man that he was, Conor complied, sucking, kissing, and nibbling up and down the column of my neck.

He slipped his hand under the top of my panties, holding his palm over my mound and his fingers just *sitting* on top of my folds. I spread my feet, trying to get his fingers to slip *into* the folds, to at least rest on top of my aching clit, but Conor seemed content in just holding me, kissing my neck, and holding his hand possessively over me.

"Conor." My voice came out a little whiny, and it was a bit embarrassing.

"Mia." His voice was barely a whisper in my ear. He turned me in his arms and leaned in to kiss me. As much as I actually enjoyed being pregnant, I would be happy when this bump wasn't between us. I wanted to be completely pressed up into Conor.

His beard scratched against my chin and I wound my hands loosely around his neck. His tongue slipped into my mouth and our kiss was heated but not frantic. I lifted my eyelids, needing to watch Conor, and wasn't at all surprised to see his hooded eyes fixed on mine.

He grinned boyishly against my lips as he pulled back. "God, I love you."

My heart stopped beating for a second, only to flutter rapidly against my ribs shortly after. I should say it was too soon. We didn't know each other.

But we did.

We spent a month getting to know one another again. He wasn't the Conor from my childhood, just as I was no longer the little kid who hung out at his house before he left for college. We were two different people and while I was probably a little too sweet for a guy like Conor, and he was probably a little too gruff and hard for a woman like me…

I liked who we were together.

So I whispered the three words into the air, feeling them with every piece of my being. "I love you too, Conor."

His grin was what fantasies were made of. Daily, he showed me how excited he was for this baby, and this grin right here told me how excited he was for us. Needing for us to be *more*, I reached between us and started to work on his pants.

"Naked, Conor," I said, drawing the zipper down.

I pushed down on the denim of his jeans, not at all surprised to see he'd gone commando, and before I could kneel to get the denim the rest of the way off, because hello, I couldn't bend at the waist these days, Conor put his hands over mine and finished the act for me.

"I can't have your mouth so close to me right now, Mia baby," was his gruff response and I couldn't help but grin. Someone was feeling needy.

After he straightened up, I had to chuckle at the sight he was. He was naked from the hips down, still sporting his bar tee on top. "You're cute."

Conor scoffed and peeled his shirt off over the top of his head. "That was fucking ass-backwards," he said, referring to the order in which he lost his clothes.

"Nah, it was good," I said, grinning. I reached out to trace the tattoo on his side. I knew the Gaelic knot he had on the back of his shoulder, and I had previously studied the lines and shapes of his sleeve, which had homages to his siblings and heritage intermixed, but these words were new.

"This is new." He must have gotten it sometime over the last few days.

He nodded, looking down to where my fingers traced. He lifted his arm a little to allow greater access. "Got it Thursday morning."

Which explained why it was still slightly red. Not badly, but just enough.

"What does it say?"

"*Dá fhada an lá tagann an tráthnóna.*"

The Gaelic lilt of his tongue was sexy and almost enough for me not to care what it meant. But, "Which means...?"

Apparently he was all about multitasking, because he dropped to his knees to peel my panties off, pressing a kiss to the underside of my belly, the top of my thigh, the top of my mound, all before answering, "'However long the day, the evening will come.'"

I lifted a brow. "You work nights, bud. Does that mean you don't like your days with me? You crave the bar at night?" I was grinning and there was a slight lift to my voice.

"No, smartass." He slapped my ass before standing and I stepped out of the lace pooled at my feet. "It means no matter how bad, no matter how long, the good will always come."

"Wow, Conor O'Gallagher has a philosophical side."

He just chuckled, shaking his head. "You really are a smartass." He reached behind me to undo the clasp of my bra, but when he did and the material didn't fall, the change in his face, from gleeful to confused, was comical.

"How the fuck does this come off?" Both of his hands went to my back to hold out the ends, but because it was a multi-way bra and I crisscrossed the straps...

"What, a man with your sexual prowess hasn't encountered a multi-way bra?"

"This a trick question?" His brows were down in concentration, but he still looked determined.

"Over my head, cowboy."

I reached in front of me to pull the cups over my breasts, which spilled out when unconfined, and started to shimmy and twist it off over my head when Conor got with the program and finished the job.

"Finally," he said on an exasperated sigh, making me laugh. His hands went straight to my over-sized breasts and he kneaded them in his hands. "God, watching these get bigger and not being about to do anything with them..." He cut off his thought when he bent low to suck on one of my nipples. My head fell back at the feel of his mouth over me and I put my hands in his hair, keeping him pressed closed.

"God, Conor."

He chuckled against my flesh and when he ran his tongue over my now hardened peak, I damn near came. "Oh my God."

"Damn," he said, pulling away from my chest. "If I knew abstinence after a really good fuck would get you to start talking, I'd have done it sooner."

I lifted a brow. "Really, Conor? We had sex, didn't talk for five months, had sex nearly twice in one day, and then spent a month not touching. How much sooner do you think you should have planned to abstain?"

He grinned, then shrugged. "Should've gone with my gut when I was still thinking about you a week after the first time. Should have found you. I could have figured it out."

"With what information?" I was trying not to, but I couldn't help but grin at his determination. "You didn't have my name, you knew nothing about me..."

"Stop being so smart about this, Mia." His grin was wide. "I should have figured out a way. Now stop talking. I want to feel you around me." He put his hand between my legs and flicked the tip of his finger over my clit, causing me to moan.

"Yeah, baby, just like that." He circled those fingers around the nub then strummed it back and forth before slipping his fingers further back. I fully expected him to sink two, if not three, fingers into me straight away, but he surprised me by starting with one.

"Gotta be sure you're ready," he said, watching my face as he moved his finger in and out slowly. "You're pretty fucking slick here, Mia baby."

"More," I said, grinding my hips against his hand.

"Ah, you're greedy today, yeah?" He pulled his finger out and went back to tormenting my clit.

I growled. Yes, I growled. "Conor."

"Tell me what you need." He lowered his mouth to my shoulder, where he pressed small kisses over and over again. His finger between my lower lips continued to play and he put his other hand on the side of my swollen belly. If I weren't so aroused, I would be smiling with happiness over the fact he always had a hand on my belly, but damn, I waited a long month for this night and I needed him.

"I need your cock, Conor. Your thick, freaking cock. I need you in me," I said sassily, annoyed with him and so freaking turned on, I would surely burst the moment he filled my pussy with his cock.

Conor threw his head back with a short, loud laugh. "God*damn*, Mia."

"Well…" The shyness was back. I used my words like he asked me to, but maybe not in the exact way he wanted them.

He must have seen my face shut down because he put his lips to mine, kissing me deeply and thrusting two fingers into me. When my mouth opened, he took the opportunity to sweep his tongue into my mouth, kissing me thoroughly.

He continued to kiss me as his fingers thrusted in and out, scissoring inside me and curling against the walls. Faster and faster, he moved his hand until my legs felt like they were going to give out from under me.

I put my hands on his shoulders and pulled my mouth back, squeezing my eyes shut to focus on both the sensation happening between my legs, and on staying upright. Conor slide his free hand from my belly to my lower back, pressing me just enough to give me additional stability. He slipped a third finger inside my tight space and relentlessly moved his hand, faster now, and at an angle that allowed his palm to get my clit in on the action.

My jaw dropped open as the impending orgasm started. I could feel it coming and knew if I just squeezed against his fingers, adding just a little more tightness to the mix, I would fly over that edge.

I needed it, though.

So I did.

"Yeah, baby, take what you need," was Conor's response when I clamped down over his fingers. No sooner than the words were out of his mouth, and I was gone.

"Shit," I said as my body shook and shuddered against him. My chest was heaving and my legs were shaking. If it weren't for Conor's arms, I would be a puddle on the ground.

I opened my eyes as the true high finally finished, even with my body shuddering and the aftereffects of my orgasm still sending shockwaves of pleasure through my body.

"You're fucking beautiful." Conor slipped his hand from between my legs, his eyes fixed on the sight. As his eyes raked back up my body, they lingered on my chest. When they stayed there, I looked down as well.

"Oh my God!" I moved my hands to cover myself. I was *leaking*. Oh my God! Everyone always talked about how they had a baby and they were waiting for their milk to come in; what the fuck was this?

This was so embarrassing.

"Oh my God. I can't... Oh my..." I tried to step away, but Conor put his hands to my hips yet again, holding me in place.

Then, without a word, he did the one thing I never in my wildest dreams would have imagined, and quite frankly, had I thought of him doing it, I would have been mildly grossed out. He *licked* me.

"Conor!"

I tried to step back but he just moved to do the same to my other breast, his hands squeezing my hips.

"It's normal, Mia," he finally said as he straightened. "And oddly erotic."

"But... You... No! No, you can't do that. That's... *weird*, Conor."

He just grinned, his bearded cheeks lifting and this eyes twinkling in the dimming light of the room. "It's fucking hot." He turned me to face the bed and walked us right up to the edge before he covered my breasts with his hands, kneading them. "I read about it. Maybe watched a video or two, too."

I frowned, looking over my shoulder. "You read about it?" I hadn't even read about it! I pretty much just skimmed the 'what your baby looks like now' web pages and just rolled with it all. But Conor was *reading* about my pregnancy? What universe was this?

"Yep. Read about it."

"And by watching, you mean…" I thought about it for a moment, then my eyes widened. I couldn't turn toward him because he was holding me in place but my jaw still dropped. "You watched *porn* about lactating women? Oh my God, Conor!"

He chuckled lightly. "I was curious about the fetish. Didn't quite get it. Even watching it, didn't really get it, but with you?" He nodded. "Totally get it."

"Do you watch porn regularly?" That could be a problem. Not a big problem, because it wasn't like I had never watched it, but if he was going to go that route instead of with me, that would be a problem.

"Mia. Babe. I just went a month without sex. Yeah, I watched it pretty regularly." His grin grew and he lifted a hand to swirl a finger in my face. "And you, miss, can't say a damn thing about it, because one of those times was on your laptop, and one of the sites was already archived."

I blushed even though it really wasn't anything to be super embarrassed about. The man knew I had toys so it shouldn't be that big of a deal but women and porn was just so… Taboo.

"I'd much rather be fucking you, though, if that's what you're worried about. But maybe someday we can watch together." He added his sexy wink and I decided to let it go.

Because he had a point.

"Enough talk. You had your turn, it's mine." To prove his point, he held his body close to mine, his thick, hard cock trapped between our bodies and pushing into my back.

"How do you want me, then?" I was going with bravado tonight. He wanted me to be more vocal, I was going to certainly try.

"What do you think is going to be comfortable? You haven't been sleeping on your back." He *would* notice something like that.

I thought about it, trying to figure out which position would feel the best. When I stepped away from him this time he let me, and I crawled up on to his much-too-big bed, my belly hanging low, and grabbed a pillow to put under my chest. I lowered my upper body and looked back at him. "Good for you?"

His hand was on his cock, squeezing it and pumping from base to head. He licked his lower lip and his grin was wicked and visceral. He moved to kneel on the bed behind me, between my spread knees, and palmed my ass. "Damn, you're fucking gorgeous."

Putting his finger at the center and top of my ass, he lowered it slowly. My ass clenched when he ran over the bud there and I bit my lip when he rimmed my pussy opening. I was still soaked from earlier, more than ready for his thick girth.

His finger left me and, glancing over my shoulder again, I saw him take himself in hand, moving even closer. He swept the head of his cock over the path his finger just took and ran his other hand up my back, reaching up to clasp around the back of my neck. He squeezed once gently just before he pushed in fully.

My head dropped to my crossed forearms, my mouth open on the soundless plea his entering me always seemed to provoke. With his arm at my neck and his cock deep inside me, his body blanketed mine gently. He dropped his other hand to rest on knuckles beside me, giving me the feeling of being completely enveloped without his body weight directly on me.

"Goddamn, I missed this," he grunted as he pulled out slowly. He squeezed my neck once more before moving that hand to mirror his other, allowing him to press kisses up and down my spine as he started to work his hips against mine.

Wantonly, I pushed back against him every time he thrust, needing him deeper and harder than he was already going.

"More, Conor."

He chuckled against my back before pushing himself up straight, his hands at my hips. If anything, he slowed his thrusts down, letting his pull drag deliciously against my inner walls.

"Oh my God, Conor." I moved my arms so they were beside me in push-up position, only so I could keep my open mouth gasp muffled against his mattress. He pulled back and cocked his hips, twisted the angle enough to cause small moans of ecstasy to crash through my mouth. I didn't feel him move a hand from my hip, but soon my hair was being pulled gently, enough to take my mouth from his bed, my head back and neck exposed.

"I want to hear it, Mia. Tell me what this does to you. Tell me what my thick cock in this tight pussy does to you."

"God, Conor, it's fucking..." I moaned again, my eyes closed. "Right there, Conor. Right there." I pushed back onto him, which earned me a chuckle and slight swat to my ass.

"Tell me, don't take, Mia baby."

"Harder, Conor."

"Like this?" He let go of my hair and gripped my hips with both hands again, slamming hard up into me.

"Oh God, Yes, Conor." The feel of his thickness inside me, the slick and quick push past my muscles, had me incredibly close to coming again.

He did it one more time, but I needed more. "Faster, Conor. Fuck me like you want me."

He held himself in me so incredibly deep and didn't move. "Don't ever think I don't want you, Mia baby. Fuck, I want you. I fucking need you."

Before I could respond though, his hips were pounding into me ruthlessly, giving me everything I needed and more. I muttered his name over and over, mixed in with high moans and senseless words, squeezing my eyes shut against the onslaught of feeling.

I was so close.

So damn close.

Knowing, God he knew me so fucking well, Conor reached around me and held his finger over my clit, our rocking hips causing his finger to move ever so slightly.

But just enough to send me over.

"Oh, fuck, Conor!" Rather than bury my head in the mattress, I threw my head back, my arms and neck straining with my release.

"Yeah, baby. Just like that." His hips continued to work against me, his thick cock pushing against the resistance my orgasm was causing until finally his loud grunt matched my quiet mews of pleasure.

And then it was over too soon.

Conor pulled out and I moaned at the loss. Rather than him leave to clean himself up though, he lay beside me, pulling me onto my side yet facing away from him. He then pulled me close and wrapped his arm around me, his hand resting on my belly gently and kissed my shoulder.

Here we were in this huge bed, and he wanted to keep me close. I couldn't stop the onslaught of tears from filling my eyes, even though it was a stupid thing to get teary about.

I closed my eyes, hoping Conor wouldn't notice, but the damn man seemed to notice everything.

"What's wrong?" I felt him push up behind me so he could look into my face.

"Nothing, I'm fine," I said, not really lying. I put my hands under my cheek and tried to settle in for a nap. I winced when the baby chose that moment to kick something vital but I kept my eyes closed.

For a second, I thought Conor was going to drop it but instead he climbed over me. I opened my eyes, which of course caused a tear to spill, and saw him sitting on his knees, looking down at me. The sight was actually quite comical, big burly, bearded, tatted man sitting on his knees while naked, looking down at me.

"Ah, I knew it!" He pointed at my face but then his own face fell. "Why are you crying, Mia?"

"It's stupid," I said, while trying to grin. "They're not sad tears, I promise."

Conor moved so he was lying down on his side, facing me this time, but kept his upper body propped up on his arm. He brushed a finger down my cheek, tracking a tear.

"What's wrong, Mia baby?" he asked quietly.

"I was just thinking about how you have this huge bed and you choose to stay wrapped up close to me. See? Stupid. Nothing for you to worry about."

He ran his thumb over my cheek and grinned crookedly. "Yeah, well, I told you. I like your bed. This fucker's too big for the two of us."

"I like your bed though." It turned out I enjoyed cuddling, but I was sure there would come a day that we would need our space in bed.

"And I like yours. You lose this argument, Mia." He relaxed his arm and lay down fully beside me, his eyes just taking in my face and features. I nearly wiggled from the uncomfortable perusal, but I refrained.

Finally, after a few quiet moments, Conor spoke up. "We have to talk baby things soon."

Chapter Fourteen

Conor

I may have only had sex with Mia a handful of times, if even—but hey, it was still more than I could say I did with any other individual woman—but I knew without a single doubt that this woman, wrapped in my arms, was who I wanted to be with for the next fifty-plus years.

The sex just got better and better. Each time, Mia vocalized what she needed and wanted a little more, which only turned me the fuck on more.

But tears in her eyes afterward? I was not prepared for that.

Then when she gave the line about the bed, I wanted to laugh out loud. She was crying because I had a huge ass mother fucking bed and I wanted to keep her close instead.

Depending on how many kids we'd have, yeah, maybe we'd get a bigger bed than her queen someday. You know, to accommodate bad dreams and stuffed animals, but I was absolutely content with her smaller mattress.

Which brought up the point, where were we putting the bed?

Her place didn't even have a fucking separate *room* to put the baby, and my place, even though it had rooms unlike her studio, wasn't exactly prime real estate for a baby. Not above a bar, and not with a room the baby could someday call its own.

Then there was the fact we didn't have a name yet. I was cool with the whole not finding out the sex thing, but the kid needed a name.

"We need to talk baby things soon," I finally said out loud.

"What do you mean?" she asked. I reached down to maneuver the covers around us and as much as I wanted to have her pressed as close as her back to me allowed, I needed her face and eyes more. I moved so my abs pressed against her belly, grinning when the kid kicked or pushed or whatever it did, and Mia entwined our legs together.

"Names. Where we're going to live. Those things."

"Oh." She nodded a few times as if thinking. "I don't think living here is that great of an idea, to be honest."

I agreed, but wanted to hear her reasoning. "Ok. Why?"

She lifted her brows and moved to sit up, pushing against the bed and moving to allow her belly space. I loved watching as her movements changed to make way for her belly.

I moved to my back and pushed back so I could rest against the headboard, watching her. I crossed my arms over my chest and waited for what she had to say, loving the fact that she didn't bother to pull the sheet with her to cover her tits.

"Well first, it's over a bar. Not exactly a great environment for a child. As an infant, it wouldn't be bad, but I don't think it would be so great with a toddler." She shrugged. "I have no problem with the baby hanging around downstairs while you're opening and whatever, but definitely not anywhere near the place when it starts to get busy."

"I agree." I didn't think she was expecting me to agree so easily.

"O-kay…"

Nope. She definitely didn't think I'd agree so quickly.

"Well, also, there's not really room for the baby. Like, there's not a physical room for it."

Again, I agreed, but just to be a fucker… "I could always frame out another room, take away some square footage from this room and the closet."

She thought about it, her eyes scanning the room as she pondered that. "Yeah..." She nodded in that thoughtful way of hers. "Yeah, I guess that could work."

She continued to look around the room before pointing to the door to my room. "You probably had some woman right there against the door."

I grinned. I hadn't thought about that, but yeah, she would go there.

"And probably in your bathroom, too. Not to mention the kitchen, the couch. Hell, you probably even got some on the stairs leading up here."

I chuckled. "I get it. You don't want to live where I had my...looser ways."

She frowned. "Is that bad of me? I mean, I know you swear you're a changed man, and I really do believe you, but for me personally, the reminder is all over."

I reached for her, pulling her by her neck until she crawled to sit right next to me. "I was thinking about finding an apartment or a house with you. I just wanted to hear what you had to say."

"You want to move in together?"

I barked out a laugh. "Mia. We practically live together already, just without the change of address form."

Mia smiled wide. "Ok. Yeah. Maybe tomorrow after my appointment, we can start looking? Do you have to do book work tomorrow?"

I was about to shake my head, because I had been intending to get that done, but remembered I fell asleep before I could. I made a face and nodded, "Yeah, but it can wait until after everything."

Again, Mia smiled. "Ok. Sounds like a plan then."

Mia

The next day, everything happened quickly. Conor had woken me up a number of times through the night, to 'play,' as he called it, and we finally got out of bed with an hour to spare before my appointment.

The appointment itself went smoothly, with my OB-GYN just asking about birth plan things and asking Conor how he felt about everything. She also wanted to see the baby's position, saying that in a few weeks' time, the baby would be in what should be its final position for birth. She had concerns of the baby potentially being breech.

She ordered a quick ultrasound to check, and if Conor and I had been hopeful about not finding out the baby's sex, well…

Our baby had other ideas.

The moment the wand was placed on my belly, our baby was all about showing what it was.

Conor laughed out loud. "That baby is all boy."

My doctor smiled. "I know you wanted to wait. I'm sorry, Mia. But yes, like Conor said, your baby is definitely all boy."

"Look at him. He's showing off."

"Like his dad," I said, when I finally found my voice. My eyes were tearing up and when Conor looked at me, I was afraid he was going to think I was crying because I was disappointed. I held my hand up and shook my head. "I'm fine. Overwhelmed, but really, really happy."

Conor leaned in and kissed my lips sweetly as my doctor started to clean up her equipment. "Well, I can say that I think he will be fine. We'll keep an eye on him, because he is getting pretty big and is going to run out of room, but everything looks good."

I smiled and thanked her, and after she left with brief instructions on what to do in the coming weeks, Conor pulled my shirt down and helped me stand.

"You're really ok?" he asked.

I nodded. "I am. Yeah, I wanted it to be a surprise, you know, the last great surprise a person could get, but…" I shrugged and grinned, shaking my head. "He's going to be such a little hellion."

"Just like his old man."

I reached up on tiptoes so I could kiss him once. I wanted a long, thorough kiss, but my OB-GYN's room was so not the place.

"Let's go look at places to live so I can take you home and ravish you senseless." Conor squeezed my hip and grabbed my purse, not afraid to put the strap over his shoulder, and helped me out of the room.

That day, we toured two nicer apartments and, after Conor's urging, a little starter house located on a cute cul-de-sac. An apartment was a one-year commitment. A house? That was a serious commitment, as both a homeowner and for a new couple.

On top of that, I was afraid a mortgage was going to put us over our heads, but Conor assured me we could afford it.

We.

He referred to us as a 'we' and while I knew he said he was in for the long haul, it was those little reminders that made my heart so incredibly happy.

It was a three bedroom, two bath ranch-style home with a small yard, but the neighborhood itself had a little park. Conor said we could convert the third bedroom into an office for now, allowing him to work from home even more.

So finally, a smile on my face, I nodded. "Ok. Let's do the paperwork."

And we started the next adventure in our life.

Epilogue

Mia

Conor was running late again. Saturday afternoons always had him walking in the door almost two hours after the end of his shift, but I knew the man only had eyes for me. That and I knew he tried to get as much Sunday paperwork finished before he came home, preferring to focus on us when he was home. After talking with Brenna, I found myself at O'Gallaghers.

The place was crazy busy and a glance at the bar itself told me why. The Enforcers were starting to trickle into town. According to Conor, camp was opening up this week and apparently the veterans of the team were having a bonding day.

I had gotten to know a few of the players, but it was easy to spot Jonny and Caleb Prescott. Jonny, with his curly blond hair, and Caleb beside him.

I waddled over to them, my baby belly bigger than ever, and squeezed between the brothers, tapping them on their shoulders. "Hello, gentlemen."

Jonny looked over at me and grinned as he lifted his beer to his lips. "Miss Mia."

Caleb grinned at me as well. "Look at you, all glowing and shit."

I grinned wide. "How's Sydney? I haven't seen her in a bit." After the wedding, and after things started to settle into a sweet, regular motion with me and Conor, I grew to be good friends with Sydney Prescott. She was a fun girl.

Before Caleb could answer though, Conor came over to us. He started switching out his O'Gallagher shirts for shirts that showcased he was taken. Today's said, boldly over his chest, "I Make Cute Babies." Today he also wore a backward ball cap with a bumble bee over his brow. I knew the front of that hat said "Daddy to Bee". It was a favorite of his and honestly, made me laugh.

"What the hell are you doing here, Mia baby?" He was grinning wide, absolutely no malice in his voice. "You know I don't want you here when you're ready to pop like that."

I grinned and rubbed my belly. "I was just curious why you weren't home. I now understand why."

He glanced over his shoulder. I followed his gaze and saw he was looking at the clock, but my eyes landed on the pictures he placed there. He wasn't shy about showing he was taken and happy about it.

There was also the fancy 'm' on his ring finger, silly man.

"Shit. Sorry, babe." He looked back around and pulled his towel from his pocket. "Stone, man, I gotta fly."

"Conor..." It really wasn't that pressing.

"I got a date with my baby mama."

This earned a chuckle from not only the Prescotts, but a few of the other players nearby.

"Jeez, Conor." I could feel my face heating.

He winked at me and crooked his finger at me. I followed him to the end of the bar, where he took my hand and pulled me into the back. "Hey, I could have said I had a date to fuck the labor out of you."

I slapped his back. "Conor!" He had said it in what was supposed to be an empty kitchen, but Rory came out of the stairwell from the upstairs apartment. We got the house, and Rory took over upstairs.

"Way too much fucking information," Rory said, shaking his shaggy head.

"I'm a lucky fuck, you know it," Conor said with a laugh, pulling me into his office. He clicked the door shut, locking it twice, because *there* was a story, and pulled me to the couch.

He tore his hat off with one hand while removing his shirt with his other, behind his back and over his head in the way men did, and unfastened his jeans. "You wearing panties today?"

I was wearing a dress, and going panty-less wasn't exactly the most comfortable but, "No, I am not." We had limited time these days.

"How long did Brenna—" Conor had added a really nice leather couch to the office here at the bar recently, one that was deep and gave the two of us more than enough room. He sat down and pulled me to him. I lifted a leg over his hips as he laid back, settling down over him, my wet heat rubbing over his thickness. I rolled my hips once, dragging myself over his rigid length.

"An hour."

Conor leaned up to kiss me, guiding my hips until he slipped into my warmth. We moaned in unison.

The last few weeks hadn't been very kind to my sex drive, but I was ready for this baby to come out. Labor-inducing sex, it was then.

It was over quicker than we usually went, but that was due to going weeks without sex, and the contractions toward the end.

Holding his hands over my sides, feeling the contractions for himself, Conor looked up at me, his eyes a mixture of glee and worry.

"Is it time?"

I laughed. I really didn't think one session was going to do it. "Nah, I think they're just Braxton hicks. She's pretty comfy-cozy in there." I groaned when she kicked. "She's probably never going to come out."

If I thought I was huge with Aiden, I was not prepared for this pregnancy. With Ava, I felt her up in my ribs all the time, and my belly needed a Wide Load sign.

I pushed up onto my knees, allowing Conor to slip from my heat, and with my hands against his chest, moved to stand.

Conor sat up and looked at the clock. "Bren has Aiden for another thirty minutes. Want to get food?" He reached for his clothes and started to pull them back on as I reached for a tissue to try to clean up as best as I could.

Which was hardly at all.

Conor chuckled and reached for my hand, taking the tissue and going to task, before finishing dressing.

The past few months had been a whirlwind. Aiden Rory O'Gallagher was born, weighing in at ten pounds, eleven ounces, and twenty-two inches. He was *big*. And because of that, I tore pretty decently.

Conor had been a hands-on dad the moment we walked into our little house on the cute cul-de-sac, and had been incredibly great at making sure I stayed comfortable. I tried breast feeding, because goodness knew I had the supply for it, but Aiden hadn't been a great latcher, and after a week of trying, failing, and therefore crying, I moved to just pumping and bottle feeding. It allowed Conor to feed him too, and there was nothing I loved more than to watch Conor and Aiden together.

After two months of pumping though, we had more than enough milk to get Aiden to his one-year birthday. I was a super-cow, I joked, to which of course Conor took offense to.

The whole calling myself a cow thing.

Anyway. I stopped pumping pretty early in the game.

Conor had been afraid of 'down there.' Not because I gave birth. No, it was because I tore so badly. He was afraid he would hurt me or worse, I would somehow just randomly tear again. One day we'd been messing around, not having sex yet because regardless of Conor's fears, we still didn't have the medical go-ahead, and Conor jacked off on me.

A month later, while doing my yearly blood panel for insurance purposes, boom. Pregnant.

I'm not making this stuff up.

So our kids were going to be hardly ten months apart. When I told Conor the news, his face blanched so quickly, I thought that my big man was going to faint on me.

He then called my OB-GYN to be sure that everything was going to be ok, that *I* was going to be ok. She reassured him, saying that it definitely wasn't the best thing for my *body*, but I should have a normal pregnancy. She just was going to keep a closer eye on me.

As we left his office hand in hand, Conor said his goodbyes to his brother and Stone, and the few hockey players still lingering around the bar. We went to my car, leaving his new truck in the back lot. Conor helped me in before going around to the driver's side.

"Grab something and head home, or ask Bren to stay a little longer and sit down somewhere?" Conor asked as he started the ignition.

We didn't have too much time to ourselves these days. Hard to with a nine and a half month old at home who was sure to skip the walking stage and go straight from crawling to running.

But I also hated being away from Aiden. Going back to work had been incredibly hard, but I was lucky to be able to spend weekends and summers with him.

"Maybe just pick something up. Brenna said she had plans later tonight."

"With a guy?" Conor looked at me, a brow up, and I grinned.

"Even if she were going on a date, it would be of no business of yours, Conor."

"Hey, she's my baby sister."

"And she's a grown woman."

Brenna and I had gotten incredibly close over the last year, too. We were obviously two very different people than we were when we were friends before, but I definitely valued her friendship.

"Speaking of grown women... I talked to your dad."

I whipped my head in his direction. "You didn't."

Conor had been teasingly threatening to talk to my dad about taking my hand in marriage. Conor wanted me to marry him, and as much as I wanted to marry him too, as much as he'd proven himself over and over again these last few months, I still felt like everything was too fast.

Sure, we were on our way to having two kids, but marriage...? That was a really, *really* big step. I mean, kids were a big step; they linked him to me for the rest of our lives. But something about marriage scared me a little.

"I told him that eventually you would be ok with the idea, and that I wanted to be sure I had his permission." Conor reached for my hand and squeezed it before placing our hands on his thigh. "I got it. So I'm just waiting on you, baby." He said it with a grin. Conor was so incredibly supportive of me and I could tell he loved me above all else. "Whenever you're ready, I'll be right there with you," he said, pulling our hands to his lips to kiss my knuckles.

He was really a great guy.

Great in bed, too, yes, but his heart and how he was with me, with Aiden, that was what kept me going day after day.

"I love you, Conor," I finally said. No, I wasn't ready for marriage, but soon. Definitely, soon.

"Love you too, Mia baby."

ABOUT LAST NIGHT

book 2

Prologue

The last job I ever saw myself in was working as a barmaid for an extremely popular Irish-American pub. Hey, nothing against waitresses and bartenders. It just wasn't something I ever saw for myself.

At seventeen, I graduated high school a year early only to go straight into nursing school—with many of my Gen Ed's already completed.

My big plans, the ones that worked so damn well on paper, had me graduating with my Bachelors of Science in Nursing by the age of twenty, with even greater plans of continuing on to eventually become a Certified Nurse Anesthetist. Ideally by twenty five.

I had such great plans.

But just like plans—and life—tend to do, everything sort of fell through the cracks my freshman year of college. My years of overachieving had me burning out by the end of first semester and with failed classes came lost scholarships. I had to drop out of my classes and work double overtime to afford my rent and expenses. I was a nursing assistant at a fairly nice assisted living facility, making bonuses on top of bonuses, and overtime on top of that.

But eventually I burned myself out there too and needed to go back to school.

I was now twenty-four with no degree to my name, but thankfully I was only a semester away from the first one. On paper, my *new* plan had me graduating the anesthesia program in another three years, so not too far from my original hopes, but I wasn't placing any bets these days.

While I loved my job and the people I worked with, namely my residents, I needed something that worked better with my schedule and paid extremely well.

Selling myself or finding a sugar daddy were not options.

I was walking down the street and came across O'Gallagher's, an Irish-American pub near both my apartment and school, when I saw a Help Wanted sign in the window. While not something I saw for myself, if I were to work at O'Gallaghers I could get rid of my car—I had nothing against Uber or Lyft—and hopefully make enough in tips working four to eight hours *most* nights, rather than working twelve hour shifts at the nursing home *every* night.

I didn't have any sort of experience in the service industry outside of what I did in health care, but I sucked it up and walked into the doors, applying and interviewing on the spot.

Turned out, the O'Gallagher siblings lost a couple of their barmaids with the end of the previous school year and were hoping to expand the business.

Conor, the oldest of the three, was a hunk with his big body and bearded face, tattoos up and down one of his arms, and his sexy ease of wearing a tee and ball cap. Brenna, the youngest, was incredibly sweet and just a bit younger than I.

Then there was Rory.

I'd heard about Rory O'Gallagher. He had a reputation that preceded him.

Rory was the type of guy who made money, flaunted money, and was, frankly, a rude piece of shit.

If you were talking to the girls he dated.

And even dated was too nice of a term.

The girls he fucked.

And left.

He took what he needed from them, gaining respect in their little circles, and then dropped them all like bad habits.

Rory O'Gallagher was not a nice guy.

Sure, he put on a pretty front, but under it all, lay a dirty, rotten, conniving man.

And it would be in my best interest to forever stay clear of him.

Chapter One
September

Rory

The first thing I always noticed upon waking was the sun trying to cut through my eyelids.

It was fucking obtrusive. Let a man sleep, yeah? Especially a man who worked until the early morning hours.

Damn sun and its insensitivity.

I know, I know, room darkening shades. But those things cost money, and my money was better spent elsewhere. Well, that and my last apartment had a tiny ass window in the bedroom and didn't warrant the black curtains. The apartment above the bar, where I'd just moved into a few weeks prior, had much better glass to the outside world.

The second thing I noticed was the leg wrapped deliciously around my hip.

Which, of course, led to the third thing, the lovely phenomenon known as 'morning wood.'

Let's be completely open and honest here. I noticed that one every day.

Of the three, it was the leg wrapped around me that gave me slight pause though. I almost *always* walked my women out at night.

I lifted my eyelids, squinting against the sun, and looked down and over to the body attached to the leg. She was on her stomach, leg up over my hip and face down in the opposite direction. Her contortion didn't look comfortable but then again… I chuckled, remembering the acrobatics of last night.

This chick here swore she'd been an Olympic hopeful in gymnastics and damn, she had the flexibility to go with that statement, but I highly doubted at twenty-three, Team USA was going to take her. Any other country, sure, but the United States gymnastics team had standards.

And I knew her age because I checked her ID before serving her last night.

Could it have been a fake? I mentally shrugged. Sure, fakes could be damn convincing but as a guy who had a business in college making forgeries, I was going to go ahead and say her license was legit.

She'd been really fucking cute last night, with her halter top and short skirt. This morning though her hair was a bit of a mess. I frowned to myself, taking in the chick's white blonde hair. She was face-down in the bed, the sheet draped low covering her ass, and she was wearing a tank top with those small spaghetti straps. When the fuck did she put clothes on?

I reached down to reposition my dick and frowned when I encountered my boxers. When the fuck did *I* put clothes on?

I wracked my brain, trying to piece together the night.

I closed the bar last night with Emily. After she left for the night, I talked Cute Halter Top upstairs when all was said and done. She nodded, giggled, and stuck around for me to finish closing up.

We went upstairs, got it on like Donkey Kong…

And then I walked her to her car.

And Em—

I quickly looked down at the girl beside me. *Shit.*

I leaned over the woman as to not wake her, and lifted her hair gently to confirm my fears.

Yep.

Fuck.

Emily.

I sat back and rubbed my palms over my eyes roughly, trying to recall more of the night. We both had clothes on, so it wasn't like I fucked her. That wouldn't go over real well with Conor.

I chuckled. Fuck. That wouldn't go over real well with Emily, either. She fucking hated my guts.

What happened, what happened, what happened…?

I opened the back door for Cute Halter Top, not really paying attention to her as she gabbed on and on. She was a fucking screamer in bed, but she really had to shut her trap now. Too fucking talkative.

I stepped out onto the back step and nearly tripped over something.

"Fuck." Damn homeless people.

But when I looked down, everything jerked to a stop.

"Isn't that your waitress?"

Barmaid *was the term we used, but, "Yeah. Here, let's get you to your car." Cute Halter Top and I walked around a sleeping Emily, and I got the girl to her car. I scratched at my chin, trying to figure out what the hell Emily was doing back here, and sleeping on the back stoop no less.*

When I reached Emily again, she hadn't moved. In the dim light the back lantern provided, I saw her face streaked with tears and an unfamiliar, unwelcome, clench happened somewhere in the vicinity of my chest.

I knew the girl didn't like me. She wasn't quiet about it. Take tonight, for instance. She didn't normally close with me, but Stone and I switched shifts as a favor to him. When she found out it would be she and I, I almost expected her to walk out.

But I knew her story. I knew why she'd been at O'Gallaghers for the last year. It wasn't because she liked passing out lagers and getting her ass slapped, that was for damn sure.

When she wasn't ignoring me, she was shooting daggers my way and saying some snide comment or another. She wasn't exactly quiet about her distaste of me and my affairs.

I couldn't very well leave her sleeping out here, though. It was September in San Diego; it was starting to get chilly at night, and she was only wearing the tank and shorts she'd changed into after her shift ended.

I bent down and lifted her willowy form. She was tall for a girl, probably around five-eight, maybe only five-seven, with clear blue eyes and long, white blonde hair that, I swear to fucking God, reached her ass when she let it down and straight. She usually wore it in those big curls girls liked and pulled back in a pony-tail.

She was gorgeous, I wasn't denying it. I just knew she didn't like me so I didn't go out of my way to be overly nice to her.

When I straightened to my full height, she sleepily turned her head into my shoulder, her nose rubbing against my neck, and fucking damn if my dick couldn't seem to remember it was just getting some twenty minutes ago. I was harder than a fucking rock, and all she did was put her nose against my neck. And she didn't even know she was doing it.

Jostling her legs so her knees draped over my forearm comfortably, I made my way back inside, carrying her upstairs. She could sleep in my bed tonight.

But fuck if I was sleeping on the couch.

Playing nice guy fucking sucked. Regardless if she woke up right now, with me staring down at her with a fucking raging hard-on tenting my boxers, or if she woke up after I left to meet with Conor, she would fucking know where she was the moment she found the front door.

I couldn't worry about that now. I had things to do, and Emily could be late for her fucking review with Conor and me. I wasn't about to wake her up and deal with her wrath.

I glanced at the clock. Ten.

Fuck.

I *had* things to do. As in past tense.

Conor was going to fucking kill me for being late.

Again.

My brother used to be all chill and shit about being late when it dealt with the female variety, even more so when it was him and his dick sunk in some chick's pussy, but then he went and became a dad and now he wasn't so fucking cool any more.

It wasn't like our meeting this morning was all that damn important. We were literally only sitting down and getting ready for yearly reviews.

Woo-fucking-hoo if I was late. I think the only person we were scheduled to sit down with today was the blonde currently in my bed. I couldn't stop the grin at the thought of her in my bed for other reasons. I'd totally do her if she weren't such a bitch to me.

I stretched my arms up above then behind my head, linking my hands and allowing my fist to tap against the wall. When that stretch was in the middle of glory to the heavens, I stretched my legs, pointing my toes, loving the feel of each muscle stretching taut. My movement caused Emily to stir.

When she removed her leg, I crunched up to sit and swung my legs off the bed. I looked over my shoulder as I stood, and saw that my face-down girl stretched long against the bed, her face *still* buried in the mattress. The stretch allowed the sheet and her shorts to slip just a bit, just enough to show a small feather tat on the top of her right ass cheek. Emily didn't seem the tattoo type. Hmm.

Turning, I headed into the bathroom to piss and try to start and resolve the morning.

Chapter Two

Emily

The very last thing I could remember about last night was sitting on the back stoop of O'Gallaghers, bawling.

My life just went from shitty to shittier.

I don't suppose it was really all that bad, but after working a double at O'Gallaghers, I had raced home so I could study for my first major test in my nursing lecture course, only to find out I misplaced my keys somewhere during my walk home.

After starting at O'Gallaghers, I did indeed get rid of my car. Between not having television or a car, and working doubles at O'Gallaghers, I'd been able to afford school *and* something more than ramen and Kraft Macaroni Dinners. I splurged on Shapes though, because yeah, they were better than the Original.

I would cut out the internet expense too, but I needed that for school.

Anyway, I got home at one in the morning only to discover I hadn't grabbed my keys in my hurry to get a few hours in of studying. I *had been* planning on studying until two, sleeping until nine, then going to my review with Conor and Rory, before finally heading to class. Everything worked out in my head.

I should have freaking known better. Nothing ever worked as planned.

I got home, couldn't get in, and had to turn back to the pub. Unfortunately, by the time I got back, Rory had already locked up. Having no place to go, I sat on the back stoop, put my head in my hands, and cried.

Cut corners, and eventually they bite you in the ass...and I'm pretty sure mine just did.

So, that was the last of what I remembered.

Somehow, though, I ended up in a bed. I started to come to when the body I had thrown myself against started to move, but it wasn't until the body moved and I could hear someone peeing in a nearby bathroom that I opened my eyes and looked around.

The bedroom was huge. I frowned.

Why was I in a bedroom?

Frantically, I looked down to reassure myself I was in my clothes.

I was.

Thank the good Lord.

What *happened* though?

I turned around and sat up, rubbing my hand over my face and then looked around the room for a clock.

Ten.

Shit!

Ten!

I was due to meet Rory and Conor like... now!

I scrambled out of the bed and looked around for shoes, spotting them tossed carelessly at the foot of the bed. I pulled myself to stand and just as I was about to slip my feet into my well-worn Birkenstock sandals that had been a gift...

Rory O'fucking-Gallagher came walking out of the bathroom.

Oh my God.

Oh my flipping God.

I spent the night in Rory O'Gallagher's bed.

I *threw* my body over his. Ok, just my leg, but oh my God, my leg *touched* something on him!

I swallowed hard, staring at him as he stood in the doorway of what must have been the bathroom. He stood there, all hard body, messy reddish-brown hair, with a delicious morning shadow.

And smirking.

The ass.

"What," he finally said. "No thank you?"

I snapped my head up to look at him from across the room. "For what?" Just like that, he had the ability to piss me off.

"Oh, I don't know," he said, leaning against the doorjamb with his arms crossed over his bare chest, and his legs crossed at the ankles. Everything about him just screamed cocky.

Over-confident.

Asshole.

"Saving your ass last night?" he finished.

I stood straight and started to chew on my thumbnail as I replayed the night prior. "I just remember coming back and sitting on the stoop when I realized you had locked up already," I said, lifting my chin in the air. I wasn't going to tell him I bawled my eyes out.

"Yeah, you fucking fell asleep on the stoop." Rather than anger though, he sounded... Concerned?

Rory O'Gallagher, concerned? Psh. No. Never. That didn't fit his MO.

"Why did you come back?" Still, he stood there, ever so patiently. We didn't have time for this! I had a review with him and Conor, as well as a test that I was likely going to fail at this point.

If I failed this class, I was done. This wasn't me being dramatic; it was the school's rules. I'd be damned if I worked this hard for this long, only to fail one class in the end.

"I don't have time for this," I finally responded, heading toward the bedroom door. I'd see myself out.

"Em." He must have moved from the doorjamb, because I could hear him padding after me. "Emily."

Ignoring him, I reached for the doorknob of what I assumed was to the stairwell leading down to O'Gallaghers, but before I could pull it open, Rory caged me in against the door. I rested my forehead against the wood and squeezed my eyes shut.

I was going to fail my class.

Not only that, but Conor was likely downstairs and he'd see me leaving the apartment with his brother and, oh my God, if I lost this job, I would really be paddling up shit creek.

"You're a smart girl, Emily," Rory stated to my back.

Ha. Smart girl. Right.

That's why it took me this long to get where I was. Look at the prime example behind me. The guy who made six figures by the time he was twenty. If anyone was smart, it was Rory. Even if he didn't get his money by being a PhD in something extraordinary, he was at least smart in his entrepreneur ways.

"You know better than to sleep outside—behind a bar, no less. Why did you come back?"

I could continue to ignore him. It's what I did best, anyway. And besides, why was he being so...not-Rory-like right now?

Then he really surprised me by grabbing my arm gently and turning me around to face him. I leaned back against the door, defeated, and looked up the minimal inches to stare directly into Rory's green eyes.

I had never noticed how pretty they were before. They were a rich emerald green with an even darker ring around them. His left eye had a slight bright blue speck in it, taking up about a quarter of the bottom of his iris. Add to that his thick, long black eye lashes, and he really was beautiful up close.

He lifted a brow over one of those beautiful eyes, wordlessly urging me to answer him.

"I left my keys here."

Rory frowned now. "What do you mean, you left your keys here? I saw you leave. How'd you get home?"

That was the other thing.

I don't think any of the O'Gallaghers knew I didn't have a car.

"I walked," I answered honestly, jutting my chin up and preparing myself mentally for Rory's response. We may not get along, he may be a cocky asshole, but one thing the O'Gallaghers were was protective of the people who worked for them.

When one of the barmaids was continuously harassed by a customer and it started to affect her outside of the pub, the boys helped her file a restraining order. When Matt's, one of the weekday bartenders, kid fell ill, only to learn he had a genetic disorder, the O'Gallaghers set up a benefit for his family and the expenses they were starting to see.

Conor did these things because beneath his cocky exterior, he was truly a big softy, something that was painfully evident when you saw him with his baby boy, Aiden. Talk about exploding ovaries. Pair that with how much he loved his girlfriend, Mia, and you couldn't help but fully take in what those closest to him meant to Conor.

As for Rory? I'm sure it was an image thing.

The look of disbelief that passed over his face now would have been comical if it weren't for the fact I was mentally exhausted about how my day was already going.

"At one in the morning? You walked. You're fucking kidding me, right?"

I ground my molars. "No, I'm not fucking kidding you, Rory. I walked. I don't have a car. I walked home like I do every night, just like I walk here every day. I was too busy thinking about a test I have to take today and didn't realize I left my keys here until I got home. Therefore, I had to turn around. But by the time I got back, you had already locked up."

"Emily, you don't walk home at one in the morning around here!"

"It's a decent neighborhood, Rory."

"Yeah, with a couple bars in either direction and therefore, shady as shit people. How long have you not had a car?"

"A year," I grumbled.

"You've worked for us for a year." His voice was eerily calm, as if he was working up a good mad.

I turned my head, avoiding his gaze. *Yep, that's right, Rory O'Gallagher.*

"You mean to tell me. You have walked here and back. At least four times a week. For a fucking *year*?"

I snaked my arms between us so I could cross them under my chest, and tilted my head to the side, sighing heavily. "Rory, I have places to go and things to do, so let's not continue this. You don't really care anyway. Thank you for the place to sleep, even though I wish you would have just woken me up. I'm sorry for...anything I may have done in my sleep." My words came out cold, but that seemed to be my only temperature where Rory was concerned. I thought back to the erection my leg brushed against and I felt my face flush.

Maybe there was some intermixing heat in there, too.

My eyes quickly glanced down to be sure he wasn't up any longer. That would be so, so awkward right now.

But.

Nope.

Oh my God. Oh my God, Rory had a boner and he was talking to me while almost holding me up against the door and it was much too late in the game to be considered morning wood any longer.

Oh. My. God.

There was a new panic stirring in me, fighting over the panic of the fact my future was about to go down the drain incredibly fast because I was going to fail my class.

"Oh that?" Rory chuckled, this time his own voice cold, before looking down and grabbing himself. I fought against the gasp.

"Natural, baby." He squeezed himself and let out a groan, biting his lip. His eyelids dropped, his gaze heavy, as he kept his eyes locked on mine.

He was so...so...*crude*.

I turned and pushed against him to try and get the door open, my butt pushing back into him. I nearly jumped out of my skin with the feel of his hardness against me.

Finally, he stepped back and I swung the door open, scrambling down the stairs without looking back.

Chapter Three

Rory

I chuckled to myself as Emily ran down the stairs, her messy white blonde hair billowing behind her as she made her hasty exit.

When she reached the bottom, she glanced back up the stairs and caught me watching her. Her face scrunched up in a disgusted frown, her brows drawn together—her lips puckered angrily, too—and she pushed through the door to the kitchen.

God, she was so fucking easy to get going.

I stepped back into the apartment and closed the door, needing to put on clothes before meeting Emily and Conor downstairs. I made my way back to the bedroom and glanced at my bed, remembering the feel of Emily, all soft and warm, next to me. The room smelled like sex and I found myself kind of wishing it had been Emily earlier in the night, instead of Cute Halter Girl.

I started my night with a boner and one cute girl, and ended the sleeping hours even harder, with Emily's snark and sass filling my head. She was so cold all the time, that just once I wanted to feel her, *see* her, all hot and bothered.

By this time, I knew that Emily would have entered Conor's office. He was bound to ask her about her attire. Emily was the type who was always made up. When she wasn't in her ass-hugging jeans or sexy short-shorts with an O'Gallagher's shirt, she was in a sundress or nice jeans with an even nicer top. Her hair was always done and her face always made up.

Conor would probably be shocked to see her in her after-work clothes, messy-assed hair, and makeup smeared face.

He'd ask her about it. She wouldn't lie. I didn't think the girl knew how to lie, she was that fucking pure and genuine.

Which made her obvious distaste of me so incredibly true and real. From the moment I met her, I knew she didn't like me.

"Rory, this is Emily," Conor said from his desk as I stepped into the back office prior to a shift. I preferred to do more of the behind-the-scenes marketing aspects of running the pub, but lately I was working behind the bar more than usual. "I hired her to fill some of the holes on the floor and she'll likely do some closings, too." Sitting across from Conor was a gorgeous blonde with clear blue eyes, eyes I could probably find myself lost in. Her hair was down and over a shoulder, showing off its thickness while the light played off the light blonde hues, making it appear almost white.

In my quick perusal, I didn't notice any tattoos, no necklaces, no bracelets. She did wear a pair of simple diamond-like studs in her ears, but other than that…

She was a complete blank canvas.

I stepped closer and offered my hand. "Rory O'Gallagher." I flashed a grin at her, wanting to win her over. Fuck, I'd give up a week's worth of easy pussy for one night with this one here.

The sweet, genuine smile she had on her face when I walked in changed just slightly, but in the direction of cold rather than warm. "I've heard of you." She offered her hand and I tried my damnedest to ignore Conor's smirk-y chuckle. "Emily Winters."

I took her hand in mine, trying to ignore the coldness of her smile, but when our hands touched for only the merest of seconds, she slipped her hand from mine and turned back to Conor, promptly dismissing me.

What the actual fuck?

At that moment, I decided that Winters was the perfect surname for her. Not only was her hair the color of winter, but she was just as cold.

From then on, I spent my few moments with her riling her up and she took the opportunities to send subtle jabs my way, things like I "whored myself for money" and that I stole from the poor.

Subtle like that, yeah?

Whatever she'd heard about me had to have been slightly exaggerated. I certainly didn't *whore* myself for money, but I would definitely admit to sleeping around. And I definitely didn't steal from the poor. Convincing people of where to spend their money was a gift, and it wasn't my fault that some people didn't pay attention to their own bottom lines.

I shook my head. I had things to do and sitting here reminiscing about Emily and whatever she thought were my wrong-doings wasn't going to get my day going.

Thankfully, my cock decided that thinking about Emily wasn't a good idea and I was able to change comfortably into my favorite pair of Left Field NYC jeans, pairing it with a well-worn Henley shirt. I ran my hand through my unkempt hair, splashed on a dash of cologne because any more and Conor would send me to the showers—the dickwad—and brushed my teeth quickly before heading down to face the firing squad that was my brother.

By the time I got to the office, Emily was standing and smiling for Conor—the ass—and Conor was laughing at something she said. Apparently Conor gave her the news we were giving her a raise. She was due for one and besides, she was a good employee and deserved therefore deserved it. Then he handed her a pair of keys.

I frowned and caught the last part of their conversation, standing just outside the door while neither caught on to my presence.

"—I'll return it in three hours tops."

"Don't worry about it. Keep it for the rest of the school week. My bike is still in the back if Mia needs me for anything today."

Emily frowned, but not like the frowns she gave me. This was more of a concerned one. "But if Mia needs you for anything, she can't very well get on the bike! And what about Aiden?"

"You just worry about passing your test, Em. We'll be fine here."

She worried on her lip and glanced around the room in what I had learned was her way of trying to come up with an alternative to whatever was being said. Unfortunately, I wasn't quick enough to pushing away from the door and her eyes locked on to mine.

And yep. There it was.

That quick look of disdain in my direction.

Fighting the urge to roll my eyes and shake my head, I stepped into the room. Even Conor's open face turned to one of scorn. Fuck, I couldn't do anything right with anyone today.

"Rory. You're late."

"I overslept. I was busy rescuing damsels last night." I winked in Emily's direction and earned myself the scowl I knew was coming.

"Emily, you can go," Conor said kindly to her. "You don't need to stick around for Rory's ass-whoopin'."

Emily laughed—she fucking *laughed*—at Conor before moving around the desk to give my big, burly brother a hug. When she moved to step past me, I turned sideways to allow her through. She turned as well, making sure to leave a fucking-assed huge gap between our bodies.

"Watch out for sleeping bodies on the back stoop!" I yelled after her as she headed toward the back door. Emily didn't even bother to turn, instead just giving me the bird over her shoulder.

I chuckled and shook my head as I stepped into Conor's office completely.

"Shut the door."

Well, then. Conor meant business today.

Fucker couldn't fire me. I paid for half of this joint, and it was my fucking ingenuity that kept patrons coming in the doors *and* our asses above the red line.

I shut the door anyhow before moving to sit in the seat Emily had just vacated.

"What's up, big brother?" I sat back casually in the chair, allowing my feet to rest under Conor's desk from my side, my ankles crossed.

"I asked you before Aiden was born if you were going to be able to step up here, but Rory..." He shook his head and ran a hand down his face. "Fuck, Rory, I know you do a lot for the place, but I really need you to be more accountable for your time. I can't fucking rely on you. For your shifts, sure, but this morning? You being late for a fucking meeting with an employee? Regardless of whatever the fuck happened with you two, I need to know that I can count on you for the business side of things. Fuck, Rory, I'd love it if I could cut back another day but I can't do that if you aren't going to be reliable."

I crossed my arms over my chest and feigned indifference. "It was just a review meeting with Emily. Fuck, I already knew we were giving her a raise; what the fuck did you need me here for?"

"To do the fucking review, Rory!" Conor roared. It wasn't very often that my big brother lost his cool; he was pretty laid back in that regard, but obviously something was stressing the big guy. "If I can't fucking rely on you to do business ended things when I can't be here, who the fuck can I rely on?"

"Allow Brenna to buy in," I shrugged a shoulder, essentially dismissing Conor's concern. Sure, Brenna never showed an interest in the business side of the bar, but hell, it was her namesake, too.

"Always have an answer, don't you? Such a fucking smart ass." Conor leaned forward and shook his head. "Even if Brenna did buy in, she isn't ready for the business side. Fuck, Stone has more knowledge on this end than she does. But that's beside the point. When can I count on you, Rory? When are you going to grow the fuck up and be an adult?"

"Woah-ho-ho," I held my hands up, palms out. "Hold up a second." I sat up straight and pointed at myself. "Me? Me, grow up. Are you fucking shitting me right now, Conor? Look who's fucking talking! Up until Mia showed up fucking five months pregnant, you were just the fuck like me!"

"Yeah, and I owned up to my shit and I grew up. You're fucking twenty-nine years old, Rory."

"And you were thirty-two!" I couldn't believe he was pulling this. "Who the hell comes up with ideas for raising our revenue, huh? Yeah, that's right, fucker. Me," I said, pointing at my chest. "My ideas have allowed you to work the fucking bar three fucking nights a week and do the cushy thing the other four."

"I have a family."

"Yeah, and a woman who won't marry you." As soon as the words left my mouth, I knew I hit the wrong button. Conor's face went blank so fucking fast and his eyes closed down. Fuck me.

Conor pushed away from his desk and grabbed his bike keys from the top drawer. "Just grow the fuck up, Rory." When his voice went from heated to so incredibly cool, I knew that it wasn't going to be easy to get back in my brother's good graces again. It was going to take a little bit longer than an hour run on his bike.

"Look, Con—"

"I hope I can trust you to open the damn bar on time." Without another word, Conor stormed out past me, opening the back door and allowing it to slam shut behind him.

Well shit, that didn't end exactly well.

Chapter Four

Emily

When I first started at O'Gallaghers, I would be lying if I said either of the O'Gallagher brothers didn't scare me. Shoot, Brenna even scared me to a degree. She was all sweet but there was definitely more lurking behind her eyes.

But Conor had changed over the last year, all thanks to his girlfriend. Mia took Conor from the womanizing brute he'd been reputed to being, to the type of guy you could easily go to with your problems.

When I entered his office this morning, he took one look at me and told me to sit. I told him everything from the past eight hours and how I was terrified I was going to get kicked out of my program for failing a test—if I failed one, I only had room to fail one more; two times, and you were out—and he offered me the keys to his truck. It was also a relief to know he had been intending to offer me a raise, minimal as it was, but I knew that it would help.

Then, while he didn't scold me, he was pretty firm about the fact that had he known I was walking to and from the bar, he would have offered *me* the apartment above the bar, not Rory, because "that fucker already had a place." Conor also offered to change my hours around so that I would still be on the floor during peak times, but not so incredibly late that it would interfere with my school schedule and studying. These were all things I'd been too terrified to ask, for fear I'd lose my job. There were more senior barmaids on the team, so it made sense to me that they would have first bill for hours, but knowing that Conor had my best interests in mind definitely helped calm some of my trepidations.

With the benefit of Conor's truck, I managed to get back to my apartment, shower and change, grab my notes and notecards, and fly to the school, where I was then able to cram for an hour before the test. I felt confident going in, and felt even better coming out.

When I returned to O'Gallaghers to thank him, I was surprised to see that Conor's bike was gone. Was something wrong with Mia?

I entered the pub through the back and waved hello to the weekday cook, Mike, on the floor before heading to Conor's office to write a note to say 'thank you.'

When I exited the office, Mike held up a hand as he dropped something in the fryer. "You want something, Em?"

I had nowhere to be and I hadn't eaten yet today. "Sure, what's your special today?" The cooks always worked with the menu Rory and Conor thought up, but were allowed an additional special every day.

"Just homemade mini tacos today," Mike said with a purposeful chuckle. If there was one thing the O'Gallaghers grumbled about with the menu, it was non-American or non-Irish items.

"Ah, deviating from your Cheeseburger Shalaylees." They were the most delicious thing on the menu; ground beef in a wonton wrapper boat, sprinkled with cheese and dipped in a Guinness barbeque sauce. Whenever Mike brought out the mini tacos—which were nearly the same thing, except with spices and sour cream—Conor went on and on about them and about how if he wanted a Mexican version of his menu, he'd change the name of the place.

But Conor and Rory agreed to give the cooks their menu item and, in all honesty, the main items sold more than the special items.

That, and Conor was a fair guy.

And he liked the mini tacos. I've seen him stuff his face with them a time or two—or twenty.

"I'll do an order of those, sure," I told him, but before I could find a place to sit, Rory came through the kitchen doors.

"I need to talk to you," he said, looking at me but addressing no one in particular. Ass could at least use my name.

He stalked past me to the back office, assuming I'd follow.

I didn't want to, but he was one of my bosses so on principle, I did.

I noticed it earlier—hell, I noticed it a few times over the year but I really appreciated it now—but the way Rory wore jeans that molded to his ass, making it mouth-watering, and the white long-sleeved Henley that still showed off the groves of his shoulders and back, further adding to his appeal. Where Conor was big and bulky in muscle, Rory had more of a swimmer's body—but was definitely still well-endowed in the muscle department.

Rory only stood a few inches taller than me, but his muscle gave me that odd sense of security.

Which was incredibly disconcerting, seeing as I didn't much like the guy.

When I entered the office, I deliberately left the door open but Rory took my wrist in his hand and pulled me from the door, shutting it one handedly. Before I could open my mouth about him manhandling me, I was pushed against the door and his mouth was on mine.

I opened my mouth and put my hands to his chest with the intent to pull away and tell him to stop, but instead I brushed my tongue against his probing one. My hands moved up and were in his two-months-past-due hair, fisting against the locks and holding his face to mine. My eyes were closed but I could feel him all around me, one hand on the side of my neck, curling over the back, and the other grabbing my hip, keeping me pulled close.

I hated him but, oh my God, the way he kissed. The way he took control of my body.

What in the ever loving hell was I doing? And why did I enjoy it so much?

I wanted to hate him. This was the man who dated women long enough to get them to leave raving reviews for O'Gallaghers, only to dump them twenty-four hours later.

This was the man who pretended to support his community, only to be a twelve-year old ass about it later, leaving terrible reviews and slandering the other companies.

This was the man who participated in those stupid pyramid schemes for weight loss companies, supporting the fit and beautiful, only to push down and be cruel to those who didn't fit in with his ideal.

Rory's social media presence was everywhere and in it, he went on and on about how sometimes making money took time, that being an entrepreneur took patience, and how every single person had something to offer, but his actions were always so incredibly different from his words.

These were the very reasons I didn't like him.

He was a fake.

He was a fraud.

He was an asshole.

But my God, he kissed me like he wanted me.

I had to remind myself that this was simply him.

This was Rory O'Gallagher at his finest.

I needed to push away. I needed to put us back on our even ground.

Instead, I pulled him closer. I was going to hate myself in ten minutes, but I was going to enjoy him for the time being.

Chapter Five

Rory

I was through with Emily Winters spitting nails at me.

I wanted her fire and fury utilized in a different way, and damn if she wasn't proving she could hand it out in spades.

I'd been wiping down the bar while one of our newer bartenders, Jordan, manned the bar itself, when I heard her voice coming from the kitchen.

I'd always been drawn to her voice, even though whenever she used it for me it was cold. I could pull her voice out of a rambunctious crowd, always able to pin-point her by following the melodic notes in her tone.

For the second time that day, it was ice cold Emily Winters who gave me a raging hard-on. The morning wood didn't count but when I held her against the door? That was all her, no matter what I told her.

So when I heard her voice, when her voice gave me this new reaction, I knew I wasn't about to let her get away. I would take everything she gave me, and turn it into a passion burning so bright she wouldn't know what hit her. She wouldn't remember why she hated me.

Her hands were in my hair, her mouth fighting mine for control, and I was in fucking seventh heaven. Her willowy body molded against mine in a way that made me want to keep her close. Her hips lined up perfectly to mine and when she lifted her leg to wrap around my hip, opening her groin up to fit snug against mine, I had to stop myself from grinding into her, pushing her even further into the door.

Blindly, I stumbled for the double locks on the office door.

I walked in on Mia and Conor once. What I saw burned my retinas. Sweet Mia had a dirty side, and I would never be able to get that image out of my head.

There wasn't any way in hell someone was walking in on Emily and me.

Unfortunately, my actions caused Emily to apparently fall back into the present, because with her hands still fisted in my hair, she pulled my head back and stared at me, mouth open, chest heaving as she fought for air.

She stared.

And stared.

And stared some more. It was a little unnerving.

Still, I didn't break the silence. I wanted her with my entire fucking being and I wasn't about to let my mouth run and have *her* run in response.

I expected her backlash. To be honest, I expected a knee in the nuts.

I didn't get either.

"Once."

"Once?" I repeated, my eyes searching hers and dropping to her mouth. She licked her lips before continuing, making me groan out loud.

"One time, Rory O'Gallagher. And then I'm going back to hating you."

Not giving her room to change her mind, I grabbed her ass and hoisted her up, pulling her clothed pussy close to my hard cock as she wrapped both legs around me. She lowered her mouth back to mine as I made my way to the couch.

I rearranged my hands so one cupped her ass, freeing my other to grab my wallet from my back pocket. I tossed it down on the couch as I sat, and when she rolled her hips over me, I moaned into her mouth. *Fucking heaven.*

I wanted my hands on her skin, all over her body. I quickly pulled her shirt up and off over her head, our mouths parting for only the mere seconds it get rid of the garment. Her mouth immediately fused back to mine, her tongue sliding swiftly against my own. I wasn't able to truly appreciate the fact that she didn't wear a bra, but my hands quickly found purchase against her slight chest.

Emily was built like a dancer, willowy and toned. She was tall, but everything else on her was small. Her hips. Her waist. Her tits.

But her little nipples were rock hard against my palms as I rolled them. I slid my hands down so I could pluck at the taut peaks, rolling them simultaneously between my index fingers and thumbs. Emily's groin rolled against mine in time to her little mewls of pleasure, all muffled by my mouth.

I squeezed one of her nipples hard enough to have her rip her mouth from mine. She moaned out loud, her head dropping back, exposing the long column of her neck to me. I leaned in, scraping my lower teeth against her skin and sucked in a kiss right below her chin. I released some of the pressure my fingers had on her, gently rolling the nubs once again.

Moving my mouth, I pressed kisses up her jawline and toward her ear. I sucked her earlobe into my mouth, my tongue playing against the stud she wore there before I gently bit down. Her body shuddered against mine and I felt as she moved her legs, her knees pressing harder into my hips.

I wished she were still in her cotton shorts from earlier so I could feel her heat, feel her wetness pooling against me. Fuck, I wish she'd changed into one of her summer dresses instead of these jeans, as great as they looked on her. My hand itched to palm her bare ass. Instead, I settled with holding her hip, my thumb rubbing gently over her hip bone.

Her hair was in her signature ponytail, and I wrapped the long tresses around my other hand, pulling back lightly so I could move my mouth from her neck, to her ear, to her chest. I pressed a kiss over her sternum, between the slight mounds that made up her chest, before traveling over to her tit. I opened my mouth, but rather than suck her into my mouth, rather than devour her little pink, hard nipple, I gave her slow lick.

The feel of her against my tongue…not a word to describe it.

Emily's moan, the sigh that ran through her body, was long and drawn out.

I moved to her other nipple and licked her there too, slower this time. I felt her stomach quiver against my thumb and I just fucking knew she was going to come.

All from a little action on her tits.

I moved back to the first nipple, licking it once more before flicking my tongue over it quickly. Her hips began their restless movement against mine, her body seeking release. Her breathing became heavier, her hands in my hair tightening more.

Her breaths were coming out in quick little pants, her mewls sounding around the room. Quicker, I flicked my tongue until finally I gave her the release she was looking for and I bit, ever so gently, on the peak.

Emily's knees drew up against my sides and her body straightened, pushing impossibly close to my face, as she came.

Fucking damn.

I grinned against her chest, letting go of her nipple and pressing a kiss to the side of her lips, her mouth open as she fought the release taking over her body. I sucked on her lower lip, her body still shuddering.

I kept my eyes on her closed ones, willing them to open so I could see the heat behind the cool blue depths.

C'mon, Em… Open those eyes…

When she did, her pupils were dilated and her nostrils flared with her gasps of breath. Her face was flushed and damn if I hadn't ever seen a more beautiful woman in the throes of passion.

Chapter Six

Emily

I should really hate myself right now.

I totally just came all over Rory's lap like any number of the girls he convinced to sleep with him. But, my God, I wanted more.

Rory O'Gallagher was addicting

If this was how he was with his lady friends after he turned on the charm, I could totally see why the girls lined up to sit on his cock, even knowing he'd leave them sooner than later.

I needed to remember who Rory was outside of sex, but I would get back to that thought later. Right now, I wanted my hands on his skin and his hard cock between our bodies.

To start.

My breath was still trembling out of my parted lips and I could feel my pussy pulsing from the ebbing release, but I was ready to move this on to the next step.

His hands were still on my hips and he didn't seem to be in any sort of hurry to get naked.

So I was going to fix that.

I reached down to pull up on the hem of his Henley shirt, my eyes fixed on his body as I exposed his tan, muscle-filled flesh. As I cleared the middle of his chest, I wasn't all that surprised to find he was bare of hair.

He probably waxed.

Or had it removed by a laser.

Pushing the negative thoughts about him out of my head, I continued to pull his shirt up until finally, Rory got with the program and reached behind his head, removing the shirt completely.

I put my hands on his bare chest, taking a brief moment to drink him in. His normally messy hair was made even worse by my hands, and he still wore the shadow on his cheeks and chin from this morning. I briefly wondered what the stubble would feel like on my lady bits.

My body shivered involuntarily over him, which only caused a grin to spread over Rory's features.

Not wanting him to open his mouth with some arrogant comment, ruining the moment, I busied my hands with the fly of his designer jeans. They probably cost the same as one of my classes alone.

I hurriedly unbuttoned the fly, reaching in to pull his hardened cock free of his jeans and briefs. Needing some sort of upper hand, I gingerly rubbed my thumb along the ridge of its head, before moving off his lap to kneel between his legs, my hand never leaving his shaft.

I glanced up at him to gauge his reaction. He moved his arms so they spanned the back of the couch, giving him a look of complete and utter comfort.

Like this was an everyday occurrence.

Then again, it probably was.

Willing girl on her knees between his own, angling his cock toward her mouth.

I really had to get out of my head before this entire thing took a sour turn.

I lifted up on my knees, letting my elbows rest easily on his thighs, before enclosing the head of his cock with my mouth. Just the tip.

Just enough so that when I sucked against him, I could revel in the tightening of his thighs under my arms.

Just enough so that when I added light teasing with my tongue, I could hear his breathy groan above me.

I pulled off him and tilted my head to the side, allowing me to run my tongue up his length without teeth getting in the way and once I reached his head once again, I dropped my mouth, sucking him back deep. My hand grasped him low on his shaft and I added quick, short pumping movements at the base of him.

I pulled back, sucking with all I was worth, ever so slowly, my fist slowing but lengthening its pumping. I felt more than saw as Rory adjusted his ass on the couch.

This time, when I bobbed on the upper half of his length, my palm working the lower half, his hips tightened and he began thrusting up into my mouth, further working my actions against him.

Rory's hands dropped beside him on the couch and from the corner of my eye, I saw as he lifted his hand, moving it toward my head, before dropping it back beside him.

His fingers clenched into the leather cushion of the couch, all while I worked him over, loving the sounds this man was making above me.

He let out a long groan before moving his hands toward my head again, only this time he threaded his hands into my hair. His long fingers cradled the back of my head and I could feel my ponytail loosening.

His hands tightened before he pulled back on my head, surprising me. I honestly would have figured he'd be the guy to hold a girl's head down as he thrust relentlessly into the back of her throat, paying no attention to her gagging.

...and part of me was secretly upset that I didn't experience the unabashed side of Rory.

I allowed him to pull me back but of course I had to make it hard for him by squeezing and sucking him, his cock finally leaving my mouth with a resounding *pop*.

"God, no more," he groaned. "I'm about to fucking come. God*damn*,

Emily." He let go of my head and I could feel how loose my ponytail had gotten. I reached up to just pull the damn thing out.

As he stood, he pulled me up to stand as well and moved me aside so he could quickly shuck his pants and briefs. I quickly lost my own jeans and panties, excited for this to continue.

He reached for me again as he sat, pulling me to him, guiding me to straddle him. His hands palmed my ass.

"You have a tattoo," he said as his hands kneaded me.

Not what I was expecting him to say. I frowned and looked over my shoulder; how had he seen it anyway?

"The other morning," he answered, as if I spoke the question out loud.

"Oh." Still, I frowned. What was with the question? He was hard and throbbing between our bodies; I was wet and hot, waiting to sink onto him. Why was he holding back?

"What's it mean?"

"That I was twenty and drunk and wanted something small." I shook my head. "What's with the questions?"

"Just curious," he answered, reaching for my hair and pulling it over my shoulder. Then he winked. "Needed to recharge a second." There was that Rory I knew and…well, I knew.

With my hair over my shoulder, the length brushed over my erect nipples. The slight feathery feeling had me moaning, but that was quickly changed to a lustful groan as Rory angled my hips so his cock rubbed deliciously against my folds.

Apparently the feeling was nearly too much for him as well. He groaned and squeezed his eyes shut against the feeling.

With a crooked smile on my face, I rubbed over him again. I bit my lip, absolutely loving the feeling of his thick girth between my pussy lips. I couldn't wait to feel him inside me.

I continued to roll my hips against him, my grin fading as my breath quickened and my brows drew in. The ridges of Rory's cock running over my pussy, my clit being rubbed deliciously by his velvety shaft, was almost too much. I let go of my lip as I closed my eyes, my hands finding purchase on his shoulders and I let my head drop back.

His hands were on my hips, his fingers flexing against me, and I nearly jumped from my skin when I felt his lips against the column of my throat once again. Between my grinding against him and the pull of his lips and teeth against my neck, I was ready to come again.

Rory's hips were flexing up under me, thrusting his cock against my folds. He wasn't even in me and this was the best damn sex I had in my sexual history. No wonder he had a reputation.

No wonder girls would do just about anything to be with him and didn't seem to care when he dropped them like yesterday's bad news.

Suddenly, Rory's hands tightened against my sides, his fingers biting painfully into my hips. I lifted my head to search his face.

"Stop. Stop, we gotta stop. I'm gonna fucking come." His voice was thick and the veins in his neck popped as tension wracked his body. "Need to be in you. Fuck, Emily, I need to be inside you."

He loosened his hold on me and shifted me back slightly, just enough that I could feel the cool air filtering between our bodies. Rory reached over for his wallet, quickly flipping it open and pulling out a condom.

I watched as he expertly ripped it open, sheathing himself in a quick downward motion, and pulled me back to him. I lifted up as he angled his covered cock with one hand, his other hand at my lower back.

I put my hands back on his shoulders and sank down on his hardness slowly, my eyes closing at the feelings of complete bliss as my body stretched to accommodate him.

"Fuck. God, fuck!" Rory was saying, well before I fully took him in my body.

I still had a small ways to go but Rory took care of that by thrusting upward into me forcefully. "Fuck. God-fucking-damn, you feel so—"

And then he let out a long groan, his hips bucking under me twice before pushing into me once and holding still.

I could feel him throbbing inside me, but more than just excited throbbing. This was the full deal, pulsing and throbbing.

Were you..?

Did he..?

"Are you serious right now?" I asked, opening my eyes. I was sure disbelief was all over my face.

He fucking came.

For all his sexual prowess, all the women who courted him, he fucking *came* and we hadn't even truly started!

Rory's face was squeezed tight, the frown between his brows was definitely more than just from his relief, because when the rest of his features relaxed, the creases remained and he squeezed his eyes shut more. "This is so fucking embarrassing."

I wanted to cry.

My body was strung tight and need coursed through my body. I wanted to come around his cock; I wanted his thickness to be the instigator to my orgasm, because there was something about being filled to the brink when you came that really pushed an orgasm through the body.

My eyes never left Rory's closed face, needing for this to be a joke. Maybe he was one of those guys who could cut off their orgasm, splitting it into two or more.

Surely this wasn't over.

This was a one-time thing, and if this was the end of it...

Rory's eyes finally opened, the green orbs looking straight into my own eyes. His pupils were dilated but the look in them was weary. "I am so sorry."

Chapter Seven

Rory

I finally get into her tight body, and I fucking come.

Even my first time *ever*, I had more fucking finesse and control over my orgasm. How in the hell did I just...lose my load the moment her pussy started to take me in?

I mean, I held back. The first two inches of her sinking on me.

But it was all gone from there.

It was so fucking embarrassing.

"It's ok," Emily said, her face starting to shut down. She lifted off of me, my slackening cock sliding from her wet, warm sheath. She stood and I watched as the cold front that was Emily Winters fell back into place.

This had been well on its way to my best lay and I had to go and be a prepubescent teenager with his first pussy.

"God, this is embarrassing," I said again, letting my head fall back onto the couch while I pressed my fingers into my eyes. I could hear as Emily sifted through clothes on the floor and decided to man up and open my eyes, only to see her bent forward, her long hair shielding nearly every part of her body as she worked on getting her panties back on.

With a sigh, I took off the condom and stood to discard it, thinking twice before putting it in Conor's waste basket.

But because I was already on his shit list, I moved to the small powder room attached to the office and disposed of it in there.

When I got back into the office, Emily was already in her jeans and had her arms behind her back as she was putting her bra back on. Completely nude still, I moved behind her to try and help her, but she stepped away from me.

Still, she said nothing.

With a heavy sigh and no idea what to say besides 'I'm sorry' or 'I'm embarrassed' yet again, I moved to my own clothes and started to pull them on. Emily had just reached for her shirt when I broke the silence. "You want to do dinner, maybe later tonight?"

I had to do something to make up for this. Shit, I had to try and find a way back in her pants so I could get a do-over.

"No, Rory." She shook her head and pulled her shirt back on. When she pulled her long hair from the collar, letting it fall down her back, I nearly groaned aloud. Damn, I loved her hair.

No sooner than I thought it though, she was pulling it back and up high in a knot that sat at the top of her head. Now I couldn't even watch the locks swaying as she walked away.

I quickly finished dressing and ran a hand through my own hair.

"It's just dinner, Em."

"Yeah, and I said this," she waved a finger in a circle in the space between us, "was a one-time deal." Yep, Ice Cold Emily was back.

Shit, I definitely preferred her hot and bothered over this ice queen persona she did so incredibly well.

I sat on the couch to slip my shoes back on, my finger nearly getting stuck behind my heel as I stepped down in a hurry. Emily was heading toward the door. I hopped up and bounded across the room to reach her before she could pull the door open.

"Dinner," I said again, my lips brushing against the back of her head.

She didn't bother turning toward me. Still facing the door, she shook her head, her hair brushing my lips as she did so. "No, Rory."

I refrained from dropping my forehead to the back of her head, instead stepping back and allowing her to open the door.

This wasn't over.

Oh no.

It was far from over.

I was just going to let her think she won.

Because Rory O'Gallagher didn't lose.

Chapter Eight

Emily

That entire next week, every day I worked at O'Gallaghers Rory was there.

No, not working. We rarely worked together.

Oh no. He was there, seeking me out.

Couldn't the guy just take a hint and go? I told him that sex between us was a one-time deal and while yeah, sure, we didn't actually get to *complete* the deed—at least, I didn't—what was done was done. I gave in to my moment of weakness where he was concerned and I was finished.

Maybe it had been gratitude for him giving me a bed to sleep in the night before, or maybe it was just me being stupid and wanting to see Rory's charm turned to me, but I gave in and did dirty things with the one person I said I'd never let near me.

And now he wouldn't leave me alone!

Oh, he wasn't annoying or obnoxious about it, not really.

But he was *there*. Throwing those sly, cocky smiles my way. Leaning in toward me while I was at the bar giving one of the bartenders an order.

And damn, the man smelled wonderful.

He started to keep the stubble look, which only allowed my mind to wander to those dirty thoughts of what it would feel like on the more sensitive areas on my body. He started to pull his hair back into a stubby pony tail and I had to say, the long hair, man-bun look never did anything for me but good God, Rory was fucking gorgeous and pulled it off so damn well.

I clenched my jaw against the thoughts, trying to redirect my mind elsewhere.

You know, to things that were important.

Like my next test. Or, more presently, the order Stone just slid my way to deliver.

I grabbed the two glasses and lone bottle, putting them on my tray, all while avoiding Rory's gaze on me. I deliberately turned in the direction away from him in order to deliver the drinks, praying for another table to flag me down. Something for a little more time away from Rory.

My prayers were answered when I heard my name over the music.

"Emily."

I glanced toward the sound and saw that Conor had just walked into the pub from the front door. He was heading toward the back but looked over at me and waved me back. "Let's talk."

Assuming it had something to do with the truck I was borrowing, I delivered the drinks and hurried back to the front. Placing my tray in its home spot, I still managed to avoided Rory.

"Talking to Con, Stone," I told him as he poured another lager.

"Got it." Stone flashed his eyes toward me momentarily while completing his task, letting me know it was me he was talking to.

I could feel Rory's eyes on me as I walked through the swinging kitchen door, until the door swung shut behind me. With a relieved sigh, I walked down the kitchen and around the corner to the office.

Conor was just sitting down, closing a desk drawer he must have dropped his bike key into.

"How's everything going with school?" he asked as I stepped into the room. When I moved to sit on the couch, I fought a blush as the memories of the last time I was in this office flooded my mind.

"Good. I passed my test last week by a few points, but I think I'll be good. Did you need the truck back?"

Conor stretched back in his chair, slouching some and crossing his arms over his chest. "You can keep it for a bit longer. Mia and I were talking and she came up with an alternative. You can absolutely say no, but I want to start out by telling you this isn't a gift. I know you have pride and we don't want to step on toes."

I sat up straight, a frown deepening on my face. "Ok?"

"Mia and I want to help get you into a car of your own. I know you said you couldn't do the payments right now, and I completely respect that. You're only a semester out and while I don't want to think about the fact I'm close to losing one of my better barmaids," he said this last part with a grin, "I know that your plan is to do nursing. If you're afraid of your credit, I can co-sign on the loan. Either way, Mia and I can help cover payments until you're on your feet and you can pay us back."

I nibbled on my lower lip. This was a phenomenal deal and I'd be silly to pass it up but...

"I don't like the idea of owing you." I shifted in my seat only to sit up taller. "It is incredibly generous of you guys though. Thank you."

"Just take the damn car."

My head flew in the direction of the door. I didn't see it open, but standing there, leaning against the jamb in the way Rory tended to do, was the man himself. How long had he been standing there? How much did he hear? Certainly enough for him to tell me to take what Conor and Mia were offering.

I felt my face flush. This time, it had nothing to do with the two of us in this very room but with mortification. I mean, I knew that Rory knew about my troubles. He was partially my boss, after all. But dealing with Conor was so much easier than Rory, the guy whose achievements made my once upon a time plans look like rubbish simply because I failed and he soared. Pretending that all we had between us was cold distaste, but oddly hot chemistry, was much easier to deal with than the knowledge that this cocky, self-entitled, wealthy guy was well aware of my financial failings.

I shifted again but before I could get a word in edgewise, Rory pushed himself from the frame and entered the room, respectably closing the door behind him.

"It's just a car, Emily. You can't keep walking at one in the fucking morning."

"Conor's changing my schedule," I said as Conor looked at his brother, brow raised over his right eye, and said, "Her schedule is changing."

"That was awesome. Do it again," Rory replied, but with a deadpan expression on his face. "It's like you two practiced that." He walked to the edge of the desk and propped his tight ass on the corner, arms crossed over his chest. While Conor took the slouched, comfortable, *welcoming* position at his chair, Rory in front of him like he was, was like putting up an invisible wall between Conor and I. Rory demanded my attention and again, I hated myself for wanting to give it to him.

"You want to finish the semester without failing, you need to be better about your time," Rory was saying. I had never seen him take such an authoritative stance when it came to the pub and their employees.

Would it further make me a heel if I said it turned me on a little bit? You know, just a tiny bit.

"You spend, what? Twenty minutes walking here? Another twenty home? If you drove, you'd be cutting off damn near seventy-five percent of that time. That gives you another thirty minutes of study time. So long as you're not cramming it all in one session, that's another great chunk of time to get your brain to focus and to retain everything you're teaching it. I'm willing to bet your scores will improve, from that extra thirty minutes alone."

I glanced over at Conor to see what he was making of all this, but his eyes were on the back of his brother's head and he wore a smirk on his face. Apparently he was amused.

Well, I wasn't.

"I'm doing fine right now. With my hours changing, I have more time in the evening to attend study groups with my peers. My scores on projects have already improved, and it's only been four days."

"You're being obstinate."

That sexual tension I was feeling by his authoritative self?

Yeah.

It was gone.

I couldn't sit up any straighter than I already was, but I refused to get to my feet and close the distance between us. Instead, I screwed up my face in my best bitch face and let it all out, "And you're being an ass. You think you know everything and honestly, you don't. What the hell do you know about studying, Rory? You probably slept with half your teachers in college!"

Conor smothered a chuckle behind his hand.

Rory just gave a menacing smirk. "Yep. It was pretty damn hot, too. Some of the best sex I had until recently." I'm sure it was only because Conor wouldn't catch the movement, but Rory shifted his eyes to the couch beside me before winking at me. "It was pretty much the most exciting sex I'd had, the fear of being caught, you know? But lately...sex has been pretty exciting."

I fought a smirk. Yeah, so exciting he couldn't hold himself back.

"Just take the damn car," he repeated.

"Why do you care?" I could feel my anger deflating. Really, it was exhausting fighting with him. That and I had already been leaning toward accepting Conor's offer.

Rory just stared at me. Not a single emotion crossed his features. His body was still strung tight as he leaned on the desk with his arms crossed. But he stared, and he stared.

"Just take the car," he finally said, pushing himself off the desk. "I'm out. Stone's got the bar." Without waiting for a response from Conor, he left the room, closing the door behind him quietly.

I puffed out my cheeks, waiting for the tension to leave the air. Surely Conor would take that outburst from his brother as more than boss-to-employee concern.

And sure enough—

"You want to tell me what that was about?" But rather than sounding pissed, Conor was...

Amused?

I wiped my palms on my shorts and shook my head. "Nothing. Rory has just decided to turn his non-existent game on to me."

Looking even more amused—if that were possible—Conor grinned crookedly. "Do you want me to do something about it? We don't have a fraternization policy, but if he's bothering you, I can do something."

I sighed. I could end all of this right now. Conor would make sure Rory would leave me alone. I wouldn't have to deal with his advances.

But just at that moment, I could smell his cologne in the air and my pussy clenched involuntarily. Damn body. I mean, what was the deal? I spent a *year* disliking him and one day, I decide to give in to his charms, he doesn't even *finish the deed*, and still I wanted him?

I sighed again and shook my head. "No. It's fine. I can handle him."

The look didn't leave Conor's face though. Instead, his grin deepened and he nodded upward once. "Ok." He sat up and uncrossed his arms, leaning into the desk. "But the car. Mia will kill me if I tell her I couldn't talk you into it. Have you seen my woman lately with her hormonal outbursts?"

This time I grinned. Mia was a hoot.

She was sweet and quiet, and honestly, pregnancy did her good. She glowed in the way I often just thought was hooey nonsense. But her temper...

Who'd have thought the Irish one in that relationship would have the calmer disposition?

"Are you afraid of Mia?" I asked, my grin filling.

Conor smirked. "You don't live with her."

Changing the subject off of me, I asked, "Are you guys ready for a second baby? I'm guessing that Aiden doesn't understand."

He was probably too young and, while I was an only child, I could only imagine that the deeper the age gap between babies, the more likely resentment would occur. But at nine and a half months, I was sure Aiden didn't know any different.

"Nah, he's too young," Conor confirmed. "I think it might change after Ava's born though." And unfortunately, Conor wasn't letting me off the hook that easily. "You've only got what, five months until graduation? Take the car, Emily. It'll make Mia feel better."

"Just Mia?"

Conor shook his head, chuckling. "Probably Rory too."

I couldn't stop the growl that resonated in my chest, which only had Conor barking out a laugh. "You two are fucking great to watch." Conor stood and pulled on his jeans. "Good luck, Em."

I took my cue to stand as well and shrugged a shoulder. "There's nothing to watch."

"Sure, keep telling yourself that." Conor walked me to the door, the shit-eating grin on his face still in place. "You're not on the schedule tomorrow. How about you take the truck, pick up Mia, and go find yourself a car. Mia can take the truck home after."

Fully realizing this was a battle I wasn't going to win, I nodded. "Ok. I will. Thank you, Conor." As much as I hated it, I wasn't ungrateful.

We walked back to the bar where I resumed my shift, and Conor sat at the bar, talking with Stone. The rest of my shift flowed easily, probably because everything was starting to fall into place. That and I wouldn't feel terrible if I had their truck and Mia went into labor.

And then there was Rory.

And for the first time since meeting him, his name brought an unwanted smile to my lips.

I'd have to think about that.

Chapter Nine

Rory

I may have talked Mia into having something to do when she and Emily were supposed to go car shopping.

Just may have.

I mean, I wasn't the pushy type, so if I admitted to myself that I was finding ways to be in Emily's presence, I would have to double check the status of my man card. The only action my cock had gotten in the last week, since she and I got together—yes, I was choosing to forget the issue I had that day—was from my hand in the shower.

Yesterday in Conor's office, seeing Emily's sass and fire directed at me wasn't anything new, no, but there was a little more passion in her voice. She was weakening toward me and I was going to take full advantage of that.

Starting by hijacking her car shopping trip with Mia.

After checking my email and corresponding with my clients and team members alike, I checked my online back-office for new orders of protein powders and muscle building e-books. I loved the pub, don't get me wrong, but this little side business I had was what truly paid the bills, and had been since I joined the company six years ago.

And I only really paid attention to it once, maybe twice a week.

I went from making a pretty penny with fake IDs and doing the occasional DJ-ing at house parties in college, to making a much shinier one by selling my muscle building knowledge. This day and age, all you needed was a good looking body and an Instagram account, and you could pull anyone in who wanted to look better.

After I printed my latest order sheet, I shut down the computer and headed down to the pub. Mia had planned on Emily meeting her here, so it made the whole, "Mwah-ha-ha, I'm coming with you" ordeal easier to accomplish.

It was early yet, so while the doors were open for business, we only had one customer sitting at the bar. His eyes were glued to one of the televisions, which was only airing the local news. I looked around, unsure of who was working today.

Jordan, a new kid we hired a few weeks ago, took that moment to pop up from whatever he was doing under the bar. Probably dropped something.

The kid was clumsy as fuck, which was the exact reason we were keeping him on the opening rotation for a bit. He was great with the customers and could mix a mean drink—he just had to work on his hands and keeping glasses *in* them.

"Hey, Jordan. How's it going?" I asked as I rounded the back of the bar, grabbing a bottle of water from the cooler.

"Good." The kid was a bit scrawny but in a hipster kind of way, which actually worked well with the early afternoon crowd. He was working on cutting limes when the front door opened. Expecting it to be Emily, I turned in my stool to see.

Nope.

Brenna and Stone.

Brenna and Stone?

I stepped off my stool and rounded the bar again, water in hand, to look at the schedule. Stone wasn't due to be in until three, but Brenna was Jordan's second man. I was going to shout hello to them but when I turned back toward the open bar area, they were nowhere to be found.

I scanned the bar, my water to my lips, and eventually saw the two of them in a corner near the dart boards, having a quiet, but seemingly heated, discussion.

Stone was a good guy. So whatever the issue, it wasn't him. Brenna probably lost her temper and was pissed to run into him. If Emily and I had our glaring moments, Brenna and Stone were just the opposite. They both flirted ruthlessly with one another, but then again they both flirted with just about anybody. They were the example of harmless flirting.

I narrowed my eyes.

But what if it wasn't harmless flirting?

Fuck, if Stone was…

Nope.

Wouldn't happen.

I shook my head and chuckled to myself. Stone may not be as obvious in his ways when it came to sex, but the man went out almost nightly. He always had plans with a female. I was pretty sure he was seriously seeing someone, but Stone was quiet about his personal life.

Had been since the moment we hired him.

"Yo, Bren," I shouted over the bar, finally earning their attention.

"What, Rory?" she called out, a bit of bite to her voice, as she crossed her arms and shoved around Stone, walking toward me.

I chuckled, watching as my sister essentially stomped toward the bar. "Leave the poor guy alone. What the hell did he do to you?"

She mumbled something under her breath but before I could have her repeat what she said, Emily came into the pub.

And her hair was down.

And straight.

Fuck me.

Why the hell did Mia get this version of her? What did Mia do to deserve Emily's fucking gorgeous hair down and swaying toward her ass?

Before I could walk toward her though, Stone, the stealthy fucker, managed to end up behind me and slapped my shoulder. "What are you doing here so early on a Saturday?"

I held up a finger and with what had to be a shit-eating grin, I looked toward Emily—who was almost to Stone and me—and lifted my chin as I spoke with her. "You ready to go get a car?"

She stopped, dead in her tracks, and her brows lowered in that way I was sure was reserved for me and me alone. "Where's Mia?"

"Last minute doctor's appointment?" I said but thought better of blowing it off with a shrug. I mean, it didn't matter if she figured out I set today up, but I had to at least get her to go with me before she did.

Because let's be honest, she figures it out and she's walking.

"Yep." I nodded. "Baby Ava's getting ready to join the masses."

Emily's frown deepened. "Why didn't she just call to reschedule? She or Con needs to be there to co-sign if I find a car."

Fuck. She was going to figure this out.

I had to get her in my truck before she did. She was so fucking smart. Nothing got past Emily. I should have been better prepared for this.

"Mia said she or Con would be able to stop by the dealership when you were ready," I said on the spot. I reached out and put my hand on her lower back, guiding her back toward the doors. Behind me, Stone coughed, but I'm pretty sure the asshole was covering a laugh.

Emily stumbled as she walked in the direction I was guiding her. I bit back a groan when she turned her head toward me, which made her hair brushed my forearm. "But—"

"Nope, she wanted to be sure you found a car today. Earlier the better, too, because you know, salesmen get pushy toward the end of the day when they've not met goal. So we need to get you out there early and if we find you something, Mia and Con can meet us and help with the paperwork."

Emily was still frowning but she pushed through the front door willingly. "...Ok."

I was kind of surprised she wasn't putting up more of a fight but I was good with this scenario. If she refrained from being pissy with me, maybe I could talk her into dinner later tonight.

She had said no every day this week, but surely one of these days she'd succumb to me, right?

Outside, my Emily returned and she stepped away from my hand. Hey, no big, so long as she wasn't throwing daggers at me. I mean, yeah, I'd rather be touching her, but as long as she was going along with every other part of my plan, I could refrain from touching her for a little longer.

We passed Con's truck and I have to say, I was impressed to see she parallel parked that beast. It was an F-350 with a SuperCrew cab, so yeah, her parallel parking it? It was impressive.

So much so that maybe my dick was a bit impressed too.

But having a hard-on right now wouldn't do me any good, so I ignored it as I followed Em to my truck, parked a few spots down from where she parked Conor's truck.

Now, my truck wasn't nearly as big and impressive as Conor's but it was still a big truck. I only had a SuperCab, but I didn't have carseats and shit to pile in the cab so the half door to the backseats was more than enough for me.

I reached around her to pull the door open, which earned me one of Emily's signature glares. At this point in the game, I was thinking it was exactly that—a game. I was beginning to think she simply *preferred* to be cold and indifferent toward me, so she put on the farce in hopes to steer me away.

I wasn't going away.

Emily stepped up into my truck and when her ass hit leather, I closed the door on her, rounding the front to get in on the driver's side.

When I turned the ignition, I looked in her direction to see her staring straight ahead, her hands clasped in her lap, all while nibbling on the corner of her lip.

The movement plumped and pushed her lower lip, and I had to look away.

Goddamn, I didn't think the girl knew what she actually did to me.

"You have a make in mind?" I asked instead as I pulled away from the curb.

I glanced over at her while I repositioned my body, wrist on the steering wheel and leaning with my arm on top of the center console.

Her eyes glanced at my wrist before meeting mine. I fought against the desire to keep looking at her and turned my attention back to the road. It wasn't a busy road and it was pretty straight, but it wouldn't do me any good to injure her in an accident.

"No," she finally answered. "I figured just one of the larger dealerships would be fine. Just a car with good mileage."

"There's nothing you haven't seen and thought, 'Hmm, that's cute'." The last was said in a high falsetto and hearing her answering laugh made me grin wide.

"I guess maybe the new Fusions."

I grabbed my chest with the hand not steering the wheel. "A Ford girl. Be still my heart."

Again, Emily laughed and I had to shift in my seat. My jeans were growing uncomfortably tight.

Emily directing a laugh at me was something I didn't realize I was missing in life.

"It has nothing to do with Ford, and everything to do with the body style."

I had a joke on the tip of my tongue about body style but decided to keep it to myself, instead saying, "Alright. Well, to Mikkelson Ford we go."

Chapter Ten

Emily

By mid-afternoon, I found myself in a white Ford Fusion with all the works. I didn't *want* all the works, would have been fine with cloth seats and a regular CD-radio unit, but Rory worked his male magic and I was the proud owner—*co-owner*—of a car with leather seats, satellite radio, and a rear camera.

At employee family pricing.

I felt pretty guilty about the last point, but Rory assured me that they were ripping me off by the tag price anyway.

Conor came out and helped with the paperwork, as Rory said he or Mia would, and when the three of us left, Rory pulled me aside and helped me into my car.

This wasn't the cocky Rory I knew. Self-assured Rory, yes, but not cocky. All day, whenever I tried to put the wall between us, he would go and do something or say something that made me smile and question what I thought about him.

Maybe he was changing.

I don't think he'd ever fought so hard for someone's attention before and it wasn't as if I were playing the cat-and-mouse game. But seeing him vie for something that wasn't coming to him as easily as everything else in his life did, was certainly shaping him into a different person.

"Dinner?" he asked me again, this time while I sat in my brand new car. He had his forearms on the top of the car and was leaning in toward me. I kept my eyes on his, searching for answers. I needed to know if this was a game.

If I was just a conquest to him.

I wasn't built like the girls he slept with. I thought I'd done really damn well over the last week, putting up the cinder block wall between the two of us, but I could feel it crumbling down.

I didn't want to be like the other girls.

When Rory was nice and kind, he was *really* nice and kind. I found myself liking him more and more when he left his cocky attitude at the door.

Still looking him in the eye, I sucked in my top lip and bit on it, concentrating. I watched as his pupils dilated and his nostrils flared, but still he said nothing.

"Ok."

It was barely spoken, hardly heard over the pounding of my heart, but Rory heard it loud and clear. His smile was movie-star worthy, showing that the man had a surprising dimple under his right eye, one that sat along his cheekbone. It added to the boyish quality he had.

"Awesome. Do you think you could be ready by seven?"

I nodded. "Sure. Is there going to be a dress code?"

"Just wear something nice. Not formal, just nice."

Because it was still warm in the evening, I chose a sleeveless sundress in white and turquoise. I did find a cardigan to pair with it if it started to get chilly. I debated on heels before finding a pair of slightly heeled sandals that wouldn't put my height over Rory's.

I had a thing against being taller than guys I was going out with.

Being tall my whole life, it was one of those things that I could either let bother me, or just go with. I let it bother me.

There was a knock on my apartment door just as I was applying lip gloss. I twisted the wand back in and headed toward the living area, grabbing my purse on the way. I pulled open the door and couldn't stop the smile from spreading when I saw Rory.

The man wore designer jeans to the bar, so it wasn't that he'd dressed up for me; he was wearing an outfit I'd seen him in before, even. It was that he paired it with a sport jacket and held a bouquet of daisies in his hand.

"You look great," he said, his eyes dropping and taking me in. "These are for you," he added, thrusting the flowers in my direction. It was slightly comical, the way he did it. I wasn't so sure that he was a flowers-to-girls guy generally.

"Thank you," I said, taking the bouquet from him. "Let me put these in a vase. You're welcome to come in." I moved to the kitchen, finding a vase above the fridge, and situated the white and baby pink blooms. I loved their simplicity.

Rory stood in the middle of my living room, his hands in his pockets which allowed his sport jacket to part in a way that had him looking all GQ-esque.

Not that he didn't any other day.

He still sported the stubble look and I was beginning to think it was just a new look for him, that he was going to keep it. It certainly didn't hurt his image. His hair was pulled back in the stubby ponytail again, but like I said, it didn't hurt his image.

"Ready?" I asked, stopping a little ways away from him. If I took a deep enough breath I could smell him from where I was. Any closer and I couldn't be held responsible for my actions.

"That's my line." His grin was crooked and he held a hand out to me, urging me closer to him. Without extra preamble, I took his hand in mine and allowed him to pull me close. I closed my eyes when I stood in front of him, allowing the moment to seep through my veins. When Rory pressed his lips to my temple, my lips lifted in a closed-lipped smile and I opened my eyes again, turning my head this time to look at him.

We were incredibly close. I could count the blue flecks in his left eye; there were five that made up the orb I previously thought was simply one blue piece in the sea of green. His eyes held mine captive and when the corners of his eyes crinkled, I could tell his grin was genuine.

"Let's eat."

Rory brought me to a nicer American Steakhouse near the coastline. We were seated on the patio, making me glad I grabbed my sweater. The breeze was gentle and the night was beginning to cool, but the atmosphere of the place was truly euphoric. They strung circle wicker lights throughout the patio and had patio heaters throughout.

After looking through the menu, I looked across the table and over the glass hurricane, toward Rory.

"You really do look beautiful tonight," he said, leaning onto his forearms. He linked his fingers together in front of him.

"Thank you."

"Thank *you* for finally agreeing to dinner." He chuckled lightly. "I'm enjoying spending time with you, Em."

Quietly, I admitted, "Me, too."

A week or two was awfully quick to change his ways, but maybe having a larger responsibility with O'Gallaghers did Rory some good. This entire week while pursing me, I hadn't noticed him checking out other women. I didn't see him persuading others to do things at his bidding.

I was about to tell him that I noticed the change in him when our waiter came.

"Thank you for joining us tonight. My name is Rick and I will be your server tonight. Have we decided on our entrees this evening?" he asked.

I nodded, as did Rory, who gestured toward me. "You go ahead."

Picking up the menu again to be sure, I found my item, reading it off for Rick. "I'll do the...ten ounce prime rib, please."

Rory's brows rose and I fought a giggle. I liked a good piece of red meat. I wasn't about to order a salad at a place like this.

After handing my menu to Rick, he turned his attention to Rory. "And for you, sir?"

Unlike me, Rory didn't need to open his menu. "I'll take your Maine Lobster Pot Pie."

I nearly bugged my eyes out of my head. I had seen that item on the menu; it was the one with the highest price tag.

And there Rory went, flaunting his money.

"Very well, sir. Any appetizers for the two of you?"

I shook my head but Rory answered, "An order of your caprese, please."

"All right." Rick took Rory's menu and folded them together in his hands. "We will have that appetizer out to you shortly."

"You've been here before, haven't you?" I asked, amused.

He nodded. "I have. When they opened, they brought some promotions to the pub and I checked it out."

"It's a very cute establishment," I said, glancing around the patio again.

The sun was a mere spot of orange over the water-filled horizon, and the beginning of a star-filled sky was starting to blanket above us. I watched as a plane's red lights flickered, flying in toward the mainland.

"The food is fantastic, too. I think you'll enjoy it."

His voice brought my eyes back to him. He held a hand out on top of the table and I allowed myself to place my hand in his. I couldn't stop the girly grin from starting as he lifted our hands to his lips, kissing my knuckles.

I had to remind myself that this was Rory's game.

But was it?

Was I different?

Or was I being a fool for allowing myself to be so drawn to Rory and his seductive ways?

I know I told myself one time with him, but I would not be opposed to bending that rule tonight. He was being incredibly kind and sweet, and it brought his sexy factor up to an eleven out of ten.

He lowered our hands back to the table, rubbing his thumb slowly over my knuckles now.

"Thank you again for finally agreeing to come out with me. I know we haven't had the best history, haven't started out on the right foot, but thank you for giving me this chance."

I internally battled with the need to tell him why I had kept my distance, but decided now wasn't the time or place. I wasn't sure that there ever would be a time or place, to be honest—unless he were to come out and simply ask.

Until then, I'd probably just keep my reasons to myself.

We were in the middle of discussing my school work and plans once the semester ended when Rick returned to the table. I let my fingers slip from Rory's as I returned both of my hands to my lap, allowing Rick to place the caprese between us.

"Here is your caprese. I also wanted to extend an apology," he was saying as he straightened. His attention was focused on Rory. "I was just informed we have run out of truffle. We can still make your meal, it would just be without that ingredient."

And that was when the Rory I had come to know, the one I'd heard about and hated, came out to play.

Chapter Eleven

Rory

God, she looked beautiful tonight.

Emily left her hair down. She curled it, sure, but it was down and I wanted nothing more than to run my fingers through the long locks.

The turquoise of her dress looked great against her skin, and it dipped just enough to show what minimal cleavage she had.

But it was still fucking beautiful.

She was fucking beautiful.

I didn't know how I got lucky enough for her to finally say yes, but I was certainly grateful.

There was also promise in her blue eyes that tonight might end my week-long celibacy streak. I couldn't wait to show her what I was truly capable of, to show her that last weekend was a fluke, a direct response to a year's worth of want and excitement.

Not that that made it sound any better.

Premature was premature, and was meant to be kept in the early teenaged years.

When Rick returned with our appetizer and Emily slipped her hand from mine, my body—my fucking *soul*—felt her leaving me.

"I also wanted to extend an apology," Rick was saying. I turned my attention from Emily to him. "I was just informed we have run out of truffle. We can still make your meal, it would just be without that ingredient."

I frowned, sitting up higher in my seat. "How do you run out of a key ingredient in your featured menu item?"

"I do apologize, sir."

"You'll be comping me for that cost then, I assume?" I didn't notice as Emily slouched further in her seat.

"I can certainly speak with the manager."

"How about you do that." The dry sarcasm in my voice was plenty evident, as was my displeasure in the situation.

How the hell did a restaurant run out of something that was a staple for their menu? Did they not have competent people running their ordering? You *always* planned for sales, and being short top ingredients was not the way to keep patrons walking in the doors.

Rick left and I shook my head. "Imbeciles," I muttered to myself in response to my last thought. I reached for my water glass, taking a sip before shaking my head again, grinning toward Emily. "Who runs out of ingredients?"

She sat up but her smile was nowhere to be found. She simply shrugged a shoulder, a frown on her face, as she looked down at the napkin in lap. "It was an honest mistake, Rory. Maybe they didn't plan for a high ordering of one of their more expensive dishes."

"But you always plan. You always make sure you have enough and then some. Do we ever run out of items at O'Gallaghers? No," I answered for her. "We don't. And you know what? We stay in the black. They have these prices for a reason, Em. They can afford an extra few pounds of damned truffles."

"I don't know," she responded quietly, as if she had nothing else to say.

The caprese grew cold between us, as did the night. I wasn't sure exactly what was up with Emily. She went from happy and sexy, to her cold, withdrawn self. I reached for a piece of the appetizer to fill the gap of time. I tried to restart our earlier conversation about her schooling when she placed her napkin on the table.

"I'd like to go home now." Her voice was quiet and her body language was completely closed down.

I frowned. "We haven't even gotten our entrees yet."

"Rory, what you just did was embarrassing." Emily's voice was still quiet and she leaned into the table as if she were attempting to keep her voice from traveling. Her eyes were widened yet weary. "You could have been more effective by simply saying 'ok,' rather than make that man feel like a heel for something that wasn't even his fault."

"But—"

"No," she cut me off, holding a hand up. "I'd like to go home now."

I stared at her, fucking baffled. What in the ever loving hell just happened?

She stood, opening her purse while doing so, and dropped a couple twenties on the table.

"Jesus, Em, I'll cover the damn bill," I said, my irritation starting to come to surface. I stood, pulling my wallet from my back pocket, and replaced her bills with my own, holding hers out in front of me. She reluctantly took them and started for the restaurant, leaving me behind.

I shrugged into my sport jacket and followed, still confused as all get out as to what just happened. So she was embarrassed? Didn't mean she couldn't enjoy her dinner. We could laugh about it later. Why did we have to go without enjoying ourselves a little more?

I reached her in the middle of the inside dining area, but when I moved to place a hand on her back—possessively, yes; fuckers were looking at her—she stepped away from me.

I could feel those same fuckers laughing behind my back.

She wanted to play this way? She wanted to go back to bitch mode? Well so fucking-be-it.

We waited in silence by valet as my truck was retrieved. Valet helped her into the cab, so I just walked around to get in myself. After being sure she was situated, by quick glance only, I threw the truck in drive and headed back to her place.

The entire drive was made in silence. It allowed me to stew on her words and her reactions.

She fucking *stepped away from me*, putting more distance between us when I had been pretty sure that wall was fucking eradicated.

She was unbuckled before I could even turn the truck off at her place, out her door before I could get my own belt to unlock. "Goddammit, Emily," I said, frustrated, as I moved after her.

"You don't have to walk me to my door." She was looking through her purse as she walked. She pulled out her keys as she reached the stairwell, jogging up them in a pretty impressive fashion, seeing as she was in heeled shoes.

"I'm walking you to your damn door," I muttered, only a few steps behind.

Emily unlocked her door in probably the quickest time I'd ever seen a key insert and twist, and she was sliding through the doorway. I pushed in after her before she could slam the door on my face.

"I don't want to talk to you right now." Her voice was still devoid of emotion, very much the Emily I had known for the last year.

"What the hell is your problem?" I let my irritation come through, but I didn't fucking care.

She whipped back toward me, her hair flying. "You are, Rory! *You*!"

"Me? What the fuck did I do?" My voice was raised as loud as hers.

"You're such a goddamned *child*, Rory. You don't behave like that in public. You are a grown man. Not only that, but you run a respected establishment. *Just like that restaurant*. How would you like it if someone acted the way you did?"

"We don't run out of shit." I stood in my spot, arms crossed over my chest.

"Oh, so O'Gallaghers is better than everyone else. Just like you fucking think you are."

I lifted my brows, but kept my arms crossed. "Oh-ho, tell me how you really feel, Emily."

She threw her purse down on the couch and came up to me, toe to toe, eye to eye. Her slight chest brushed my forearms and I watched as her mouth tightened in anger, her chest heaving with pent up anger and emotion.

Well guess what, Cupcake? You and me both.

"You are a cocky asshole who thinks he's better than everyone! You are the least genuine person I have ever had the misfortune of knowing. You are all about the bottom line and don't care how you get what you want. You're self-centered, materialistic, and *heaven forbid* you take on a client for your," she waved her hand in the air, "other business—*who actually needs your fucking help*. But no, because they don't fit in with your ideals and who you think is worthy of your time, you push them aside to figure things out on their own."

"At least people know what they're getting with me. I don't lead people on. The women all know what I'm about, and my clientele and team *thank me* for what I bring to the table, because I'm helping further their careers. You, on the other hand, are a fucking block of ice. Who the hell knows what they're gonna get with you? Sweet in the middle? I thought so, but apparently that was all a fucking façade too. Embarrassing is leaving a restaurant before they've even given you your meal."

She just shook her head minutely, not saying a word as her eyes stayed locked with mine.

Finally, she spoke up, her voice strong, but quieter than before. "You need to grow up and become an adult, Rory." She stepped away. "I'll be sure Conor knows to not put us on the schedule together, ever. I don't want to deal with you anymore."

She turned away and part of me wanted to follow her, to finish this fucking fight, but the other part was as done with her as she was with me.

Good fucking riddance.

Chapter Twelve

Rory

That night was fucking hell.

I tried scrolling through my phone for a quick hook-up, but every time my thumb hovered over the connect button, it was Emily's face I saw.

No, not the yelling one I recently encountered, but her shining blue eyes, her wide smile as she laughed, and her fucking gorgeous blonde hair.

I really hated conceding to people's opinions, but I spent the entire night—no joke, the entire fucking night—replaying her words.

Was I really that shallow?

Like I said, the women I slept with knew the score going in.

And I really didn't see anything wrong with choosing clients who were well on their way in their fitness journeys. It made sense. You give them a product, they have a quick turn-around time, they post the hell out of that shit on social media, and you had more orders.

But maybe I should look into taking on a client or two who actually, truly, needed the service. It would take longer to get to the end goal, but maybe that wasn't such a bad thing.

I went through every fucking email, deleted ones too, trying to find people I could add to my client base. It was three in the damn morning, but I still responded to their emails.

I ended up finding five additional people to add to my clientele. What was adding five more going to do for my time? Not a whole lot. It wasn't going to eat much more than my current base was.

At four, I emailed the owner of the Steakhouse, apologizing and offering a hefty tab at O'Gallaghers if he ever wanted to stop by.

I suppose part of this was easy because I wasn't doing it face to face, but there was one face to face I was going to have to do.

That I wanted to do.

Putting aside my laptop for the night, I closed my eyes and took a nap.

She was opening tomorrow. I'd find her then.

Chapter Thirteen

Emily

I arrived to O'Gallaghers early the next day, thankful to see Stone was opening with me. He didn't do many early shifts so I didn't get to work with him often, but he was a fun guy. He made everything light and easy.

Things I was definitely needing today.

I was under a bit of an emotional hangover today after letting out every single thing I'd been holding back with Rory. I should have known the good was going to fade, that he couldn't be as great as he was showing me over the week.

I entered O'Gallaghers through the back, not thinking about the fact I'd be passing Rory's staircase, but thankful just the same when I didn't see him. The kitchen was quiet but music was playing in the bar area. Stone was probably setting up his coolers 'just the right way.' It was funny to me how such a big guy could be so OCD about something as trivial as lemon and lime placement.

"Hey, Stone," I started, as I pushed through the doors, but my words were cut off by the man sitting at the bar, facing the doors as if he were waiting for me.

"Emily."

I clenched my jaw and lifted my chin. "Rory." I moved down the bar toward Stone, who was indeed working out his coolers. "What can I do to help?"

"If you want to get towels together, that would be great."

Ignoring Rory, I moved to the back to do as Stone asked, grabbing enough for the first hours before they were due to be changed out. As I was about to push through the door again, it opened back toward me and Rory stepped in.

I was expecting a pissed off look on his face; instead, there was a thoughtful one.

"I'd like to talk to you." Before I could answer, he added, "Stone is aware and is ok if you take a few minutes."

This was a really difficult place to be. On the one hand, I wanted so badly to tell him off again. I didn't want to—couldn't—deal with the emotional backlash again. But on the other, he was my boss and I did need this job for at least the next few months. There was only so much Conor could do; he wasn't the only one running O'Gallaghers.

I set the towels and bucket of sanitizer water down and headed toward the office, the only place we could shut the door and have privacy. I refused to think of other things we did in this very space.

"About last night." He took a deep, audible breath. "I did some thinking."

I crossed my arms. He could think all he damn wanted. He could keep thinking for all I cared.

"I want to change."

I stuck my tongue in between my teeth, biting down gently. I wasn't entirely sure how to respond so I didn't. I wasn't expecting him to say that.

"You helped me come to the realization that I have room to grow as a person. You and Con, really. He said something earlier in the week that rang along the same lines as what you said." Rory stuffed a hand in his jeans pocket and ran the other through his hair, holding it against the back of his head as he kept his focus on me.

"I really enjoyed the time we had together. When I wasn't being a dick, that is. I'd like to work on being a better person, a person who *you* believe in. I never had a hard time looking in the mirror until after you told me what you saw negatively in me. It really had me thinking."

I shook my head and sighed. "Rory, no. We can't…" I shook my head again. I felt myself completely thaw toward him. There wasn't anything worse in the world than feeling like you had to change for someone and I hated that I did that to him.

I was glad he wanted to make the changes, but I didn't want him to make them for me. We didn't have a future. The moments we had, short as they were, had some fun mixed in, but I was leaving in a few months. "It would probably just be better for everyone if we just ended this here and now. I'm done in four months. I don't know where I'll go after graduation, if I'll be staying in San Diego or if I decide to go elsewhere for school. Heck, it depends on where I get into the anesthesia program. You're my boss and it's just better, *healthier*, for everyone involved if we just kept it that way."

I wasn't sure what his reaction would be, but the thoughtful look on his face wasn't what I would have bet on.

"Ok."

I couldn't help it; I frowned. "Just like that?"

His smile wasn't coy, it wasn't cocky. It wasn't full and assured, either. It was actually kind of sad. "I'm going to prove to you that I can change. I'll give you your space but I'm not going to let this go."

I couldn't stop my grin this time. There he went again, all sure of himself.

"Rory, no." I uncrossed my arms and stuck my fingers in my back pockets. "Do you, Rory. When you're not being an ass, you have a certain energy about you. Don't change that for me. Don't change that for anyone. You have the ability to be a great guy, but I just don't think you and I could be healthy together. Too much negativity between us."

Rory stepped close to me but I held my ground. I wasn't sure what his next move would be.

I was honest with my words.

When Rory was being a good guy, he truly was an awesome man to get to know. If he stuck with that, he'd make *one* lucky woman very happy.

He'd have to figure out the monogamy thing, sure, but I thought he was on his way to being an adult.

"Whatever you want to think, Em. But I'm going to prove you wrong." With that, he put his hands on my shoulders and leaned in to kiss my forehead.

Before I could react, he was gone.

Epilogue
Eighteen Months Later

April

Emily

I graduated my nursing program with honors.

Surprising, yes.

But with the help of a changed schedule, and the ability to get places faster, I was able to put more energy into studying and passed my remaining tests with flying colors. One of the prerequisites for the nurse anesthesia program was a minimum of one year in a critical care setting, so I chose to apply to a number of ICUs in the Bay Area, eventually accepting a position in a pediatric ICU. It was extremely difficult to work with critically ill children, but it also was incredibly rewarding.

When it was time to apply to my next school, I was quickly accepted to a Nursing Anesthesia program in Arizona, thanks to my previous grades and letters of recommendation from peers. With my new income, I was able to get my auto loan out of Conor's name and fully into mine too. Conor joked that he was sad to be cutting yet another tie with me, but I assured both him and Mia that I would come back around. The O'Gallaghers had become a pseudo-extended family of sorts, and I enjoyed spending time with them.

Rory too.

Over my final months in San Diego, not once did he approach me about furthering this…*thing*…we had between us, and if he was continuing with his sexual endeavors the way he had before our little office party, he'd become incredibly secretive of it.

He'd been in the pub more often, doing more of the day-to-day tasks while Conor took over much of the bookkeeping. With two babies at home under the age of three, Conor and Mia had their hands full.

Rumor had it Rory was also doing more one-on-one coaching with his clientele.

I suppose it wasn't so much of a rumor, as I saw him spending time at the beach helping a heavier woman with exercises she could easily do without equipment or a gym.

I was proud of who he was becoming.

But that was now all in my past.

O'Gallaghers, and its people, was now a piece of my history and I was moving on to the next phase of my life. I'd been in Arizona for about twelve weeks and I found I loved my new surroundings.

Nursing anesthesia school was no joke, and the last few months proved it. Between work and studying, I had little time for a social life, but that was something I was used to.

I was coming home from my day of classes, folders and papers and syllabi in hand, completely prepared to get a head start on studying for my finals that were scheduled for next month. It would be just about another year until I received my clinical experience, but I wanted to be absolutely sure I knew the science behind everything I was going to learn.

I parked my car in the driveway of the house I was renting and was a little concerned that there was a car parked along the street that I didn't recognize.

But then again, I was new to town and didn't recognize many of the cars in the neighborhood yet.

After parking my car in the garage, I stepped out, shouldering my backpack, and was rounding the end of the car to head inside when a tall shadow fell into my garage.

With a startled yelp, I put my hand to my chest and turned, hoping to God it was just a friendly neighbor and not some psycho out to get the new neighbor.

I maybe watched a scary movie last night.

In my dark house.

With minimal furniture.

I don't know what I'd been thinking, either.

"You startled me," I said to the faceless stranger, only to gasp aloud when the person moved from the shadows, showing his face.

Rory

I spent a lot of time giving Emily her space.

And in that time—eighteen months, to be exact—my hand and arm got a little sore because that was the only action my cock was getting.

I was hell bent on proving to her that I could be a good guy, a guy she could believe in, and hell, a fucking grown up.

I certainly proved it to Conor, who gave me more responsibilities at the bar because he trusted I would run the bar as he would. And because of that, I felt like shit when I gave him the news.

I had one last person to prove myself to, and I hoped to fucking God she would be as understanding, as open, as Con had been.

Emily left O'Gallaghers a year ago. She stopped in on occasion, but she no longer worked for us. And then she moved.

She fucking moved, and I felt that shit.

I knew that I was hung up on her, knew it the week I begged her to dinner. But her moving did things to me.

Sure, it was only a few states and only a five hour drive, but I wanted her close.

Shit, that made me sound like the insensitive ass she accused me of being earlier last year.

I wanted her close and I was willing to make those changes to have it happen.

Better?

Thought so.

I moved out of the apartment above the pub and it actually stood vacant right now. Brenna stated her living arrangements worked for her and Con and I didn't exactly want a stranger living up there.

So I vacated the apartment.

I gave Con my news.

And I hopped on a plane.

Arizona was warm in the early spring, not much different than San Diego, but I didn't find myself sweating over the heat as I stood outside the house my GPS brought me to.

No, I was sweating over fucking nerves.

How would she react? What would she say? Should I maybe have called instead?

Probably.

Fuck.

She'd go and probably say how self-assured I was, when really this was the most fucking vulnerable I'd been in *years*.

When the little white Fusion came pulling into the garage, I walked around, wanting to see her. I didn't intend to scare the girl and when she gasped, I took a step back and held up my hands. "It's just me, Em."

She dropped her chin and frowned. "Rory?"

Her hair was pulled up on top of her head so I couldn't get my fill of that. Instead, I was able to appreciate just about every other facet of her. She wore white shorts and a flannel, and was sexy as hell in the ensemble.

Arizona looked good on her.

"Hey, Emily."

Hey, Emily?

You mean to tell me, after all the thinking on the plane and the drive over here, all I could come up with was *Hey, Emily?*

She dropped her backpack to the ground beside her and, still frowning, made her way toward me. "What are you doing here? Why aren't you back home?"

"I don't currently have a home." Hey, it was the truth. Go big or go... Well, you know.

If anything though, her frown deepened. I reached out and smoothed my thumb over the ridges. "That'll get stuck, Em."

She shook her head, which had me pulling my thumb away, but she didn't look pissed. No, she looked confused. "Why are you in Arizona? Why aren't you back in San Diego?"

I took a deep breath and launched in with the words I wanted to say. "I have tried really hard over the last year, year and half, to be the type of man you could count on. You don't need a man, hell, you'll probably tell me you don't have time for a man, but I want to be there for you. I want to show you I've changed. I want to hold your hand. I want to make you dinner on those nights you're scrambling to figure out how you're going to juggle food and work and studying and walking the dog."

"I don't have a dog."

I grinned and held up my finger. "We can take this at your pace, Em, but this is something I want to do. A journey I want to take. Please give me that opportunity."

She was quiet, staring at me. I had the gut sinking feeling she was going to say no.

Conor would take me back. Hell, he'd probably welcome me back with open arms. Brenna had taken some of my responsibilities, but I wasn't sure how that would pan out in the end. I also had a place to live above the bar.

But what was life without the person you had a feeling you were meant to spend it with?

When she still didn't answer, I took a deep breath, letting it out slowly. With a sad grin, I reached for her hand, needing some sort of contact with her one last time before I walked away. I squeezed once and stepped back.

"Ok. Alright."

I took another step back and when she still didn't move, I turned.

I was going to leave with my pride. I wasn't going to beg.

The desert looked a little drier, was a little warmer, and was definitely browner, as I made my way back to the rental car.

Emily

This was all so surreal.

Rory was here.

Rory was here, in Arizona, at the house I was renting.

And he was walking away.

He was walking away and was going to head back to San Diego.

Did I trust that he could have changed? Well, yes, actually. I witnessed the small changes. Did I think he could keep those small changes?

Would I hate myself if I didn't at least give it a shot?

Hell, I really didn't have time for a relationship! But who was to say he'd still be around in three years when I graduated? The fact that he apparently waited a year and half was damn impressive.

I heard a car start and I shook my head, forcing myself back to the here and now.

He was leaving, and it made me come to a realization.

I couldn't let him leave.

I bolted out of my garage and ran down the slight drive, jumping in front of what had been the mysterious car, all while praying he wouldn't gun it, leaving this place in his haste.

I stared at him through the windshield.

He stared back.

And when I smiled at him, he smiled back.

And he knew, just as I did, that I was giving him his chance.

We would figure it out. And if it didn't work, it didn't work.

But we could at least say we tried.

Because when his cocky side was gone, and my cold indifference melted, I really enjoyed being around him.

This wasn't going to be easy.

We had hardly been anything other than friends over the past year and half, and we were jumping into something more.

...but it was going to be worth the ride.

ALL NIGHT LONG

book 3

Prologue

For as long as I could remember, I've lived under the protective shadow of my older brothers. We were all fairly spread apart in age, at least in comparison to my friends who were one or two years, three years at most, apart from the other kids in their families.

But for my brothers and me? We had the four year gap.

Well, technically Rory and Conor were three years apart but their birthdates were on opposite ends of the year.

So pretty much four years.

That meant I never went to the same school as Conor, who is eight years older than me.

It also meant that there had only been two years in elementary school, no years in middle school, and one four-quarter period in in the space of life that was known as high school, that I had with Rory.

That did not stop the two of them from threatening every kid they ran across though.

People knew who I was.

If there were such a thing in our little beach town, I would have been considered royalty with the way my brothers watched over me.

By ten—ten!—I decided I needed to find a way to step away from the pampered role everyone saw me in, so I set out to do just that.

Away from my brothers' eyes, of course.

Which only made their unwavering faith in me feel like a dagger through the heart, with every omission of truth I told them.

Or the little parts of my life that I didn't tell them. The little parts that made the large sum of who I was.

The things that they considered rumors.

I pushed away good friends so I could fit in.

I'm ashamed to say I spread my legs to ruin that 'good girl' reputation my brothers molded for me.

By day, I was Sweet Brenna O'Gallagher, the girl who could do no wrong in her brothers' eyes.

But everyone else knew who I really was.

They knew the slutty girl, the one who wore low cut tops and too much eye makeup.

The girl who was known behind hands as the one who fucked a senior in his van her freshman year.

Then rumors spread about other things.

STDs. Drugs. Pregnancies.

While most of those rumors I could give a big 'fuck you' to, there was one rumor that hit incredibly close to home, one that wasn't a rumor at all.

And every time I heard it, every time I saw someone whispering behind their hands, their eyes avoiding mine but looking for the tell-tale signs, the pain in my gut, in my heart, was so incredibly agonizing that I could not bear to be that person anymore.

So I vowed off men the year I turned nineteen.

Nineteen.

The time most girls were starting to find who they were.

I had already found who I was and I didn't like her. I didn't like what she did to her body, what she did to her head, what she did to her heart.

I was successful at keeping men at bay for two years. Granted, the rumors turned into 'cock tease' but that was infinitely better than what they had been.

For two years, my vow of celibacy, of staying away from men, wasn't even tempted to change. But then my brothers hired him.

Greyson Stone.

Stone to everyone. Grey to just me.

Behind closed doors.

Behind our hands. Away from public. Away from my brothers.

Just like every other aspect of who I truly was, I was extremely good at hiding this relationship from my brothers.

But Grey was threatening to change that.

Five years, he let me have him in secret.

Five years, and he knew who I really was, who I hid from my brothers. He knew and he wanted to expose me.

Expose us.

So, what could I do but try and push him away?

Chapter One
Five Years Ago

Brenna

I walked into the pub that had been as much a part of my life as the family home had been, ready for my first shift working under my brothers' reign.

Conor and Rory re-opened the doors to our parents' pub last year, but between my age and, let's be honest, the desire to not work for my brothers, I respectfully declined every offer they gave me to be a barmaid.

A barmaid!

In my family's bar!

Just call me Cinderella, then.

At least give me a good job. Books or something. Don't make me start from the ground when the two of them were just...handed the place!

They saw me as some weak creature in their world, but I suppose some of that was my own fault. They often mistook my pain of the rumors that swirled about me as just that—pain of rumors—when in all actuality, the pain was because the truth they all spewed.

 But I needed a job and this was one I didn't have to apply for.

I did the community college thing after high school. My brothers thought I got a 'feel good' degree, an associates in something like graphic design or something, but really I was now the proud owner of an Associate Degree in Business Management.

I was keeping that card close to my chest though.

I did also have some graphic design knowledge because come on, my brothers thought I was taking the classes—I had to actually take some.

I may not be telling them about my business knowledge anytime soon, I wanted to learn the ins and outs of our particular setting before I showed my hand, but I could at least prove my worth with menu and ad design.

If they let me.

In the meantime though, I was going to do the Cinderella thing and wait tables because goodness knew, my brothers didn't want me to even think about getting my bartending license until I was twenty-one.

The law was twenty-one, yeah, but I could at least start looking at the materials.

This bubble they put me under?

It effing sucked.

But I went with the flow, letting them think whatever they wanted to think because that's what I did best. It's what made me...me.

Through the back door, I stepped into the kitchen and made my way to the office. There were pegs and lockers for other staff members, but Conor told me I could use the office with him and Rore.

It was early yet, ten on a Friday morning. O'Gallaghers wouldn't open for another hour and even then, it wouldn't be hopping. The kitchen was devoid of people, but I could hear some sounds.

At first I thought maybe Rory turned on a game in the bar, but as I neared the office, I realized the sounds were coming from in there. Voices.

Two of the voices I recognized as my brothers.

The other was unfamiliar. It wasn't as low as Conor's, but certainly wasn't a high pitched voice, either. It was a 'just right' kind of voice, the type that you knew would whisper gruffly in your ear one moment, and laugh jovially with you the next.

Not that I had any recent experience.

I walked into the office, realizing that my brothers were currently interviewing this beautiful voice.

Or had been.

The three of them were all smiling and laughing now.

"Morning boys," I said, walking into the room.

The laughing faces all turned toward me, and Conor, in his office chair with his hands on his belly, grinned wide behind his beard. He started wearing it when he was seventeen; I don't remember what he looked like without it anymore.

"Morning, Brenna. Stone, this is Bren, our sister. Brenna, Greyson Stone."

Stone stood from his chair and stepped forward with one foot, closing the small distance between us in a respectable way, still close enough to his chair that he could sit after introducing himself to me.

With his hand held out, he flashed me a beautifully crooked smile, showing off straight white teeth in his square jaw. "Stone."

I gave him a welcoming smile, taking his hand in mine. "Nice to meet you. Brenna." I took in his clear, clear gray eyes. I had only ever seen the clearness in blue, the type of color you felt you could see right through.

But Stone's gray eyes...

I could fall in the never ending clear depths.

I mentally shook myself.

I was done with men. Falling for this one wouldn't do me any good.

Besides, my brothers probably gave him an ultimatum.

"You as well," he said, pulling me from my thoughts. I slid my hand from his and smiled wide toward my brothers as Stone sat again.

Rory, at twenty five, was finally growing out of his baby looks and looking like a real live adult. If only he acted like one.

"What would you boys like for me to do?" I went to the filing cabinet, opening the bottom drawer in the metal monstrosity. I grimaced at the scratch of metal on metal. This beast was here when I was a baby.

I dropped my purse into the empty drawer and faced my brothers again.

"We're just about done here with Stone. He's our new bartender. He'll be working with me and you this afternoon," Conor said. I often felt that while this whole re-opening adventure was credited to both Conor and Rory, Conor was the one manning the expedition. Rory simply stood back and was a presence.

"In the meantime, if you want to get glasses set, that would be a great help."

"Sure thing." I turned back to the door to leave. I almost stopped to say something to Stone, something along the lines of 'nice to meet you,' but thought better of it.

Especially seeing as he and I would be working together.

Today.

I was going to have to repeat my no-men mantra over and over today, there wasn't a doubt in my mind.

Stone

I tried to watch Brenna leave from the corner of my eye.

One of the first warnings I received was that the youngest O'Gallagher was starting today too, and that she was strictly off limits, which only made me want to meet her more.

I knew she was going to be gorgeous.

Her brothers weren't bad looking dudes, so I had a feeling she was going to be right up there with them. I wasn't prepared for the knock I received when she walked into the office, all raven-colored, wavy hair and bright smile. Her eyes were green and stood out against her face, framed by thick dark eyelashes.

She was one of the most gorgeous women I ever had the pleasure of laying my eyes on. Staying away from her, on a personal level, was definitely going to be a challenge.

"So, we good?" Rory asked Conor. The kid looked like he had other places to be.

Conor nodded. "Sure, yeah. If you could just work on coming up with promotional things, that'd be great."

"Will do. Great meeting you, Stone. Look forward to working with you." Rory slid past the desk, seemingly in a hurry to leave.

When he left, Conor shook his head with a chuckle. "That kid. I swear—the actual act of working would kill him. But he's pretty brilliant on the other side of things."

I offered a crooked grin. "It's the age. You're either ready or you're not." Like Rory, I was twenty-five, but I definitely thought I was more adult than he was. The way he dressed stated he cared a great deal about what people thought. The way he held himself gave off the vibe that he put himself higher than others. And there was nothing wrong with any of that; everyone's experiences shaped them differently.

Mine just included a dad who beat on me until my mom got the courage for us to leave when I was thirteen. You grew up fast in that life and learned that appearances were rarely what they seemed.

"You need to do anything, grab anything, before hitting the floor?" Conor asked as he stood from the desk. I took that as my cue to stand as well, more than ready to get started. I didn't like sitting around doing nothing. I preferred being active as many hours of the day as possible.

I hadn't gone to college so my options for working tended to be on the slimmer side. I started bartending at twenty-one, at a pretty busy bar downtown. Found I loved not just the atmosphere, but talking to the people. Some places were better than others, sure. One of the reasons I left the other bar was because a friend and I had come to this one a few months ago and I fell for the aura of the place. It was modern yet rustic. Hip but had a huge range of patrons.

I'd been at the other bar for two years but was ready for a change. I left on good terms, something that was incredibly important to me.

I didn't believe in burning bridges.

You never knew when you'd need one of them again.

I had already done a walk-through of the pub when I first arrived, so Conor simply led me into the main bar area. I glanced at a table where Brenna was wrapping silverware and occasionally glancing up toward the TV. There was a hockey game on and I was impressed to see she was actually paying attention to it.

"The Enforcers have made this place their spot," Conor said, nodding toward the television. "Occasionally we'll see a Padres player or a Charger, but the place is almost always littered with hockey players." He moved toward the end of the bar, where the coolers and such were. "When you're on, feel free to organize all this however works best for you." He went to one of the chests and pulled out empty containers, as well as a few that were covered. He took the covers off and revealed lemons, olives, and other condiments.

"I'll leave you to this. Have some book work to do and need to get your paperwork submitted. You good?"

I nodded, stuffing the tips of my fingers into the pockets of my jeans. "Absolutely."

Conor nodded once and moved past me, clapping me on the shoulder. "Good to have you here."

As I began to prep the bar to my liking, I kept an ear on the game over my shoulder and an eye on the black-haired beauty semi-in front of me. She really was fucking gorgeous.

She had that classically beautiful face, the type that you couldn't tell if she wore makeup or not. Her lips were the perfect cupid's bow and her nose was a smaller, daintier version of the one that was on both Rory and

Conor's faces.

She wore a tight O'Gallaghers shirt that showed off her ample chest. She was large on top but didn't look disproportionate. Her legs were encased in skin-tight skinny jeans and on her feet were heels.

She was wearing heels to a bar.

To work.

Her feet were going to kill her before the night was over. I chuckled and shook my head which, while not my intention, caught her attention.

Her eyes narrowed. "What's funny?"

I shook my head. "Nothing. I was just thinking to myself."

She nodded upward once, slowly, her eyes assessing me. "Sure…"

Still grinning, I looked down and started cutting lemons and limes, the sizes perfectly similar. I heard as Brenna stood and gathered her box of wrapped silverware, just as I heard her heels clicking to the back of the bar where she deposited them in what I assumed was the basket that housed them.

Her clicking moved and glancing to my left, I saw that she moved to a lower fridge. She was kneeling now, her knees to her chest as she went through the fridge.

She glanced over at me with just her eyes before turning her entire head.

"Do you have a problem?"

The left side of my face was tight in a crooked grin. I turned my attention back to my task. "Nope."

The door to the refrigeration unit shut with a solid thump and her clicking came close. It was difficult, but I kept my attention on task even though I could smell the vanilla peppermint combination of what had to be her soap or shampoo. There was no way that was a perfume.

She smelled sweet.

I had the feeling that sweet wasn't who she was.

I continued my task even though I could feel her standing next to me, facing me, staring at me. I scooped up the last of my slices and deposited them in the tub before grabbing a towel and wiping my hands. I stuffed an end of the fabric into my back pocket and turned toward her.

Her arms were over her chest and her chin and nose were both angled up. Her body language said she was impatient with me, annoyed with me, but her eyes…

The green emeralds shining up at me showed she was intrigued, but more than that?

Curious. Want. Need.

And maybe a hint of timidity.

"What's your problem?" she asked.

I mirrored her body, my arms crossed over my chest. Her eyes flickered to my forearms which were now exposed. When we were in the office earlier, the sleeves of my shirt were down but now after working with my hands, I pushed the sleeves of my long-sleeved tee up, exposing the intricate colorful designs on both.

I nodded down toward her feet. "You work a bar in those before?"

She scoffed at me, shifting ever so slightly in her spot. "No. But they are my shoe of choice and I've worn them for hours on end. What I wear on my feet should be no concern of yours."

I just grinned at her attitude. "Sure thing. Just don't come crying to me when your feet kill."

"I don't go crying to anyone."

I simply stared at her. I heard a world of truth in her words and damn if that didn't make me want to be the person she could come crying to.

Damn. Hold up.

I just met this girl and received the equivalent of a death threat from her brothers if I touched her.

Yet I didn't seem to care.

"Oh, but you will."

"Will I?" She lifted a perfectly shaped brow in challenge.

I leaned down and in so we were nearly nose to nose.

She was easily six inches shorter than me in her heels, which had to put her at around five-three without. "I think you will."

She stared at me, her face tilted up and her expression unwavering. From here, I could see gold specks in her eyes. There was a light dusting of freckles over the bridge of her nose.

And those lips of hers.

That cupid bow mouth with a plump lower lip.

They were begging to be kissed.

She smelled sweet and looked it too, and I knew without a doubt I would have this woman—someway, somehow.

In secret, in public, I didn't care.

I was making it my mission to win her over, her brothers be damned.

Chapter Two
Four Years Ago

Brenna

When I say that keeping Stone at arm's length was difficult, I mean it was the equivalent of trying to keep a ticking bomb—with a remote detonator you did not have—from going off.

For a year I managed to avoid his advances.

Hardly.

Instead, I flirted back with him, trying to prove to him just where his place was. I was the sister of his bosses and he wasn't getting anywhere with me.

Even if I wanted those thick, colorful arms around me.

His spicy, musky cologne near me.

His beautifully crooked smile aimed at me.

Stone and I fell into an easy rhythm, which turned out to be incredibly important, as he and I worked many shifts together. He may have flirted with every person with tits, but he saved a special brand of flirting just for me.

Just as I did for him.

With it, I found myself having an absurd amount of fun with him. I looked forward to working with him for more than his good looks, but for the way he made me feel.

"Hey, gorgeous. What've you got for me?" Stone said, moving down the bar to where I set my tray down to remove old bottles and glasses. Today he wore a light blue shirt that had his gray eyes popping, but I tried to not focus on that, instead focusing on work.

"I need you—"

"I've been waiting for that." His grin was smug.

I lifted a brow. "*I need you,*" I started again, "to pour me a house lager, please...oh kind sir," I added with a hint of sass. I couldn't stop the corners of my lips from angling up.

"Anything for you." He wiped his hands on the towel hanging from his side before doing just that. He glanced past me to the kitchen door before lowering his voice, speaking from the side. "When are you going to agree to go out with me?"

Every shift, without fail, he asked.

Every shift, without fail, I told him no.

But it was getting harder.

"When the sky turns orange." Still though, I smiled, watching as his large, capable hands worked the tap system.

"I heard a storm is coming. It may turn orange before you know it." He smirked, placing the glass on my tray.

"Don't hold your breath." I couldn't wipe the silly grin from my face though, even if the entire thing baffled me.

I didn't get it.

How did one manage to go two years without finding any guy attractive, only to be blindsided by someone who was technically off limits in every sense?

I didn't want a man in my life. I was tired of being that Brenna.

On top of that, I had two very protective older brothers.

Stone didn't have a chance.

But good God, I wanted him like I wanted my next breath.

Generally, my shift ended before Stone's, but for whatever reason, today he left the floor at the same time I did.

"Rory's covering for me," he said when I slid him a side glance. He followed me to the back and I almost expected him to follow me into the office as well when I went to grab my purse, but he didn't.

He was waiting by the back door, though. "So that sky? It's kind of orange right now. You see, Bren," he said, his eyes locked on mine as I neared the door and therefore, him, "regardless of a bad storm, the sky turns orange at night with the setting sun. I think you wanted to go out with me."

I continued walking toward him, slipping past him when he held the door open for me.

I may have brushed my arm along his stomach in doing so.

Maybe.

Not on purpose though.

...but maybe, yeah.

"I meant green." I tried not to chuckle.

"Ah-ah, you can't go back on it." He was behind me and, without touching me, moved his arm over my shoulder and pointed toward the horizon.

O'Gallaghers may have been in a fairly populated place, but you could still make out the ocean horizon. And just past the ink marring the space beside me, just beyond the finger he pointed, was one of the most gorgeous sunsets I had the pleasure of viewing from this spot.

"Orange." His voice was low and dangerously close to my ear. "You owe me a date." He dropped his arm back to his side and I was surprised that I missed the almost contact.

There was no point fighting something that I wanted, something that I craved. I could be proud of myself for holding off men for two-plus years, and this particular one for twelve months.

I hoped like hell I was safe from disappointment though—that I learned something from my time being single.

One date.

I didn't have to sleep with him, much like I would have had we met one another even four years ago.

Just a date.

Resigned,

 yet excited at the same time, I took a deep breath and shot him a coy smile over my shoulder. "You got time tonight, Greyson Stone?"

Stone

Twelve months, I spent trying to work down this girl, and it was fucking worth the wait.

For the sake of her brothers, we took separate vehicles back to my place, where she hopped into my Jeep and we spent an hour driving up and down the coast.

It was fun.

It was light.

We laughed and joked, talking about nothing important but, for whatever reason, that felt important.

"We're near my place, if you want to go there? We can order something?" she asked, looking at me from her spot in the passenger seat.

The roof was off and her black pony tail was blowing every which way around her face. She reached up to grab the end, holding it to her shoulder as she waited for my answer.

I was a healthy twenty-six year old man. I would be lying if I didn't say I was hopeful that going back to her place meant more than just eating.

But I also realized Brenna kept me at arm's length for the past year, and there was likely a reason other than her brothers. She never talked about dates or guys or, hell, anything, in her past.

Recalling the timidity in her eyes when we first met, I was willing to bet there was a story there.

I wasn't going to push though.

"Sure, we can do that."

I turned the music down slightly so it could still be heard over the roaring of the passing road and cars, but also so I could hear Brenna's directions.

During a straight shot, Brenna sat up straight in her chair, a huge smile on her beautiful face. "I love this song!" She reached for the dial and turned up the volume. It was Old Dominion's "Song for Another Time."

As she began to sing with the words, I chuckled to myself. This was my favorite CD at the moment. When the song finished, the CD shuffled to my current favorite song, namely because it felt real to what I was doing with Brenna right now.

Not knowing these words, Brenna sat back, listening to the words of "Til It's Over," nodding her head and swaying during some of the bigger instrumental points. Still, she was good about pointing me in the right direction and with awesome timing, the song ended just as I pulled into her duplex.

"Let me open the garage so you can park inside. You know. In case." She hopped out of the Jeep before I could say something, but I shrugged mentally. She was a little paranoid about her brothers finding out we went out for a little while, but I'd let her have it. For now.

If this was going to continue, there was no way in hell I was keeping her a secret.

She was the type of girl you showed off. Not just because she was beautiful, but because she was fun. She was sun and laughter all wrapped into a pretty package.

When the garage door lifted, I pulled the Jeep in, shutting off the ignition and climbing out just as she hit the button to close the door again.

Following her into her place, I looked around at the largeness. It was open and had a staircase that led to a lofted area. "You live here by yourself?"

She nodded. "Yeah. I shared it with a roommate up until a few months ago but she moved out and it's all mine now. Rent's not terrible for being in this area."

The garage door led right into the kitchen and dining area, which looked fairly updated with the slate floors and nice counters. Even the cabinets looked to be more modern than I would have thought for a duplex in this area.

"It's really nice."

She nodded. "Yeah. It was one of Rory's projects a few years ago. Well, not the actual renovation, but the planning of it. After, it was what gave Conor the inspiration to completely reno the pub."

I walked around the space slowly, taking everything in. If the kitchen and dining were the back half of the house, with a door leading to what I could only guess were the laundry room and a bathroom, the front half was the living area. The floors there were a natural wood and her furniture was incredibly nice too.

Shit, did these people have money and I didn't know it?

I stuffed my hands in my back pockets and turned back toward her, putting a smile on my face. So she had nice digs and a nicer place to sit down at night. But knowing what I did about Brenna, little as it may be, I didn't think that any of this was for show.

"Food?"

Brenna gave me her full, real smile, the one that brought out a dimple parallel to the bottom of her left eye, and nodded. "Sure. What would you like? I have pizza on autodial."

And that was what we ate for our first meal.

Nothing terribly special.

Nowhere fancy.

But comfortable, and cozy, and enjoyable.

 After the pizza was eaten and everything put away, Brenna and I sat on her overstuffed leather couch in absolute silence. She lost her heels right after the pizza arrived.

She wore heels every shift. Sometimes I wondered if it were just her being stubborn, trying to prove a point after our first conversation about them. Still, I never caught her grimacing or even toeing them off during her breaks. She wore them like she was born in them.

If she were turned, I'd probably offer her a foot rub. I could only imagine her moan of pleasure as I dug my thumbs into her arches.

But I was rather comfortable right here, right now, with her curled into my side.

I noticed she didn't have a television, but I didn't want the obtrusion anyway. At some point, Brenna grew more comfortable with me and was now curled up into my side, her head on my shoulder and my arm around her. Her fingers traced lazy circles on my denim covered thigh but every now and then, her hand would pause and I would feel her tremble.

For all of her laughter and smiles, I got the sudden feeling that maybe her holding me back had a shit-ton to do with her, rather than her brothers.

"Dance with me?" I asked, picking up her hand in mine.

She sat up and smiled slightly. "Sure?" Her brows drew in for a moment, making me chuckle.

"Don't worry about the music, Angel."

If anything, that made her frown deepen, but still she rose from the couch when I pulled her to stand, willingly moving into my body when I brought her closer.

With both of her small hands in one of mine I brought her closer, my other hand to the small of her back. She was pressed against me everywhere and I fucking loved it. She was a little stiff, but my guess would be she simply felt awkward. Hell, there was no music—it *was* slightly awkward.

But I brought my A-game tonight.

I was no Justin Timberlake, but I could sing when needed.

With my voice low and soft, I sang to her, our bodies rocking slightly back and forth in the light of her living room. I sang to her a classic Sinatra song, and led that into "Till It's Over," my version a little more sensual and slower than the version she swayed to in the Jeep earlier. When I got to the 'naked making out' part though, Brenna pulled back laughing.

It was the most alive I had seen her face in the short time I'd known her. "They don't say that!" Her eyes were bright, her smile wide, but she didn't pull her hands from the cage mine put them in.

I grinned crookedly. "But they do. You've interrupted my song." My hand on her lower back rubbed in small circles. "*...or keep our clothes on. Don't—*"

"But those aren't the words. It's 'makin' makin' out.'"

I barked out a laugh, my own smile growing wide. "This isn't Chitty Chitty Bang Bang, Brenna."

"Seriously though? 'Naked makin' out?'"

Reluctantly, I let go of her hands to pull my phone from my pocket. I was more than pleased when she kept her hands on my chest, spreading her fingers over me. I kept my hand on her back though, not wanting to let go of any more points of contact. Quickly, I pulled up a search result for the lyrics to the Old Dominion song and double-tapped the screen, zooming in on the first verse.

With my thumb under the words, I showed her the phone. "See? Naked makin' out."

She spoke through her wide smile, shaking her head. "That's ridiculous."

I tossed my phone toward the couch, kind of thankful it actually landed on the couch and not the hardwood floor, and wrapped my arm around her shoulders, pulling her impossibly close. Lowering my head toward her ear, I swayed us back and forth to the music in my head. "But it's true," I whispered to her.

She burrowed into me, slipping her arms around my waist, and swayed with me as I sang her the rest of the song.

Chapter Three

Brenna

Stone scared me.

Things I felt around him were things I hadn't felt before, not in my teenaged years, nor my twentieth year, of surrounding myself with guys.

Much like the words he sang to me, he didn't try anything more than to sway with me in my living room. The feel of his hard body pressed against mine had my heart fluttering like mad. Add to that the fact that he was clearly aroused yet tried *nothing*...

My goodness, this man.

Eventually, he grabbed his phone and turned on a Spotify station and I found I missed his low, raspy singing voice, the grit in his words, his voice in my ear. But having music to sway to helped to keep the moment light.

After what had to be the tenth song, I leaned back from his arms and searched his face. What I was looking for, I wasn't entirely sure.

His gray eyes bore down into mine, but he said nothing, did nothing. Not that I did either. We stood and stared at one another for a few long moments and rather than feel awkward it felt...

Freeing.

Stone was unlike any man I had been around and while, like I said, it scared me, it also had me excited and curious. What would it be like to be in this man's arms in the primal sense?

I dropped my eyes to my hands, spread on his broad chest. With a deep breath, I found the courage to fully break my clause, putting my trust in this man I didn't fully know but who made me feel like something, someone, I hadn't felt ever before.

Moving my green gaze back to his gray one, I slid my hands up his chest, brushing along the sides of his thick neck, and placed them gently on his scruffy cheeks. Still, my eyes searched his, this time looking for a reason to stop, a reason to step back into my safe walls.

There weren't any.

I pushed up on tiptoe, gently pulling his face down to meet me. His eyes never left mine.

Before I could press my lips to his though, he spoke. "We don't have to, Bren."

So I whispered against his, "But I want to."

His lips pressed to mine, not giving me the chance to close the small gap myself. His hands moved from my back down to my ass and before I could prepare myself, he lifted me up. I gasped into his mouth which only served as an opening for him to sweep his tongue into mine.

The feel of the thickness in my mouth had me moaning. I moved a hand to the back of his blond head, wrapping my other arm around his neck. Between my arm and my legs wrapping around his hips, I was entwined around him like a monkey, I was sure, but I gave two fucks. My body was pulsing, my core was wet, and I wanted nothing more than to be completely engulfed by this man.

"Upstairs," I whispered against his mouth.

I felt him pause and knew without a doubt that this man here was a good man. He was considering what I was telling him.

But I gave him permission already. I wanted him, us, upstairs.

Finally, he moved us toward the stairs without further direction and excitement coursed through my body. He kissed me until we were about halfway up the steps, where he stumbled.

I laughed as he mumbled, taking the rest of the stairs with his mouth away from mine.

I wanted to pull his lips back to mine when he reached the landing, but he moved us directly to the bed. With me still wrapped around him, he moved onto the bed, knees first, moving to the middle and lowering us.

We probably made out, fully clothed, on that bed for an hour. It was the most delicious hour I had ever spent with someone's hands roaming over my body, under my clothes, as we learned one another.

When our clothes finally made their way to the floor, Stone stopped me from trying to climb over him again, instead pushing me back and laying his mouth to my pussy before I could stop him.

With one long sweep of his tongue, I was nearly in ecstasy.

I ground myself against his mouth as his tongue and lips worked magic over my clit. When he thrust his tongue into me, I had to grip the sheets at my sides. I was so incredibly close to coming.

Again, his mouth was at my clit and he hummed against me, bringing a whole new set of feelings down there. I clenched down on my muscles to try and stop my impending orgasm. I closed my eyes, focusing on his mouth on me, and I felt as he trailed a finger over my pussy lips, feather light.

Goodness, I was going to come so hard.

The softness of his finger and the magic of his mouth had me fighting toward a high I'd never reached before. All it would take was one bite, one thrust, and there wasn't going to be any way I could stop myself from jumping over the edge.

And sure enough, when Stone slowly, so freaking slowly, pushed his thick finger into me, I shattered around him. "Stone!"

Stone

Her body bowed in ecstasy was a sight I couldn't have imagined. Her responses were better than I could have thought up.

My middle finger wasn't even completely buried in her and she was pulsing around me, her back arched and body tight. Keeping my finger in her, I moved up so I could kiss her, needing my mouth on hers. Her body relaxed slightly but her breathing was still heavy as I locked my mouth over hers. Her hands went in my hair and her tongue met mine, thrust for thrust. When I felt her wet channel slow down, I began to thrust my finger in and out of her, slowly, mimicking what I so badly wanted to do with my cock. I bent my finger, just enough so I could explore her walls, all while kissing and swallowing her moans.

Her hips shifted under us, her legs spreading as she fought to find another release.

Good fucking lord, I could love on her all night.

I added another finger to the mix, moving slowly again to get her used to the added width. She was tight and slick and I just fucking *knew* I was going to have a hard time holding my shit back when I finally sank into her.

"Stone," she moaned, pulling away from my mouth.

I had been Stone to everyone for a long fucking time—to family and friends alike—but for the first time since I left my first name behind in high school, I wanted someone to call me by my given name. I kissed her cheek, allowed my lower teeth to scrape over her as I moved my mouth toward her ear. "Grey."

She didn't ask for me to elaborate, she didn't question it. No, instead she turned her head toward mine and locked eyes with me. "I need you, Grey."

If that wasn't a boost for the ego...

Her using my name was like my own type of Kryptonite. Her husky, sex-heavy voice saying my name had my spine tingling but I'd be damned if I was blowing this soon.

I leaned back on my haunches and, after reaching for my pants on the ground and fishing out a condom, grabbed my hard girth and covered myself. I lowered the head to notch right where I wanted to be, where she wanted me to be.

Needing a moment to fully appreciate everything, I slid the tip up her wet folds, gathering moisture, before positioning myself once again, pushing into her slowly as I lowered my body to hers again.

I was going to love on her slowly this first time.

And then I was taking her every which way until the morning light.

I kept my thrusts slow, cocking my hips up every time I sank fully home. Every time I dragged out, Brenna bit on her lip. Every time I pushed all the way to the brink, she closed her eyes and moaned. She was going to end up with a sore lip, so rather than let that happen, I dropped my mouth to hers, kissing her slowly and in time with my thrusts.

There came a point though that I needed more. I could feel my orgasm coming again and I needed her closer to her own peak. Holding her body closer still, I quickened my pace, my open mouth breathing roughly against her ear, hers doing the same. Little mewling moans broke through her gasps and fuck if I didn't love them.

I reached between us, finding her clit with my thumb, rubbing circles over the nub as I pushed myself in and out. "Come on, Brenna. Let go, Bren," I told her, kissing her cheek.

Her breath hitched once, twice, and finally her jaw dropped open and her body bore down as her orgasm took her. I held myself in her deep, kissing her eyelids, her nose, and finally her mouth, as I waited for her body to calm before I continued, needing to find my own release. Holding myself deep in her, feeling her pulsing, squeezing against my hard cock and *not* coming right along with her should have won me a Goddamn medal.

When her body stopped moving, she opened her eyes and smiled up at me.

"You ready for more?" I asked her. When she nodded, I sat up to kneel between her legs, never dislodging my cock from it's warm, wet home. I slowly started to grind my lips, allowing the drag to be slow before I grabbed her behind the knee, holding one of her legs up. She put her foot on my shoulder and with a hand on her hip and the other on her knee, I began a ruthless rhythm. I watched her tits bounce with each thrust for a bit before she covered them with her hands, only to pluck at her nipple.

Her slick channel was growing wetter and she was moaning again, her fingers playing herself expertly and my cock driving into her again and again.

"God, Bren, I'm gonna..." I grunted, trying to hold back a few moments longer. I didn't want to leave her; I didn't want to end the feeling of her enveloping me. Goddamn, this was close to the best sex of my life and I didn't want it to end. "Fuck, I can't..." With a shout, I thrust into her once more, harder than before, my body shuddering as my own orgasm overtook me.

I didn't think she'd have it in her, but Brenna's body was taut under me again, her fingers pinched tight over her nipples and her eye squeezed shut in ecstasy. I could feel her squeezing against my cock as it fought to rid itself of cum.

Hands down, best sex of my life.

Three more rounds later and it was nearly four in the morning. The hours just flew by, between rounds of sex and quick catnaps.

Brenna lay against me and my fingers traced over the swirls and lines covering her back.

They surprised me when I took her from behind. It wasn't a tattoo I would have imagined for a girl like Brenna.

It was a huge piece, taking up her entire back. Rather than angel wings or butterfly wings, it was an abstract line piece of a whole butterfly.

"What's your tattoo mean?" I asked. Someone like Bren wouldn't get a huge-assed tattoo for no reason. An infinity somewhere, sure; peer pressure and all that, but this was a serious piece.

Brenna froze against me as if I'd said something that upset her. I lowered my chin to look down at her, trying to gauge her reaction, but she just gave me a tight smile.

"It's just pretty," she finally answered.

I honestly didn't think that was the full answer, but I'd let her leave it at that for now. Her hand had found its way to my cock and I wanted nothing more than to go through another round with this woman right here.

Serious questions and serious answers could wait.

Chapter Four
One Year Ago

Stone

"That's the last of my shit," I said after depositing a box in the bedroom Brenna and I would now be sharing officially.

My girl sat on the bed, grinning that wide, beautiful smile of hers, the one that made her green eyes dance.

The one that had me wanting to strip her of her clothing and love on her all night long.

We were good with the all-nighters. I suppose it helped that we were both night owls, but there was nothing I liked more than laying in her bed, waiting for her to come back to me, when I knew I was going to get sweet loving for hours on end.

Or even vice versa, knowing that I was going back to her place where she'd be waiting for me.

But now her place, her huge lofted duplex, was now our place.

We still hadn't told her brothers, which definitely didn't sit well with me. Brenna and I had been seeing one another, dancing around this, for *three damn years*. It was fucking difficult to keep on the down-low. I wanted to shout on the rooftops that I was in love with this girl, but I had to keep it to myself.

Well, and to Brenna. As far as I knew, she didn't know that I loved her; I hadn't told her yet. I was afraid that the words would send her running for the hills.

For three years, we went on occasional dates and had a number of secret sleepovers, either at her place or mine. We even went on vacations twice a year, she and I.

Brenna always had to come up with our excuses though, so her brothers wouldn't catch on. I had waited until I was completely moved in to her place before asking her about it though. Now was that time.

I knew my question was going to take the smile from her face, so I decided to kiss on her first, needing her full, open happiness for a moment longer.

I stalked toward her, loving the giggle she gave as she scrambled back to the middle of the bed. She was such an open and free spirit when it was just she and I. I wished, for her, that she would let go of the things that weighed her down. I knew a little about her past but I had a feeling that it only grazed the surface, that there was more to it than being the sheltered, over-protected sister of Conor and Rory O'Gallagher.

I crawled over her, grinning down at her. "You happy, Brenna O'Gallagher?"

Her smile grew smaller, but the joy was still written all over her face. She hooked her hand around my neck. "Absolutely, Greyson Stone."

"So," I said, finally broaching the subject of her brothers as she and I lay in bed, just a sheet draped over us after another marathon hour of sex. "I'm going to have to update my address on file."

Here's the thing.

Brenna was fucking smart. She had a degree in Business Management and was working on her Masters in the same field, yet, for whatever reason, hadn't told her brothers that either. When I brought it up to her, back when she first started the online program, she simply shook her head, saying that she wasn't ready for her brothers to know. I let it sit at that, but it was yet another thing about this woman that I didn't understand.

She was bright as the fucking sun. As beautiful as the sun setting over the beach.

But she kept so much about herself back from her brothers and I didn't understand why.

She told me once that if I wanted to be with her, I was going to have to be ok with her walls and because I *did* want to be with her, I overlooked them.

Didn't mean it didn't kill me a little inside, though.

I figured that my statement would have her realizing that we were going to have to tell her brothers about us, but no, her brilliant mind came up with a different alternative that I didn't see coming.

"Then just tell Con you want to pick up your statements. He'll be happy to save the pub forty-odd cents," Brenna said with a shrug.

I sighed but covered it up with a kiss to her forehead. "Bren," I said against her forehead. "How do you see this working? Us living together and them not finding out eventually?"

"Time, Grey." She looked up into my eyes. "I just need a little more time."

I thought three years was plenty of time, but what was a few more days?

Chapter Five

Brenna

With Grey working today but being off myself, I found myself at the mall.

Just as I was leaving to head home though, I was nearly plowed down by a pregnant woman.

Ok, so plowed down may be a little overzealous. I wasn't paying attention, she wasn't paying attention, and then BAM! I ran into her. Or she me.

But when I looked into the woman's shocked face, I knew without a doubt, mine mirrored hers.

"Mia Hampton?"

Mia had been my best friend growing up. She and I had been thick as thieves, getting into mischief and taunting my older brothers relentlessly. We stopped being friends when we were ten though, but while we hadn't hung out, I still saw her now and then throughout the halls in school.

But this was the first time I'd seen her since graduation.

When we were younger, people would sometimes make the rude comment about how much of a pretty girl I was and how *not* pretty Mia was. Heck, my brothers even had some not very nice names for her, but looking at her now? Mia grew into herself extremely well.

Gone was the insecure, thicker girl and in her place was a gorgeous woman.

She gave me a timid smile. "Hey, Brenna."

"Oh my God, it is you! You look fantastic!" I knew that probably wouldn't go over well. One of those true rumors from my past was that I pushed Mia aside because she was the fat half of our friendship. I knew that was a rumor she knew too well.

Her smile lifted a little. "Thank you. You do too."

"God I love your curls." I reached out mindlessly to pull one of them, allowing it to bounce. "Remember when we were kids and we got a lock stuck in a fan?"

Her smile filled into a laugh. "My mother wasn't too happy about that. The bowl cut doesn't work too well with this hair."

I laughed too, remembering the time when we were eight and life was carefree, easy... There weren't worries about popularity or boys, or who you hung out with.

After a moment though, I recalled the fact that she was pregnant.

Very pregnant.

"Oh my goodness, look at your baby bump! You're so freaking cute, Mia. Where's your husband?" I peered around her, sure that whoever was with her wouldn't let her stay away for long.

Her smile fell this time and she shook her head. "I'm not married."

My brows rose a fraction. Mia was single and pregnant? Not that that was an atrocity in our world these days, but it simply wasn't something that fit in with the person Mia had been.

"The baby was an accident." While a seemingly negative comment, Mia said it with a small smile. "But a good one." She rubbed her swollen tummy.

I had so many questions for her, but standing outside of a maternity store wasn't the place to have them. "Do you want to go get coffee or something? I mean, decaf for you."

She stared at me for a moment, her eyes searching mine, before she finally nodded. "Ok. Sure."

Chapter Six

Brenna

What a whirlwind of thirty-six hours.

After Mia confessed just *who* her "baby daddy" was, I concocted a plan to get her and Conor back in the same place. Sure, it was at my birthday dinner, but I wanted them face to face once again.

Sure, I wanted Conor to own up to what he'd done, but more so, I wanted Mia to tell Conor. Conor deserved to know, but I also couldn't help but want to see my oldest brother with my once best friend. It didn't surprise me that Mia had liked Conor once upon a time, and I was willing to bet there was still a small part of her that wanted to see if she could like him now.

The only problem with all of this though, was the blow-up that happened after the re-meeting.

I hadn't thought there would be anger and pinched faces. I should have figured, knowing Conor's personality, but I really honestly hadn't thought it would get to the point it did. Just when I thought I could potentially find a friend—again—in Mia, I went and screwed that up.

Watching Mia cry, watching as she pointedly glared at me, had the past all rushing back to me. Back to when I pushed her away. Back to when I started making stupid decisions.

Back to when I started to close off who I really was from the world.

It was time to start letting that out.

But there was only one person I wanted to talk to.

Even if the conversation would kill me.

Stone

When I got home from the pub, I was surprised to see Brenna's car in the garage. It was early yet for her to be done with dinner with her brothers.

"Hey, Bren, what's up?" I asked, walking into the living room where she sat on the couch, her legs folded under her. I dropped my keys and wallet on the kitchen table, moving toward her.

"I want to talk to you." Her voice was void of emotion, but her eyes were sad.

Shit, what the hell did I do?

I may be annoyed with the keeping things secret thing, but damned if I wanted this to end now.

"Ok, yeah. Sure." I moved to sit on the loveseat adjacent to the couch Brenna occupied and my racing heart calmed a fraction when she unfolded herself to sit next to me on the much smaller couch.

I angled myself in the corner so I could face her and Brenna sat completely sideways, her legs under her once again, and her head resting on the back of the couch.

"So I invited Mia to dinner tonight."

"Mia, as in the girl you ran into at the mall?" Yesterday, Brenna explained to me, in excitement, about this meeting of her once best friend. That excitement wasn't anywhere on her face now though.

"Yeah, but she's a little more than just a once-friend." Brenna took a shaky breath and I was hit with the knowledge that this was it.

No, not as in the end of our relationship, but as in she was going to completely open up to me. I was going to learn about her walls.

"I know I told you Mia was once my best friend and that we sort of fell apart, but that was only a half-truth." Her hands were folded in her lap and she looked down, her raven hair blocking her face from me.

I didn't want her hiding herself from me, so I reached out and pushed her hair back behind her ear. She may not give me her eyes right now, but I could at least see her face to a degree.

"When I was ten, I decided Mia was too...different from me to stay my friend." Her words were choked. I could feel the disappointment in herself, behind her words. She was ashamed of herself and that had me frowning.

I reached for her chin to lift her face toward mine. "You were ten. It happens."

Brenna shook her head and pulled back from my hand, her eyes sadder than I had ever seen them before.

And she had me sitting through some pretty gut-wrenching movies in our time together.

"No. It was incredibly mean of me. She was fat and I wasn't, and the cool kids wouldn't talk to me with her hanging around. So I pushed her away. I pushed her away so I could hang with the cool kids." She took another one of those shaking breaths, her hands fisted so tightly together that her knuckles were pale. I reached for her hands and gently pried them apart, allowing her time to speak when she was ready.

"Well, the cool kids have a way of biting you in the ass and not giving a shit," she said around a sad smirk. "I started smoking when I was twelve. I stopped, but it happened. I had more boyfriends than I could count by the time I was fourteen."

The more she refused to meet my eyes, the more I realized I didn't want this truth any more. I didn't want to watch her break herself open.

"Brenna." I tugged her close, glad when she willingly crawled into my lap. "It doesn't matter. None of it matters, Angel." I rubbed my hand up and down her back but she shook her head against my chest.

With her face buried into my shoulder, her body shaking, she gave me a truth I would have never guessed. "My tattoo isn't because it's pretty. It's in memory of the baby I lost."

Chapter Seven

Brenna

His hand froze on my back.

I knew it.

I just *knew* that if he knew the truth, he'd likely pull away.

I swallowed, begging in my mind for him to keep holding me a moment longer, to not let me go for just a little while longer.

I chose butterfly wings for the little girl that I named Nova. I didn't have a lick of Native American in me, but the name meant 'chasing butterflies' and that's what I wanted for the baby who wouldn't ever see a birthday. I wanted to imagine her somewhere bright and happy, chasing butterflies and being a regular, beautiful little girl.

"Ok," Grey broke into my thoughts.

That was it. Just 'ok.'

I pulled my head away from him to frown up at his face, surprised to see it wasn't contorted in disbelief or disgust, but rather…concern?

"So are you sad today because you ran into an old friend who's pregnant? Or because of something else?" His question only held curiosity and had me pausing before answering him. When I still hadn't, he started rubbing small circles over my back again.

I searched his eyes, but had a feeling I wasn't going to find what I was looking for. I wasn't going to find judgement from his man. Not once in the four years knowing him had I seen him being judgmental about anyone.

"Do you want to talk about it?" he asked instead.

Not really but, "I was seventeen. I couldn't tell you who the father was." I burrowed back into Grey's chest, not wanting to have this conversation but knowing that because I started it, he deserved to hear the rest.

To learn why I needed to keep things from my brothers.

"My brothers thought I was some freaking angel, but really I was spreading my legs for any guy who smiled at me. Heck, they didn't even have to smile." My voice caught in my throat when Grey's hand stopped yet again but rather than push me away, he hugged me tight.

It was his silence that urged me to go on.

"I lost her at twenty-two weeks. A spontaneous late miscarriage," I whispered. "It was winter, so I could hide my belly behind baggy sweatshirts and no one thought anything of it. Well, except the kids at school. Someone found out I'd been pregnant and it was all over the school in the matter of a day. When I never showed, it didn't stop the rumors from circling but every time I heard it, it crushed me.

"I wasn't ready to be a mom, but I felt that me losing my baby so late was God's way of punishing me. Or karma. Really bad karma." I squeezed my eyes shut, picturing the day I had to deliver her. The day I delivered my dead baby, all by myself, not a single person who mattered to me, standing beside me. "I delivered her and held her. She was so tiny, but so, so perfect." My breath hitched again. "Her tiny nose, her hands. She wasn't any bigger than my hands but, in that moment, I knew what it was to love and lose, and I hated it."

I took a deep breath and pushed back from my spot, wiping at my eyes with the palms of my hands before staring into Grey's eyes yet again, still on his lap for as long as he'd let me stay.

"I got over the hurt by sleeping around more. When I was nineteen, I realized I didn't like the girl in the mirror, so I stopped. I vowed to not allow myself to be that girl ever again, to not find comfort in a set of arms."

Grey nodded, reaching out and wiping at my tears with his thumbs. "And your brothers don't know." He said it with such quiet calm.

I shook my head. "No. They don't know who I was in those years. And they never questioned that I stopped dating, that I never brought guys around."

"I think you should tell them," he said, still without a drop of judgment on his face, only concern, as he looked into my eyes.

Still though, I shook my head. "No. I don't want them to know. Ever."

I was thankful when Grey let that sit. The mood was incredibly somber but I was grateful he hadn't put me aside and left me here to deal with these emotions alone.

"What made you break your vow?" he asked, sometime later.

I could finally smile. "You. Just you."

Chapter Eight
This Year

Brenna

It had been nearly a year since Grey moved in, a year since he learned my most heartbreaking secrets, but still our relationship was strong.

In that time, Conor became a daddy for the first time. Aiden Rory O'Gallagher was the cutest little button with his daddy's hair and eyes. Watching as Conor went from playboy to loving boyfriend, even further to doting dad, was one of the best transformations I had the pleasure of watching.

In that time, Mia and I grew incredibly close again. I shared with her some of my past secrets, keeping the biggest ones to myself. The night I confessed them to Grey was one of the worst nights I'd ever experienced. More than once, I woke up in a cold sweat, crying from dreams I couldn't remember, but could only imagine they dealt with Nova. Grey simply held me tight, kissing away my tears, and loving me back into oblivion.

While our schedules were all over the place, we never missed an opportunity to be in one another's arms, a place I found I loved more than anything. The way Grey made love to me, owning my body and driving my needs to completion, had me falling for him in ways that scared me. And because of that, I started worrying that someday this wouldn't be enough for Grey.

But, right now, it seemed like it was plenty for him.

He had me pressed against the counter, a hand kneading my breast over my shirt and bra, and his mouth on my neck, nibbling in ways that had goosebumps trailing up and down my body.

"Grey, my brothers are coming!" I said, trying to push him away from me. One of us had to be the levelheaded one. "You have to go."

He groaned but pulled away. I shivered at the loss of his warm mouth on my skin, even though the distance was what I needed right now.

"Jesus, Bren," he said. I knew he was annoyed with this part of the situation. He started talking about bringing us up to my brothers about a month ago. "Can't we just tell them yet?"

I shook my head.

No.

My brothers liked Grey and if they found out he'd been sleeping with me, let alone living with me for the last year, they would surely blow a fuse. Both of them.

"We have to put your stuff away," I said, my mind in frantic mode as I looked around the duplex for any signs of Grey.

He was all over.

He lived here; of course he was all over.

I stuffed things in the cubes under the coffee table, more things in the hall closet, knowing my brothers wouldn't go in there. I barely noticed when Grey shook his head and headed to the kitchen.

Hopefully to remove any evidence he lived here in there too.

I ran down the hall to be sure all of our clothes were put away, then into the bathroom to move his products into the linen closet.

When I moved back into the living area, fifteen minutes before my brothers were to arrive, Grey was standing by the front door, his shoes on and shrugging into a jacket.

"I hate this, Bren."

"It's only for a little while longer," I lied. I wasn't sure when I would be comfortable telling my brothers.

And as much as I trusted Grey, cared for him, there was still a small piece of me that was terrified of what would happen to me when he decided he'd had enough of me.

When he decided to walk away.

At least whenever that happened, if my brothers didn't know about us, he could go on living his life the way he had been.

"I want to tell them."

My eyes flew to his. "Please don't. Not right now."

"Brenna, they deserve to know everything you've gone through."

A mind of their own, my hands covered my flat stomach and I shook my head. "No."

He stared at me a little longer before shaking his head sadly. Without a word, he turned and left the duplex.

I took a deep breath, trying to calm the racing of my heart.

However, the racing came from a whole different type of anxiety than my brothers finding out.

No, the racing was because suddenly I was very afraid of losing Greyson Stone.

"Isn't that Stone's?" Conor asked as he walked into the kitchen, pulling out a chair at my tiny table. He sat down with Aiden in his lap. I followed his eyes and saw what his had landed on.

Sure enough, Grey's hoodie was in the corner, where he had thrown it off me earlier.

"Um." I looked around frantically. "I borrowed it last night." I refrained from nodding and looking like a crazed person. "When I left the pub, it was chillier than I anticipated, and he let me wear it home."

Thankfully, that answer seemed to appease my brothers, as the subject dropped and changed to the upcoming get-together we were planning for our parents' return to San Diego.

Rory decided he wanted to order pizza, and the two of them stayed longer than I thought they would. By the time they left, Aiden had been napping on the living room floor for an hour.

I sent a text Grey, letting him know it was safe to come back home, but when he didn't answer—when I went to bed alone—that earlier anxiety of losing Grey came rushing back.

Chapter Nine

Stone

Angel: *They're gone. You can come home now.*

I stared at my phone, wanting above everything to just tell her off. I was sick of this.

Five years.

Five years I've known Brenna and have essentially been doing just this. Sure, it was ok at first, but shortly after moving in with her, things started to take a much, much more serious turn for me.

Five years was a long time to be with someone.

And it was mentally longer when you had to do it in secret.

I didn't want to date her in secret any more.

What was I going to do, marry her in secret? Send her away on year-long vacations so she could have babies in secret?

Because that's where my mind, my fucking heart, was right now.

I didn't play along with this game for five years just to say goodbye to her, no. I played along because I knew she was it for me.

The four hours that I wasn't allowed in my own fucking place, I mindlessly drove around the Bay. I spent a good amount of time at La Jolla, sitting and watching the seals sunbathe.

I still hadn't answered Brenna's text when the sun started to sink over the horizon but she hadn't tried to get back to me, either.

I stood from my perch on a rock and headed back to my car, squeezing the bridge of my nose.

Knowing Brenna, she was probably mentally preparing for me to say goodbye to her. Whenever she revealed a piece of her past, it was like she curled herself into a coat of armor, waiting for me to decide I was done.

As if her past did anything other than make me love her more.

Did I hate that she kept her life so far apart from her brothers? Yes.

But I admired her for the things she shouldered, for the things she went through—alone.

The fact that I waited so long to respond now—well, to *not* respond—probably had her head in some insecure headspace.

God, I loved her so much and I physically ached for her and the pain she went through by herself for so many years. I wanted her to open up and tell her brothers. I wanted her to take that weight off her own chest.

She had nothing to be ashamed of.

Me: *I'm on my way home*

I pocketed my phone before I could talk myself into waiting for her response.

Brenna

I was already in bed by the time Grey came home.

I didn't roll over, didn't greet him. I could feel his frustration the moment he cleared the loft stairs though.

Squeezing my eyes shut, I forced my body to relax. I could hear as he moved around the room, discarding his clothes before walking into the bathroom to brush his teeth and get ready for bed.

The lights clicked off in the bathroom and his footsteps fell softly on the carpet. I felt the bed dip behind me and I fully expected him to turn his back on me, to sleep apart from me.

I understood why he was upset.

It wasn't the first time he'd asked me to come clean to my brothers, about my past, about us.

But I was terrified.

Absolutely fucking terrified.

If my brothers knew what a slut I was growing up…

I couldn't bear to think of what their faces would look like.

And then, if they found out I'd been a pregnant teenager? Oh my God, Conor would probably be most pissed for that offense alone.

And like I thought earlier, if they knew about Grey and me…

Grey didn't deserve the wrath of Conor and Rory.

But what did that mean for Grey and me?

I was going to have to force him to bow out. I was going to have to convince him he didn't like me anymore, to get him to move out and away.

I stifled what would have been a sob. It ended up being more of a muted hiccup. I squeezed my eyes shut, hopeful Grey wouldn't notice.

The good thing with what Grey and I had been doing was that when he walked away, we could just continue going on like we had been in public. No one would know the difference.

He'd still flirt with everyone in a skirt, with a special brand for me, and I'd still give him eye-rolling hell.

And I could cry in private, because it was going to hurt to tell him goodbye.

Tomorrow.

I'd have to do it tomorrow.

I couldn't keep doing this.

I parted my lips to take a deep breath, releasing it shakily.

Resigned to my plans, I cuddled deeper into my pillow, willing the tears that threatened to stay at bay. It would do me no good to cry right now. I could do it tomorrow after Grey took his things and left.

But when he reached toward me, pulling me into his bare chest, I nearly lost my resolve. The tears that had been a mere threat before were now burning behind my closed lids, threatening to spill.

And when he pressed his lips to my shoulder, the words he spoke absolutely shattered my soul.

"I love you, Brenna."

Chapter Ten

Stone

When I crawled into bed with Bren last night, I knew she'd been awake, but she put on a good game.

I didn't know what was going through her head, but her slight trembles and shaky sighs fucking killed me. I knew right away I shouldn't have stayed away so long.

Fuck. I shouldn't have gone in the first place.

When I woke, Brenna was no longer in my arms. I looked around the room, not noticing any signs of her but seeing the door to the bathroom closed. Focusing, I could hear the shower running.

I didn't have to be in to the pub for a few hours, but Brenna had an early shift. I could get in the shower with her, save water and hopefully save whatever was crumbling in our relationship, but I had a feeling Brenna wouldn't be completely open to that at the moment.

With a resigned sigh, I rolled out of the bed and pulled on yesterday's jeans.

"Brenna, you're not listening to me." I'd been trying to get through to her since the moment she stepped out of the shower. When it was time for her to leave for the pub, I refused to end our talk at the standstill where it was currently at. She fought it, but eventually allowed me to drive her in to work.

Not that we got any further in our standstill.

"We aren't telling them, Stone!" She pushed out the Jeep's door and my heart tumbled not just her hasty retreat, but by her calling me Stone.

She never called me Stone when we weren't at the pub, putting on a disguise.

"Brenna, it's been five fucking *years*!" I slammed the door after I exited the Jeep.

"If it's too much for you, then you can take your things and leave." She stomped up to the front doors of O'Gallaghers, pushing through them.

I had to quicken my step to get to her before she got into the back. If she did, that was going to be the end of this conversation and, potentially, the end of us.

I wasn't about to let that happen.

I didn't date her in secret for damn near five years, living with her for one of those years, for this to all just go and disappear.

I did it because I thought that, at some point, she would change her mind and be open to telling her brothers. I didn't think it would take this long, in all honesty, and it was beginning to look like Brenna would have kept it like this until we ran our course.

But I didn't have plans on our relationship 'running its course.' Oh no. This course wasn't ending for another fifty or sixty plus years.

"Brenna. C'mon, Angel, let me talk to you." I took the steps two at a time and caught her hand, sliding in behind her before the door could close on me.

"We're not telling them!" Her voice was lowered but definitely full of heat.

"Why, Bren? Why." I pulled her into a darker area of the pub near the dart boards. I noticed Rory by the bar and as much as I'd like to tell him I was dating his sister—shit, living with her—I was going to let Brenna do it. Or let her give me permission to do it. But fuck if it was going to take more than today to get there.

"Because I'm not ready!"

"When will you be, Brenna? Seriously. It's been five fucking years. I *live* with you!"

"Then move out." She crossed her arms over her chest and while her words were defiant, there was a world of sadness in her eyes.

"That's a cop out, and you know it."

"They like you, Grey." Thank fuck she called me Grey. "If they found out what we've been doing, what we are doing, they're not going to like you anymore. You're going to be out a job, friends..." She shrugged a shoulder.

"Who the fuck cares, Brenna? It's *you* I want. Not the pub. Not your brothers. I would think that was made clear by the fact I've played this your way for this long. I also think you're not giving your brothers enough credit."

"Grey—"

"No. I'm not done. Do you need to tell them about your biggest mistakes growing up? No. Should you tell them the real meaning behind your tattoo? Yeah. Yeah, I think you should. Do I think they've put you in a bubble and are a little blind when it comes to you? Sure do. But that's on you just as much as it's on them. You are one of the strongest, *feistiest* women I know; you could have stepped out of that bubble at any time."

She shook her head again. "You don't understand."

"No, Bren, I don't think *you* understand. You've fallen into this victim's mentality when it comes to your past and I understand where your head's been, but you have support. You have your brothers—if you let them in. But you also have me.

"God, Brenna. I am so over the moon in love with you, but I can't keep doing this. I can't love you in secret and pretend nothing is going on during the day, not when all I want is to put a ring on your finger and a baby in your belly." I stepped back and put my hands in the air, resigned.

"Can't do that in secret."

Again, Brenna shook her head. Or maybe she never stopped. "I can't right now, Grey." She looked defeated and while I hated I did that to her, I was glad I got my words out.

Now, to see how she would sit on those words. To see if she would accept them or pack my shit for me, because I'd be damned if I was moving out on my own.

Brenna

"Yo, Bren!" sounded from the other end of the bar. I looked away from Grey and his determined expression, toward the source of my name calling—Rory.

"What, Rory?" There was a bit of bite in my voice, but I was annoyed with the men in my life. Rory, for being his regular self, and currently Grey because he...

Well, because he loved me and that didn't fit in with the plan.

I pushed around Grey, needing the space but also needing to get ready for my shift.

"Leave the poor guy alone. What the hell did he do to you?"

I shook my head, mumbling to myself, "He just wants a little bit more from me than I'm ready for."

The earlier hours at the pub were surprisingly busy today and when Grey came on for his afternoon shift, I tried to avoid him. Well, as best as I could. We were working together for my last hour on the floor.

My thoughts last night about ending things with Grey, but everything being normal at work? Yeah, not sure how that was going to happen.

He refused to talk to me, other than when he and I had to deal with drink orders. He stayed on his end of the bar and I stayed on the floor.

Every time I glanced over at him and saw him flashing his smile at a woman, my heart cracked a little.

This is what I wanted.

I wanted to push him away.

Thankfully, I didn't have to think about it too much longer. I slipped into the back room when my shift was up, grabbing my purse and phone. When I left the office, I nearly ran into Conor.

He grabbed my arm, steadying me from my bounce back. "Hey, Bren. Mia wanted to know if you wanted to come for dinner."

I glanced toward the bar, then back toward Conor. I didn't have a ride home; I rode in with Grey. Besides, I needed a little bit of space.

"Yeah, sure."

When we got back to his and Mia's place, a squirming ten month old was thrust into my arms and my hair was pulled on, but the liveliness of the house had my spirits lifting.

I sat in the kitchen with Mia as she waddled around, her big baby belly getting in the way of everything. My heart swelled, watching my oldest brother put his hands on his very pregnant girlfriend's waist, putting her aside with a kiss on her temple, and telling her he'd finish getting dinner ready.

Conor fell into the domestic thing pretty quickly, but it fit him so well. He was a different guy these days than he was when he opened the pub. As much as Mia may have hated me when I threw the two of them together, forcing her to tell him who she was and that she was pregnant with this cutie pie sitting on my leg, I didn't regret a single moment of the piece I played in their getting together.

Mia, Aiden, and I moved to the living room where Mia sat on the couch and I on the floor with my nephew, rolling him a ball that he would promptly attempt to put in his mouth.

Aiden was all Conor. He had the same pitch-black hair that my brother and I shared, but also the startling blue eyes. He did have Mia's nose and chin, but there was absolutely no doubt who this kid's father was.

"Is Miss Ava getting ready to come out?" I asked, rolling the ball another time.

Mia groaned, putting her hand on the top of her large belly. "I sure hope so."

I laughed lightly and moved to my knees to crawl over to my nephew, scooping him up with one arm and moving back to sit. He giggled the entire time, his gummy, two-toothed smile wide and infectious.

God, I loved this baby and I knew without a doubt his baby sister was going to be just as lovely. I didn't envy Mia and her baby belly, no; I heard all too often how uncomfortable this pregnancy was making her, but the baby in my arms and the one who was due to make her appearance any day now?

They had flashes of blond haired, green-eyed babies in my head.

I never really thought about kids, not after losing Nova. Heck, even before I lost her, I never thought about kids. But being surrounded by babies and, damn him, Grey mentioning me having his babies...

The panicky feeling overcame my chest again, making it hard to breathe. I tried to keep it from Mia but the woman was incredibly perceptive.

"What's wrong, Bren?" She scooted to the edge of her seat and I didn't have a doubt in the world that if she could maneuver to the floor, and then get back up again, she'd be right next to me.

I shook my head, focusing on deep breaths. When I was sure I was going to be ok, I gave my friend a small smile. "Nothing. I'm fine."

Mia's eyes narrowed and I could tell she wanted to press, but thankfully, she let it be. "Alright well... I'm going to go check on Con. You good with Aiden?" With a hand on the couch beside her, she lifted herself to stand.

I fought to stop the grin from spreading on my face as I watched her. She was a fucking cute pregnant woman.

"We'll be fine." I turned Aiden so he faced me, having him stand on his chubby legs. "Won't we, boy-o?" He squealed his delight.

Once Mia left the room, I sighed and gave Aiden a small smile. "You're pretty cute, you know that?"

He bent his knees in a jump, and I allowed him to dip before pulling him back up to stand on my legs.

I glanced over my shoulder to be sure Con and Mia weren't within earshot. "What am I going to do about Grey?" I whispered to Aiden. He gave me a babbled answer. "Yeah, I know." Next, Aiden's hand went into his mouth. "You're tellin' me, buddy…"

I flipped him around so he sat in my lap, his back to my front, and reached for my phone. Regardless if I was putting distance between us, it would be rude of me not to let him know where I was. He was my ride to the pub and he'd likely expect me home tonight. I shot him a quick text that I was with Con and Mia, and that I'd be there for the night at the least, before turning my phone off. I didn't want to hear his response. Not yet.

Chapter Eleven

Brenna

I avoided Grey another day.

But I had a good excuse; Mia was having contractions throughout the day, so she and Con asked if I could stick around to help with Aiden in case they had to leave. The day didn't bring a baby, but there was hope that the night would.

At around three in the morning, Conor tapped me on the shoulder, effectively rousing me from sleep.

"I'm bringing Mia to the hospital."

I sat up straight on the couch. "Now?" I frantically looked around. Mia was by the door, a pained smile on her face, and a bag by her feet.

"You're still good staying here with Aiden?"

I nodded. "Absolutely. Yeah, sure."

Conor stood and pointed to the coffee table, where he put the video monitor. "He'll probably sleep for another three or four hours. I'll call you when it's go time. Mia's keys are on the hook; you can just take her car. Aiden's seat is already in it."

I smiled sleepily. God, this was exciting. I stood up and gave my brother a hug before moving to Mia, hugging her tight. "Go have a baby, Mia."

She laughed, hugging me back. "Thank you, Brenna." I could hear in her voice that her thank you was for more than just watching Aiden for the next few hours. I leaned back and gave her a smile.

"You are more than welcome, Mia."

"Someday you'll find your happy, and I can't wait to be there for you," Mia said, squeezing my shoulder. The squeeze got painfully tight as her face contorted.

"Shit, Mia, that's four minutes. We've gotta go."

Her face was still tight, her eyes shut, but she managed to hold up a finger for my brother. One second, she was saying.

I couldn't help but grin.

God, I loved these two.

Conor moved to grab their bag and wrapped an arm around Mia's back. "You let me know when you're good, Mia baby." I stepped away, giving them room, and after a moment longer, Mia nodded.

"Ok. Yeah. Let's go have this little lady." Mia smiled up at Con, who bent down to press a light kiss to her lips.

I had to look away.

What would it be like to have that?

Shit.

I had that.

And I, more or less, was throwing it away.

The anxiety in my chest was starting again, but I managed to hold it back until after I saw Conor's truck leave the drive.

God, what was I doing?

Five years ago, I met a man who made me feel things I hadn't in a long while before that point.

Four years ago, I took a chance and went on a date with that same man, a man who became a constant in my life.

Three years ago, one date turned to two, which turned into a once a week thing. We even threw a vacation or two in there.

Two years ago, we decided that the occasional date wasn't going to be enough, and we were at one or the other's place nearly every night.

One year ago, he and I decided life would be easier if he just moved in, like it was no big deal.

Cohabitation was completely normal. People did it all the time.

One day ago, I got scared because he told me he loved me.

So I pushed him away.

The only person in the world who knew all my secrets, knew all my faults, yet still fucking loved me. He loved me and I pushed him away.

When I looked at Aiden, I wanted something like him in the future.

When I looked at Conor and Mia, I was envious of their relationship.

But why?

I had what they had; I just refused to acknowledge it in person.

So what if my brothers decided he wasn't good enough for me, if they fired him and never looked at me again?

When did I get to start living my life, for me? When did I get to start loving my life, and let go of everything that held me back?

I moved back to the couch and picked up my phone from its spot next to the monitor. I looked at the monitor screen, making sure Aiden was still sleeping, before opening my text log.

It didn't surprise me that Grey never responded before. If there was one thing I was sure of, it was that I hurt him by walking away from his declaration.

If there was one thing he proved over the years, it was that he was willing to play things my way—but eventually he was going to stop playing.

Me: *Mia's off to have baby Ava.*

Not expecting a response—he closed and likely went to bed an hour ago—I turned off the screen and tried to settle back into sleep, knowing it likely wouldn't come.

I stared at the dark ceiling, my eyes tracking the slow moving fan as it whirled around in circles.

I didn't want to be alone. I didn't want the quiet.

I wanted laughter.

I wanted hugs, kisses, love, and I knew just who I wanted them from.

Chapter Twelve

Stone

I couldn't sleep.

It had been a long fucking time since I went to bed alone, or without the knowledge that Brenna would be coming to bed, to me, in a matter of hours. And to do it two nights in a row didn't make it any better.

It fucking sucked.

I lay in bed, my arms back behind my head and the sheets down by my hips, my ears open and listening for her. Surely she would come home tonight.

She wanted me to pack up everything and leave?

No.

I wanted her to come home and fight it out with me. There had to be more to her reluctance to tell her brothers her past, other than simply she didn't want to ruin what they thought of her. To hell what they thought of me! I could give two fucks if they decided they didn't like me simply because I was in love with their sister.

I didn't think they'd be too pissed, anyway.

Not with Conor becoming Dad of the Year, and Rory doing...whatever the hell Rory was doing with Emily.

There was a story I couldn't wait to watch unfold.

I sighed heavily and tried closing my eyes, even though I knew sleep wouldn't come. I tried counting sheep, counting backward from one hundred, purposely relaxing every part of my body, starting down at my toes…anything that I had been told worked for someone somewhere.

But all with no such luck.

I let my eyes open again, staring at the white ceiling. Two sleepless nights were no joke.

When a Luke Bryan song started wafting through the duplex, I frowned momentarily. It was Brenna's ringtone for texting.

Shit.

It was Brenna's ring tone.

I jackknifed off the bed and moved to the other side of the loft, where we kept the charging dock for devices. I picked up my phone and ran my other hand through my hair, thumbing open the message.

Angel: *Mia's off to have baby Ava.*

I started a response and erased it probably five times before I just pressed call.

As the phone rang in my ear, I walked back to the bed, hoping against all hope that she would answer. *Please answer, Bren.*

Just when I thought it was going to go to voicemail, where I'd at least get to hear her voice, the call clicked on.

"Hey, Grey." Her voice was unsteady, unsure.

"Hi, Angel."

There was a moment where neither of us spoke and I could hear her breathing through the line.

"Do you want me to come over?" I asked finally.

She took a moment to respond. "You don't need to."

She could be so stubborn. "Do you want me to come over?" I repeated.

"Yes."

It was whispered, but the single word packed a punch.

"Ok. Alright." I stood again and, holding the phone to my ear still, starting pulling out clothes to put on. "I can be there in ten minutes."

Ten minutes later, I pulled into the drive of Conor and Mia's house. I cut the engine and got up to the front door in record time. At three thirty in the morning, the little neighborhood was quiet, the only activity being maybe a plane flying overhead. Otherwise the night was silent, still.

I started to knock, not wanting to wake Aiden with the doorbell, but just as my knuckles hit the wood, the door was pulled open.

There she stood, in all her raven-haired beauty.

Her hair was loose and wavy around her shoulders. Add to that her bed attire of a tank and shorts, and her unsure face, and she looked tired in more ways than just from lack of sleep.

"Hey, Bren."

She stayed standing there, a hand on the door, staring up at me. I stayed put, waiting for her to tell me what had her pausing.

Finally, she said, "I'm sorry, Grey."

I shook my head. "You have nothing to be sorry about, Angel."

"No, I do," she said, shaking her own head. She stepped back, allowing me into her brother's home, and I took her hand in mine. I squeezed it once, and after the door was closed and locked, she led me to the living room.

We sat next to one another, her bare thigh pressed to my jean-clad one. I kept her hand in mine, not wanting to lose more contact.

"I'm ready to tell my brothers." She looked at me. "About us," she clarified.

I nodded. "Ok." I could take that. "Eventually, though…"

She shook her head, knowing where I was going. "They don't need to know, Grey."

I tugged her closer until she was sitting on my lap and I had my arms locked around her. "Their opinion of you is not going to change, Brenna. You are still their sister."

She dropped her eyes from mine, watching as she traced a finger down my chest. With her voice low, she said, "I don't want them to know. I don't want to open up that hurt again."

That I could understand. The night she told me about losing her baby, she definitely shattered in my arms. There were only so many times a person could do that and still find a way to put the pieces together again.

I took her chin in my fingers and lifted her face toward mine. "I do not judge you. You know this." I pecked her lips before finishing what I had to say. "If and when you decide to tell them, I *will* be there to help you pick up your pieces. You are strong, Angel. You can get through any of it."

She offered me a half smile which I gladly covered with my lips. We kept the kiss light and appropriate for our surroundings.

I wasn't about to make love to her in her brother's living room. Not happening.

"I love you, Brenna O'Gallagher," I said against her lips.

She pulled back this time, a hand on my face as she stared at me. She brushed her thumb over my lips, her eyes on the movement, before she shifted them back to mine. "I love you too, Greyson Stone."

My lips lifted on their own accord. "Yeah?"

"Yeah."

Before I could celebrate that news though, her phone chimed through the dark.

"Oh! It's probably Con," she said, scrambling off my lap. I took the moment to adjust myself, then stood to move toward her. "It's time. Oh good, it's time!"

"That wasn't long. We going?" I asked, unsure of what her plan had been.

She nodded, heading toward Aiden's room. "Yes. I just need to grab Aiden. Could you start the car? Mia's keys are on the hook."

I did as she asked, finding myself surprisingly excited to get to experience this with Brenna and her family.

Brenna

Just as we parked, Conor texted to let me know that Ava Grace O'Gallagher made her entrance. With a sleeping Aiden in tow, Grey and I made our way to their room. I was excited to meet my little niece.

Grey held Aiden against his side and had my hand in the other. I was anxious to walk into the room like this, I wasn't going to lie, but I was going to go through with it anyway.

"Congrats, Mama!" I said as we walked through the door, me leading my small pack.

"Thank you," Mia said from her perch on the bed, a smile on her face as she looked down at her bundle. But when her face lifted to us in the doorway, her eyes dropped to mine and Grey's linked hands, then back up to my face. Her own face dropped, her eyes wide and mouth open.

"Brenna O'Gallagher!"

Con, whose back was to us as we walked in, looked over his shoulder, frowning at Mia's outburst.

And then, to make the whole fiasco even more fun and exciting, Rory stepped into the room behind us.

"Guy uses the bathroom and comes back to squealing. What's going on?"

"Are you...?" Mia asked.

Grey's hand in mine tightened.

Support.

He was always giving me his support.

"Yes. We are," I answered.

Conor stood and Rory stepped around us to join him. Both had matching frowns on their faces.

It was funny how those two looked nearly nothing alike, but their expressions were mirror images.

"How long?" Conor asked, crossing his arms over his chest in that big, puffy way men sometimes got.

"Dude, they're holding hands. It's probably been awhile. Or else they'd have just walked in together." Rory, ever the thinker…

"We're not here to talk about Bren and me." Grey shifted Aiden in his arms, but the boy still slept.

"But let's!" Mia was giddy as all get out and I couldn't help but laugh lightly at her reaction. She should be tired after pushing out a baby but she was excited for me.

"And Bren's giggling. So maybe it's new. That's a new relationship sign."

I shook my head at Rory. He wasn't all that bright in the women department, which was probably why he had yet to secure Emily in his life.

I looked over to Grey only to see him looking at me. He was letting me decide how long. Because really…how long? Five years? That's when it started. One year? That's when it got seriously serious.

"Five years," I said, my chin rising.

"Five years?" Conor's face was contorted in confusion. "That was when—"

"Shit—" Rory started, but was interrupted by Mia yelling 'ears!', "You mean, every time I covered a shift for you so you could go out with a girl, it was with my *sister*?"

"Seriously. Five years?" Conor couldn't seem to get past that.

"It was casual for the first few years, yeah, but I moved in last year," Grey offered, putting all our cards on the table.

Conor's eye swung to mine and where I semi-expected anger, there was just confusion. "Why the secrecy, Bren?"

I shrugged. "I wasn't ready."

And I left it at that. They could too.

"I'm so excited for you, Bren," Mia said. "Come here and look at your niece."

What she really meant was she and I were having a discussion apart from the boys.

Grey let go of my hand and when I moved to Mia's bedside, he moved closer to my brothers. Con reached for Aiden and took him from Grey, cuddling him into his chest. The anxiety was back; I was afraid of what my brothers would say to Grey now that we were apart.

Unfortunately—or fortunately, depending on how you looked at it—Mia stole my attention.

"Would you like to hold her?"

I smiled at my once again best friend. She looked tired but absolutely radiant. When Mia handed me my niece, I cuddled her close and lowered my face down to her sleeping one.

"Hello, little lady."

"Tell me," Mia said, her voice low. I looked over at her, a frown on my face. She lifted her brows and moved her head to the side slightly, signaling the boys. "Tell me!"

She scooted over on the bed, patting a spot next to her hip for me to sit and face her. I did as she wanted, keeping the baby between us and my attention on Ava's face.

"I love him."

"Awww."

I grinned to the side and looked up at Mia. "I have my reasons for keeping everything quiet. I know that that's probably going to irk Con and Rory, but most of it is going to stay between me and Grey."

"Grey?"

I grinned. "Yes, Grey. I stopped calling him Stone in private a long time ago."

"I love it. Tell me more."

Chuckling, I glanced back down at the baby in my arms, running a finger down her cheek.

I held Aiden at this age, but holding Ava, a baby girl, was hitting me a little bit harder. I took a moment to compose myself before looking back at

Mia. "He's been my rock. I haven't always been the kindest. But he's been there, and he supports me. Heck," I said with a laugh, "he let me keep us a secret for this long. If I knew there wouldn't be fists flying, would I have been willing to share it sooner?" I glanced at the boys, who seemed to be more relaxed, if Grey's laughing was any indication. I turned my attention back to Mia and shrugged. "Maybe. But maybe not. Maybe the road we took is what we were supposed to take to get here. What's done is done and there's no reason to think about the what ifs."

"God, Bren. You're so fucking adorable." My eyes widened at Mia's swearing. She stopped swearing, at least in public, the month before Aiden was born.

Her eyes were misty. "I wish you would have felt comfortable telling me, but I understand why you needed to keep it to yourself."

Now I could feel *my* eyes getting misty. "Oh, Mia. Me keeping it from you had nothing to do with our past." Because that was where Mia was going with that comment. I knew it without a doubt in my mind. "It was more because I was afraid you'd tell Con."

Her laugh was a little watery. "Yeah, I probably would have."

Chapter Thirteen

Brenna

Just like we had done when Aiden was born, Rory and I had a fruit bouquet and a meat and cheese tray catered into the room while family and friends filtered in and out through the late morning and early afternoon to meet the newest O'Gallagher. When the crowd was dying and it was down to just my brothers and I, as well as Mia, Grey, and the babies, I started to clean up what was left.

Grey walked up behind me and brushed his hand over the small of my back before leaning down and whispering in my ear. "I love you."

I smiled.

It was as if now that he'd said it and I responded in kind, he couldn't stop saying it. And I, well…I loved it.

"I love you too," I whispered over my shoulder, smiling when he pressed his lips to mine.

"No making out in corners, kids," Rory said, pocketing his cell in his back pocket. "Shoot! That's what you were doing the other day, wasn't it? You too like a little heat with your sweet." He chuckled to himself. "Ha. Poet and I didn't know it."

Conor groaned, shaking his head.

"No, we were just fighting that day," Grey told him, picking up a pile of paper plates and tossing them.

"Sure, sure..." Rory shook his head and walked over, snagging the last cantaloupe and pineapple flower from the bouquet before I could put the remaining fruit in a container.

"Speaking of fighting," I said, putting the lid on. I stacked it with the other container of what was left of the meat and cheese before turning to my brother. "I heard you and Emily got into a fight."

Rory took a bite of his flower and shrugged a shoulder, chewing slower than necessary.

"Yeah, I want to hear what's going on with you and Emily!" Mia shouted from the bed. Conor sat in a chair adjacent to her, his socked feet propped on the bed and Baby Ava bundled and curled at his shoulder. Aiden slept in the bed next to Mia.

"There's nothing to tell about me and Em," he finally said after finishing—yes, *finishing*—the fruit in his hand.

"You were awfully cozy with her at the dealership," Conor offered.

"But she was upset yesterday," I added, looking to Rory. "What did you do to her?"

"We just got into a disagreement, I said some words, she said some words, which echoed some words Con said—"

"Don't bring me into this."

Rory gave him a pointed look. "I just said she had words that were similar to ones you gave me." He shrugged again and turned to the containers, opening the meat and cheese to grab a cube of cheddar. "AndImaybeamgoingtomakesomechanges."

The room was quiet, everyone trying to process what Rory mumbled as he popped cheese into his mouth.

Mia, bless her pretty heart, said what we all wanted to. "Say that again, slower this time."

Rory groaned and looked up to the ceiling. "I'm going to make changes."

"For a girl?" Conor asked, his face splitting in a huge grin.

"Yes, for a girl."

Rory went to toss a cheese cube at him but Mia put her hand up. "Sleeping babies. You hit her with that, you will be hit with the wrath of Mia Hampton."

Rory pointed at her, palming the cube as he did. "Good point." Instead, he popped the cheese in his mouth.

By this point in the conversation, Grey pulled me to a chair and into his lap. I was surprised at the ease I felt. While Grey and I weren't *new*, putting us in this kind of environment was, and I would have assumed I'd feel some sort of unease, but I didn't.

My oldest brother shifted in his seat at Mia using her last name and I glanced at him, watching him. It wasn't a secret that he wanted to change Mia's name.

Just like it wasn't a secret that it would happen eventually.

But I knew he wanted it done sooner than later. He was so in love with her.

He caught me staring at him from across the room and raised his black brows. I felt like he was trying to tell me something, ask me something, but I couldn't figure it out.

Finally, he nodded his chin down toward Ava. "Av and I are going for a walk." He took his feet off the bed and put his shoes back on, one hand on the baby's back at all times. "You want to walk with me, Bren? You can be my hands." Then he addressed the room. "Anyone want a beverage?"

"You can leave her," Mia said with a frown.

Conor gave her a crooked grin before bending to kiss her on the lips. "As her mama, you get her more than me. Just let me hold her for a little longer."

Mia smiled up at him and laughed lightly. "Ok, burly man."

He gave her one more kiss and rounded the bed. Grey patted my hip before I stood. I trailed my fingers over his shoulder and he took my hand when I was behind him. Pressing his lips to my knuckles, he let me go when Conor reached us.

Conor winked at me and slapped Grey on the shoulder in a friendly manner—it was still probably a bit harder than necessary—and walked with me out of the room, Ava still secure to his chest.

"Can't let her go, can you?" I asked my older brother, a big smile on my face. There was nothing like seeing him with his babies. He made such an awesome father.

His chuckle was quiet, his lips still pressed together, but Ava shifted on him at the slight movement. He turned his face into his daughter's and pressed a kiss to her forehead, walking with me in the otherwise quiet.

I pursed my lips in an action that was probably too duck face, so I quickly pulled my lips in. I sighed heavily as we walked to the open refreshment area. When he still said nothing, I stuffed my hands in my pockets.

Still, nothing.

"So," he finally offered the moment we reached the juice and water machines. "You and Stone. For five years."

Rather than feel the anxiety I imagined, I couldn't help but smile slightly at Con's voice. "Well, not really five years."

"That man back there has been dating you on the low for five years, Bren, regardless of when it was 'serious.'" He lifted his free hand to do air quotes and I couldn't stop my slight smile from filling all the way.

Conor wasn't an air quotes guy. Rory, sure, but not Conor.

"Why didn't either of you say anything?" One hand still on Ava, Conor opened a cupboard, revealing Styrofoam cups and lids. I reached in to grab them, knowing there was only so much he could do with Ava in his arms.

I shrugged, pulling down enough cups for our family. "I had some things I had to get over. Personal things."

I knew Con wouldn't be content with that answer. "Personal things? What, like all the rumors you lived through? Bren, you gotta know that none of that shi—stuff mattered."

I filled the cups, half with water and the rest with an assortment of the available juices. "It mattered to me. I wanted to make changes to who I was." I shrugged again, still filling cups. "For what it's worth, I said 'no' to Grey the first few times he asked."

"But eventually you said 'yes' and you still didn't feel the need to tell your brothers."

"I didn't want him to lose a job. O'Gallaghers needs a bartender like Grey, and that's not me being biased," I added with a pointed stare at my brother.

He let that go.

"But he's good to you." It wasn't a question; it was clearly a statement. I lidded a cup before looking at my oldest brother, the guardian of much of my youth, and took in his raised brows and concerned blue eyes.

I nodded once slowly and while my smile was much smaller, it felt like it had much more emotion behind it. "He's good to me."

"Then that's all I care about." Con opened another cupboard, taking down a disposable tray. I helped place the cups on it and when the task was complete, he and I headed back to the room.

Right before we reached the doorway, Conor stopped, his hand in his pocket and a frown marring his face.

"What's up?" I asked him, my back to the propped door.

His hand dug in his pocket for another second before he nodded, seemingly to himself. "Nothing. We're good."

Chuckling, I shook my head and pushed with my back through the door. "You're weird."

"Right back at'cha, Brenna."

Stone

I would have thought that the first time I was in the O'Gallaghers' presence after our announcement, with*out* Brenna, I'd have been uncomfortable to a degree.

Let's be honest. For as carefree as Rory sometimes acted, in the years I've known him, where his sister was concerned? He could be pretty fierce.

But it wasn't like that at all.

No, Mia and Rory joked with me like they did at the bar. Again, I found myself with Aiden in my arms, to which Rory took offense to.

"I'm the kid's uncle. You're not."

"Yeah, well..." I looked at Aiden and winked at the chubby ten-month old. "Give that a year."

Mia gasped. "Yeah?"

I shrugged, shaking my head at the same time. "Yeah. I'll give her time, though."

"Please not another five years."

I chuckled. "I said a year, Mia."

"Ah, yes. You did. Pregnancy brain."

"I don't know if you caught it, but pretty sure you *had* the baby already, Mi," Rory, ever the smartass, said.

"Fine. New baby brain." She stuck her tongue out at Rory. The teasing quickly turned to smiles as Brenna and Conor came back into the room. I stood to help Brenna with her full tray of drinks, giving Mia back her son, and taking the tray from Brenna to place it on the room's built-in desk.

Brenna, standing beside me, hugged me from the side and I wrapped my arm around her shoulders. "You good?" I whispered down to her. I could only imagine that her and Con's walk was more than just grabbing water and juice.

"I'm good," she answered, turning her smiling lips up toward me. I took the opportunity to kiss her lightly.

"Don't drop her..!"

Brenna and I collectively turned at Rory's voice, only to watch as

Conor shook his head, readjusting Ava in his arms.

"I'm not going to drop my kid. She's not the first one."

"You weren't supposed to admit you dropped Aiden, Con," Mia whispered from the bed. My eyes swept to her, only to catch her laughing and holding up a hand. "I'm kidding!"

"I wouldn't drop my kid," Conor grumbled goodheartedly. "Rore, can you take Aiden please?"

Rory's auburn brows rose but he did as he was asked. "Sure. Hey, kid. It's your *real* uncle," he said, picking up the boy from Mia's side. Aiden babbled and pulled at Rory's hair, making him wince. "Yeah. Alright. Watch the hands."

"I think she's hungry," Conor said, offering a very much sleeping Ava to Mia.

Mia lifted a brow but accepted the baby. "She's sleeping, Con."

Conor shifted after standing. "Well...she was fussing a little out there."

Brenna shook her head against my side, her arms still wrapped around me. "N—" she started, but Conor cut her off with a glare.

Yeah.

A glare.

Like, she would have been struck by lightning if she dare speak a word otherwise.

"I love seeing you so concerned," Mia said, her words laced with laughter. She glanced around the room and shook her head before looking back down at her newest baby.

"We should probably start to get going though, so if she does wake up, you can do... you know, your thing," Rory said, waving toward Mia. "I've seen your boobs one time too many."

"Rory!" Brenna exclaimed but Mia only grinned at him.

"Hence the extra locks," Conor said. "You guys should stay for a few more minutes." He seemed fidgety. I had never seen the man anything other than overly secure in his spot in the world.

"Knocking works wonders too," Mia told Rory. Then, looking down at Ava, she added in a smaller voice, "Doesn't it, baby girl?" She brushed her finger down Ava's cheek, down her neck, and over her shoulder. Her finger caught on something under the blanket though and she turned her face up toward the group then Conor.

"Conor…"

He nodded at her, then gestured with his chin toward her hand. Mia placed Ava on the bed between her legs, slowly unwrapping the swaddle Ava was in. I felt Brenna jump slightly against me. Her excitement was coursing through her and I couldn't figure out—

"Oh!" Mia said, just as Conor lowered to a knee right next to the bed, reaching for Mia's left hand as her right picked up a ring that was in the swaddling blankets.

"Mia Hampton. You've made me the happiest man in the world, not once, but twice. Heck, a hundred and two times. I don't have a pretty speech because frankly, I'm a little afraid you'll shoot me down again but please. Please, Mia baby, will you marry me? Take the same last name our babies have? Let me love you forever?"

While I wasn't privy to all the details, I knew that this wasn't the first time he had asked, but I was pretty sure this was the most formal time he'd popped the question.

Brenna let go of me, only to move around and stand in front of me, leaning back. I wrapped my arms around her shoulders, loving that her chin rested on my forearms.

"Yes, Conor." It was whispered but it was through tears.

Conor shot up from his kneel, leaning into his now fiancée and mumbled against her lips, "Fuck yes," before kissing her soundly. It was almost embarrassing to watch.

"It's about time," Rory mumbled.

"You're next," Conor said, pulling back from Mia with a huge-assed grin on his face.

Rory shook his head. "Nah. I've got some time. But those two..." Rory pointed at us. "You shoulda heard Stone. He's planning on—"

"Close it," I told him. It took me five years to get Brenna to admit to us as a couple in public. I wasn't about to throw a proposal on her without talking through some things first.

Brenna grinned over her shoulder at me. "You're planning on what?"

I kissed her temple and shook my head. "We'll talk about it later."

I should have realized she'd never let it be.

"What were you planning?" she asked when I got into Mia's car after getting Aiden. We were headed back to Con's house for the moment. Brenna's mom and dad were sticking around the hospital for a little longer but then would meet us at Con's house and switch guard of Aiden.

I couldn't wait to get Brenna back to our place.

God, I missed her there, what with the last two times I went to bed and she wasn't there.

"Don't worry about it," I said around a chuckle, turning the ignition. "I'll tell you later." I looked over my shoulder, pulling out of our spot.

I caught Brenna looking at me, her brows up, before she looked in the back where Aiden was already fast asleep.

"God, I hope I have kids as good as Aiden," she said.

"You want to have more kids?" I asked her, glancing over her.

She nodded, still looking at Aiden, before turning her attention back to me. "I do. Holding Ava was a little hard, but there wasn't any room in that maternity suite for sad feelings of things that weren't meant to be." She offered me a smile and I reached over to take her hand, squeezing it once in support.

She squeezed mine back. "Do you?" She paused, as if weighing the silence. "Want kids? I mean, I know you said..."

It may not have been something I thought about at length before

Brenna, but, "Yes. I do." I grinned over at her, winking once, before turning my attention back to the road.

"You know," she started, looking out her window. "Five years is a long time. And we *have* been living together for a year."

"Mmhmm." My lips tightened, the corners lifting.

"Maybe..." She glanced over at me then shook her head. "Never mind."

I let her have her silence, knowing without a doubt what she had on her mind—because it was on my own, too, and by the end of the day, I was going to ease her thoughts.

Chapter Fourteeen

Brenna

His hands roamed under my shirt, his tongue sweeping into my mouth. My own hands were fisted in his hair.

We made it back to our place a little bit ago and no sooner than walking into the duplex, Grey tossed me over his shoulder and headed for the stairs, carrying me up to the loft while I laughed into his back. Rather than tossing me on the bed though, he slowly dropped me to stand in front of him, my body rubbing against his deliciously on the way down.

"I love you, Brenna O'Gallagher," he said against my mouth, pulling back so he could lift my shirt over my head. I let go of his hair to allow him to do so. When it was off, I went to work on his jeans as he took off his own shirt. We undressed one another in hurried silence.

Still standing, he pulled my body close. I stood on tip-toe, my chest pressed to his, so I could pull his lips down to mine.

With our lips connected, he lifted me, an arm under my butt and the other banded around my back, and this time, brought me to the bed we shared—the one we spent many all-nighters in—to lay me down gently. I kept my arms wrapped around his neck, loving when he lowered his body to press mine into the bed.

I ran my toes up his calf slowly, causing his body to flex into mine.

His hard cock trapped between our bodies twitched and I smiled into his mouth.

"You like that, do you?" he asked, a grin on his own face. Pulling back and kneeling between my legs, he grabbed his cock in his hand and slowly stroked his length. "Do you want this?"

"Yes, Grey," I said, but two could play this game. I shifted slightly, just enough to spread my legs more, and brought my fingers to my core, rubbing a slow circle over my tight clit. "Do you want this?"

"Fuck yes, baby." He squeezed himself once more and went to bring his mouth down to me but I covered myself with my hand completely.

"No, Grey. I just want you right now. I need you right now."

He pressed his lips to the back of my hand. "I need to taste you, Bren. God, I've missed this. Missed you."

I couldn't help the smile. "It was only two nights."

"Yeah." He kissed my hip bone. "Two nights where I stared at the ceiling hoping you'd come back to me."

I pushed up onto my elbows, peering down at him. "I'm sorry," I said softly.

"Don't be." He moved up to kiss between my breasts, making me lie back down. "You needed time. I got that. I pushed you, I should have expected it." His arms caged me again as he loomed over me, his face directly over mine. "But I'm not going anywhere."

I smiled up at him, reaching to place both my hands on his now day-old scruffy cheeks. "Thank you for being my rock. For not giving up on me."

"Never giving up on you, Angel," he said quietly as he lowered himself, his mouth closing over mine. We did some of his favorite "naked making out" before he reached for a condom at his bedside table where the boxes had lived, and had been utilized, since we began this adventure.

Thinking about our earlier conversation, I put a hand on his forearm to stop him.

He wanted babies. I wanted babies.

We should probably do things in the correct order, but I wasn't anywhere near my fertile window, and I was protected in other ways.

"We don't...have to use one," I shrugged, suddenly slightly self-conscious. Immediately, my head went through all the times I slept with men, some safely and others not. "I'm clean," I rushed on to add. And I was. Thank goodness for that, with my history.

He lowered his reach to place his elbow on my side, laying half on me, half off. With his other hand, he brushed wayward strands of hair from my face, staring down at me. "Are you sure?"

I nodded. "I'm clean."

His face split in the crooked grin of his that was incredibly endearing to me. "Angel, I wasn't questioning that."

I sunk into my pillow, slightly embarrassed that that was where my head went. "Ok."

He leaned into me again, licking the seam of my lips before kissing them once, sucking on my lower lip. "I know bareback isn't a big deal to some people, but it's a big deal to me," he offered.

"I'm sure," I whispered against his lips.

He moved himself over me again, lifting one of my legs as I did the same with the other, wrapping my ankles at his back. With slight guidance from his hand, he thrust into me, rocking us slowly at first, our mouths fused and kissing as slowly as our bodies moved with one another.

Eventually the pace picked up though and with my arms wrapped tightly around his neck, I pulled myself close and pressed my open mouthed moans to his chest.

"Fucking...love...you," he said with each hard thrust in the mix of his short, quick ones. His hips moved against mine and I release my hold on his neck to hold on to his ass with one hand, feeling his muscle bunch with each quick thrust.

He rolled us, wrapping his arms around me this time, keeping me close and unable to sit up and ride him properly. With his feet bracing against the bed, he pounded up into me again and again.

I let out moans, most louder than the previous, as the feel of his corded cock continuously hit nerve endings in my pussy. I was so close.

With one of his arms banded around my hips and the other, my shoulders, I wasn't going anywhere. My open mouth was still pressed to his shoulder, my breaths coming out hot against his skin, the moisture from my breath mixing with his sweat. His grunts in my ear told me he was getting close too.

"Squeeze down on me. Squeeze, Angel. God, come all over my cock," he demanded between grunts.

I did what he asked, squeezing my muscles down around him, making the feel of him that much greater, sending me that much closer. Two, three, four more thrusts and my jaw dropped further and I fought to move my head to press my forehead to his shoulder. My moan as I came echoed through the duplex.

"God." Thrust. "Damn!" He thrust up into me one last time before his hot cum jetted inside my walls, his cock twitching and pulsing in me. "God, I love you, Brenna," he said against my ear, a shiver running through his body as his cock emptied.

Stone

Brenna lay in my arms, completely sated. I could do this for the rest of my life—love her, love on her, and hold her through the night.

Knowing what I wanted to do, I pulled away from her with a kiss and moved to the closet. Brenna sat up, holding the sheet to her chest for no reason other than the open windows in the place allowed a cool draft to circle through.

"What are you doing?" she asked as I went through a few of the boxes I had stashed back there, full of off-season clothing.

"Looking for something."

Before I moved in with her, I knew that this was the direction I wanted to take.

That Brenna was it for me.

Maybe it had been presumptuous of me, especially seeing as she hadn't allowed us to be in public for so many years, but I knew in my heart this day would eventually come. Finding what I was looking for, I took the ring from its box and carried it back with me, closed in under my fingers.

Brenna moved to sit against the headboard, watching as I returned to her. I tapped her legs and she folded them to her, allowing me to sit across from her. I kept one leg on the floor and the other folded between us, completely naked and not giving two shits about it.

"Brenna."

She turned her head and narrowed her eyes playfully at me. "Grey."

I grinned at her and held out my free hand for hers, which she placed in mine quickly. I squeezed her fingers, never taking my gaze from hers.

"You know I love you."

This time she grinned. "Yes. Yeah, Grey, I know. You know I love you, right?"

I lifted her hand to my lips to kiss her fingers. "Yes, Angel. I know." I kissed each finger before bringing our hands back down.

"I want to love you forever."

Her breath hitched and her fingers tightened in mine.

"I know you just got around to accepting who we are in public, but I'd love nothing more than for you to say you'll marry me. We can take our time; it doesn't have to be fast." I paused, actually fearful that she might say no.

But she smiled and there were tears in her eyes as she nodded her head. "Yes. Yes, I'd love to marry you, Greyson Stone."

My smile was the widest it had ever before gotten, I was sure. "Yeah? It's not too soon?"

Her smirk was cute and her words were mimicking. "It's been five effing years, Grey."

I chuckled, pulling her to me. She scrambled close, allowing the sheet to drop, and curled her body into mine.

"You did just get around to admitting us to your brothers, though."

"And they took it really well. I was worried for nothing." She traced her hand down from my shoulder to my closed fist.

Shit. My closed fist.

With a grin, I turned my fist upward and revealed the ring I had chosen for her two years before. I hadn't seen it in that time, but it was still as radiant, still as "Brenna" to me, as it was when I first bought it.

It was a simple square cut diamond, but the band had its fair share of the brilliant stone too.

"It's beautiful," she whispered, staring at my hand. I leaned back from her so I could pick it up, holding it between us. "It reminded me of you. In a sea of all things radiant, you stand out. You always have."

She smiled, then bit her lip. "Put it on me?"

"With pleasure."

Then I slid the ring on its rightful home.

Epilogue
Eight Years Later

Brenna

"Bren! Come on, we're going to be late!" I heard as I scrambled to get the baby's bag together. At some point today, Chris, our eighteen-month old, thought it would be a really good idea to hide the baby's diaper bag.

I still couldn't find it.

So rather than continue to search for the missing bag, I was putting together a new one. I just couldn't find...

Aha!

I closed the closet in the nursery after finding one of Mikey's favorite two binkies.

They were all the same, but for whatever reason, the boy fell asleep better with one of these particular two.

"Bren! Angel, come on. The boys are getting antsy!"

"I'm coming!" I hollered back, running down the stairs to our renovated farm house. We moved a little way away from San Diego, but still close enough that we could go in to the pub when needed.

These days, I did a lot of the business minded things, while Con handled more of a human-resources roll. We didn't need to both keep working at the pub; I could have left or he could have, but we both liked to keep busy. Grey had been the head trainer for many years, right up until we had Matt four years ago. He *asked* to be a stay at home dad.

Grey was not afraid of me being the breadwinner, something that had me laughing a time or two.

I had two boys with black hair and gray eyes, but I was pretty sure baby Mikey's hair was going to keep turning lighter. I wasn't destined to hold another baby girl and call her mine; Grey and I were done having kids and I was completely ok with the fact I was going to be a boy mom. Nova was my baby girl and she'd always be my one and only.

When I rounded through the mud room, Grey was standing in the doorway with the door propped open, grinning at me. "You find what you were looking for?"

"I had to pack a bag! I told you this." I lifted the bag to show him.

"Why?" Grey frowned, allowing me to step past him and into the garage where the Pilot was running and waiting for us.

"Because Chris moved the other one. My goodness, Grey, I'd think *you* had baby brain." I shook my head and got into the passenger side, setting the bag between my feet.

Grey got into the driver's seat and shook his head, his face amused. "Chris didn't move the bag, Angel." Grey chuckled to himself and put the SUV into reverse, pulling out of the garage.

"He did! It was near the car seat and then it was gone. You know how Chris likes to move things." It was true. Many a pair of sunglasses and shoes have gone missing since Chris learned to walk.

And he started at ten months.

That was a lot of missing sunglasses and pair-less shoes.

Grey, still chuckling, hit the garage remote and moved the car into drive, heading toward the Bay. "No, Angel. *I* moved it."

I frowned. "But…"

"You never asked if I knew where it was. You would have saved yourself a lot of trouble." Grey openly laughed at me now.

"You could have said something," I grumbled, crossing my arms and looking out the window.

Grey's hand wandered over and found its way to my thigh, squeezing gently. "You just said you were looking for something." The smile was still evident in his voice, the bastard.

"Mmhm."

Again, he laughed. "Now we have two. You know," he paused, and I could imagine him shrugging a shoulder. "In case Chris moves the one." I glanced over at him and he took the opportunity to wink at me.

He was mocking me.

The bastard.

"Mmhm," I repeated through tight lips, but I moved my hand to rest on top of his, intertwining our fingers when he turned his hand over to hold mine.

"So, Con doesn't know? You're sure Mia didn't slip?"

I shook my head, looking back at my husband. "No. According to Mia he's completely clueless. Just thinks we're meeting him at the pub for a quick lunch."

Trying to surprise my oldest brother hadn't been an easy feat for Mia and me. Most of our ideas, Conor seemed to figure out but for whatever reason, when Mia told him about today's lunch, he hadn't batted an eye.

He was going to be surprised to see our parents there as they were supposed to be on another cross-country trip, but likely more because Rory, Emily, and their son would be there. Caleb and Sydney Prescott, too. We still wanted to keep it intimate, so we kept our numbers low. There were also going to be ten littles running around, so we were trying to keep a pretty decent ratio of kids to adults. If we started inviting every employee and every close friend, the pub would be so full the littles would easily get lost.

"I don't know, Bren," Grey said, shaking his head. "I think he knows something's up. He was talking about seeing Rory and Emily."

I scoffed, shaking my own head. "No. I think he and Mia were talking about taking a vacation without the kids, and Scottsdale was the main idea."

"Either way," Grey retorted with a shrug, "it'll be good to see everyone. Hear any more news on the Prescott front?"

Caleb and Sydney didn't have family here, outside of Jonny and the team, and because of that, they did a number of family dinners with Conor and Mia. Their kids got along incredibly well with Aiden, Ava, and Ali, but they hit a terrible rough patch recently.

My heart broke for them.

I shook my head. "No, but they did confirm they would come out with the boys for a little while."

"Good. They need an hour or two away," Grey said, nodding.

When we heard the news, Grey and I sat up all night talking about what we would do if we were in their shoes. It wasn't an easy place to put yourself.

I glanced over my shoulder, checking on our boys. All three were zonked out.

I turned back around with a small smile on my face.

No, I couldn't imagine what Caleb and Sydney were going through, but I wasn't taking a single day for granted.

Stone

I pulled our Pilot into the back lot just as Conor and Mia were getting out of their truck, Aiden and Ava arguing as they hopped down as well. Little Ali climbed down quietly, reaching for her mom's hand the moment her feet hit the gravel.

After parking, Brenna took care of Mikey's car seat, hauling him in it, and I unbuckled Matt, lifting him out of the SUV and allowing him to run to his mother.

God, I loved calling Brenna that.

Wife, too. That was another favorite.

I walked to the other side to release a sleeping Chris from the confines of his car seat, hoisting him out and carrying the sleeping boy into the pub behind everyone else.

Brenna had placed the car seat with a still sleeping Mikey on a table, freeing her hands so she and Mia could pull a few of the lower tables together.

O'Gallaghers' opening staff was already in, which worked perfectly with the plan. Con would never guess something was off, that the girls had pre-planned for the pub to be closed until three, leaving the place available to us for a few hours.

I looked at my watch before heading toward Conor, who was helping Aiden shoot darts in the back. It was my job to keep him distracted.

Thirty minutes, and it would be go time.

Rory

We were soaring above the sky, just reaching altitude. It would only be a matter of minutes before the plane began its descent once again. I looked out the window to see if I could make out the lights of the towns below us as we flew through the dark sky.

It was a short flight home, only an hour, but Em hadn't thought she could handle sitting in a car for five and a half hours.

To be honest, I didn't think I could handle sitting in a car with her for five and half hours. She had to pee every twenty minutes. We would have never made it home.

I looked to my right, where my wife of a little over three years, curled up beside me. She pulled up the arm rest to her far side, so she could pull her feet on the seat beside her, and the arm rest between us so she could lean into me. With my arm around her shoulders, she slept against me peacefully.

How she fell asleep so quickly was beyond me. One of the first times she did, I was in the middle of a conversation with her, post-sex, and thought she'd gotten pissed at me.

Nope. She'd only been sleeping.

I grinned at the memory, then reached for her hand resting on my thigh. I let my thumb play over the rings there before reaching further over to place my hand on her swollen belly.

I would be forever thankful for the chance she gave me.

After I first got to Arizona to be with her, she and I fell into a very easy rhythm, which surprised me. I had never lived with someone other than my siblings and Emily and I hadn't had a lot of alone time in the months, year, prior to me arriving.

I helped her study.

I walked the dog—that we ended up getting some months after I moved down and in. Teddy was a Golden Doodle, more golden than doodle, who definitely favored her mama to me, but was a sweet dog all the same.

Emily graduated from her CRNA program at the top of her class. I was so fucking proud of her. When she was looking at jobs, we discussed moving back home but then a position opened at the pediatric hospital she'd been working at, and it was her dream position, so we stayed.

Which was fine.

O'Gallaghers ran fine without me there—because, low and behold, my sneaky sister had more up her sleeve than just a secret relationship. Girl was a genius in business.

Not that I'd tell her that.

I took my weight loss, muscle gain, and supplement knowledge to a new level, and started my *own* company. It was a move that I questioned, as all of my clients were loyal to the company I found them in, but the move turned out to be a great one.

Between the two of us, Emily and I were able to move to one of the better neighborhoods in Scottsdale and on the day we moved into our home, I proposed.

She said yes.

If you hadn't caught that part yet.

We made a baby that day; I would swear that was the day of Will's conception until the day I died.

William Alexander O'Gallagher was every piece of his mother.

Oh, he was a hellion. He had to get something from me other than the waves in his white blond hair, but he was definitely Emily in a little boy package.

Emily shifted against me and I looked down, seeing she was still sleeping. I felt the baby kick and soothed my hand over the spot before falling back into my reverie.

It probably wasn't the most *ideal* being away from my siblings and parents while I had my own family starting, but it was working for now. Two weeks ago, my parents came and visited Em, Will, and I, staying in the house for a week before offering to drive Will with them to San Diego.

Emily and I took Will on a plane once.

Yeah.

We weren't doing it again for another few years.

I grinned at the thought. I loved knowing I had years and years of happiness ahead of me. Sure, I knew life could change in an instant but I wasn't going to do anything to change the path Emily and I were on. Did we have our fights? Absolutely.

But more than anything else, we had love and the love Emily had for me?

It was fucking amazing.

Emily

When we landed in San Diego, we were met by my parents-in-law, who had our three year old box of mischief, Will, by the hand.

Will tugged on his Mamaw's hand until she let go, and he barreled his way toward us.

"Pick up your toes," I whispered with a grimace, seeing in my head him falling face first into the ground. It wouldn't be the first time if he did.

Rory chuckled beside me and rubbed the small of my back. I closed my eyes in brief ecstasy before Rory grunted. Opening my eyes, I knew what I'd witness.

Will launched himself at Rory's legs and now my husband was lifting him in the air, settling him in front of him as Will wrapped his little legs around Rory's hips.

"How's it going, little man? You be good with Mamaw and Papa?"

Will nodded. "Yes huh. I got a Paw 'trol toy. Wanna see?"

I ran my hand through his getting-too-long hair and we moved to meet up with Rory's parents.

"The drive was ok?" I asked them, even though I'd asked them the same thing the other day when they made it to their hotel.

"It was," Rory's mom reassured me with a smile before hugging me. "And the flight? How's this one holding up?" She put her hands on my ever-growing belly. I was thirty weeks but so ready to have this baby.

"Baby's well."

"Everyone's at the pub and waiting on us," Rory's dad said, breaking in. It was Conor's forty-third birthday, and we were having a get-together for it.

According to Mia and Brenna, Conor didn't know so that would be fun.

I reached my hand out toward Rory, who took it more than willingly. Then, as three, my little family followed Rory's parents.

Conor

My wife was up to something. She'd been co-conspiring with Brenna for the last few weeks and every time I'd ask or say I knew what was up, Mia promptly denied it.

"Bullseye!" the board's robotic voice said, and I looked down to see my boy doing a dance in his spot. He had no moves.

Chuckling, I ruffled his hair. "Good job, Aiden."

I let him be, checking on Ava at the pinball table, her almost-five-year-old sister Ali looking on. When she shooed me away with her hand, I grinned and joined Stone and his boys.

"They're up to something," I told him as I took a chair, turning I backward, and sat down. My eyes were on my wife and sister at the bar, whispering something to Jon, the cook who was working our opening shift a little later.

Stone, with a bored look on his face, just shook his head. "Those two are always up to something."

"Isn't that the damn truth," I mumbled.

Suddenly there was a lot of commotion.

I glanced over my shoulder at the sound of music playing from the kitchen and watched as my parents walked, in followed by...

"No fucking way," I said around a grin, standing. Remembering I was near my nephews, I grimaced to Stone. "Sorry, man." He just chuckled and stood but I didn't pay any attention to him from there. My kid brother was home.

We saw Rory and Em usually about once a year, but this was definitely a surprise. I walked over to them and pulled Rory into a hug, grinning and patting him on the back. "Hey, kid. What brings you back?"

My nephew Will wiggled from Rory's arms to be let down, scrambling to join Matt and Chris.

"Hey, Em," I told her next, leaning in to kiss her forehead. "You look ready to pop."

She smiled, her face absolutely lighting up. "Don't I wish."

"That baby's cookin' for another ten weeks. Don't jinx it," Rory said, pointing at me.

I chuckled but went back to my earlier question, "Seriously though. What brings you home?"

Then the commotion was at the front of the bar and I turned and watched as Caleb and Sydney Prescott and their brood of boys—seven year old Brandon, five year old Brody, and eighteen month old Brooks—came through the doors. My friends looked tired but the fact they were here instead of where they likely had been before?

Something was definitely up.

Before I could question it, the music changed, this time to fucking Happy Birthday.

I turned in a circle, taking in my family and friends before my eyes landing on my wife, standing by Brenna. I playfully glared at her and stalked toward her. The music was loud, and everyone was singing, but it didn't stop me from leaning down at talking in her ear, "I told you no birthday shit."

She smiled up at me, that beautiful fucking smile that still knocked me in the gut after ten years. Rather than coming up with an excuse, my sassy wife just smiled and pulled my face down, pressing her sweet lips to mine.

"Happy birthday, lover," she spoke against my lips.

I smiled against hers. "Thank you, Mia baby."

Mia

Our time was wrapping up.

I was happy with how things turned out. Brenna and I managed to surprise Con, something I wasn't sure was possible.

I looked around, taking in our family and friends, seeing everyone so happy.

Even Cael and Sydney had smiles on their face, as Sydney had a sleeping Brooks on her lap, her chin resting on his brown hair, while Caleb sat with his hand on Sydney's thigh. Brody and Brandon were playing with Aiden, but it didn't miss my attention every time Cael or Sydney's eyes lingered on one of their babies longer than normal, and the fact one of them wasn't well enough to be here.

My heart broke into a thousand little pieces every time I saw Sydney look at my girls, knowing that I couldn't help fix her hurt. That nothing I could do, nothing Con could do, could help their family.

I liked to think that this helped, getting their family out and moving. It was probably hard, but I hoped it was at least healthy for them.

Before tears could burn my eyes, I moved to my husband, hugging him from behind. He angled his body, so he could reach behind him, curling an arm around me and bringing me to his side.

"Thank you, Mia," he said, bringing his lips down to my ear, the beard he still wore to this day, tickling against my ear.

"For?" I snuggled into his side.

"Everything, Mia baby. Everything."

HOT HOLIDAY NIGHTS

Dear Reader:

This holiday novella takes place the holiday season after Rory finds himself on Emily's driveway in Arizona. Due to some spoilers in regards to All Night Long, Hot Holiday Nights *needed to be released 'last' as to not give away one of Brenna's secrets.*

I hope that those who enjoyed Rory really enjoy him now, and those who felt Rory and Emily's "happily for now*" wasn't enough for this couple...*

I hope this eases that for you.

xox Mignon

Chapter One
December 22

Rory

"Grrrr-UH!"

My head jerked up at the sound of distress coming from the living room, quickly followed by something heavy thumping down on what I assumed was the coffee table. I saved the e-mail to my newest client as a draft, and moved from my lean-to against the counter to my full height—checking behind me to make sure the water on the stove wasn't boiling over—before calling out.

"...Em?"

I ran a hand through my hair, missing its once pony-tail length. It was still longer—a good two or three inches in length—but I kept the sides short these days.

Turning the heat down on the burner, not wanting to burn the rotini I had going, I cautiously walked into the living room of the house I moved myself into about seven months ago.

I had to admit, I'd been a bit surprised that Emily allowed me to just drop my shit in her rental, further allowing me to stick around, but I rolled with it and in all honesty, this cohabiting thing was the shit.

Had someone to talk to every day. Someone to watch stupid movies with, even when she groaned the entire time.

And I do mean *the entire time*.

Someone to sleep with every night.

That one took a few weeks to work up to, but eventually I stopped sleeping on the couch and moved my ass into her bedroom.

At her request, I'd like to add.

Sex was still off the table, but Emily was warming up to the idea. I mean, it wasn't like my last performance was all that stellar; of course she wanted to work up to the idea again.

Twenty five months was a long fucking time to go without sex—I was pretty much a born again virgin. But I would relive every one of those days again, knowing that I would eventually get to this spot, right here.

I walked through the large archway all the houses in Arizona seemed to have, into the living room where Emily was sitting on the couch, cross legged, with her elbows on her inner thighs and her head in her hands. Stepping into the two foot area behind the couch, I crossed over to stand directly behind her and put my hands on her shoulders.

She was fucking tense as hell.

"What's up, Em?" I squeezed her shoulders, digging my thumbs into the knots that had formed there.

She answered, but with her head down and in her hands, I didn't catch a fucking word. I refrained from chuckling, instead gently putting a hand to her forehead and pulling her head back. "Say that again?"

"I don't fucking *get it*!" she yelled, kicking a leg out at the table. This time I couldn't stop the laughter from passing my lips if I tried.

This wasn't Emily's first studying temper tantrum since I moved in. The girl was smart as hell and beat herself up when she didn't grasp a concept the first time she read it, but even I knew that she'd sleep on it tonight, and like magic poofed and fucking pixie dust sprinkled around her, she had the shit memorized in the morning.

She jerked away from my hands, no doubt because I was laughing at her. "You're a jerk," she pouted, reaching for the large book she must have thrown down. She finished uncrossing her legs, both feet on the floor now, as she reopened the large textbook and picked up a pink highlighter.

I leaned over the couch, moving my hand until it was surrounding the mass of blonde in a half-assed knot on the top of her head, gently pulling her back. When she hit the back of the couch, I kept gently pulling until her head rested on the top, making her stare up at me.

Her clear blue eyes looked tired and she had slight bruises under her eyes. She hadn't been sleeping this week. She was tired and free of makeup and damn if she still wasn't the most beautiful woman I had ever come across.

I let go of her hair, putting my hand back on the couch and leaned down, pressing my lips to her upside-down ones. "Take a break," I said against her mouth.

Emily first kissed me at a Halloween party under the ruse of our costumes, and you bet your ass I ran with that shit. This whole living together thing when we weren't really dating but weren't completely friends had had the potential to get awkward fast but it didn't.

I moved in, plopped my ass on the couch, and showed her, up close and personal, all of the changes I had made in the previous year and a half. Three weeks of being a constant for her—feeding her, helping her study, cleaning the place up so she had less to worry about—and she offered me half her bed. Then, when one of the guys I met at the gym, Matt, invited me to a Halloween party at a trendy bar in Scottsdale, telling me if I had a girl she was more than welcome to come too, I maybe coerced Emily into attending with me.

...and by coerced her into going to the Halloween shindig, I mean I came home with a couple of costumes and told her she was going or I was burning her books.

I wouldn't actually burn her books, but the girl needed a break. Her nose was in a book all of the time. I completely understood it. I mean, I read some of her texts over her shoulder and the fact she was acing her classes impressed the hell out of me. But I was just a guy with a business sense and marketing strategies. Medicine and pathways and whatever hell else she was studying went way over my head.

I had to deal with her mumbling and grumbling over costume choice for two full days after I brought them home, but she was too busy to come up with something different, so we arrived to Matt's party as Batman with his sexy sidekick, Robin.

She made a really fucking sexy Robin. Red corset pushing her tiny tits up, making them look bigger than they were; short green skirt that cut up high on her hips paired with thigh high black lace stockings, making her mile long legs seem longer...

Shit, she nearly killed me—or at the very least, kicked me out—when she saw the ensemble but she did it. But oh-ho, the joke was fucking on me because there were more men at that damn party than women and all their damn eyes were on her. And when some douched muscle head started hitting on her, Emily just turned toward me and laid one on my lips.

Claimed me in the sea of testosterone.

So like I said, I wasn't letting that one go and I've been kissing her ever since. If only we could do more of that when between the sheets...

"I'm going to kill someone the first time I administer meds," she mumbled against my lips. "And you want me to take a break."

I grinned crookedly against her mouth and stood up again, pushing her head up gently. I dug my fingers into her knot, finding the hair tie, and started to unwind her hair. I learned over the last few months that the regular circle hair ties were the devil, but these fabric things with a tied knot on the end were great.

Emily could only wrap it around her hair twice, too, which made it easier to take out.

Her hair free from the confines of her knot, I gunshot slung the tie across the room—earning me grumbling—and finger combed her hair. I'd always been slightly obsessed with Emily's hair and it certainly didn't get any better once I had access to it.

"Take a break," I repeated when my fingers got to the ends of her blonde tresses. "Your book's not going anywhere."

"But I have a test when we get back from break!"

"Yeah, in two weeks." I let go of her hair and walked around the couch, pushing her book away from her and closing it again. "It's winter break, Em. Take the holiday off."

"But—"

I put my fingers over her lips. "Emily." I lifted my brows, staring her down. "Take a break."

"I—"

My lips curled up and I shook my head. She just couldn't stop. "How 'bout this. You have plans for New Year's Eve?"

"You know I don't," she said against my fingers, causing electrical currents to shoot down my core, my cock twitching behind my zipper. I wasn't sure if I should take my hand away from her mouth and shake out the tingles in my arm, or keep my hand where it was and beg her to do it again.

Even though we were living together, and hell, catching z's together, we were pretty much just glorified roommates.

Who kissed and slept together.

It was a different situation, that was for damn sure.

"Well neither do I." I plopped my ass down on the coffee table, finally moving my hand from her mouth. "I propose," I started, taking a dramatic pause for effect, "that we stay up on the New Year's and study. Put the books aside until the thirty-first, Em, and I will study with you for hours, welcoming the new year." I smiled, pretty damn happy with the plan.

Hell, during her two week break I was going to be getting a lot of one-on-one time with her and I was pretty damn happy about *that* too. No distractions of work or school. This could work in my favor.

When she stared at me, not giving me an answer, I lifted a brow. "You know you like studying with me. Admit it."

I watched as she fought her smile. It ticked up in the corner and she pushed it down, only for it to curl up again shortly after. "I guess that would work."

"Good." I slapped my thighs and stood. "'cause we're heading to Flagstaff tomorrow and your books aren't allowed to come. Merry Christmas." With that final statement, I went back to cook her dinner.

Chapter Two

Emily

Flagstaff? Tomorrow?

The muscle between my eyes was tight and I focused on relaxing my frown before standing and following Rory into the kitchen. "I thought we were driving to San Diego?"

When Rory moved in, I wasn't entirely sure what was going to happen between the two of us. We were friends but more...but still not quite *everything*. He was surprisingly easy to live with and he held up on his end of the bargain, or what he offered when he begged for me to allow him to stay.

He cooked, he cleaned, he grocery shopped. He put the toilet seat lid down and replaced the toilet paper. He even did my laundry, *and* hung my bras and laid out my shirts that needed to dry flat. We did everything that couples did but have sex and I was pretty sure that was going to be happening sooner than later—sooner if I had a say. There were only so many nights I could go with him wrapped behind me before I decided to take him in his sleep.

It didn't appear that Rory was going to be making any moves. It looked like his 'big move' was the literal move of relocating. *I* had to kiss him first. I had to offer him half my bed.

Apparently I was going to have to undress him, too. That was ok; I had a plan.

With a silly grin on my face, I shook my head mentally. Not only did he help around the house, but he helped clear my mind of everything else because just like that, worry over a test I had in two weeks was pushed to the back of my mind.

It was still there, but it was no longer the forefront of my thoughts.

I knew I was a bit of a freak about studying but this degree was a big deal to me. Yeah, the job came with a lot of zeroes behind the dollar sign, but more than that it was a career that I knew would keep me on my toes. While I didn't want my hands literally *in* a surgery, I liked the idea of helping out during traumas and run-of-the-mill surgeries.

"We *are* going to San Diego," Rory said, his back still to me as he futzed with the stove top. I sat at the high top style kitchen table and watched him. His back muscles flexed under the fabric of his shirt and I wished I could put my hands on them. Unfortunately, we weren't to that point in our relationship...friendship...whatever you wanted to call it. "But first, we're going to Flagstaff."

"What's in Flagstaff?" I reached up to gather my hair but when I went to put it in a high bun, I realized I didn't have my hair tie on me. *Dammit Rory*. I let my hair go and twisted it in a long coil, rolling it and twisting it into a true knot at the base of my head.

"Snow."

"So we're going to stop in Flagstaff on the way home for Christmas, for *snow*."

"Mmhm." Rory took the pot off the burner, shutting it down. He brought the hot pot to the sink to drain the water and I lifted my chin up to try and see what type of noodle was in the pot. Rory was pretty consistent with what he cooked.

Marinara only went with spaghetti or angel hair noodles. Alfredo or pesto only went with fettuccini. Macaroni was, obviously, mac and cheese, but Rory baked that. And rotini was buttered noodles.

Rory made a lot of noodles, but I didn't have to cook so I wasn't complaining.

Looked like buttered noodles it was tonight.

"When did you plan on telling me we were making a stop on the way?"

He transferred the noodles into a large bowl and walked to the fridge, pulling out an entire stick of butter. My eyes widened in fear he was going to use the full stick.

Only half went in.

Only half. I smiled to myself; because that was so much better.

"It's just a night, Em." He stirred the noodles and butter, the movement bringing my attention to the muscles corded in his forearm. The very first weekend he was here, we went up to Sedona and did the tourist thing, it had been a lot of fun! Shortly after that, the man tattooed the red rocks on his arm, saying tattoos were meant to be personal and that it signified a big life event for him. It was hard not to look too far into that. I mean, I knew his intentions; he hadn't been quiet about that when he scared me in my garage last spring but hearing him say things like that did things to a girl, you know?

"Thought it would be a nice change," he finished, turning to his spice rack—yes, *his*, because I didn't do much beyond salt and pepper—and grabbing two glass jars. "It was meant to be a surprise but..." He didn't measure the spices as he put them in.

Surprise, my left foot. Rory would be more upset if his "surprise" was ruined.

"I see," I answered, a small smile on my face as I nodded slowly. Rory had something more up his sleeve, but what? "So what time are we leaving?"

"Probably ten?" Next he went into the fridge, pulling out a shredded white cheese mix.

I really enjoyed Rory's buttered noodles. Garlic, salt, cheese...the works.

"Hey, can you do me a favor?" he asked as he finished mixing everything together and grabbed two bowls. "Double check the reservation." He tipped his head toward his laptop.

He totally had something up his sleeve.

I stood and walked over to the counter where his laptop was set up. On the screen was an email to a client and it gave me warm fuzzies inside. Arizona was a big fitness place so it was definitely the right place for him to work on his own brand. He'd been doing extremely well the last few months and I loved listening to him get excited about it. The best parts though were when he got excited for his clients' victories. Rory was no longer the self-centered guy he was two years ago; just another reason why I was glad I decided to give him his chance.

"Where am I going?" I asked, my hands poised over the keys.

"Just my email. Double check that that email is saved though first then in search, find 'confirmed trip.'" He started splitting the noodles into two bowls and I did as he asked. When the confirmation email appeared, I didn't click into it, simply saying, "It's there."

He looked over at me before bringing the pot to the sink. "Open it and double check the time?" I swore I caught a cocky grin on his face as he turned his head away from me.

Although my eyes narrowed, I did as he asked. Quickly, the email loaded and soon the screen was filled with what had to be the most gorgeous one-room cabin I had ever seen.

"Oh my gosh," I whispered, leaning into the counter.

I scrolled through the email, taking in the pictures. Nestled in the pines with a panoramic view of the always snow-capped Humphreys Peak was a tiny wood cabin. It looked cozy and warm, with its cute little wrap-around porch and on the inside, a large bed, a tiny kitchenette, and giant whirlpool tub.

It was incredibly romantic.

Maybe I won't be the one to initiate sex after all…

I startled when Rory's hands came to my hips, holding me in place as he rested his chin on my shoulder. "Merry Christmas, Em," he whispered before running his tongue up the shell of my ear. After a quick nibble on the top, he stepped away, leaving me wanting more.

I wasn't even sure that we were walking the fine line between friends and lovers any more. I was pretty sure we took the step over but were simply being cautious with the next leap.

"You're going to relax tomorrow night," Rory continued as he brought our bowls to the table. "And then you're going to spend Christmas Eve with your family relaxed, and Christmas day with my family, relaxed. You can go back into frantic mad-woman mode on the 26th, but not a moment before." He turned toward me with his arms crossed over his chest, leaning back into the table. "And it would be preferable if you waited until nine or ten in the morning, but I'd understand if you went all Cinderella and her pumpkin on me and busted out your study guides at midnight."

I laughed lightly. "You said no books and that we would study on New Year's Eve."

Rory lifted a brow. "Em," he deadpanned. "You have that shit on your phone."

He had a point, and he proved he knew me well. "I'll wait until midday," I said. "I'll try anyhow." I could put aside my studies for three and a half days. I could.

Before I pushed away from the counter and Rory's laptop, it dinged with a notification. Rory jogged over in a comical, over-exaggerated way, and leaned around me to see. Why he didn't move me out of the way was beyond me but I liked these little moments.

"Gotta close up my clients for the holiday," he mumbled, both his arms around me as his fingers played over the keyboard and touchpad, opening up the latest notification.

The email opened; it was an ordinary email and I wasn't about to be nosy so I wasn't going to read it, but as soon as the page fully loaded, showing a picture at the bottom of the page, my eyes dropped to it.

Who was sending Rory pictures?

And of...

Puppies?

"Fuck," Rory mumbled behind me, slamming down the top of his laptop. I frowned over my shoulder at him. An email, pictures of puppies, and that reaction? What in the world?

"Let's eat," he said, not elaborating on what the heck just happened and instead, tapping my hip and walking toward the table.

"Rory?" I walked slowly toward the table, climbing into my seat.

"Spam," he said, looking down at his bowl as he grabbed a napkin from the center of the table. He picked up his fork and took a giant mouthful of noodles. "There's some Trojan going around right now with pictures. Heard about it yesterday."

I nodded once slowly, trying hard to contain my grin.

Sure, Rory...

He was a terrible liar.

"Don't you think we should talk about pets before you actually go and get one?" I asked him, seeing right through the man's bull.

His green eyes stared through me as he chewed. He was thinking really hard and it made me a little giddy. We were getting a puppy! It was one of his argument points when he first arrived out here; I should have known it was going to happen sooner or later.

Cabin retreat, puppy, going home for the holidays...

A girl could get used to this treatment.

"I knew you'd get excited and want one, but the woman only had one and Con asked me to pick the pup up on the way to San Diego. It's for the kids. We'll pick her up after we leave your parents."

My excitement fell. "Oh," I said, my fork playing in my noodles. "It's probably not a great time to get a dog anyway." I speared a noodle and smeared it around the bowl, scooping up any seasonings that stuck to the sides. "Maybe in the summer. Not that summer semester is any lighter than the regular school year."

Rory's socked foot found my shin under the table, where he lightly kicked me twice. "We can leave our number with this lady and maybe the next litter we can pick one out."

I nodded a few times, bringing the seasoned noodles to my lips. "Sure." I closed my mouth around the fork, hoping that we could be done with that conversation. I didn't know why I was so disappointed.

We were living together, but it was my name on the lease. We kissed and hugged and did couple-y things, but we weren't really a couple. I guess maybe getting a dog would feel like a step in the couple-y direction. A semi-long-term type commitment.

Seven short months ago, I left Rory—a co-worker slash friend—and San Diego behind, intent on starting a new life with bigger dreams and aspirations than I had ever set out to accomplish before. Then he was here, asking to prove that he could be the commitment type and pretty much on a whim, and totally out of character, I gave him the chance.

And now I wanted some sort of sign that long-term was doable with this man.

Maybe it was because I knew who Rory had been. In the past, he wouldn't wait even two days to take a girl to bed. Him waiting the weeks I put him through had been a big deal for him. Now, not only had he grown up and showed he could be a real live adult, he waited *twenty-five months*—and counting—to take what we had to the next level.

Me going that long without sex was no big deal, but Rory? The man who had been a man-whore two years ago? I guess maybe I was comfortable with our arrangement but feared that he would get antsy.

I liked what we found together over these last few months. I liked the comfort and the ease, and I wasn't entirely sure what I would do if he decided that Arizona—that I—wasn't enough for him anymore.

"We'll get a dog, Emily," Rory said around a chuckle, taking another bite of noodles. "But let's get you through your first couple of semesters first, 'kay?"

Chapter Three

December 23ʳᵈ

Rory

Emily had been in a mood last night after I told her the dog was for Con and Mia's kids but what was I supposed to do, tell her her entire fucking Christmas present before the actual holiday? I chuckled to myself as I zipped up the large duffle we were both using for clothes. She was so predictable.

"You ready?" I called out. She was in the bathroom packing up our toiletries in a separate bag. She was in a much better mood this morning but even if she were still pissy over the dog, I was sure that the moment we hit snow up north, she'd be happy again. Because who the hell didn't get excited over snow?

"Did you want the green or blue bottle of Axe?" she replied. I grabbed the overstuffed duffle and walked toward the bathroom, dropping the bag to the floor and stepping into the small space. It was tiny and really couldn't fit the two of us, but I found I liked small spaces with Emily. She was currently standing outside the standing shower stall, glass door wide open, as she considered the bottles in the hang-up caddy.

I stepped right behind her, keeping a small distance from her body. I loved the way her tall, willowy body aligned with mine and my cock twitching under my jeans wasn't ever shy to tell her, so I kept my distance. "Green," I answered.

She leaned into the shower, stretching in and thrusting her ass out toward me and I fought a groan. I wanted nothing more than to run my hand up her back, around her side, down her front...

But I was taking my damn time with her. I waited this long—after royally embarrassing myself—I could hold myself back until she was completely ready to take this to the next level.

I wasn't going anywhere.

Even if I teased myself mercilessly in the meantime.

She stepped back and into me, stumbling and reaching a hand out toward the glass door jamb to steady herself. "Rory!"

I helped steady her by grabbing her hip with my hand. "Sorry," I said chuckling. "I thought you heard me come in."

"I did," she said, turning in my arms. Her upturned face brought her lips so incredibly close to mine. I could lean in, take the sweetness that was presenting itself...but I want going to. Not yet. "I just didn't think you'd be that close." She stepped around me and put the bottle in the bag holding all our other bathroom items.

"We need a bigger place," I answered, hoping it came off in a semi-off-handed manner. Like the puppy, I was trying to give her some long-term items in hopes she'd be willing to take the next step.

"Maybe when I graduate in fifty bajillion years," she grumbled as she zipped the bag.

"Less than two, actually."

She turned her head toward me, her face twisted in amusement. "You're keeping track?"

"For when you get out of the terrible twos and temper tantrums? Fuck yes," I joked, reaching for her hips and pulling her in, easing the jest with a quick kiss to her lips, finally taking a fraction of what I wanted.

"I'm not that bad," she said against my lips.

"Oh, Emily." I shook my head, pulling my head back but keeping my hand on her, sliding it to her lower back. She was currently in leggings and a long-sleeved t-shirt of mine, allowing me to still feel the dips and grooves of her lower back and spine under the cotton. In the matter of a few hours, she'd be in a bulky sweatshirt. I had to get my feels in while I could. "You are that bad."

I let my hand linger at the small of her back, fighting the urge to slide it down and cup her ass.

Emily was so fucking cute when she pouted. "It's an expensive program—"

"To fail, yeah, I know," I finished for her. "But you're not going to fail. I shouldn't have even brought it up," I chuckled. "We aren't supposed to be talking your classes right now. Right now," I said, pulling her close, this time allowing my body to rub up against hers, enjoying the feel of her pressed against me. "Right now we're getting in my truck and driving north." I was sporting a semi and refrained from rubbing myself against her hips the way I ached to do. I didn't need to be hard and driving. It would be a long assed drive in that state. But leaving her in an uncomfortable state...

Hell, if it got her closer to taking the next step with me, I was all for it.

Giving myself the go-ahead, I dropped my hand to her yoga-firmed ass and squeezed the globe before smacking her gently. "Let's go."

And before I could give in to anything else—like lifting her on the counter and grinding myself against her opened core—I grabbed the bag from her and left the tiny room.

Chapter Four

Emily

"Wake up, Em," came from my left as a hand shook my leg. With a yawn and my arms stretching in front of me, I opened my eyes to a white winter wonderland.

"Oh my gosh," I said in awe, fully awake now. I leaned forward, bracing a hand on the dash, as I took in pines and trees surrounding us. Rory was still driving but had slowed as we climbed what I assumed was the mountain side. "It's so pretty."

Rory chuckled from the driver's seat, taking his hand off of me. Immediately, I missed the contact. "I figured you'd want to see some of it before we got to the cabin. We're about a mile out."

"Did you know," I asked, still in amazement as I looked out the windows, "I haven't actually ever stepped foot in the snow? My entire family is in southern California and my parents never had any desire to travel north." My voice did little to hide my awe at the sight surrounding us.

"I did not know, no," he answered, both hands on the wheel as he glanced over at me. "Happy I could do this for you then."

The remainder of the drive was done in silence as I took in the snow around us. It was absolutely beautiful. Snow in trees, snow on the cabins.

There were cabins with Christmas lights strung and smoke puffing from chimneys. We hadn't even made it to ours, and already I wished we had more than a night here.

With the click of his truck's blinker, Rory turned into a small drive, heading toward the cabin that was ours for the night. Like some of the others, this one was decked out with white lights. I couldn't stop the grin from spreading across my face if I tried.

"I'm so excited," I whispered, sitting up straight in my seat. Rory laughed lightly beside me, putting the truck into park.

"Time to relax, Emily girl," he said, turning the key out of the ignition. He quickly jumped out of the truck and rounded to my side, opening my door before I had a chance to break from my stupefied state and unbuckle. He reached for my hand and helped me down.

"Before we go inside," he started, his hand in mine but not pulling me into him, "I do *not* expect anything tonight. I just wanted you to relax away from home."

Two years ago, and I would have thought that was a line. But now I knew Rory better, or rather, Rory had changed and I knew without a doubt he was speaking the truth. Besides, what was the difference between us cuddling in my bed, versus in a romantic secluded cabin in the woods?

He may not be expecting anything to come of this little side trip, but I most definitely was. Call it his Christmas present...

"Thank you," I said, smiling up at him as I thought of my plans. I straightened my legs just enough to bring my lips up to his, brushing them over his lightly. "Let's see this place."

Rory really had this entire night planned.

About an hour ago, a catered dinner arrived to the front porch, left only with a knock. Before Rory could open the door to retrieve it, the delivery person was roaring back down the drive.

In the few hours since we arrived, Rory and I built a snowman and drank hot chocolate on the wrap around porch, wrapped in warm clothes and a single giant blanket that huddled us close. And that was just outside, the first hour we were here.

Inside, he had built us a fire and we currently rested on the oversized couch, Rory lying back with me between his legs and against his chest. My ponytail loosened from using him as a pillow, but I didn't care enough to fix it. Everything was comfortable and sweet, but I knew more than anything that I wanted *more*. I was sure that Rory wasn't going to make the next move but I was more than prepared for it. I didn't have any fancy gifts for him, nothing that could even compare to a romantic hideaway cabin in the snowy woods, but I had a feeling that what I planned to give him tonight would more than make up for it. I just had to be certain I knew where he was standing first.

"Are you happy with Arizona?" I asked, breaking the silence around us. I kept my gaze fixed on the fire, listening for the crackles at the same time as listening to Rory's even breathing below me.

His arms tightened around me. "Couldn't be happier."

"You made friends quickly so I'm sure that helps."

His arms stayed tight around me and he rubbed his perma-stubbled chin over my temple lightly. "Only friend I need, right here."

I laughed to myself lightly, shaking my head but still burrowing back into him. "Sure, Rory."

He turned his lips in and while he didn't dispute the comment, I did feel his lips turn up into a grin as he pressed them over the spot his chin was.

"Surely you miss your family though, right?" I mean, heck, *I* missed them.

This time he pulled his face away from mine so he could crook his head to look at me. "What are you getting at, Em?"

I shrugged a shoulder, shifting against him so I could angle my body and look at him. "I just wanted to be sure that your rash decision to move to Arizona was…going the direction you wanted it to." He more than proved himself to me, but I just didn't understand why he didn't try and pursue a sexual relationship with me. Was he interested in another woman? I didn't think so, not really, but when a guy and girl were living together, *sleeping together*, one would just assume other things would be happening in that bed other than fully clothed cuddling.

His green eyes stayed locked with mine, but the stare down didn't feel uncomfortable in the slightest. After a grand pause, he finally said through a serious face, "I would do it again."

"Yeah?"

"Yeah."

He stared me down again and with his eyes looking so intently in mine and his hands locked over my hip, I knew without a doubt he spoke the truth. But it still didn't sit right with me, the fact he hadn't made any advances sexually. With as hard as he pursued me before, one would think that *surely* he'd find a green light in there somewhere.

I needed to know why.

I pushed myself up, hearing him grunt when I elbowed his stomach in the process, and blurted, "Then why won't you sleep with me?"

Rory pushed himself up to a sit, one leg falling over the side of the couch. "What do you propose I've been doing in your bed every night, Em?"

He could be so frustrating.

I crossed my arms over my chest, a mix of hurt and pissed off that I wasn't aware I was feeling. "Don't be a smartass, Rory. Why won't you fuck me? Is that better?"

Chapter Five

Rory

I will be the first to admit that I love riling Emily up. I love pushing her buttons until she explodes. It was a game when I first met her, trying to get her to warm up to me, and now I just liked to see the woman flustered.

But even I knew that there was a time to push buttons, and now really wasn't it. Still though, I had to push one. Just one.

Looking up at her as she sat there, crooked and on a hip between my legs, I pushed myself to sit up. "What do you propose I've been doing in your bed every night, Em?" I've been sleeping with her. And it was fucking torture, but I was doing it.

Emily crossed her arms and a mix of emotions crossed her face, telling me that I should have stuck with my gut and not pressed this particular button. Someone wasn't feeling very much like joking at the moment.

"Don't be a smartass, Rory. Why won't you fuck me? Is that better?"

If I hadn't already sat up, that would have done it. *Fuck her*? She wants to know why I won't *fuck* her? How about because I was falling in lo—

Woah there. Slow your jets, Rore. Let's not let that cat out yet...

I could feel energy coursing through me and I wanted nothing more than to pace it off, but I was going to sit my ass right here and make her face what she just said.

"One," I started, holding a finger between us. "When we get there, it will not be *fucking*." I may have sneered the word.

No, I definitely sneered the word.

"Two." A second finger joined the first. "I thought we established we were, *I was*, doing this different with you. I'm proving to you that I can be a good guy, someone you can count on and rely on. Me *fucking you* right out the gate certainly wouldn't prove that."

It had been a long time since I'd gotten so easily heated over a discussion, but I could feel it happening. Were all my efforts the last few months—the last fucking *two years*—for naught?

"And three—" I folded my index finger down, holding up my back three fingers. Before I could come up with something on the spot, because I had nothing, Emily threw her body forward, knocking me backward and causing my head to hit the wall behind the arm of the couch.

"God*damn*," I mumbled, reaching for my head, all while Emily lay over me, her laughing face buried in my shirt. "Yeah, yeah, laugh it up," I said, feeling a smile try to break out on my face.

Emily pushed herself up, her hands in the center of my chest, with hair falling all around her. Half was still in a loose, low ponytail, and the other half had wrestled itself free. Her face was split in a huge grin and I couldn't help but think she was freaking beautiful.

And she was afraid I wasn't happy in Arizona, just sleeping beside her?

Shit. I'd do it again and again.

I mean, I might have to revise my statement in a few more months—a guy had needs and two years was already a long fucking time—but I would not trade the last few months for anything. Sure, Arizona brought me new success in business but again, I had Emily to thank for that too. She opened my eyes and I fought to find a different pathway.

Her face still smiling, she reached a hand out, cupping the back of my head where I'd hit it against the wall. "You ok?"

My own grin was crooked and I shook my head. "I'm fine. Thanks for the concern." Her fingers gently scratched over the spot, slowly and mesmerizingly. My eyes started to feel heavy, but I wasn't through with this conversation.

Gently, I took her wrist in my hand and pulled her hypnotizing fingers from my hair. I pressed my lips against her knuckles before placing her hand back next to the other. "I haven't *done the dirty* with you because I need you to know that I'm in this for the long haul," I finally answered. While the phrasing was done in jest, the sentiment was serious. "That, and I might still be a little bit embarrassed," I added with a wink, feeling an immense need to lighten up the mood again.

With a heavy sigh, but still a smile on her face, Emily seemed to accept that. "Ok. For what it's worth, you've proven yourself a hundred times over." She leaned down to peck her lips against mine before pushing away and standing. "I'm going to change for bed."

I glanced at the clock. Shit, it was eight already. I sat up fully, swinging both my legs over and resting my wool socked feet on the floor. Turning my head, I watched as Emily walked over in her own wool socks to the giant bed where our bags were sitting. My eyes cut over to the whirlpool tub that I may have fantasized about—not the tub, the actions in the tub—when booking this place a few weeks ago.

In all honesty, I'd been hoping we would have gotten to the sex part of our relationship by now, but it was looking like a lot of the features of this place would go wasted. Still though, Emily seemed the most relaxed I'd seen her in the last few months, so I could at least chalk most of this night up to a win.

With my own heavy sigh, I stood just as Emily stood, clothes close to her chest, as she moved toward the bathroom. "I'll be out in a minute."

I nodded. "Yeah, sure." The door closed behind her and I walked to our bags, pulling out night clothes from the duffle that held both mine and Emily's clothing. I stifled a yawn, not realizing how tired I was until now. When I had what I wanted, I took the clothing bag and placed it on the settee at the end of the bed and grabbed the second bag with our toiletries, walking it toward the bathroom. I'd just leave it outside the door to bring in when I changed.

I knew Emily's night routine so I was a little surprised she didn't grab at least her face wash but maybe she wasn't planning on going to bed yet. It was a little early, after all. I'd be cool hanging out on the couch a little longer. There was a TV that we could watch. Not once in the hours since we arrived had it been turned on, but maybe it would be a good way to ease through the night hours.

Surely there was a Christmas movie showing. I'd stomach through the corniness if it meant holding on to Emily a little bit longer outside of bed.

I rapped my knuckles on the bathroom door. "Toiletry bag is out here, FYI." Emily mumbled something in response that I didn't catch, and I moved toward the couch once again. Tossing my lounge pants and long-sleeved tee on the table, I plopped down on the couch, fishing out my cell from my back pocket for the first time since arriving. I double checked my emails, sending an appropriate response to one of them, and quickly shot off a text to Con, asking—again—if he and Mia needed us to bring anything when we arrived. Not waiting for a reply, I shut down my phone and tossed it on the table beside my clothes.

The fire was starting to dwindle, so while I waited I put a few more logs on. Shit she was taking a long time. And she hadn't even opened up the door to grab the other bag. What the hell was she doing in there? Getting herself off?

I chuckled to myself and sat back on the couch, closing my eyes as I thought about Emily leaning against the wall, one leg propped up on the bathroom sink counter, and her long fingers between her folds. She'd have her other hand on a tit; girl liked her tits played with. One time with her and I knew that for certain.

I imagined Emily dipping her fingers into her pussy, gathering the moisture there and bringing it up to her tiny clit, where she'd move the wetness around and make a sweet, slick friction. The more I pictured it, the harder I got under my jeans. My cock was digging into my zipper, begging to be let free.

The last time we were together, I hadn't had the pleasure of tasting her. Definitely was rectifying that the moment she said go.

And just like that, that was where my mind went.

Me in that bathroom, on my knees between her spread legs. Her foot resting on my shoulder now rather than the bathroom counter. My mouth up against her, my tongue—

"Rory?"

I sat straight up, startled out of my daydream, and looked over to where the bathroom door was now open but Emily wasn't anywhere to be seen.

"Yeah?" I croaked out. Clearing my throat, I stood and adjusted myself, knowing there wasn't a whole lot I could do about the major bulge in my jeans. "What's up, Em?"

"Can you come here?" Her voice was coming from the confines of the bathroom so I made my way in that direction. After crossing the few feet of space, I pushed the door open the rest of the way and damn near swallowed my tongue.

Where the fuck was the sweatshirt she brought in here? I saw a fucking sweatshirt against her chest. And her short-assed boxer shorts. Where were they?

My eyes were glued to her; I couldn't sweep the room and find them if I tried.

I did try though—really fucking hard—to keep my eyes on hers, but I couldn't stop myself from dropping my gaze. In front of me, in the probably the most sexy fucking get-up I had ever seen in my thirty-two years, stood Emily. She had her hips cocked to the side and a hand in the dip of her waist. A black see-through triangle did nothing to hide her nearly bare mound and her top half was covered by the same material, the flowy hem of the teddy she wore moving slightly with her deep breaths. Further up, her chest was covered with a less see-through material but there was no padding, allowing me to see just how turned on she was in this non-outfit.

Finally, my eyes finished traveling north, taking in her bottom lip between her teeth—was she unsure of my reaction? Because *shit*, my reaction was most definitely positive—and her eyes watching me take her in.

And then her hair. Her beautiful fucking blonde locks, were long and loose down her back, begging me to gather it in my fist.

"*Fuck*," I finally breathed out.

Chapter Six

Emily

After staring at my reflection for what seemed like hours, I still couldn't get up the nerve to walk out of the confines of this bathroom. I was tempted to say screw it and throw on my actual pajamas, but I *knew* Rory wanted me. Even without the questions I spewed out at him, I knew it. I mean, his body wasn't exactly great at hiding it.

But Rory was good at keeping his distance.

After pretty much getting the go-ahead from him, I decided that I was most definitely making my move tonight. When I packed my items earlier, I threw the black teddy set in on a complete whim, making sure to hide it in a bulky sweatshirt just in case Rory would move items to put his own stuff in the bag.

With a deep breath, I consulted my reflection before cracking the door open and calling out for him, my gaze back and locked on my reflection. I sucked in my top lip in thought, battling the urge to throw on my clothes.

"What's up, Em?"

His voice was still far enough away for me to change my mind. I could do it. I could change my mind.

But what the hell? This wasn't the first time I gave in to an urge where he was concerned and I'd be damned if I was backing out now.

The man wants you, Emily.

And good intentions, be damned. I was going to have to make this move.

With a nod toward my reflection, I turned my body toward the door. "Can you come here?"

I crossed my ankles then decided that made me look like I had to pee. I crossed my arms, trying to push up when minimal boobage I had, and decided that that was doing nothing for me. Finally, with a hand on my waist, I popped a hip and waited.

I bit down on my lip, nerves racking through my body.

You're on the same page, Em. Even if he didn't want you—No. He wants you.

I licked my bottom lip, nervous, and bit it again. Waiting. Waiting.

And then he was there.

And he was staring at me.

And staring more.

My heart pounded in my chest. Was this the right move?

I watched as his green gaze dropped and took me in, inch by slow inch, until finally his eyes locked with mine. "Fuck," he said on an outward breath. Still, he made no move toward me.

Inwardly I groaned. What the hell happened to men taking the initiative in these things? And while I loved that Rory had made changes in his life, every now and then a girl needed a man to take control of the situation. In that regard, I kind of wish the man whore that was once Rory would show up. Just for tonight. And maybe for forever, so long as it stayed in my arms, my bed, my life.

Before Rory, I had my sexual encounters. High school puppy love, college boyfriends. Drunk sex, sober sex. Around the time I started at O'Gallaghers though, I had been so focused on school that finding time to be with a man was nonexistent.

Sure, Rory had taken control of that first kiss, that first semi-time, but it was probably the only time I had had crazy, uninhibited sex. That vixen wasn't someone I thought I had in me, but I proved it once—I'd prove it again.

I dropped my hand from my waist and walked toward him slowly, barefoot, my eyes locked on his. With my toes next to his socked ones, I lifted my chin the slightest of inches.

"I want you," I whispered brazenly. I stretched upward to press my lips to his stubbled chin. "Take me."

Chapter Seven

Rory

I didn't need a brighter green light.

I'd been waiting for this day for a long fucking time, and I was taking what was being offered.

My white hot Emily.

I reached my hand out, cupping the back of her neck, and held her where she was while I dropped my chin and took her lips. Prior to Emily, I loved fucking with chicks much shorter than me but Emily was damn near perfect for me.

No. Not damn near.

Just was.

Her tall, willowy body. Her tiny waist and sharp hips. Her barely there chest.

I wouldn't trade any of them for a fucking second.

Her mouth parted under mine, allowing my tongue the access it probed for. With my arms wrapped around her and my hands on her ass—and they were on her *ass*; this get-up included a fucking thong—I kept her pressed close, no longer caring if she felt my arousal against her.

I ground my hard cock against her all while kneading the cheeks of her ass, swallowing the little mewls she made. I needed to feel her naked against my own skin though.

I moved us backward and Emily, completely with the program, kept up in the movement, not once breaking the seal of her mouth over mine. Backward, I walked us toward the bed, occasionally stumbling over feet or haphazardly placed shoes but damn if that didn't make the moment that much more real.

There was no true preamble. Nothing like any other woman I'd been with.

But damn, that was just Emily.

Last time, I took her kisses quickly and freely, leading us to the next step. Just like the then, she and I went from zero to sixty in two seconds flat and I'd be damned ok if that were the way things were whenever we got together.

Maybe slow down eventually but hell, thirty was the new twenty; we could keep this up for a few years yet.

When the back of my knees hit the mattress, I sat and pulled Emily down with me, twisting us until she was on her back, our mouths parting.

But of course Emily wasn't having any of that.

Immediately she sat up and reached for the bottom of my sweatshirt, tugging it upward. With her hands working the front, I grabbed the back and lifted it over my head, grabbing enough of the material to ensure my under tee came with it. My hands went to the button of my jeans, slipping it through the hole, but before I could lower the zipper and step out of the denim, Emily pushed me back and was straddling me.

She brought her nails down my chest gently, causing my abs to suck in when she reached the bottom of my six pack, and leaned down to restart our kiss. Her hair was all around us; I could smell the sweet spice of her shampoo intermixing with her arousal.

God I needed my mouth on her pussy.

I hooked a leg around hers and forced her to her back again. I pressed one more kiss to her lips, lingering, before pressing kisses down her neck, between her tits. I rubbed my chin over the sheer fabric. When my stubble snagged, Emily grabbed my hair and lifted my head up.

"Don't ruin your Christmas present," she said around a mischievous smile.

"It's a damn good Christmas present," I said, pushing up again to press my lips to hers a moment before resuming my position. "But if it's mine, I want it off you."

"I've only had it on ten minutes," she pouted but still, that glint was in her eyes.

"Do you want to wear it again?" I spread her knees and kneeled between them, gently moving up the lower part of the teddy to expose her stomach. Placing open mouthed kisses over her stomach, I moved them until I was at her navel, dipping my tongue into the slight divot.

"Maybe one more time," she whispered.

Chuckling, I sat back on my folded legs. With my jeans partially unzipped, the position had my cock fighting to free itself from my pants but first...

First I was freeing her from the confines of all that lacey goodness.

I reached for her hands and pulled her up to sit. Immediately her arms went around my neck and we were kissing again, tongues fighting for dominance, lips fighting for the upper hand, or rather, the sucking of the lower lip—the best damn lip to suck on. Emily's legs bent and she wrapped them around my thighs, pulling herself close to me. I fisted my hand in her long hair, tilting her head back so I could kiss her more comfortably. My tongue plundered in her mouth, momentarily forgetting what my current end goal was.

But then her hands were in the top of my briefs, her fingers brushing over the head of my cock, and I was quickly reminded.

I pulled my hips back from her. "Uh-uh. No."

She had the nerve to pout. "But—"

"No, Em," I said, pointing at her. "No. We're doing this right this time."

And that was the last I was talking about my embarrassing miss last time. Emily was not getting near my cock until I was ready to sink in her. God only knew how excited it got around her and her pretty mouth.

Carefully, because she had ideas of wearing it again, I removed the teddy from Emily, tossing it back over my shoulder as I took in her chest. Before I could get my fill though, her arms were back around my neck, her mouth fighting to find mine again. I gave her the kiss she searched for but then dropped my lips to her shoulder and with an arm around her back, lowered her back to the bed.

Again, I moved my kisses down over her collar bone and over her sternum but this time I stopped in line with her tiny mounds. Her nipples were pebbled, begging for my mouth to play with them. I angled my head to take one of her slight breasts into my mouth, sucking the whole of it in and pressing my tongue flat over the erect peak. I grazed my teeth back gently, keeping the scrap gentle as her nipple popped from my mouth. Below me, Emily moaned. It wouldn't be long...

I turned my attention to the other side, this time suckling on her tit, altering pressure on her nipple. Her legs moved restlessly under me and her fingers dug into my lower back. She pressed her chest up into my face, begging for more without actually asking for it.

I shifted between her knees, allowing myself room to put my hand between her legs. The lace there was soaked. Pushing the fabric aside, I ran my finger up her wet slit, lingering at the swollen bud at top, and moved down to sink two fingers up into her. I turned my hand up, crooking my fingers inside her and pushing them in and out of her in time with my suckles up top.

"Oh, my God, Rory," she moaned breathlessly above me. She slid a knee up and the other fell open as I continued my slow glides in and out of her, letting my fingers pull even slower over the area of the rumored G-spot.

Just before I could push my fingers back in and restart the process, I could feel her body start under me. *Found it.*

Now, to focus on that spot. I pressed my palm to her mound and let my fingers stay dug into her, only moving the tips of my fingers over the spot that caused her body to react. Slow, slower, quick. Slow, slower, quick.

Her pussy was so fucking wet; I couldn't wait to slide in and out of the slick confines. But first, she was getting off. She was almost there... Just about there.

I bit down gently on her nipple and flicked my tongue over the very tip.

"Oh... Oh my..." Her hands were in my hair now, fisting tight, and her hips were moving impatiently, trying to find her release. I quickened my fingers and bit down just a little bit more until finally her body was quaking under mine.

She shouted my name and arched her back, her hips pulling away just slightly. Keeping my mouth on her tit, I looked up and took in her long, graceful, exposed neck. Fucking beautiful.

And fucking mine.

I released her nipple, licking over the hurt, but kept my fingers in her wet, pulsing heat, loving the feel of her body milking them all while she grew warmer and wetter. I pushed up the slight distance to take her mouth with mine, pressing easy kisses to her lips until she lifted her lids.

Her pupils were dilated, the icy clear blue nearly a stormy gray. When her eyes were on mine, *that* was when I pulled my fingers completely out, bringing them to my lips.

The part I'd been waiting a long damn time for.

Well, part of it anyhow.

I sucked the two digits in my mouth, licking off every bit of her with my tongue. After, I sealed my mouth over hers and thank God, she participated. Her mouth was open again, taking in her essence off my tongue and not at all put off by it, if her actions were any indication.

Again, her hands tried to find purchase below my waist.

With a laugh—who the fuck knew you could laugh during sex?—I pushed back to my knees yet again. "Keep your hands to yourself, Em!"

"Then hurry the frick up and undress yourself," she told me, and damned if she didn't growl the words. My girl was antsy.

Yeah, well, so was I.

Screw redeeming myself. I just needed to be in her, loving on her.

Chapter Eight

Rory

I pushed myself off the bed and quickly shucked my jeans and briefs to the floor, my cock out and ready to play. I gripped myself near the base of my shaft, giving my cock a long pull. I wanted nothing more than to sink right into her heat, right now, but first…

Condom.

Shit.

Everything in me paused. If we couldn't do this because I wasn't prepared…I'd fucking shit bricks. Turning on my heel, I found my wallet near our bag. Surely there was one in there. It might be expired though.

Fuck. It would totally be fucking expired. It had been two years since I got any. Hopefully though…

"In my makeup bag," piped up from the bed. I looked over my shoulder at Emily, on her side and pushed up on an elbow as she watched me. With her bare top and those barely there bottoms, she looked like an angel.

I cocked a brow.

The outfit, packed condoms…

She was totally planning on this.

"You knew…"

Her smile was wide and she sat up, crossing her legs in front of her. Her hair fell over her chest, hiding her from me, but that was ok. I could deal.

For now.

"What? That I had to kiss you, and had to invite you to my bed, so I was going to have to obviously go the next step? Yeah, I had thoughts. Now hurry up, Rore."

Bless my girl and her planning.

I pulled the toiletry bag close and found her makeup bag inside, unzipping one of the compartments and hoping against all hope that it was the right one. There were so many zippers on this thing.

Sure enough, nestled inside near brushes and mascara was a good handful of condoms. Woman came prepared.

I grabbed them all and walked back to the bed, ripping one open and dropping the others to the ground, sheathing myself quickly. I crawled back over her until I lay beside her on my side, a hand on her stomach and my lips to her shoulder. She turned on her side, facing me, and placed her hand on my cheek.

"Merry Christmas," she whispered around a smile.

"Merry Christmas, indeed," I spoke into her shoulder. I pressed another kiss there before rising above her yet again. Back between her knees I kneeled, this time with the intent of pulling off the now drenched lace from between her legs.

I tugged and she lifted her ass, allowing me to pull them down. She brought her knees up and I fully pulled the lace off, tossing them somewhere along the floor to reside with the lost teddy. Who the hell knew where? Not me, not when Emily dropped both her legs open, exposing her glistening pink folds to me.

I tasted her on my fingers but I needed my mouth on her. It was one thing I hadn't been given the last time we were together and I was damn well taking it now. At least for a moment.

I ran my fingers up her slick folds, the very tip of my middle finger playing along the underside of her clit.

"Rory…"

Emily's eyes were closed again and her hands were fisted in the sheets.

"You want more of that, Emy?" I nearly choked on my tongue with the stutter of her name but she did nothing to correct me so I let it go. I flicked my finger over her clit again and she groaned.

"Rory…" she said again. "It's sensitive."

Not wanting to hurt her, I moved my hand so the pad of my thumb covered her, pressing lightly then rolling. "That better?"

She moaned her approval and with my thumb on her, I rearranged my body to lay between her legs with a prime viewing spot.

I breathed her in. Even if I didn't know how wet she was, I could smell her and it was fucking intoxicating. I pressed a kiss to her inner thigh, then her other, before moving my hands to hold down her hips.

Then, with slow precision, ran the flat of my tongue up her folds, the tip of my tongue circling her clit. Again I did it. And again. Until finally I sucked the engorged bud into my mouth.

Emily's hands moved from the sheets to grip my wrists, keeping my hands in place on her hips. I was cool with that. My hand already discovered her. It was my mouth's turn and damn if I wasn't enjoying myself.

Wanting to give her clit a reprieve, I moved my mouth back down to her pussy opening, dipping my tongue inside and lapping up her wetness. I sucked on her pussy lips, moved my tongue over her, then dipped my tongue back in. Quick little thrusts with my tongue all while breathing her in.

Her nails were digging into my wrists. Wouldn't be much longer now…

But I needed to feel her coming around my cock. I deprived myself of that last time with my prematurity—Goddamn, I wasn't going to remind myself of that—so before I could let her find her release, I pulled my mouth away.

I fished one hand out from her grip so I could guide the head of my cock to her entrance, coating the head with her slick juices before nudging myself right. There.

I took her hand in mine and, as I lay over her, thrusting deep into her warm envelope in one long push, brought our hands up to the pillow beside her head, my fingers interlocking with hers.

Her open mouthed moan echoed my own. She released my other wrist, putting that hand on my shoulder, and I took the opportunity to put my free hand under the small of her back, angling her just enough...

Good God, she felt like heaven.

I wanted nothing more than to blow my load now, but I'd be damned if that was happening. Not again.

Granted, Em seemed to be looking for a repeat performance so I guess it wouldn't be too horrible.

I could feel her heart pounding against my chest as we were pressed together, just as I could feel the slight ebbing pulse of her pussy walls, ready to take that final plunge.

Keeping my hips slow and close, I started a gentle thrust, absolutely thriving on the feel of her walls squeezing my cock. Fast, and I was more than positive we'd both come, but I wanted—no, *needed*—this to last.

This first time needed to last.

With slow thrusts, I was able to focus on kissing every inch of Emily's face.

Her eyelids, closed over the clear blue orbs that I was damned lucky to look into every day.

The tip of her nose, turned up just ever so slightly in a button type way.

Her high cheek bones.

The corner of those pretty pink lips.

Then finally over her open mouth.

God I loved kissing this woman. Her tongue danced against mine in the same slow fashion as my cock did down below. I let my own eyes close for a moment, taking in everything by the sense of feel.

The feel of her mouth loving against mine.

The feel of her warm walls enveloping my cock.

The feel of my heart swelling in my chest.

Two years was a damn long time, but to get to here? Damn well worth it.

Emily brought her knees up, squeezing against my hips. Her mouth began to try and find a quicker dance to mine and one of her feet pressed against my ass. She wanted this to hurry up.

I pulled my mouth from her with a slight grin and quick chuckle.

"You in a hurry?" I asked her, holding myself inside her, deep to the very root of me.

"I need more," she whined, trying to lift her hips.

"Not yet, Emy," I said, bringing my mouth back down to hers. What the fuck was wrong with me and her name? It was like, all of a sudden I couldn't manage to get the L in there.

With my mouth against hers, but before I could resume our kiss, she whispered, "I like that."

I pulled my head back. "Like what?"

She paused, searching my face. "Emy."

Ah, she liked my blunder of her name. I couldn't very well tell her it was an accident now. But hell, if she liked it…

"Alright, *Emy*." I kissed her lips. "Now let me do what I was doing. I'm enjoying myself." I said the last part against her lips and began the slow thrust again.

This slow push and pull was torture, but what exquisite torture it was.

But of course, Emily wasn't going to let this go on for long. Soon her hips were moving under mine again, both feet pressed to just below my ass, trying to get me to move faster.

But it was when she put her hand between our bodies to get herself to where she needed to go, that I drew the line.

"No." I pulled back and moved her fingers from herself.

"I'm right there, Rory! Just...just *fuck* me already!" she pouted.

"Not fucking," I growled at her, by no means upset with her but really hating the term. This? This was not fucking. "I'm making love to my girl."

That gave her pause.

With wide eyes on mine, she stared at me a moment before opening her mouth again. "Am I? Your girl?"

"Fuck yes, Emy." Why she doubted that for a second was beyond me. What had we been doing the last seven months? Playing glorified house? Friends with not-so-many benefits? Shit no. I was living with my girl, helping her get through some of the hardest classes she'd ever take, with the end goal of forever.

Yes, she was my girl.

And no, I wasn't fucking her.

Sure, fucking had its place in the bedroom but right this moment, I was *making love* to her. This slow, sweet sex was full of more emotion than I had ever felt, in or out of the bed. And she damn well was going to know the   difference   before   this   night   was   through.

Chapter Nine

Emily

His girl. Making *love*. It was all almost too much.

But it wasn't. Not at all.

It was just enough.

With my heart a few sizes too big for my chest, I brought our linked hands to my lips and pressed a kiss to Rory's knuckles.

With a cheeky grin hiding behind our linked hands, I told him, "You may continue."

"Oh may I?" he responded with a light laugh and a quick roll of his hips. "Are you sure? You have any more questions? Because I've got all day…"

I let go of his hand so I could frame his face with both of mine, bringing him down again. I held on to his green gaze, lifting a fraction to press my lips against his, feather light, and whispered, "Make love to me, Rory. I'm almost there."

"Yes, ma'am." His own whispered reply brushed his lips over mine before he took my bottom lip between his teeth in a gentle bite, then a long, healing suckle. I slid one hand to the back of his head, dropping the other down his neck and between his shoulders, loving his mouth on mine.

When he started to move his hips again, I squeezed my legs around him, my inner thighs pressed close to his flexing hips. I could feel his ass clenching with each slow, agonizing thrust.

But then he changed the angle. Just slightly, but in a way that had his groin brushing my clit with each full sink into me. Just two times of feeling him press and roll over my clit and my entire body was shaking.

"Rory!" My legs tightened around him as my thighs quivered with my release. I wrapped my arms around his neck, pressing my forehead to his shoulder as my body let go.

Apparently it was almost too much for Rory, too. "Fuck, Em," he groaned out. He was impossibly full in my tight pussy and the feel of my body flexing around his rock hard cock had my orgasm going on and on.

"God, I can't..." He pulled out once more, pushing in slowly, before he started rocking his hips quicker, small, little thrusts with his face pressed against the side of mine. "God, Emy, you feel so fucking good, squeezing my cock. Milking my cock," he murmured around grunts as his hips pistoned into me, fighting against the tightness. Then, with a shout, his own orgasm overtook him.

His hips flexed and his cock jerked with his release. I kept my legs tight around him, not wanting him to leave me just yet.

When his body stilled and his muscles relaxed, with his body weight pushing me into the mattress, I finally let my limbs loosen from around him. I took a deep breath, loving the feeling of Rory's weight on top of me. There were few pleasures in life, and for me personally, this was one of them.

His body lax and content on top of mine.

Sure, he'd get heavy soon—the man was a lot of muscle—but for the moment, I was enjoying this.

"I can't move," he mumbled into the pillow beside my head, making me laugh lightly.

"Yeah, well, I can't either," I responded back in jest. When he braced a hand beside me to push himself over, I wrapped my legs around him again. "One more minute."

I should have figured he wouldn't let that slide. With a push, he rolled us over, still inside me, and I scrambled to unhook my ankles from behind his back before they were crushed under his big body.

"One minute here." He put his hands on my hips and shifted me down just slightly, just enough so I could rest my head on his shoulder, snuggling into his neck. I bracketed my forearms beside our heads on the pillow and closed my eyes, fully relaxed. Rory's hands lazily roamed up and down my back.

After a quiet moment, the only sound in the tiny cabin being our slowing breaths and the crackle of the fireplace, Rory said, "That was worth the wait."

Smiling, I propped my chin in the middle of his chest and teased, "It made up for last time."

I squealed when his hand connected with my ass in a stinging slap. "Sass." He rubbed the spot to ease the sting before tapping both hands on either side of my hips. "I gotta get rid of the condom. Would hate to be considered the next Conor and Mia."

I froze at that.

Did he mean…?

Did he not want kids? I mean, I wasn't by any means ready for them, but I liked to look at the long-term and there was no sense wasting time with someone if there wasn't going to be a forever…

He must have seen a shift in my eyes because he tugged on my hair. "Emily."

I forced a smile and shifted off of him. "Go get rid of the condom, Rore." I moved off the bed and wished I had my bed clothes nearby but because they weren't, I walked naked to the bathroom, refraining from closing the door as badly as I wanted to, and pulled on the sleep boxers and sweatshirt I'd brought in earlier. The soft inner fleece of the sweatshirt was still too much for my sensitive nipples, but I wasn't about to walk back out to find a tank to wear under.

I was working on pulling my hair up in a top knot when Rory walked in. My eyes caught his in the mirror but quickly went back to my own reflection. In my peripheral, I watched as he discarded the condom and just when I thought he'd move from the room to grab his own clothes, he stepped behind me and slid his arms around me, his hands under my sweatshirt and on my bare stomach. I lowered my arms after securing the band around my knot and let my arms hang uselessly beside me.

I watched in the mirror as he turned his face in to mine, pressing his lips to my temple before regarding our reflections. "I just meant," he said softly, "that we wouldn't want an unexpected pregnancy right now. Someday, Emy girl, I am going to put a baby in here." He rubbed my stomach gently. "When you're through with school and are completely ready."

My eyes teared up; I couldn't help it. With a watery tilt of my lips, I asked, "When did you turn into such a good guy?"

His chuckle vibrated against my back and he pressed another kiss to my temple. "There was this girl..." Rory turned me then, and I put my arms around his naked back. "In due time, Emily. You have more important things to worry about right now."

I tilted my chin up so I could press my lips to his softly. "I'm game."

Chapter Ten
December 24th

Rory

Later, when Emily was cuddled under the blankets of the cozy bed, sleeping through the midnight hour, I reached for my phone from the bedside table. These last two days with Emily far exceeded my expectations and there was no way in hell I was watching what we had walk away—at *any* point.

What started out as a chase, the need to take the one girl who wanted nothing to do with me, turned into so much more than I could have ever fathomed. Two years of my attention being focused on Emily, on how I could be the man for her, really put into perspective Bren and Stone's situation. I would never fully understand their need to have kept it a secret for five years, but I got the whole longevity of it.

I wanted what my sister had with Stone, what Con had with Mia. And I wanted it with the woman I once felt was ice cold indifferent toward me.

I scrolled through my emails, finding the one I was looking for, and shot off a new message to the puppy lady before responding to a second message. Tomorrow Emily's Christmas would be complete—and we still had the actual holiday to go through.

Best damn Christmas ever.

Emily sat in the middle of the now-made bed, hair a freaking mess and a coffee mug in her hands between crossed legs. Her facial expression told me she wasn't exactly thrilled to have been woken up at four.

That said, I made sure to have coffee ready before waking her; I knew her well enough.

She should be happy I let her sleep all night. I sure as hell didn't, not with memories of the two of us between these very sheets—well, on top of them really. I would have loved nothing more than to take her again and again throughout the night. As it was, I slept off and on and finally woke up at three thirty to start getting our stuff together.

I glanced up at her sour expression and chuckled to myself, turning my attention back to the task at hand. "Hey, you told your mom we'd be there at ten." I reached for Emily's discarded lingerie from the floor and grinned as I stuffed it in the bag with everything else.

"It doesn't take six hours to get to San Diego," she mumbled, lifting the mug to her lips.

"From home, no," I said, standing. I tugged my pajama pants back into place. "But we're north; it actually will take nearly seven." I looked at the clock. Four sixteen. "And we're still going to be late."

Her eyes widened. "Seven hours?" She uncrossed her legs and placed the mug on the table beside what had been her side of the bed. "I have to shower!"

I watched, fascinated, as she started stripping from the two pieces of clothing that kept her body from mine all night—hell, make that *every* night I'd slept with her. Had I known she chose to be bare under the two pieces of clothing...

She carelessly left the clothes on the floor, puddled where she stood, before walking quickly to the bathroom.

God, her body. I loved it.

"We're going to be so late!" she said, talking to herself, as she stepped into the bathroom. I heard the crank of the pipes as she turned on the shower, and followed her in. She was just stepping under the spray when she caught me undressing as well.

"We don't have time for that, Rory!" she said, pointing to my growing erection.

"Save water, Em." I stepped into the shower behind her, pushing her under the spray and putting my hands in her long hair, threading the locks through my fingers and helping the water douse every inch. At the ends, I tugged until she tilted her chin up toward me.

"We don't have time for this," she growled before I put my lips on hers. She kissed back though, so I didn't know who she thought she was kidding. I stepped closer, my now hard cock trapped between our bodies, as I danced my tongue over hers.

I let go of her hair so I could cradle the back of her head with one hand, the other to her back, where I loved to put my hand and push her closer to me. This was *almost* my favorite spot to be with her.

When her arms wound around my neck though, I revised that statement.

This. This was my favorite position.

She kissed me back like she didn't have a care in the world. Like a switch, she seemed to forget *she* was in a hurry.

I had our bases covered though, so really, hurrying wasn't necessary.

Keeping her hips pressed to mine, I backed her up to the shower wall. Her back arched, bringing her body closer, when she hit the colder tile and her mouth faltered under mine, but when my hand dropped over the curve of her ass until my finger grazed over the slit of her pussy, her mouth stilled for an entirely different reason.

Her body relaxed against mine and she moaned into my mouth as I drew my finger around her opening, not pushing the digit up into her yet.

Already, I could feel the thick, slick wetness of her as it intermingled with the water dancing around our bodies. She lifted her leg, wrapping it around my hips and opening herself up for me.

I chuckled against her mouth. Oh, she wanted to hurry this up, did she?

"You in a hurry?" I asked against her mouth.

She tore her mouth back from mine, her blue eyes serious on mine. "In me, Rory."

I pushed my finger up into her now, watching as her gaze became hooded and her mouth dropped open with the intrusion. She swiveled her hips, allowing better access to my probing digit.

With my finger rubbing against her inner walls, and my lips leaving a trail of kisses from her temple down, down, down to her collar bone, I kept Emily close. Her nipples were pebbled against my chest and her breathy moans were soft under the surrounding water falling.

"I don't have a condom on me," I told her after pressing a marking kiss to her collar.

"Pull out then. Damn it, Rory, I need you."

This little vixen…

Not what I was expecting, that was for damned sure. I figured I'd come in here, play with her a bit, relax her a little bit more, and fist one out after she stepped out of the shower. But if that's how she wanted to play…

I reached between our bodies to take my engorged cock between my thumb and two fingers. I bent my knees slightly, just as she rose up on tiptoe, a leg still around me, and angled the head of my cock at her entrance, letting it drag over her clit on the slide back.

Before I could thrust into her warm heat though, Emily slapped a hand over my chest and pulled her upper body back. "This is a stupid thing to ask now, considering…" she started. Her eyes searched mine and I could feel the worry in her expression. What…? "You're clean, right? I mean, it's been a while, other than last night, right?"

Shit. That's what she was worried about?

"I wouldn't do that to you," I told her honestly. I let go of my cock and straightened my knees, but brought my hands back to the small of her back and pulled her close once again. "I had a physical before moving out here and you know there hasn't been anyone."

"Ok," she nodded. "Ok, yeah. " She brought my face to hers now and kissed me open mouthed. "Now, Rory."

Bending my legs once again, I found the spot I wanted to be in and thrust into her as she moved her hips against mine, bringing me fully into her. This wasn't my first time barebacking, although I found myself wishing it was. There was something innately intimate about it with a person you cared about.

Scratch that. Loved.

With the water at my back and pooling at me feet, I made sure I had even footing before moving my hips against hers.

This was no slow loving like last night.

Not with Emily's hands pulling at my hair, her fingers scratching down my back, her foot digging into my ass, egging me on. And I found I was ok with it.

For the longest time, I thought sex with that so-called forever person had to stay vanilla and unexciting. But I was learning that there was more to making love than sweet, slow, meaningful moments.

Just because this was fast, my cock pounding into her, pressing her against the tiles as her body reacted violently against mine—it didn't mean that there wasn't anything meaningful in this moment. If anything, the wild fucking was just as solidifying as last night's slower romp.

There was fucking to fuck, and there was fucking someone you loved. It was just a little more crazy and fun.

And I would take it.

Chapter Eleven

Emily

I think I surprised Rory earlier in the shower. After I got mine, I dropped to my knees, pulling his cock into my mouth. I was a little put off by the fact I was all over him—licking your own cum just wasn't something that I had any desire to do—but I knew how Rory reacted in my mouth.

He'd already been close so I didn't have much work to do on him. As his thickness was in my mouth, my hand fondled his balls. Just when they drew tighter to his body, Rory pulled my head back.

"Not your mouth."

If that wasn't one of the oddest requests… I thought guys went all bonkers on that?

"Well not my face," I argued with him, my eyes narrowing. Shooting a load on a girl's face was just nasty.

His fist was around his cock, holding tight. "Your chest." He tugged on his cock in a long, slow pull. "I want to see my cum all over you, Emy girl."

It was better than my face and I didn't quite understand the whole thing, but hey, it made the man happy.

We finally made it on the road at five-thirty, to which I may have done some freaking out. But Rory, being Rory, just laughed at me, shaking his head.

The drive to San Diego had us going back near our place but we continued driving through the desert mountains. We made minimal stops and were actually making great time but no sooner than we crossed the Arizona-California border and Rory was making a turn not on the map.

"Where are we going?" I asked, trying to eye the gas gauge. We'd recently stopped for fuel and a bathroom break, so it shouldn't be that, but then again maybe he didn't want to get gas again until we were headed home in two days.

"Detour." His eyes never left the road and I frowned. We didn't have time for a detour, and I told him as much.

"Just relax, Em. Your parents know we're getting there late."

I narrowed my eyes more. "What? Are you in cahoots with my parents all of a sudden?"

This elicited a laugh from him. With a smile and a shake of his head, he answered, "In cahoots. You're somethin' else, Emy girl."

I shifted in the passenger seat, trying to angle toward him. "Well?" I asked, ignoring his jest. "Are you?"

"Just relax," he said again.

Crossing my arms, I turned forward again. I refrained from mumbling under my breath, as much as I had to say to him at the moment.

It was Christmas Eve. We already were only staying with my parents through an early dinner, heading to Conor and Mia's to sleep that night, where Brenna and Stone would be staying as well.

Sure, my parents came out for Thanksgiving, but we had limited time with them today! We didn't have time for this joy riding near the *Mexican border*!

But your parents know, I mimicked in Rory's voice in my head. This detour better be worth it.

There better be a whatever numbered wonder of the world where we were headed.

It was Christmas Eve! I thought again. It wasn't like much was happening today.

When Rory pulled onto a dirt road, I started to get nervous. What in the ever loving world…?

Down the gravel and dirt road, we bumped along in his truck, but still he said nothing.

The asshat had a shit-eating grin on his face, though.

When he pulled into a driveway leading up to an older farm house, I really began to frown. What was happening?

He put the truck in park and tapped the middle console between our seats. "Get out."

I unbuckled as he did, slowly stepping down and out of the truck. "What's going on, Rory?"

He rounded the front of truck and stepped closer to me, holding out his hand. "C'mon," he said instead of answering.

…and because after the last two years, more notably the last few months, I *did* trust him, I went with him. We walked past the house and toward the back, where young crying was happening.

But it wasn't a baby's cry.

It was…

I stopped in my tracks, pulling on Rory's hand when he kept walking. With the shit-eating grin still on his face, he turned back to me. "Hmm?"

"I thought we were getting the puppy for the kids after my parents' house tonight," I said slowly.

"Who said anything about a puppy?" he asked, still trying to play coy.

He tugged on my hand and again, I followed him to the very back, where a woman was waiting with an adult Golden Retriever, and a puppy in her arms.

"I'm glad you made it," the woman said, addressing Rory. "She's the last one and she's been waiting for you."

Rory brought me close to the puppy holding woman. "We had a later start this morning than I anticipated," he answered. He let go of my hand

and I let my arm drop to my side. I watched as he reached out and took the dark golden mass of wavy hair from the woman. Awe struck, I simply watched as Rory cradled the puppy in his arms after lifting it, eye to eye, and having some sort of silent communication with the pup.

With the puppy in a football hold, Rory scratched the puppy's head while having a conversation with the dog's owner but I was stuck staring at the puppy. I'd seen Rory with his nephew and niece. Multiple times. But even cradling a puppy, he made my heart go all aflutter. Mix that with our baby conversation earlier and I couldn't wait for school to finish.

When Rory told me the other night about the puppy for Con and Mia's kids, he said we'd pick it up after my parents' Christmas celebration. We were still a good hour from their house, and they were only twenty minutes for Con and Mia. There would have been no logical way we would have back-tracked to pick up a puppy for the kids.

Which meant...

Just as my smile started to bloom on my face at the thought, Rory turned toward me. "You want to hold her?" he asked, holding the puppy out toward me. Seeing it's mama was a Golden but this puppy had some curliness going on, my guess would be it was a Golden Doodle.

"Yeah, sure," I finally said, holding my hands out. Rory handed me the puppy gently and I saw that on the back of its neck—*her* neck; she had no little boy parts and the lady did say 'she' a little bit ago—was a tiny red Christmas bow with a little note attached.

I was curious to see what it said, but I could feel Rory's eyes on me so I refrained, instead choosing to cuddle the fluff ball close to my neck. She nuzzled her nose into my neck and the cold of her nose near a sensitive spot had me giggling.

"Thank you, Meridith," I heard Rory tell the woman and he turned back toward me, putting his hand on the small of my back and turning me back toward the truck.

He took the puppy from me to allow me to climb into the truck, handing her back to me after I secured my belt. He quickly jogged around and got in, too, buckling as well before nodding toward the puppy. "What's her note say?"

He took his keys and stuck the one in the ignition, cranking the truck back to life.

I pretended to not hear him, instead continuing to cuddle the puppy and rub under her chin. She stretched her neck, offering me more to scratch and closing her eyes in bliss as I did. She had a cute white patch in the middle of her chest, and her little chin was much lighter than the darker color of the rest of her fur.

"She's so cute," I finally said as the puppy sighed and curled into my lap. "Will she be ok not in a crate?" I looked over at Rory, who was now pulling the truck back on to the main dirt road.

Just as I ignored his question, he ignored mine. "What's the note say?"

Again, I could feel my giddy smile starting to bloom. This puppy was totally ours. He screwed up on his story. I probably wasn't supposed to see the email.

Oh my goodness, we had a puppy!

"Emily!" His eyes were still on the road but his knuckles were white as he gripped the wheel. "What's the note say?"

"Is this puppy ours, Rory O'Gallagher?" I asked instead.

"Dammit, woman. Just answer my question." He was getting agitated but in a cute way. It was as if he was nervous.

Rory? Nervous..?

Deciding to give the man a break, I did as he asked. By now the pup was sleeping so I was careful to turn the tag over against her wavy golden fur.

"It says," I started, looking at the feminine writing that must have been the woman's. "Merry Christmas, Emy. Love—" Tears immediately filled my eyes and I choked out the last word. "You." I looked over at him through the blur of tears. "You love me?" I wasn't expecting that.

But my goodness, I had grown to love this man too.

Rory's body visibly relaxed again and he took his right hand from the wheel. With a glance in my direction, he reached out to cup my cheek, his thumb wiping away a tear. "Yeah, Emy girl. I love you."

Chapter Twelve

Rory

I probably should've had Emily read the tag *before* I started driving because all I wanted right now was to watch her face. When her voice choked off the last word and I could hear tears I had a slight moment of panic.

A moment which quickly receded at the awe and wonder in her tone when she asked me if I loved her.

Of course I loved her. Last night only solidified it.

One of the first emails arranging the purchase of the puppy had me adding the sentiment—I'd known how I felt for the woman prior to this trip. I nearly blurted it out any number of times but I felt that Emily deserved grand gestures, something that I didn't have all that much practice in, so I waited for this moment.

Last night's email to Meredith simply had me adding my new name for my Emy girl.

I wiped a fallen tear from Emily's face before returning my attention to the road. It would be nice if Emily returned the feelings but I would completely understand if she needed time.

Two years ago when she and I truly began this game I didn't have the best track record but I definitely thought I proved I could be the man Emily needed. But if she wasn't there yet, if she couldn't say she loved me yet, I would be ok. Things were going in a positive direction for us...

"I love you too," she finally whispered.

I glanced back at her, huge grin on my mug. "Yeah?"

Emily nodded, her face blotchy from tears but her blue eyes bright with emotion. "Yes, Rory O'Gallagher. I do love you."

We neared the highway then and as soon as I pulled the truck onto the smoother road, I reached for her hand, holding it over the center console. The puppy snoozed away on Emily's lap, not that I blamed the pup. Emily was a pretty cozy place to be.

I went from a bachelor in a huge assed apartment I didn't need, making forgeries for college kids and playing music at parties, to a bachelor living above the family bar. I had my women and I made my money, but it was this willowy blonde beauty next to me who made me re-evaluate everything.

I would gladly live in the tiny two-bedroom rental house—a house where I could put my arms out on either side of me in the bathroom, and without stretching, reach the walls; a house with an oven that was probably from the early nineties; a house with a yard made of *rocks*, as I learned Arizonians liked to do—with this willowy blonde, then go back to the way life was.

I enjoyed growing my health and fitness company while helping Emily study her ass off for a career that she was passionate about. I even enjoyed cooking her dinner and cleaning up the house, so she wouldn't have to worry about it later.

Sure, someday I'd love a bigger place with her—I wasn't lying when I told her this morning I wanted her to carry my babies. We were going to get a bigger house and fill it with a bunch of hell-raising blondes, and if our girls looked anything like Emily? Well shoot my now.

Or help me pick out an appropriate rifle.

One or the other.

We drove along the highway in silence, the roads understandably busy for the holiday. The radio was on low but couldn't be heard much over the road noise. Not that I minded. With Emily's hand in mine, I was plenty comfortable.

"So you, who thought of everything," she finally spoke into the quiet truck. "Have you thought of a name for this beauty?" I glanced over and watched as Emily lightly stroked the puppy's fur.

"Nope. I thought you would like a say in that."

"Hmm," Emily replied through a closed lipped smile. She looked incredibly relaxed and happy, and it had little to do with her customary leggings and oversized shirt. She even wore those fuzzy boots that girls seemed to like, but looked like she was walking with an animal on either foot, but hey—if she liked it...

"Well, she kind of looks like a teddy bear, don't you think?" I gave a noncommittal grunt but could do nothing to stop the slight grin on my face. "But Teddy is too masculine," she continued.

I squeezed her hand. "So what are you thinking?"

With a big wide smile aimed at me, she announced. "Theodora. Teddy for short."

I let out a short laugh. "A name *and* a nickname? She's a dog, Emy girl. Not a kid."

"Hey, I could go and give her a pedigree name. You gave me naming powers," she jested, squeezing my hand back. "Theodora, Golden light of the Arizonan sun, the Goldendoodle." Her voice was thick with laughter. Letting go of my hand to scoop the sleeping puppy up under her forearms, she went nose to nose with the quickly excitable puppy. "You think that works for you, Teddy girl?"

I shook my head, still grinning, albeit much wider now that she addressed the puppy. "You're nuts, Emily. Absolutely certifiable."

"Yeah well, you love me," she snuck in there, still looking and talking to the puppy now dubbed Teddy.

Long-assed pedigree-type name or not, I could be game with a dog named   Teddy.

Chapter Thirteen
December 25

Emily

I woke with a happy sigh. Stretching my arms over my head, I looked over, seeing Rory's sleeping form beside me. He was on his side, one hand resting on my stomach and the other arm wrapped around the pillow under his head.

Quietly, I rolled to my side to put a hand on his cheek. The man lived in scruff these days, but if he didn't trim it up sometime soon, he'd start to look like Conor with his full beard.

I trailed the tip of my finger down the slope of Rory's nose then over his cheekbone. I wasn't sure what time he joined me in bed. Yesterday when we arrived to my parents' house, I was surprised to find puppy toys and food. Apparently Rory had thought of just about everything where our Teddy girl was concerned, managing to keep her a secret with the help of my own parents.

So while I helped mom finish our middle of the day dinner, Rory and dad played with Teddy in the living room with her new toys.

We left my parents' house after dessert and drinks, arriving to Conor and Mia's after the kids had already gone to bed. Tired, I said my own goodnights while Rory stayed up with his brother and sister-in-law.

Checking over my shoulder, I saw Teddy still snoozing in her puppy crate, curled up with a blanket under her chin. My eyes sought out the clock behind Rory; it was only six. The sun was starting its morning struggle but it was still fairly dark beyond the window. I held my breath, trying to hear if anything was going on beyond the guest bedroom door but the house seemed quiet.

Satisfied that it appeared to be, I leaned forward to press my lips to Rory's parted, sleeping ones. I kept my lips light on his while trailing my hand over his waist, his hip, then dropping my hand to cup his still soft cock. Over his boxer shorts, I squeezed and pulled just as lightly, keeping my hand gentle and teasing. Quickly though his cock began to harden, waking up to my ministration. Rory groaned under my mouth and I kept my eyes on his lids, waiting for them to open.

When they did, Rory rolled over and pulled me with him. My hand left him to brace on the mattress beside him. I smiled against his lips, kissing him once more.

"Mmm," he mumbled against my lips. "Good morning." His big hands found their way under my sleep shirt and rested on my lower back. "You're being sassy this morning," he said sleepily, pushing his hips up into mine.

His sleep voice was so damned sexy. Low and rough, his voice paired with the hardness against the apex of my thighs had me wet and wanting.

With my hands on his chest, I pushed myself up, grinding myself against his hard cock. "I think everyone's still sleeping."

Rory's fingers flexed against my hips. "Yeah?"

I nodded, smiling crookedly down at him. "Mmhm. Yeah." Moving from my straddle of his hips, my hands quickly went to work, pulling his boxers down, over his erection and off his legs. I tossed them to the floor before pressing a kiss to Rory's muscular thigh. However, when I moved my hand to squeeze his hard, straining cock, Rory's hand quickly wrapped around my wrist.

"Naked," he demanded. His voice still held that sleepy quality but he was all sorts of awake now. I climbed off the bed to pull off my clothes while Rory scooted back in the bed, peeling his own shirt off and resting back against the pillows.

Laying there, his once again getting-too-long wavy hair a mess around his head, his body toned and his cock standing at attention, he was the most beautiful man I had ever seen. He'd always been a good looking guy but his cocky attitude always overpowered that in my eyes. That's not to say he wasn't cocky any more—he just channeled it differently.

"Condom?" I wanted to feel his release in me. No more pulling out nonsense. "I'm on the pill," I confessed. I moved back onto the bed, sitting on my knees beside him.

Rory seemed to think about that. Finally, he reached out to cup my face, pulling me close to kiss me once. "But if we use both, the risk of pregnancy is smaller, Em."

Slightly frustrated, I growled at him. "If we get pregnant while using a contraceptive, well then it's meant to be, Rory. I'd deal with—*we'd deal with it*—if it happened."

Again, Rory watched me and contemplated.

"Fine, whatever," I said, pushing from the bed. Not bothering with my sleep clothes, I went straight to our bag to pull out clothes for the day. When I stood though, clothes in hand, Rory's body was pressed against my back.

"Damn, you have a temper," he chuckled against my ear. "Drop the clothes, Emy girl." Powerless to him, especially now that he had an arm wrapped around me so a hand could cup one of my small breasts, and the other arm wrapped and placing his hands over my mound, his fingers dipping into my folds and flirting with my clit, I did as he said.

"I just don't want you to regret anything," he whispered in my ear as his fingers started to pluck and pull at my nipple. I let my head fall back to his shoulder as he did, the nerve endings in the sensitive peak having me close to crossing my eyes in pleasure.

He walked us closer to the wall, his hand still plucking at me while his other started a slow roll over my other bundle of nerves. I could feel how wet I was between my thighs; I needed his thickness in me.

"Brace your hands on the wall," he issued into my ear. I did as he demanded, loving that his body, his hands, never left my body. His fingers continued their slow play over my clit but his hand left my breast to press against my stomach. "Now, you have to stay quiet, Emy girl. We don't want to wake up the house, do we?"

I shook my head before resting my cheek on the back of one of my hands. I kept myself pushed away from the wall enough that I didn't feel the cold texture against my skin, which allowed me to tip my hips back toward Rory. He removed his hand from my stomach and grabbed for my thigh, lifting my leg up. I took my cue and folded my leg back and around his thigh. As soon as I did, I was welcomed with Rory's thick girth. One strong, sure stroke and he was buried to the hilt.

I groaned quietly, squeezing my eyes shut at the intrusion. I turned my head to rest my forehead against the wall now. Rory's lips were between my shoulder blades. "God, I love you," he murmured against my back before slowly pulling out. He nearly pulled out all the way before slamming back into me, both of our groans filling the room in unison.

With my hands against the wall and his wrapped around me, our thrusts against one another were like a well-choreographed dance, as if he and I had been doing this for far longer than two nights.

His fingers pinched and rolled over my clit while his other hand found it's home back against my breasts. Rory knew damn well that my nipples were my 'point,' that with enough playing there, alone, I could fly through my orgasm. Pairing that sweet nerve ending with the playing down below, adding it to the thickness inside me, and I was damn close to flying.

Rory pulled me up to stand straighter. I kept one arm out, steadying myself against the wall, and brought my other to the back of Rory's head, my fingers threading in the long strands.

"So fucking beautiful," he murmured against my shoulder, his hips flexing into me. His arm was now bracketed under my chest, holding me upright. Still though, his fingers played a lovely dance over my clit, rubbing in circles, lines... Over my clit, around my clit, occasionally pulling the hood back and having direct access to the sensitive nub.

"God, Rory," I groaned, tipping my hips away from his fingers. Rather than give in though, he simply pinched the nub between two fingers. Again, I groaned, shutting my eyes and flexing my fingers in his hair, no doubt pulling the strands.

"Fuck, Em." His fingers pressed together, squeezing my clit harder, as his thrusts shortened and quickened. "Squeeze my cock, Emy girl. Come all over me, baby."

I knew that if I squeezed against him, I would come apart in a matter of seconds.

But it was what I wanted.

So I did as he asked and with one quick push into my tightened pussy, the head of his cock hitting hidden nerve endings and his fingers squeezed over exposed ones, my body arched against his and my mouth dropped open on a silent moan.

"Fuck, Em." His cock continued its push and pull. "Fucking A, Emy girl. That's it. Milk my cock. Keep...Right there, Emy. Right...*there!*" He shouted his own release, surely waking up the house but I didn't care.

His cock was buried to the hilt in me and I could feel as his hips jerked once, twice in response, and the hot spurts of his cum filling me. His mouth was to my shoulder and his breathing was as hard and labored as my own. I couldn't help but smile.

"I love you so much," he whispered into the silence.

I turned my head toward his, smiling when he lifted his mouth from my shoulder to my lips. "I love you too."

Chapter Fourteen

Rory

Shortly after letting Emily's leg drop back to the floor, pulling my slackening cock from her warm heat, Teddy began whimpering in her crate.

"You go ahead and shower; I'll just clean up and get the dog," I told Emily, kissing her on the lips and playfully slapping my hand to her ass, rubbing the spot after to gentle the sting. As badly as I wanted to join her in the shower, I knew we had an appearance to make.

Probably sooner than later. Emily hadn't exactly been quiet. Hell, neither had I, for that matter.

Emily gave me an amused grin when I followed her into the bathroom. "I thought you were taking care of Teddy?"

"In a minute," I said. "After I clean up." I closed the bathroom door behind us and pulled open the linen closet, grabbing a bath blanket for Emily and a smaller towel for myself. "As much as I'd love to keep you on me," I started, pointing to my now relaxed cock. I didn't finish my thought but Emily smiled and rolled her eyes all the same.

As I cleaned up in the sink, Emily prepared the shower for herself but before she stepped into the steam, I pulled her back to me for one more kiss.

"Merry Christmas," I said against her lips. I loved giving her sentiments while my lips brushed against hers. It was an intimacy I hadn't allowed prior to Emily.

With a happy moan, Emily returned her love and damn, it would never get old. It couldn't get old.

I watched as she stepped into the shower, regretful that I couldn't—well, *shouldn't*—follow her in. Instead, I did my puppy-parent duties and walked out of the bathroom, leaving the door open a crack, and quickly pulled on my lounge pants and an old ratty sweatshirt. I pulled out leggings and a sweatshirt for Emily but saw a tee-shirt dress under it all. Assuming that was for today, I pulled out the dark green fabric and put it on the bed for her before moving to kneel in front of the puppy crate. Looking at the size of Teddy's paws, we would need a bigger crate soon, I mused.

"Good morning, Teddy girl," I said, unlatching the door. With a yip and a wiggle of her butt, the puppy bounded out of the small space. Not wanting her to piss on my brother's wood floors, I scooped her up. She climbed up to rest her front paws on my shoulder, happily panting in my ear as I left the room.

The hallway was pretty quiet yet with the doors to other bedrooms closed, but I could hear my brother and Stone talking down the way. Sure enough, in the kitchen in their own sleep clothes, stood my brother and brother-in-law, mugs of coffee in their hands, standing on either side of the kitchen's peninsula counter.

"Morning." I nodded in their direction before moving further into the kitchen, passing the guys and the kitchen table to let Teddy out into the fenced in backyard. All that was back there was a swing set and a sand box; she couldn't get into too much trouble back there.

As I turned back to the guys though, I saw that Stone was laughing behind his hand and Con was doing a piss-poor job of keeping a straight face.

"What's up?" I moved to grab a coffee mug of my own, filling it to the brim with steaming hot java.

Again, Stone laughed, this time the sound erupting from his mouth in an explosion of air, as if he was trying to keep it contained behind tight lips.

What the fuck was so damned funny?

"So you and *Emy* have figured things out since we last talked?" Con finally said, lifting his mug toward me before taking a sip.

"Well, yeah?" My brother fucking knew this. He knew about the puppy, he knew about the damn—

The gift she was getting today.

He knew damn well I loved the woman.

He also knew we—

Fuck.

"Oh, Emy. Fucking A, Emy," Con said in a low voice now, humping his kitchen counter.

Jesus fucking Christ. "Grow the fuck up," I grumbled into my coffee.

Stone slapped me on the back just as the hot liquid met my lips. With a curse, I put the damned mug down.

"Glad to hear it's working out for you, man," he said around a snicker.

"I, for one, am glad to hear *you* grew the fuck up. Took what you wanted," Con said, adding in his own two cents.

I sure as hell wasn't about to tell him that it was Emily who took what *she* wanted.

"How the hell did you know?" I mean, yeah, we weren't quiet but...

"I was putting Ava back in her bed after she spent the last three hours in ours," Con informed me. Ava's bedroom was the one right next to the one Emily and I were sharing.

I could be cool with my brother taunting me about sex, but I wasn't entirely sure I was ok with my baby niece hearing all that. "Did she sleep through it?"

Please say yes. Please say she did. She was only two but I couldn't imagine she wouldn't have questions. She had questions about *everything*. And I wasn't looking forward to having to pay for her therapy…

"Naw, yeah. She slept." Conor chuckled and took another sip of his coffee before pushing away from the counter. "But I'm happy for you, bro."

"Just don't bring it up to Emily," I said, pointing to Con and then swinging my gaze to Stone. "Don't. She'll get all embarrassed and shit."

"I love how you bring out your bad boy words with us. I bet it's all flowers and poetry with *Emy girl*." Conor could be such a fucking ass when he wanted to.

"And you don't?" I glared at my brother, then my brother-in-law as well because, while he didn't agree or disagree with Con's statement, I knew damn well how he was with my sister.

"Won't say a word," Stone said, his hands up in the air. "Swear it."

I stared at him, then my brother, before nodding. "You better."

Chapter Fifteen

Emily

Our bags were once again packed and the puppy sleeping in the crate beside our bed. I was sitting up against the headboard, waiting for Rory to leave the bathroom and join me. I had both the clock alarm and my phone's alarm set, both of us agreeing to get back on the road early before the post-holiday traffic started to get too thick.

Today had been a good day.

Sure, there had been some odd winks and hugs from Conor and Stone, but otherwise it was like any other time the group of us had gotten together. I really missed the O'Gallagher family, the people I called *family* the years I was in school and pushing to get by. Even without Rory at my side, these people were just that—

Family.

I guess I'd been so busy with school lately that I didn't realize how much I missed them. It was because of that that I feared that maybe Rory missed them all too.

I glanced up from my phone when Rory stepped out of the bathroom, turning off the light and fan in there before crossing the softly lit room to join me on the bed. I put my phone down and twisted the switch on the lamp, bringing the light in the room down yet another notch. Rory's lamp was still on.

I waited for him to turn his off and cuddle down with me before voicing my fears. Unfortunately, he never turned off his lamp. Instead, his hawkeyed gaze was on mine, calculating, as if he was trying to gauge my feelings.

"You ok, Em?" he finally asked.

I nodded and offered him a smile. "Yeah. It was a good Christmas."

He mirrored my nod and reached an arm out to pull me into his chest as he sat up against the pillows. "It was."

Needing the contact, I wrapped my arms around his torso, wedging the one behind his back, and resting my head on his chest. I smiled to myself when I felt his lips brush over my head in a quiet kiss.

We sat there in the quiet for some time before I opened my mouth to voice my concerns, when Rory beat me to the punch.

"I have another gift for you," he stated.

I pushed away from him, frowning. "Rory! You've already given me too much! I just got you some stupid socks."

"And you paid for next year's legal fees with the business. *And* the website."

Still, I frowned. Those things had been necessary for him and I was glad to help him out with them. I couldn't do much for the man but I'd been saving up for those for the past twelve weeks. He did *so much* for me around the house, and then to top it all off, he gets me a fancy snowed-in type retreat and a puppy. I also opened up a pretty orange, casual dress, much like the one I'd been wearing today for the holiday.

He pressed another kiss to my temple before twisting his body away from me. Reaching under his pillow, he grabbed something and brought his tight fist back out. I narrowed my eyes once again. What did he have that could fit in his fist?

"Emily Winters. This is by no means an engagement ring," he started before lifting his brows. "It can be! I just didn't want to put that pressure on you." He turned his fist over and loosened his fingers, revealing a ring with a diamond encrusted band and a blue topaz stone on top, making me gasp in awe. It was beautiful. "It's more of a promise ring. A promise to you." He took my right hand, now trembling, and slid the beautiful ring on my ring finger.

"I promise that I will always be by your side. Anything you need from me, I will deliver on. I would gladly do the last two years over again, if I knew that in the end I would still be with you." Both of my hands were in his now and he squeezed them as he looked into my eyes. "You, Emily, changed my outlook on so many things. I want to continue to be your rock, be your guide. And when the time comes, I want to be your husband."

I looked down at our hands. The way he was holding them put the ring on display and I loved how it looked against my skin. It really was beautiful. "Can I wear it on my left hand?" I asked him.

I could see as Rory took a deep breath, his breathing slowing way down. "Do you want—"

I tugged my hands from his so I could place them on his cheeks. "I like the idea of a promise ring, Rory O'Gallagher," I said softly before leaning in to press my lips against his. "I just want it on my left hand."

He kissed me back and I wanted nothing more than to deepen our kiss, but Rory pulled back. Taking my right hand in his again, he pulled off the ring and moved it to my left hand. "Someday," he said, "this will be a different ring."

"You don't need to get me an engagement ring," I told him. Seriously, how many rings was this man going to get me?

"Someday, this will be a different ring," he repeated before bringing my hand to his lips to kiss my knuckles. "And then this one can go back on your right. On your left, it tells the world that you're mine."

Which was precisely why I wanted it there.

I wanted the reminder that I was Rory's.

That beyond all my fears, Rory was truly in it for the long haul.

Something he continued to prove yet I still hadn't truly grasped onto until this moment.

He kissed me again, this time allowing his tongue to brush over my lips. I parted them, moving the tip of my tongue over his, before he pulled back. I started to ask why, but he twisted to turn off his lamp, blanketing the room in darkness. Rory lay down then, pulling me along with him and I cuddled into his side, content and happy and surer than anything the direction things with him were going.

"I love you, Emy girl," he spoke into the growing darkness.

"I love you, too." I rubbed my hand over his stomach.

"I can't wait to get you home." His face was turned into mine again and his lips brushed over my temple.

"Yeah?"

"Yeah. So I can love on you all over and be reminded of it every day."

I laughed lightly, hitting his stomach gently. "Behave."

He didn't respond but I could feel his grin. "You want it too," he eventually said, to which I didn't confirm nor deny.

No sense, when he knew the truth anyway.

"Merry Christmas, Rory."

He hugged me close and I closed my eyes, ready to drop off into sleep. "Merry Christmas, Emy love."

ACKNOWLEDGEMENTS

As I stated in the final O'Gallagher Nights book, I have truly enjoyed writing these siblings. I have absolutely loved watching the playboys that are Con and Rory find a single woman each who has them reevaluating everything they've done before, and the love Gray has for Brenna? I've loved that man since he first 'spoke' to me.

That said, this series definitely tested some limits for me as a writer, like it did for some of you as readers. So thank you for continuing on the ride and believing that men like Conor and Rory could find their forever loves, and for watching as Brenna opened up her heart and believed that what she had, could last.

Like always, to my editor Jenn. You have been such a great sounding board and again, I'm so glad to have found you to add to my team. You're a great ear and have talked me off of many ledges...

Dana of Designs by Dana. I *love* the new covers for this series. You did such a great job and I definitely feel these covers convey how I feel about the characters. Thank you, thank you, thank you!

Colleen of Itsy Bitsy Book Bits. Thank you for your continual support.

Mia and the IndieSage group. I absolutely love working with you and the company; I cannot wait to continue this journey with you guys in my corner.

Bloggers: I was once you, 'full-time' not even seven months ago. I know the work you put in and how sometimes you bite off bigger chunks than you realize you should take, rushing to get posts up and cross-posting reviews. Thank you *so much* for helping me promote my stories. You all help this indie-world go 'round.

And, lastly but most certainly never least, my readers. Seven months I've been on this journey and it is you all who have continued to motivate me to keep writing and sharing my stories. I have no plans of stopping any time soon. I have many more stories to share with you, and I cannot wait to do so!

ABOUT THE AUTHOR

Mignon Mykel is the author of the Prescott Family series, as well as the short-novella erotic romance series, O'Gallagher Nights. When not sitting at Starbucks writing whatever her characters tell her to, you can find her hiking in the mountains of her new home in Arizona.

LOVE IN ALL PLACES *series*
full series reading order

A LOOK AT INTERFERENCE

Caleb and Sydney's story

Chapter One

April, Present Day

Sydney

After a stressful day of exams, I was ready for a glass of chocolate wine. Whoever decided to put chocolate and wine together in one glass was a freaking genius.

I opened the door to my cozy, some would say quaint, apartment and tossed my keys in the bowl I kept on the table there. I quickly closed the door behind me, bolting and chain-locking it, before haphazardly dropping my messenger bag from my shoulder to the floor.

I'd move it in a little bit. The only thing in it was notes upon notes, and those puppies could burn. That class was done; finito, sayonara, adios senior-year marketing. Just a set of grades between me and a degree.

The classes were a breeze. I was just having a hard time narrowing my final direction down. I've always wanted my hands in everything; from wedding planning, to advertising, and even theater management.

Couldn't act worth a damn, but I loved all the behind the scenes stuff.

Last summer, I interned with a local wedding planner and had a blast. I definitely could see myself in that business. Granted, I hadn't experienced any bridezillas but I certainly heard the stories. While that route seemed to be my direction, a classmate of mine told me about a paid internship he was doing with a semi-big production company and it left me more than a little curious.

Perhaps some would call me an overachiever.

I would say I just liked to keep busy.

And because, you know, senior year classes and college graduation weren't keeping me busy enough, on top of my job at the college bookstore, mind you, I asked for more information. So now I was getting meagerly paid to study under some talent director out of LA. Not a bad gig, right?

Did I mention I live in Utah..? Yeah, Utah. Not California. So the logistics of this understudy thing were a little wonky to me, but in the age of the internet and Skype meetings, it seemed to be working well.

I essentially just did research for David, the guy I was working under. He gave me a name; I Googled the heck out of said person. He gave me a scripted location; I found a way to make it come alive in some back-lot studio—that I've never been to.

I was pretty sure that anything I emailed him was getting sent to the trash bin and whenever he appeared to be taking notes during our Skype meetings, he was actually just doodling...I don't know, cars or something...but I enjoyed this digging into stuff.

Maybe I should have gone into intelligence...

I digress.

It's been a few days since David last talked to me. He said he'd have a bigger project for me the next time we spoke, so I made sure all my ducks were in a row, school-wise, but the way it was looking, I was going to have a weekend to read anything that wasn't a textbook.

Or maybe I could go to a movie.

Not that there was anything out...

After toeing off my ballet flats, I walked through my white on white apartment toward the little kitchenette, pulling my long red hair off my eck and into a high messy top-knot. I grabbed a wine glass from the rack before opening up my fridge to grab that delectable chocolate wine I'd been thinking about since turning in my last exam. Just as I was about to pour though, the sound of Adam Levine singing about being locked away, in that sexy…sexy…voice of his, broke the silence, muffled as it was.

Putting both the glass and bottle down on the counter, I treaded back to my messenger bag to grab my cell from the side pocket.

The bag may have ended up back on the floor by the door.

Like I said, I'd move it later. For being such an organized person, I sure had little care over my bag. It was the one thing I tended to toss wherever.

Glancing at the screen showed me David was calling. Looked like he was making good on that so-called 'bigger project'. I slid the unlock bar over to answer the call as I fell onto my couch, surrounded by my gold and brown pillows. "Good afternoon, David. How are you?"

"I have that assignment for you," he said, cutting straight to the chase.

I sat up a little straighter from my seat on the couch and tried not to grin. I was super curious as to what he managed to put together for a student like myself. It wasn't like you needed a degree for this particular field, but if this did turn out to be the avenue I'd pursue, I wanted all the knowledge I could get.

I always kept a notebook and pen on the coffee table in front of my couch. I reached for them, narrowly missing the trio of candles that also sat there. I crossed one leg over the other, clicking the pen in place and securing my cell between my shoulder and ear.

"Ok, shoot."

"I'm going to have you do some casting. Your research ability has been pretty impressive, and I'd like to see how you fare with casting. Obviously, the final casting will go through me, but you do great leg work."

"Alright, awesome. What type of show are we looking at?"

"Dating show."

And just like that, my mega-watt grin faded a little.

Or a lot. It wasn't like I was looking in a mirror. A dating show was not what I was going for. One, dating shows were a dime a dozen and aside from the ones that had a solid fan following, they didn't do too well in the ratings. And two, the guys and girls on these shows were terribly fake.

Who the hell finds love in a few weeks? And who wants to share her man with fifty thousand other girls, as they stick their tongues down his throat? Certainly not me.

No. Thank. You.

David continued on, so I paid attention, scribbling notes as he spoke. "The single guy is going to be an athlete. We've come up with a short list of men we'd like to try out, and your job is to find them, talk to them, talk them into the idea. Get a gist for what they're looking for in an ideal partner. You know, that kind of thing."

"And the athletes?" My pen was poised and ready.

"Well, the one we really want is Caleb Prescott."

Didn't ring any bells.

"...and?" He did say athletes, did he not?

"Just work the Prescott angle for now. See what you can get; talk him into it."

"Who exactly is this...Caleb Prescott?"

There was a pause on the other line, followed by a slight sigh, and I imagined David running his hand down his face in frustration. "He's a hockey forward—"

...and that would be why my bell hadn't rung. I don't think I've ever seen a hockey game, outside of flipping past one during the Winter Olympics.

"...plays for the San Diego Enforcers. His father played NHL, won a ton of awards. Currently coaches in Wisconsin. Caleb is one of six kids. Huge hockey family."

"And if he says no?"

"We'll work on it from there, but I really want Caleb on the show." When David shot off Caleb's agent's phone number, I wrote it down. "Give him a call. Let me know by tomorrow, six p.m., the status. If you need to head out to him, tell me. We'll pull strings and get you there."

Six?

I put my pen down so I could pull my phone from my ear, the time flashing on the screen. I had less than twenty-four hours to figure this guy out, call him, talk him into the show…and what if he didn't have an answer for me? What would I do then? Make a side trip to San Diego?

But then again…did I really have a choice? It really didn't sound like it. Talk about a tight deadline.

When I put my phone back to my ear, David was going on about the premise for the show. I didn't bother to write it down. A dating show was a dating show was a dating show. It sounded clichéd—like every other show of its type. While he continued on, I mentally flipped through my calendar. I always took the week of exams off from the bookstore, as well as the following week to regroup. I wouldn't have to worry about work, and I was pretty sure there wasn't anything else I had planned.

When all was said and done, and my call with David was complete, I tossed my notebook down on the couch beside me. Pursing my lips, I puffed out my cheeks in frustration. Besides random doodling, there wasn't a whole lot going on on the page. 'Dating show' and 'Caleb Prescott' were the bolded items. The lines should be reading characters, wants, looks, actions…anything and everything more than…

…dating show stuff.

This was not going as I'd hoped.

For a first casting assignment? Quite frankly, it sucked.

Caleb

I shouldn't have gone to O'Gallaghers with Jonny last night.

I pulled my pillow from under my head and, face planting into the mattress, pushed the sides as close to my ears as possible. Anything to block out the annoying ring of my cell phone.

Last night, San Diego won. As was tradition, Jon Jon and I went out on the town. Sometimes the other guys on the team would come along but for the most part, it was just me and the kid brother. Back in our peewee hockey days, mom would take us to McDonald's; in college, the one year he and I attended at the same time, we would party in my dorm. Now, we went out, partied long and hard, and of course, shut it down. Most of the bartenders looked the other way with some of the younger athletes in town, and we could always count on Conor O'Gallagher. Rumor had it the O'Gallaghers were a little rough around the edges. Probably why Conor was willing to overlook Jonny not quite being twenty-one yet.

Both Jonny and I had been drafted to the San Diego Enforcers. During my senior year of college, Jonny's freshman year, we both walked into training camp as college kids with great stats, and walked out with spots on the roster. Sure, the Prescott name means something to the organization, but Jonny was a damn good goaltender, and my stats were better than dad's in the respect he didn't touch majors until he was in his mid-twenties, having played in the American league for a few years beforehand.

Last night's win meant the Enforcers were that much closer to Sir Stanley and his Cup. Finals were well within our reach. All we had to do was win Tuesday night's game and we'd make it into the next round. It was a close series, but the odds were in our favor. With Jonny in net, Vegas had to pull all the punches to get the puck past him.

I sighed blissfully when my phone finally stopped ringing, but just as I was about to drop off that sharp edge of sleep, Jonny slammed my bedroom door open. I lifted the pillow enough to look over my shoulder at the intrusion, watching as my boxer-clad brother tossed the cordless house phone onto my bed, bouncing off my hamstring–a little too close for comfort.

"Fucking asshole."

Jonny merely raised a dark blond brow. Oh, the perks of sharing a condo with your younger brother.

I guess it could be worse. My sisters weren't exactly the easiest to live with.

"Next time, wake up and answer your damn phone," Jonny grumbled. "There's a lady on the other end, and I don't think she much appreciated my sarcasm."

I reached back for the phone with one hand as I tossed the pillow aside with the other, before shooting Jonny the bird. As I put the phone to my ear, I watched my twenty-year old brother shuffle back toward his own room. "Caleb," I said on the exhale of a tired sigh.

"Um, hi," came the voice on the other end. Female, like Jonny said. Not high pitched, but not as sexy and throaty as some female voices were. Nervous, maybe. I didn't think I knew her voice, and the landline number was pretty locked down, so she couldn't be some weird stalker chick. I squeezed my eyes shut briefly. Way too much thinking for this hour.

"I'm so sorry that this seems to be an inopportune time. I figured you'd be up and moving, as it's ten." Was it ten already? "I thought that was the time you started practice on game days. I'm on a tight deadline and was really hoping to just leave a message." Ah, she didn't expect to actually talk to me.

"And this is…" I stated, not asked, before yawning.

"I'm sorry," she apologized again. "My name is Sydney Meadows and I'm calling on behalf of Sorenson Media Group. I tried to reach you through your agent, but he directed me straight to you."

I made a mental note to talk to Mark the first chance I got. He really needed to stop directing people to me. Wasn't that his job? To figure out what appearances and gigs were best for his athletes when they weren't doing what they were being paid to do? Fuck, Mark knew I didn't like to sign up for the extra things that came with being a pro-athlete. Events with the team, sure. Gigs at the rink, absolutely. But beyond that, it was a hard no.

"We are putting together a reality television series, and you are one of the names we were interested in having involved with the show," she stated in a rehearsed manner.

I didn't think sleep was going be coming back to me anytime soon, so I rolled over onto my back before throwing my legs over the side of the bed. As I stood, I shook my head. "Yeah, sorry. No reality TV."

"If you'd just let me pitch it to you—"

"That's all you're going to be doing, Miss Meadows. Do you really want to waste your breath? I'm not doing television."

"That's fine," she rushed to say. As she began talking about multiple women and just as many dates, I strode naked to my dresser to pull out a pair of old, worn sweatpants. I pulled them on while listening with one ear. She continued to talk, so I continued to move, walking out of my room and down the hall that was home to both mine and Jonny's rooms, a spare room, and a bathroom, before walking barefooted down the stairs. Whenever she'd pause for an answer, I was sure to give a barely verbal 'mmhm' just so she would continue her rant and be closer to done.

I had sisters. I knew how to work a phone call with the long-winded female species.

"So great," she said finally, with a smile evident in her voice, so unlike the unsure tone at the beginning of our conversation, one-sided as it mostly was. "I will meet you tonight after your game. Thank you so much, Caleb. I promise you, you won't be disappointed."

Standing in front of the fridge now, I frowned when I heard the telltale sign of her ending the call. I pulled the phone from my ear only to stare down at the 'call ended' screen, the frown not going anywhere.

Well shit...

What did I just agree to?

Chapter Two

Sydney

After calling David and talking him into extending my deadline—because let's be honest, twenty-four hours was not doable, not to talk a guy into a show he was apparently against—I packed an overnight bag and headed to Grand Junction Regional, a good hour and a half away. The only flight leaving for San Diego was at five in the evening, with a quick layover in Phoenix. After all was said and done, I arrived in San Diego at almost eight thirty. According to my calculations, that still gave me about an hour to head from the airport to the arena. Not knowing traffic, yet assuming the worst, I really hoped that was enough time.

I left my terminal and headed towards the rental car area. Seeing the line snaking back and forth, I had to fight back a groan. I moved to the back of the line and propped my wheeled bag up before digging in the front pocket to find my leather folio. In it, I had my printed confirmation codes, maps, a description of the show, random notes on the man, and any and every selling point I could possibly give Noah Caleb Prescott, award winning forward of the San Diego Enforcers. I had to convince him to sign on.

After what little I found, I wasn't entirely convinced I would be able to pull this off.

The second child of Noah and Ryleigh Prescott, he was the first to be professionally drafted in the family. Not for lack of trying on his oldest sister's part, though. She was one of the largest supporters of a professional women's hockey team in the Midwest, and I almost found more information on her than I did Caleb.

Caleb was a six foot five power forward, a player known for his speed and quick moves. He wasn't one to get into many scuffles, but he wasn't afraid to pull a punch if it was necessary. Most of the journalists and forum posters had nothing but good things to say about him.

To be honest, I couldn't find a single negative remark on the man.

That was on the ice.

Off the ice wasn't much different.

He gave back to his community at home. He participated in most of the teams' appearances at local hospitals. He was endorsed by a few brands, but from what little I could find, his name was simply attached to the companies. There weren't print or video ads, and the few interviews I found weren't extremely lengthy.

I did find a few paparazzi shots of him with models and actresses, but never with the same one more than once. And never so many pictures with different women in a span of time that would paint him as a typical athletic player. The one event he seemed to go to annually was the NHL Awards in Vegas, which I can't say I was aware was a thing. He went right before his rookie season and again last June. Like most of the attendees, he was freaking gorgeous in whatever big named suit he'd wear. Most of those pictures though, he was either by himself or with a blond male that the captions labeled as his brother, Jonny.

So what I knew was the man didn't like to be in the public eye, yet the public still loved him.

And I was supposed to convince him to say yes to a very public reality show?

I needed all the luck in the world with that one.

I triple checked my car rental paperwork before placing the folio on top of my bag. I tugged down on my brown dress pants before smoothing my hands down my thighs. My hands went to the small of my back to check the tuck of the light green, long-sleeved blouse I chose for the meeting, making sure it was tucked and tight, not billowing. I guessed I kind of resembled a tree, the brown and green thing going on, but the light green worked well with my complexion and hair.

I leaned to the side a little to try and catch a glimpse of the people ahead of me. When it looked like there would be no moving for a moment yet, I toed off one of my three-inch heeled sandals to flex and rotate my foot. Oh, that felt divine…

At five-two, every inch counted. If my body was able to handle the pain of five-plus inch heels for long periods of time, I'd wear those in a heartbeat. As it was, my baby three-inch ones killed.

I slipped the heel back on when I saw the line start to shuffle forward. Grabbing the handle of my bag, I moved with the masses, stopping yet again a few feet later. As a fan of the messy top-knot, I had tried really hard to keep my hair down for this meeting but that was so not happening anymore. The temperature difference between Utah and California was pretty significant, even at this later hour.

I leaned down to unzip the front of my bag again to find a hair tie. I opted against my go-to style for a clean, if slightly loose, ponytail in the middle of my head, part over my left eye still intact. I brushed my long side-swept bangs into place before glancing at my watch.

I was such a fidgeter. Patience was something I'd never had a whole lot of.

It was nearing nine. A full thirty minutes had passed already? That was no good.

I was that person who would have everything done yesterday if I could. I hated being late; I liked being punctual, on time, and therefore no less than fifteen minutes early.

According to the map I looked at earlier, it was ten minutes from the airport to the arena, but that was on a good day.

Again, I bent forward to the front zipper to rift around, pulling out my iPhone this time. I opened up a web browser and plugged in NHL.com to figure out where I stood in regards to the timing of the game. From what I pulled up earlier, it appeared most games ended at about nine-thirty or so. I figured that to get to the arena on time based off those numbers and the traveling times, I'd have to leave the airport in fifteen minutes to get there on time, Sydney style, or within thirty minutes at the absolute latest.

Honestly, though, the thought of getting there right on time almost gave me hives.

iPhone in hand, I crossed my arms and tapped my toes. Could this line move any slower?

As if my thoughts willed it to happen, the line moved. Two more lanes opened and two others cleared, allowing the line to move a bit more quickly.

Positive thoughts, Sydney...Positive thoughts.

I was late.

This did not sit well with me. Those hives I was thinking about before? I certainly felt a twitch behind my eye and was fighting back the urge to scratch at my arms. Granted, it sounded like the game was still going, if the cheers and loud music were any indication.

This late thing didn't sit well with me, but what was I going to do, especially with the game apparently still going? Go down to the ice and talk to him?

Ok, deep breath; maybe I really wasn't all that late.

Thanks to David, I had been able to drive the rental right up to the side of the arena, where security would watch it. No parking tickets here, no siree.

I stumbled briefly in my jog-walk from the front doors of the arena to a set of doors separating the lobby and the actual seating and bowl.

Running in heels wasn't really my forte. I left my bag in the car, but carried my leather folio with me. When I was stopped for not having a ticket, all I had to do, according to David, was give my name. Upon doing so, the ticket usher spoke into his walkie-talkie and I was given clearance. An usher walked me around the side to a private elevator, making me feel all sorts of special.

He sent me down to the lower level, where I was met by a security guard. This one was female, but she looked a bit scary to me, so I just smiled and let her take me to where I had to go.

The woman stopped with me in a long hall as echoes from the announcer ricocheted the halls, expressing the organization's thanks for coming out and that the kids in attendance were welcome to stick around for a post skate.

Well… I guess the game was done now.

A few feet ahead of me was a lit opening to the right, the tunnel maybe, and directly across from that was a set of closed, double doors. As we neared the tunnel and doors, I could hear talking and music from beyond said doors. Extremely loud music.

I let out a quick breath through pursed lips before smiling over at the security lady. "Thank you."

She nodded and turned to stand a bit further down the hall, near the elevator but still watching me.

Don't worry, I wanted to say, I won't barge into the locker room.

While I had grown up with three older brothers, barging into a locker room full of men of all ages wasn't really my thing.

Not knowing what else to do, I stood next to the wall across from the closed doors and crossed my arms over my chest. I supposed I would wait; it wasn't like I had any other choice, right?

Patience, Sydney. Patience, I repeated, over and over in my head, trying hard to refrain from tapping my foot. Granted, I wasn't too sure I could stay upright if I attempted to tap my heeled toe, so instead I shifted my weight to the other leg, wincing slightly as the pressure was released from the previous.

No sooner than the wince left my face, the double doors opened wide and men in work-out clothing, team sweats, and a few in business attire, started to pile out. Ok, maybe 'pile out' wasn't entirely accurate, but they weren't exactly coming out single-file, either.

Two terrifyingly tall men walked out, wearing identical brown wind-pant bottoms. One wore a white tee with the Enforcers' logo taking up the entire front of the shirt. The logo was either printed vintage-style, or the shirt had seen many trips to the laundry.

The other wore a light brown long-sleeved tee with Enforcers written over the right chest area. Both had wet hair and brought with them a fresh male scent; however, the smell that wafted after them was pungent, smelling of stale sweat and old gym clothes.

I tried really hard to not turn my nose up.

The man in the long-sleeved shirt quickly glanced in my direction, causing me to straighten to my full, even if short, height. He nodded upwards once at his teammate before saying in a deep voice, "See you on the ice." The other said something in return in a heavy European accent, perhaps in agreement. Man-in-long-sleeved-shirt walked over toward me; the nearer he came, the larger his tower of height became.

Taking a breath, I reminded myself that at five-two, most men towered over me. Then again, most men didn't come at me with the additional inches skates gave.

"Can I help you?" he asked.

"Um, yeah. I mean, yes, please," I stuttered, nervously glancing down to my leather folio. One of the things I needed to work on was my presence, and stuttering and using half-words like 'yeah' was not acceptable. I opened my folio and pretended to sift through papers when honestly, I had no clue exactly why I was here. What if Caleb didn't agree to meet with me? What if he was only agreeing over the phone to get me to hang up?

I couldn't look this man in the eye. He was...scary looking, with a yellowing black eye and a missing front tooth.

He pulled up the sleeves of his shirt as he waited for an answer.

"I'm looking for Caleb Prescott?" I asked, finally gathering the courage to look up at the man, painting a look of confidence on my face. "I'm Sydney Meadows; he's expecting me."

"Oh, yeah. He mentioned something about something," he said with a nod. His hard face softened just slightly, no longer as intimidating without the stare in his eyes. "I'm Winski. Trevor." He threw a thumb over his shoulder. "I'll get him for you. He's debriefing."

"Ok, thank you."

I watched as Trevor turned away and went back toward the double doors, but rather than going through them, he simply put a hand on the door jam and leaned in. "Yo, Prescott! You got a visitor." He turned back around and crossed the pathway to enter the tunnel, grinning and nodding once toward me.

Well then. If yelling was all it took…

I took a deep breath to compose myself before running my hands down my shirt to straighten it again, as well as triple check the tuck. I was about to pull my hair tie out before thinking better of it; it would likely be a crazy mess with an annoying crease where the hair band had been. To still my shaking hands, I crossed my arms over the folio and pulled it to my chest.

The next man to walk out of the double doors was a tall blond, his hair too long and too curly for most guys – but managed to work on him. The nearly white curls were extremely tight for blond hair, and they fell past his ears and were nearing his shoulders. Unlike the previous two men, he still wore his hockey pants and socks but walked out shoeless. He also was without a team tee, and instead wore a Reebok form-fitting shirt. When he walked closer, seeming intent on coming to me, I was afraid that maybe I had looked up the wrong guy on the internet.

No.

No, no. This was Jonny Prescott.

"You wanted me…?" he asked, a crooked grin on his youthful face, no doubt due to the double meaning he threw out. He looked like a baby still, maybe newly-early twenties.

I was grateful that he wasn't in skates; I didn't have to look up too much further to speak to him.

"I was looking for Caleb? He was expecting me. I'm Sydney Meadows."

"Oh," he said, drawing the single syllable out with a slow nod. "I'm Jonny. Wrong Prescott at your service." He extended his hand for me to shake.

I looked at his proffered hand before sliding my much smaller one into it. "Sydney."

"You said."

With a quick nod, I drew my lips into a tight smile before taking my hand back.

"Jonny Prescott..." he said, with a slight lift to one of his blond brows.

I simply nodded. I wasn't sure what he wanted me to say.

When I didn't respond, he looked me over so quickly I thought I imagined it. Then, with a grin he no doubted practiced on women of all ages, he said, "You're that sexy voice from this morning."

I felt my face blanch before going hot. I brought one of my hands to the back of my neck and squeezed gently in embarrassment. "Yes, I did call this morning. I'm sorry for the timing."

"Ah, don't worry about it. Look," he said, stepping back with one foot, "I'll just tell Cael to hurry his ass up. There's a post-skate tonight so he should be out of Coach's office soon, anyway."

I couldn't find words to say through my embarrassment so I just nodded and watched as he walked back toward the locker room. Unlike Trevor before him, he didn't yell for Caleb. I wasn't exactly sure how Jonny summoned him, but it was obviously a different tactic than the first time.

It wasn't too much longer before Jonny came back out, having ditched his hockey bottoms for the same wind pants his teammates before him had worn, as well as a clean tee. Walking beside him in a nearly identical get-up, the only difference being the type of skates, was Caleb.

He looked even better in person.

Jonny and Caleb may have been opposites in looks, but oddly enough I could tell they were brothers. Where Jonny had curly blond hair, Caleb's was brown and straight; maybe, if he grew it out longer than the half or so inch it was, it would have a slight wave to it if the quick flip by his ears was any indication. They had different jaw lines, too, and Caleb appeared to be slightly taller, but beyond that...

Shee-oot.

Fuck a duck. Peace out, girl scout, this wasn't going to be as easy as I'd hoped. The longer I looked at Caleb in person, the more intimidated I became by him. The elder Prescott brother was hands-down gorgeous. Paired with the sleep-thickened voice I heard this morning, I could feel my lady bits tighten and my heart rate accelerate from something other than business nerves.

Caleb grinned crookedly and shook his head at a crack Jonny made before putting a hand to the side of his younger brother's face, pushing him away. Jonny held up his hands, laughing lightly, then nodded to him as they separated–Jonny for the ice and Caleb for…

Me.

With a quick breath out, I straightened as best I could, throwing my shoulders back and putting a grin on my face. I offered my hand yet again tonight. "Caleb? I'm Sydney."

Caleb

"You could probably tuck her in your pocket. How that voice on the phone came from that pixie of a girl… Damn, Cael, you better tap that, show be damned."

I shook my head with a grin before scratching my jawline with my middle finger in a subtle jab. We turned the corner from the locker room to head out when Jonny added, "If I wasn't in a committed relationship with Jenna…" His pause was more tell-tale than I think he realized. "I'd look twice."

The name 'Jenna' was like nails on a chalkboard, so I just shook my head again at my brother. That girl sunk her nails into Jonny when he was drafted for the National Junior team and hasn't let up. The entire family could see what Jonny simply couldn't—she didn't want him for him.

"I mean, never mind the fact the girl is hot, this idea she's pulling you in for? Dating twenty chicks for a month? Damn, son…"

Jonny could talk…

Which was funny, because of my two brothers and me, Jonny definitely was the more 'tenderhearted old soul', as our mom often said. He wasn't generally one to run his mouth, but lately all he did was talk chicks and tits and pussy; I had a feeling Jenna was going to be out the door sooner than later.

God, I hoped so.

I glanced up just as I pushed Jonny away from me, hand to cheek, and saw a well-dressed redhead standing a few feet off. Jonny peeled off to the ice, not before smacking me in the back, and I neared the woman who had to be Sydney.

"Caleb? I'm Sydney," she said as she offered her hand.

"Yeah, Jon Jon said." I wanted to be skeptical of this chick, but I had manners. I took her much smaller hand in mine and squeezed gently once, rather than shake it. Goddamn, she really was a pixie.

She was even shorter than my sisters and they were easily five-four. Myke, my oldest sister, was maybe five-six. Still, this Sydney stood damn near a foot and half lower than me; sure, yeah, I was wearing skates, but on a quick look down, I saw she was wearing heels. Barefoot, the difference wouldn't be much different than now.

I took my hand back and crossed my arms over my chest. I watched as her pretty amber eyes flashed down to my chest then back up to my eyes. Well, I was pretty sure she was actually looking at my nose.

I reached up and ran a hand over my jaw shadow before scrubbing over my goatee, continuing a quick appraisal of the tiny redhead in front of me. I was pretty sure green and brown shouldn't go together as a rule, but the colors worked well with her skin tone. Her blouse was unbuttoned just enough to show what minimal cleavage she had.

Yes, I looked at her chest. I was an ass and tits guy. Didn't know many guys who weren't.

Her neck was unadorned and with quick realization, I saw that the only jewelry she wore was in her ears. Even there, though, she wore simple, tiny diamond studs. Two in each ear.

Further down, I got at least half of what I liked to see. She didn't have huge hips, but her ass...

I almost was expecting her backend to be as flat as her top but nope. She had a nice ass in those tailored pants of hers.

Afraid I was lingering too long to be considered acceptable, I moved my eyes back up to her face, where I now noted more than her eyes. The lighting wasn't the greatest down here, but I thought I saw a light splash of freckles over her nose.

It made her a little sweeter.

As pretty as she was, I had to put a stop to this reality TV nonsense.

"Look. I know I said I'd meet with you, but can we make it quick? We have a post-skate with some kids and I really need to get out there."

"Ok, yeah. I mean, yes, of course," Sydney said with a nod.

As she and I stood near each other in the cinder block hall, Sydney went over the show with me, much as she had that morning, adding a few more details. She explained that the show would be filmed during a 30-day Hawaiian cruise, with excursions being used as individual and group dates. It was like Love Boat meets The Bachelor

Film crews would start filming me in my natural element, being here in San Diego, as soon as the end of the week if I agreed. Then, at the end of the season, the true filming of the show would begin.

As she was about to rush into explain when I would board the cruise-liner, as if I had agreed to it, I held up my hand. "Miss Meadows." God that sounded too formal for a woman like her. "Sydney," I tried again, definitely preferring the taste of it on my tongue. "How about we meet over coffee or something tomorrow? Ten?"

Her eyes widened slightly, just briefly, before she nodded with a fixed smile in place. "Of course. Yes, that will give you more time to let it sink in. So long as you agree to—"

I cut her off with a grin. While yes, this show was against everything I had ever thought for myself, I had a feeling that sitting with Sydney and talking to her about the show, as if I were agreeing to it, would be the only time I'd see this gorgeous redhead again. I didn't quite know what was drawing me to this short pixie of a woman, but I definitely wanted to see her again. Tomorrow I'd have no time constraints and she could talk all she wanted.

But before I realized the words were out of my mouth though, I said, "I'll do it," agreeing to her pitch.

Shit. Fuck.

The smile filling her face wasn't one I was about to take away, and her amber eyes danced, lightening just slightly to bring out fiery red specks. "We can discuss contestants tomorrow then. Wonderful. Oh, great!"

I had to swallow a chuckle at her obvious excitement. We agreed on a place to meet and I watched her leave out of the corner of my eye while heading toward the ice.

Like I said, I liked her ass.

"So," Sydney said, sitting across from me the next morning at one of the many non-chain coffee houses near Jonny and my condo. Today she was wearing a flowy black skirt with a white fitted tee that hugged her slight chest, and one of those chunky belts. The belt was that orangey cognac brown—the only brown, my sisters had informed me once, that could be paired with black. Her red hair was down around her shoulders today, showing off blonds and browns in the wavy, long tresses. If I thought she was pretty yesterday...

Damn, I wasn't prepared for today.

Unlike most women I met, she appeared to wear minimal makeup, something I couldn't fully tell in the dim light last night. Her complexion was that peaches and creamlike color people typically attributed to redheads, but only her nose and cheekbones were dusted with light freckles. I could see a few others along her collar bone sprinkling near her covered shoulders, too.

While she was dressed to the nines, I had shown up in a comfortable choice of jeans that I'd had for probably the better part of three years, and a hooded sweatshirt, sleeves pushed up to my elbows.

"My job is to find you your potential...dates, girlfriend, wife, whatever it is you're trying to get out of this show," Sydney continued. "Rather than going about this in a completely random fashion, I thought I'd start off by hearing your preferences."

"My preferences?" I slid back to slouch a bit in my hair, reaching both hands out to wrap around my coffee cup.

"Yes. Height, build, hair, et cetera, et cetera," she answered, picking up her legal pad only to put it back down, slightly angled this time. She slid her pen off the top of the pad and flipped it once in her left hand before clicking the end, extracting the tip.

So she was a lefty. Different.

"Whenever you're ready," she prompted.

I sighed heavily, a grin tugging my lips. "My preferences..." I reiterated before truly beginning. I kept my gaze on Sydney while spewing off my ideal woman—or what had been my ideal before a short, sexy redhead walked into my life the day prior because at this moment, I'd do anything for a date with her.

"Tall. Nothing more than a foot difference. Did that once." Though, truth be told, in some ways it made sex more exciting. It was easier to work against a wall or in a shower with a shorter chick.

I watched for any change of expression on her face, but she wrote what I said with nilch, nada, nothing showing. Ok, then, I thought.

"Never really had a thing for redheads," I said, forcing a fake grimace of apology but she never looked. Again, no reaction.

And now for the big guns. I supposed it wasn't a nice spot to play, on account of some women being self-conscious about it, but, "Definitely have to have more than a handful to work with."

This time she did look up, a quizzical look on her face. "A handful?"

"You know..." My voice trailed off as I raised my hands slightly out in front of my chest. I threw in a hand squeeze with both balls of air.

Sydney's eyes flicked from my hands down to her own chest, then back to her legal pad so quickly I thought it may not have happened.

But there it was, that pink in her cheeks.

Got her.

It almost killed me to not grin in victory.

"You seem to have rather large hands, Mr. Prescott," she muttered, "but I'll try my best."

This time, I couldn't help the chuckle that escaped, but she didn't seem to notice or mind. Yet again, she was in business mode.

"Kids? I understand you're only in your mid-twenties and at the height of your career, but some women will definitely have that on their radar." She glanced up at me, waiting for my answer.

Honestly, I hadn't really thought of them. With hockey season taking up damn-near three-quarters of the year, and the rest being filled with camps and giving back and not a lot of downtime, I hadn't given a lot of thought to any sort of settling down, which is partly why this show idea was such a joke.

I told her as much.

Well, the schedule part. Not the joke one.

She nodded and wrote on her pad before tapping the backend of her pen twice against her chin, then gave me a small smile. "Do you have any questions?"

"What is your role in all of," I waved my hand near her notepad, pausing a moment before finishing, "this?"

She put her pen down only to reach for her coffee cup, taking a sip and returning the cup to the table. She then sat up a little straighter and tucked her hands down...under her ass? I wasn't about to lean and look, but I definitely thought she was sitting on her hands. "I just completed my senior year of marketing. I officially graduate in a couple of weeks. I did a summer internship with a wedding planner out of Salt Lake City—"

I interrupted her. "Utah?"

She raised an auburn brow. "Do you know of another?"

I couldn't stop my grin at her spunk. "Continue. Sorry."

"As I was saying, I did a summer internship with a wedding planner, and then a classmate was talking about an internship he was doing with

Sorenson. I've always been interested in the behind-the-scenes stuff with television and movies, so I figured I'd give it a shot, too. I don't need the internship, having completed the one in summer, but I wanted the experience. So I'm like an intern-slash-casting assistant for my boss, David, who really is a casting assistant. The director of the show gave David the spiel and he gave me your name. My other assignments have been typical assistant duties like scoping out places. I guess with movies and scripted things, the assistant helps with readings but," she shrugged a shoulder. "So here I am. Trying to pitch a show to you."

"Well, you pitched the show to me. Pretty sure I agreed to it too." I grinned over at her.

"Anything for a bunch of ladies, right?" Her smile widened. "I have brothers, I know how you boys work."

Not so sure about the 'anything for a bunch of ladies' crack, as it was truly all about the one sitting in front of me, but I'd leave that alone. It looked like we were done talking about the show, but I wasn't ready to leave yet. "Brothers? How many?"

"Three. I'm the youngest of four. Smith is twenty-eight, Sean twenty-seven and Sawyer is twenty-four."

"And you are... Twenty...?"

"Two."

I nodded. "I'm twenty-four, but you knew that. I have an older sister and four younger siblings."

After an almost awkward silence where I didn't expand and she didn't ask, Sydney smiled again and picked up her pen. "Well, I'll let you go. The paperwork will be sent to your agent and filming crews will likely be with you starting the end of the week. They'll do shots like playing, practice, hanging out at home. Couple monologues. I'll work on your cast, and I believe the cruise is set to start mid-June..." She pursed her lips as she flipped through the end of her notepad. "Or beginning of July, rather. I think they wanted to give you enough time to rest in the event you went to the championship game."

I had to hold back a chuckle at the phrase. "You don't know hockey, do you?"

Her eyes widened slightly before her cheeks flushed to a pretty pink. "No, not really, but that's neither here nor there. The temporary itinerary will be emailed to you upon your signing the agreement, but you and the filming crew will board one week prior to the women. At that point, the thirty-day Hawaiian cruise will begin. The last week, your family is invited to join.

"The end game of the show isn't necessarily a proposal, but the idea is more than just 'a date with Caleb Prescott'. It's more like the idea you'll meet someone you wouldn't get to meet otherwise. The running title of the show is Beauty. I think they need to work on it, personally but—"

"Do you know what a beauty is?" With her 'championship game' lingo, I was willing to bet the hockey slang went over her head too.

She spoke slowly, unsurely, her eyes going from left to right before settling on mine. "A beautiful girl?"

I shook my head, my grin tight but I could feel that shit in my cheeks. "No. A beauty is a player who's good with his hands, loves the game, gives back to the team... The guy the team loves. But also the guy on the team who's..." I tried to think of a decent way to word it, "good with the ladies."

She smirked a little and nodded a few times. "Makes more sense now. I get it." She shook her head in amusement. "You hockey players."

As she started to put her pad and pen back in her folio, I asked the question that had been lingering in my mind since the night prior. "Are you going to be there?"

"Where, the show?" I nodded. "Oh, no. I imagine this will be the last time we see each other." Sydney smiled again. Damn, I could probably drown on the pull of her lips on her face. "Unless of course, you made a side trip to Utah someday. I could return the coffee gesture."

"Yeah, I'll let you know." I smiled to hide my disappointment before standing. "It was nice to meet you, Sydney Meadows." I extended my hand. "Even if you talked me into something I didn't really want to do."

She stood, too, and took my hand in hers. "Let's be honest, you changed your mind pretty quickly."

"Pretty persuaders can do that," I said, knowing that it came off as a line but meaning the words. "Can I walk you to your car?" She'd gotten here before I did and I had to park what felt like a mile away.

Sydney just tilted her head down, motioning out the windows. "I'm just right there. But you can walk me out, I guess."

So I did.

And on my way to my own car, I tried to figure out a way to see her again.

From *Interference*, available now!

47116503R00248

Made in the USA
Middletown, DE
05 June 2019